# SALADIN AHMED

## of the
## Crescent
## Moon

**DAW**
No. 1575

### Book One of
### *The Crescent Moon Kingdoms*

D0035370

...ome for the sword fighting, but stay for the humane
...ssage at the heart of this terrific fantasy." —NPR.org

DAW
No. 1575

$7.99 U.S.
$8.99 CAN

ISBN 978-0-7564-0778-0

5 0 7 9 9

EAN

**Raves for *Throne of the Crescent Moon*:**

"*Throne of the Crescent Moon* is colorful, magical, exciting, and moving. Saladin Ahmed delivers a beautiful story of a demon hunter in an *Arabian Nights* setting. An excellent first novel!"
—Kevin J. Anderson,
international bestselling coauthor of *Hellhole*

"This promising debut offers a glimpse of a dusty and wonderful fantasy city through the eyes of three engaging, unconventional protagonists."
—Elizabeth Bear, Hugo award-winning
author of *Grail*

"Ahmed is a master storyteller in the grand epic tradition. Swashbuckling adventure, awesome mystery, a bit of horror, and all of it written beautifully. A real treat!"
—N. K. Jemisin, Locus award-winning author
of *The Hundred Thousand Kingdoms*

"Saladin Ahmed is not your typical fantasy writer, and this is no ordinary debut novel. With deft plotting, painstaking characterization, and fluid prose, Ahmed brings us a riveting adventure, complete with stunning magics and compelling intrigue. A thoroughly enjoyable read from one of the genre's rising stars."
—David B. Coe, Crawford award-winning
author of *The Dark-Eyes' War*

"A genuinely brisk, bold, and colorful diversion. . . . Flashing swords, leaping bandits, holy magic, bloodthirsty monsters, and sumptuous cuisine . . . what more do you want me to do, draw you a map? Read this thing."
—Scott Lynch, Sydney J. Bounds award-winning
author of *The Lies of Locke Lamora*

"Readers yearning for the adventures of Fafhrd and the Gray Mouser will delight in the arrival of Adoulla and Raseed. In addition to these two marvelous characters, Saladin Ahmed has given us the wonderful, colorful city of Dhamsawaat, ghuls and demons and manjackals, and the ferocious tribeswoman Zamia, who gives new meaning to the words 'wild girl.'"
—Walter Jon Williams,
Nebula award-winning author of *Deep State*

"*Throne of the Crescent Moon* is a strong debut novel with an exciting and classic fantasy plot, monstrous ghuls, and a marvelously-described world. If that's not enough (although it should be), then you should absolutely read it for its world-weary, sarcastic hero, Doctor Adoulla Makhslood, who is fat and old and out-of-shape and ready to retire and yet unable to do so because of his sense of duty; he is utterly wonderful because he is not like any other hero in an epic fantasy novel."            —Kate Elliott, author of *Cold Magic*

"Ahmed's writing is deft and graceful, and his characters move through a world of real stakes and significant consequences, much to their cost. Combine this with glorious setting and his careful mastery of craft, and you have a lovely fantasy read on your hands."

—Jay Lake, John W. Campbell award-winning author of *Green*

### From the media:

"Ahmed's debut masterfully paints a world both bright and terrible. Unobtrusive hints of backstory contribute to the sense that this novel is part of a larger ongoing tale, and the Arab-influenced setting is full of vibrant description, characters, and religious expressions that will delight readers weary of pseudo-European epics."            —*Publishers Weekly (starred)*

"Set in a well-detailed and historically thick culture, perhaps the most compelling piece of this tale is the richness of the environment, how well Ahmed has brought to life the town of Dham-sawaat, and the societal mores of the characters. A compelling read well worth picking up."            —*RT Book Reviews*

"Distinctive Middle Eastern fantasy from newcomer Ahmed. Equally impressive are characters who struggle not only against their opponents but against their own misgivings and desires, and accept that victory may be achieved only at great personal cost. An arresting, sumptuous and thoroughly satisfying debut."            —*Kirkus (starred)*

"This long-awaited debut by a finalist for the Nebula and Campbell awards brings *The Arabian Nights* to sensuous life. The maturity and wisdom of Ahmed's older protagonists are a delightful contrast to the brave impulsiveness of their younger companions. This trilogy launch will delight fantasy lovers who enjoy flawed but honorable protagonists and a touch of the exotic."           —*Library Journal (starred)*

"Ahmed is as good as, if not better than, anyone else out there writing fantasy today. He has created a vibrant and exciting world where his characters both live and have the adventures which form the basis of the story. While there are five main characters involved in telling us the story, the city becomes another character who lives and breathes alongside everybody else. Ahmed's descriptions are so vivid she takes on the type of distinct personality we ascribe to the places we are most familiar with."           —*Seattle Post-Intelligencer*

"Bottom line: If you're a fantasy fan—and it doesn't matter if you're a fan of paranormal fantasy, epic fantasy, dark fantasy, etc.—chances are very good that you'll find *Throne of the Crescent Moon* to be one of the best novels you read this year."
                                        —B&N Explorations

"Yes, it's medieval fantasy packed with badass Dervish ninjas, shape-shifting nomads and terrifying undead monsters; but it's also a smart, well-observed tale of corrupt regimes crumbling before a people's uprising like no other. Think of it as *Lord of the Rings* meets Arab Spring."           —NPR.org

"There's a wonderful soul to *Throne of the Crescent Moon* and, with all the skill and eloquence he showed in his short fiction, Ahmed has brought to life a wonderful cast of characters and introduced readers to a thrilling and interesting new world to explore."           —A Dribble of Ink

"As a kid I loved watching Ray Harryhausen classics like *The 7th Voyage of Sinbad* and *Jason and the Argonauts*, with their fighting skeletons and stop-motion monsters—and reading Ahmed's novel gave me that same sense of swashbuckling mythos mania. What really makes this book shine, however, are the characters and utterly riveting worldbuilding. By the end, you might even find yourself a little choked up after the dust settles. You'll love the people you meet in *Throne of the Crescent Moon* that much. I can't wait to see what Ahmed will write next."           —io9.com

DAW Books presents
Saladin Ahmed's
*The Crescent Moon Kingdoms*

Book One:
THRONE OF THE CRESCENT MOON

# SALADIN AHMED

# Throne of the Crescent Moon

## Book One of *The Crescent Moon Kingdoms*

## DAW BOOKS, INC.

### DONALD A. WOLLHEIM, FOUNDER
375 Hudson Street, New York, NY 10014
**ELIZABETH R. WOLLHEIM**
**SHEILA E. GILBERT**
**PUBLISHERS**
http://www.dawbooks.com

First Printing, January 2013
1   2   3   4   5   6   7   8   9

DAW TRADEMARK REGISTERED
U.S. PAT. AND TM. OFF. AND FOREIGN COUNTRIES
—MARCA REGISTRADA
HECHO EN U.S.A.

PRINTED IN THE U.S.A.

To my parents, Ismael Ahmed, and the late Mary O'Leary,
who introduced me to the fantastic world of books;

to my wife, Hayley Thompson,
who supported me in a dozen ways as I wrote this one;

and to my children, Malcolm and Naima,
who make this broken world beautiful enough to keep
living and writing in,
this is for you.

# Acknowledgments:

A number of people have helped me usher *Throne* from the "neat idea" stage to the book you now hold in your hands. In particular I'd like to thank:

- All of the readers who've helped me hone my writing over the past few years; My fellow students in the 2007 Taos Toolbox workshop (especially Christopher Cevasco, Scott Andrews, and Dorothy A. Windsor); the members of the 2009 Rio Hondo workshop; and the past and present members of the Tabula Rasa and Altered Fluid writers groups (in particular E.C. Myers, Rajan Khanna, Richard Bowes, and Justin Howe)
- Walter Jon Williams, the best teacher in the genre-writing business
- Kevin J. Anderson, for the precious gift of his free time
- The members of the SFNovelists listserv, for their generous mentorship
- Jennifer Jackson, super-agent extraordinaire
- Betsy Wollheim, the best editor/publisher a writer could ask for

This book wouldn't exist without your help, folks. Thank you!

to the Coin Cities
and the Warlands

The
Empty
Kingdom

Zimbuk

The
Jewel
Isles

Guardian's
Bay

The Soo
Republic

Priscilla Spencer

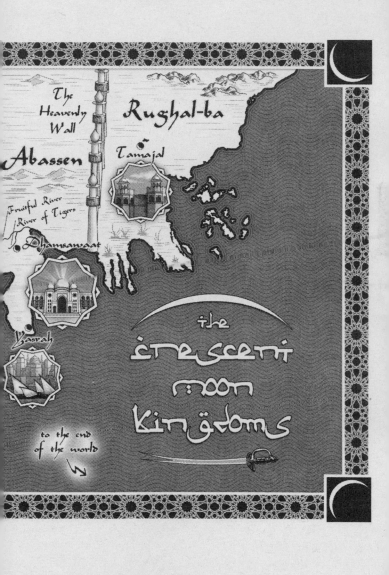

The Heavenly Wall

Rughal-ba

Abassen

Tamajal

Fruitful River
River of Tigers

Dhamsawaat

Yasrah

the
crescent
moon
Kingdoms

to the end
of the world

✣

# Throne of the
# Crescent Moon

# I.

*NINE DAYS. Beneficent God, I beg you, let this be the day I die!*

The guardsman's spine and neck were warped and bent but still he lived. He'd been locked in the red lacquered box for nine days. He'd seen the days' light come and go through the lid-crack. *Nine days.*

He held them close as a handful of dinars. Counted them over and over. *Nine days. Nine days. Nine days.* If he could remember this until he died he could keep his soul whole for God's sheltering embrace.

He had given up on remembering his name.

The guardsman heard soft footsteps approach, and he began to cry. Every day for nine days the gaunt, black-bearded man in the dirty white kaftan had appeared. Every day he cut the guardsman, or burned him. But worst was when the guardsman was made to taste the others' pain.

The gaunt man had flayed a young marsh girl, pinning the guardsman's eyes open so he had to see the girl's skin curl out under the knife. He'd burned a

Badawi boy alive and held back the guardsman's head so the choking smoke would enter his nostrils. The guardsman had been forced to watch the broken and burned bodies being ripped apart as the gaunt man's ghuls fed on heart-flesh. He'd watched as the gaunt man's servant-creature, that thing made of shadows and jackal skin, had sucked something shimmering from those freshly dead corpses, leaving them with their hearts torn out and their empty eyes glowing red.

These things had almost shaken the guardsman's mind loose. Almost. But he would remember. *Nine days. Nine . . . . All-Merciful God, take me from this world!*

The guardsman tried to steady himself. He'd never been a man to whine and wish for death. He'd taken beatings and blade wounds with gritted teeth. He was a strong man. Hadn't he guarded the Khalif himself once? What matter that his name was lost to him now?

*Though I walk a wilderness of ghuls and wicked djenn, no fear can . . . no fear can . . .* He couldn't remember the rest of the scripture. Even the Heavenly Chapters had slipped from him.

The box opened in a painful blaze of light. The gaunt man in the filthy kaftan appeared before him. Beside the gaunt man stood his servant, that thing—part shadow, part jackal, part cruel man—that called itself Mouw Awa. The guardsman screamed.

As always the gaunt man said nothing. But the shadow-thing's voice echoed in the guardsman's head.

*Listen to Mouw Awa, who speaketh for his blessed friend. Thou art an honored guardsman. Begat and born in the Cres-*

*cent Moon Palace. Thou art sworn in the name of God to defend it. All of those beneath thee shall serve.*

The words were a slow, probing drone in his skull. His mind swooned in a terror-trance.

*Yea, thy fear is sacred! Thy pain shall feed his blessed friend's spells. Thy beating heart shall feed his blessed friend's ghuls. Then Mouw Awa the manjackal shall suck thy soul from thy body! Thou hast seen the screaming and begging and bleeding the others have done. Thou hast seen what will happen to thee soon.*

From somewhere a remembered scrap of a grandmother's voice came to the guardsman. Old tales of the power cruel men could cull from a captive's fear or an innocent's gruesome slaying. *Fear-spells. Pain-spells.* He tried to calm himself, to deny the man in the dirty kaftan this power.

Then he saw the knife. The guardsman had come to see the gaunt man's sacrifice knife as a living thing, its blade-curve an angry eye. He soiled himself and smelled his own filth. He'd done so many times already in these nine days.

The gaunt man, still saying nothing, began making small cuts. The knife bit into the guardsman's chest and neck, and he screamed again, pulling against bonds he'd forgotten were there.

As the gaunt man cut him, the shadow-thing whispered in the guardsman's mind. It recalled to him all the people and places that he loved, restored whole scrolls of his memory. Then it told stories of what would soon come. Ghuls in the streets. All the guardsman's family and friends, all of Dhamsawaat, drowning in a river of blood. The guardsman knew these were not lies.

He could feel the gaunt man feeding off of his fear, but he couldn't help himself. He felt the knife dig into his skin and heard whispered plans to take the Throne of the Crescent Moon, and he forgot how many days he'd been there. Who was he? Where was he? There was nothing within him but fear—for himself and his city.

Then there was nothing but darkness.

# Chapter 1

*Dhamsawaat, King of Cities, Jewel of Abassen*
*A thousand thousand men pass through and pass in*
*Packed patchwork of avenues, alleys, and walls*
*Such bookshops and brothels, such schools and such stalls*
*I've wed all your streets, made your night air my wife*
*For he who tires of Dhamsawaat tires of life*

DOCTOR ADOULLA MAKHSLOOD, the last real ghul hunter in the great city of Dhamsawaat, sighed as he read the lines. His own case, it seemed, was the opposite. He often felt tired of life, but he was not quite done with Dhamsawaat. After threescore and more years on God's great earth, Adoulla found that his beloved birth city was one of the few things he was not tired of. The poetry of Ismi Shihab was another.

To be reading the familiar lines early in the morning in this newly crafted book made Adoulla feel younger—a welcome feeling. The smallish tome was bound with brown sheepleather, and *Ismi Shihab's Leaves of Palm* was etched into the cover with good golden acid. It was a very expensive book, but Hafi the bookbinder had given it to Adoulla free of charge. It had been two years since Adoulla saved the man's wife from a cruel magus's water ghuls, but Hafi was still effusively thankful.

Adoulla closed the book gently and set it aside. He sat outside of Yehyeh's, his favorite teahouse in the world, alone at a long stone table. His dreams last night had been grisly and vivid—blood-rivers, burning corpses, horrible voices—but the edge of their details had dulled upon waking. Sitting in this favorite place, face over a bowl of cardamom tea, reading Ismi Shihab, Adoulla almost managed to forget his nightmares entirely.

The table was hard against Dhamsawaat's great Mainway, the broadest and busiest thoroughfare in all the Crescent Moon Kingdoms. Even at this early hour, people half-crowded the Mainway. A few of them glanced at Adoulla's impossibly white kaftan as they passed, but most took no notice of him. Nor did he pay them much mind. He was focused on something more important.

Tea.

Adoulla leaned his face farther over the small bowl and inhaled deeply, needing its aromatic cure for the fatigue of life. The spicy-sweet cardamom steam enveloped him, moistening his face and his beard, and for the first time that groggy morning he felt truly alive.

When he was outside of Dhamsawaat, stalking bone

ghuls through cobwebbed catacombs or sand ghuls across dusty plains, he often had to settle for chewing sweet-tea root. Such campfireless times were hard, but as a ghul hunter Adoulla was used to working within limits. *When one faces two ghuls, waste no time wishing for fewer* was one of the adages of his antiquated order. But here at home, in civilized Dhamsawaat, he felt he was not really a part of the world until he'd had his cardamom tea.

He raised the bowl to his lips and sipped, relishing the piquant sweetness. He heard Yehyeh's shuffling approach, smelled the pastries his friend was bringing. This, Adoulla thought, was life as Beneficent God intended it.

Yehyeh set his own teabowl and a plate of pastries on the stone table with two loud clinks, then slid his wiry frame onto the bench beside Adoulla. Adoulla had long marveled that the cross-eyed, limping teahouse owner could whisk and clatter bowls and platters about with such efficiency and so few shatterings. A matter of practice, he supposed. Adoulla knew better than most that habit could train a man to do anything.

Yehyeh smiled broadly, revealing the few teeth left to him.

He gestured at the sweets. "Almond nests—the first of the day, before I've even opened my doors. And God save us from fat friends who wake us too early!"

Adoulla waved a hand dismissively. "When men reach our age, my friend, we should wake before the sun. Sleep is too close to death for us."

Yehyeh grunted. "So says the master of the half-day nap! And why this dire talk again, huh? You've been even gloomier than usual since your last adventure."

Adoulla plucked up an almond nest and bit it in half. He chewed loudly and swallowed, staring into his teabowl while Yehyeh waited for his reply. Finally Adoulla spoke, though he did not look up.

"Gloomy? Hmph. I have cause to be. Adventure, you say? A fortnight ago I was face-to-face with a living bronze statue that was trying to kill me with an axe. An *axe*, Yehyeh!" He shook his head at his own wavering tea-reflection. "Threescore years old, and still I'm getting involved in such madness. Why?" he asked, looking up.

Yehyeh shrugged. "Because God the All-Knowing made it so. You've faced such threats and worse before, my friend. You may look like the son of the bear who screwed the buzzard, but you're the only real ghul hunter left in this whole damned-by-God city, O Great and Virtuous Doctor."

Yehyeh was baiting him by using the pompous honorifics ascribed to a physician. The ghul hunters had shared the title of "Doctor" but little else with the "Great and Virtuous" menders of the body. No leech-wielding charlatan of a physician could stop the fanged horrors that Adoulla had battled.

"How would you know what I look like, Six Teeth? You whose crossed eyes can see nothing but the bridge of your own nose!" Despite Adoulla's dark thoughts, trading the familiar insults with Yehyeh felt comfortable, like a pair of old, well made sandals. He brushed almond crumbs from his fingers onto his spotless kaftan. Magically, the crumbs and honey spots slid from his blessedly unstainable garment to the ground.

"You are right, though," he continued, "I have faced worse. But this . . . this . . ." Adoulla slurped his tea. The battle against the bronzeman had unnerved him. The fact that he had needed his assistant Raseed's sword arm to save him was proof that he was getting old. Even more disturbing was the fact that he'd been daydreaming of death during the fight. He was tired. And when one was hunting monsters, tired was a step away from dead. "The boy saved my fat ass. I'd be dead if not for him." It wasn't easy to admit.

"Your young assistant? No shame in that. He's a dervish of the Order! That's why you took him in, right? For his forked sword—'cleaving the right from the wrong' and all that?"

"It's happened too many times of late," Adoulla said. "I ought to be retired. Like Dawoud and his wife." He sipped and then was quiet for a long moment. "I froze, Yehyeh. Before the boy came to my rescue. I froze. And do you know what I was thinking? I was thinking that I would never get to do this again—sit at this table with my face over a bowl of good cardamom tea."

Yehyeh bowed his head, and Adoulla thought his friend's eyes might be moist. "You would have been missed. But the point is that you did make it back here, praise be to God."

"Aye. And why, Six Teeth, don't you say to me 'Now stay home, you old fart?' That is what a real friend would say to me!"

"There are things you can do, O Buzzard-Beaked Bear, that others can't. And people need your help. God has called you to this life. What can I say that will change that?" Yehyeh's mouth tightened and his brows drew down. "Besides, who says home is safe? That madman the Falcon Prince is going to burn this city down around our ears any day now, mark my words."

They had covered this subject before. Yehyeh had little use for the treasonous theatrics of the mysterious master thief who called himself the Falcon Prince. Adoulla agreed that the "Prince" was likely mad, but he still found himself approving of the would-be usurper. The man had stolen a great deal from the coffers of the Khalif and rich merchants, and much of that money found its way into the hands of Dhamsawaat's poorest—sometimes hand delivered by the Falcon Prince himself.

Yehyeh sipped his tea and went on. "He killed another of the Khalif's headsmen last week, you know. That's two now." He shook his head. "Two agents of the Khalif's justice, murdered."

Adoulla snorted. " 'Khalif's justice'? Now there are two words that refuse to share a tent! That piece of shit isn't half as smart a ruler as his father was, but he's twice as cruel. Is it justice to let half the city starve while that greedy son of a whore sits on his brocaded cushions eating peeled grapes? Is it justice to—"

Yehyeh rolled his crossed eyes, a grotesque sight. "No speeches, please. No wonder you like the villain—you've both got big mouths! But I tell you, my friend, I'm serious. This city can't hold a man like that and one like the new Khalif at the same time. We are heading for battle in the streets. Another civil war."

Adoulla scowled. "May it please God to forbid it."

Yehyeh stood up, stretched, and clapped Adoulla on the back. "Aye. May All-Merciful God put old men like us quietly in our graves before this storm hits." The cross-eyed man did not look particularly hopeful of this. He squeezed Adoulla's shoulder. "Well. I'll let you get back to your book, O Gamal of the Golden Glasses."

Adoulla groaned. Back when he'd been a street brawling youth on Dead Donkey Lane, he himself had used the folktale hero's name to tease boys who read. He'd learned better in the decades since. He placed a hand protectively over his book. "You should not contemn poetry, my friend. There's wisdom in these lines. About life, death, one's own fate."

"No doubt!" Yehyeh aped the act of reading a nonexistent book in the air before him, running a finger over the imaginary words and speaking in a grumble that was an imitation of Adoulla's own. "O, how hard it is to be so fat! O, how hard it is to have so large a nose! O Beneficent God, why do the children run a-screaming when I come a-walking?"

Before Adoulla could come up with a rejoinder on the fear Yehyeh's own crossed eyes inspired in children, the teahouse owner limped off, chuckling obscenities to himself.

His friend was right about one thing: Adoulla was, praise God, alive and back home—back in the Jewel of Abassen, the city with the best tea in the world. Alone again at the long stone table, he sat and sipped and watched early morning Dhamsawaat come to life and roll by. A thick necked cobbler walked past, two long poles strung with shoes over his shoulder. A woman from Rughal-ba strode by, a bouquet in her hands, and the long trail of her veil flapping behind. A lanky young man with a large book in his arms and patches in his kaftan moved idly eastward.

As he stared out onto the street, Adoulla's nightmare suddenly reasserted itself with such force that he could not move or speak. He was walking—wading— through Dhamsawaat's streets, waist high in a river of blood. His kaftan was soiled with gore and filth. Everything was tinted red—the color of the Traitorous Angel. An unseen voice, like a jackal howling human words, clawed at his mind. And all about him the people of Dhamsawaat lay dead and disemboweled.

*Name of God!*

He forced himself to breathe. He watched the men and women on the Mainway, very much alive and going about their business. There were no rivers of blood. No jackal howls. His kaftan was clean.

Adoulla took another deep breath. *Just a dream. The world of sleep invading my days*, he told himself. *I need a nap.*

He took a second-to-last slurp of tea, savoring all of the subtle spices that Yehyeh layered beneath the cardamom. He shook off his grim thoughts as best he could and stretched his legs for the long walk home.

He was still stretching when he saw his assistant, Raseed, emerge from the alley on the teahouse's left. Raseed strode toward him, dressed as always in the impeccable blue silk habit of the Order of Dervishes. The holy warrior pulled a large parcel behind him, something wrapped in gray rags.

No, not something. Someone. A long-haired little boy of perhaps eight years. With blood on his clothes. *O please, no.* Adoulla's stomach clenched up. *Merciful God help me, what now?* Adoulla reached deep and somehow found the strength to set down his teabowl and rise to his feet.

# Chapter 2

ADOULLA WATCHED RASEED weave between the teahouse tables, pulling the child gently along. They came to a halt before him, their backs to the Mainway's throng of people. Raseed bowed his blue-turbaned head. Looking more closely, Adoulla did not think the frightened-looking, long-haired child was wounded. The blood on his clothing seemed to be someone else's.

"God's peace, Doctor," said Raseed. "This is Faisal. He needs our help." The dervish's hand rested on the hilt of the curved, fork-tipped sword at his hip. He stood five lithe feet, not much bigger than the child beside him. His fine-boned yellow features were delicate and highlighted by tilted eyes. But Adoulla knew better than anyone that Raseed's slender frame and clean-shaven face hid a zealous killer's skill.

"God's peace, boy. And to you, Faisal. What is the problem?" he asked the dervish.

Raseed's expression was grim. "The boy's parents have been murdered." He darted his dark eyes at Faisal but made no attempt to soften his tone. "With apologies, Doctor, my knowledge is insufficient. But from Faisal's description, I believe ghuls attacked the boy's family. Also—"

Two porters passed, each shouting at the other to go screw a pickle barrel, and the soft-spoken dervish's words were drowned out. "What was that?" Adoulla asked.

"I said that I was sent here by . . . Faisal is . . ." He hesitated.

"What? What is it?" Adoulla asked.

"Faisal's aunt is known to you, Doctor. It was she who brought him to your townhouse." Adoulla looked down at Faisal, but the child said nothing.

"Stop this mysterious monkeyshit, you stuttering dervish! Who is the child's aunt?"

Raseed's birdlike mouth tightened in distaste. "Mistress Miri Almoussa is the boy's aunt."

*God damn me.*

"Her courier brought the boy and this note, Doctor." He drew a rolled piece of rough paper from his blue silk tunic and handed it over.

*Doullie*

*You know how things stand between us. I wouldn't have bothered you if the need weren't great. But my niece is dead, Doullie! Murdered! Her and her fool marshman husband. To hear Faisal speak, it was*

*neither a man nor an animal that killed them. That*
*means you will know more than anyone in this city*
*about what to do. I need your help. Faisal here will*
*tell you all that happened. Send him back to my house*
*when you have learned what you must from him.*

> *God's peace be with you,*
>   *Miri*

"'God's peace be with you'?" Adoulla read the words aloud, a bit incredulous. Such a passionless, formulaic closing from his old heart's-flame! Mistress Miri Almoussa, Seller of Silks and Sweets. Known to a select few as Miri of the Hundred Ears. Adoulla pictured her, middle-aged and still able to fill him with more lust than a girl of half her years, sitting in her brothel office among a hundred scraps of paper and a half dozen letter pigeons.

It was true that their last meeting had not been a happy one. But was she really so fed up with him that, even in such a dire situation, she had sent a *note* instead of coming herself? The rosewater-scented memory of her threatened to overwhelm him, but he shoved it to the side. He needed analysis now, not heartsick nostalgia.

The dried blood on Faisal's rough spun shirt must have been from one of his parents. Miri had not even wasted time changing the child's clothes before sending him over. "So you are Miri's grand-nephew? I remember her speaking of a niece who lived out near the marshdocks."

"Yes, Doctor." The boy's tone was hard and flat—the voice of one who has refused to let his mind absorb what his eyes have seen.

"And why, Faisal, have you come all the way to the city for help? There's a large watchmen's barracks at the marshdocks—the Khalif has treasure-houses there, after all. Did you not tell the watchmen what happened?"

The child's features twisted with bitterness that belied his, perhaps, ten years. "I tried. But the watchmen don't listen to marsh boys. They don't care what happens outside the treasure house walls, long as the Khalif's gold and gemthread are safe. My mama told me that my Auntie Miri in the city had a friend who was a real ghul hunter, like in the stories. So I come to Dhamsawaat."

Adoulla smiled sadly. "Very little in life is like the stories, Faisal."

"But my mama . . . and my Da . . ." Faisal's tough marsh boy mask slipped and tears fell.

Adoulla was not at his ease with children. He stroked the boy's long black hair, hoping this was the right thing to do. "I know, little one, I know. But I need you to be strong right now, Faisal. I need you to tell me exactly what happened."

Adoulla sat back down, seating the child opposite him. Raseed remained standing, hand on hilt, his tilted eyes watching the crowds that walked past the teahouse.

Faisal told his story. Adoulla sorted through babbling, sobs, and the exaggerations of fear, trying to isolate useful information. There was little to isolate. Faisal lived with his parents in the marshes a day's ride from the city. While out spearfishing with another family they had been set upon by hissing, gray-skinned monsters, man-shaped but not human. Bone ghuls, unless Adoulla missed his guess—strong as half a dozen men and as hard to kill, with gruesome claws besides. Faisal had fled, but not before he'd seen the ghuls start to eat the heart muscle of his still living parents.

The blood on his shirt was his father's. Faisal was the only one who'd escaped. Adoulla had seen grisly things in his work, but sometimes it was worse seeing the effect such things had on others.

"I ran away and left them . . . . Mama said 'run' and I did! It's my fault they're dead!" He began bawling again. "My fault!"

Adoulla wrapped an arm awkwardly around the boy. He felt like a great ape coddling a new hatched chick. "It is not your fault, Faisal. A *man* made those ghuls. Almighty God willing, we will find this man and keep his creatures from hurting others. Now I need you to tell me just once more what happened—everything, every detail you can remember."

Adoulla extracted another telling of the incident. He didn't like doing it—making the child relive this horror twice and thrice over. But he had to, if he was going to do his job. Frightened people often remembered things falsely, even when they meant to be honest. He listened for new details and inconsistencies, not because he distrusted the boy, but because people never remembered things exactly the same way twice.

Still, Adoulla found Faisal a better source of information than most grown men who'd laid eyes on a ghul. He was a marshman after all, and they were tough and observant folk. No people—not even the Badawi òf the desert—lived closer to starvation. Adoulla could remember Miri's disgust a dozen years ago when she'd learned that her niece was marrying a marshman. *"What is there for her out there?"* she'd asked Adoulla over a game of bakgam. He had been unable to answer; he was as thoroughly a city creature as she was. But there was no denying that where life itself depended on spearing quick fish and raising fragile golden rice, attentiveness flourished.

Faisal's retellings informed Adoulla that three creatures had attacked, and that no man had been visible at the time. Adoulla turned to Raseed. *"Three* of the things! Commanded outside of the line of sight. This is not the usual half-dinar magus, heady with the power of his first ghul-raising. Troubling."

The Heavenly Chapters decreed that ghul-makers were damned to the Lake of Flame. The Chapters spoke of an ancient, corrupted age when wicked men commanded whole legions of the things from miles away. But those times were past. In all his years of ghul hunting, Adoulla had never seen a man make more than two of the monsters at a time—and this always from a few hundred yards away at most. "Troubling," he said again.

He instructed Raseed to cut a small scrap from the boy's scarlet-stained shirt. Other than the name of its maker, the blood of a ghul's victim was the best component for a tracking spell. The creatures them-selves would likely prove easy enough to find. But he would need to head closer to the scene of the slaying, and get away from the city's teeming, confusing life-energies, to cast an effective tracking spell.

Adoulla only prayed that he would be able to find the creatures before they fed again. As the silent prayer echoed in his mind, he felt a weary determination ris-ing in his heart. There was more bloody work to be done. *O God, why must it be me every time?* Adoulla had paid his "fare for the festival of this world," as the po-ets say, many times over. It was some younger man's turn to do this.

But there was no younger man that could do it with-out him, Adoulla knew. He had fought beside many men, but had never had the wherewithal to train an-other in the ways of his near-dead order—had never been able to bring himself to set another on his own thankless road. Two years ago he'd reluctantly agreed to take Raseed as an assistant. But while the boy's mar-tial powers were unmatched, he had no talent for invo-cations. He was an excellent apprentice in the ends of ghul hunting, but his means to those ends were his own, and they were different than Adoulla's.

In ages past, the makers and the hunters of ghuls alike were more plentiful. Old Doctor Boujali, Aduol-la's own mentor, had explained it early in Adoulla's apprenticeship. *It's an almost dead art I'm teaching you here, young one,* he had said. *Once the ghul-makers ran rampant over God's great earth, and more of our order were needed. These days . . . well, few men use ghuls to prey on one another. The Khalif has his soldiers and his court magi to keep what he calls order. And if a few fiendish men still follow the Traitorous Angel's ways and gain their power through the death and dismembering of poor people, well, that's of little concern to those who rule from the Palace of the Crescent Moon. Even in other lands the ghul hunters are not what we once were. The Soo Pashas have their mercenaries and their Glorious Guardians. The High Sultaan of Rughal-ba controls those few who still know our ways. They are part of his Heavenly Army, whether they wish it or not. Our work is not like the heroism of the old stories. No vast armies of abominations stand before us. These days we save a fishmonger here, a porter's wife there. But it is still God's work. Never forget that.*

But in the many years since Doctor Boujali had first said these words to Adoulla it sometimes seemed that the scale arm was swinging back in the old direction. Adoulla and his friends had dispatched enough fiendish creatures over the decades to make him suspect that the old threats were starting to regain a foothold on God's great earth. Yet He had not deigned to raise scores of new ghul hunters. Instead, for reasons known only to He Who Holds All Answers, God had seen fit to pile trouble after trouble onto the stooped shoulders of a few old folks. One day—one day very soon—Adoulla feared his spine would snap under the strain.

Why was Adoulla made to bear so big a burden alone? When would others learn to defend themselves from the servants of the Traitorous Angel? What would happen after he was gone? Adoulla had asked Almighty

God these questions ten thousand times in his life, but He Who Holds All Answers had never deigned to respond. It seemed that Adoulla's gifts were always just enough to keep the creatures he faced in check, but he wondered again why God had made his life in this world such a tiring, lonely chore.

Still, as tired of life as he sometimes felt, and as foolish as he found most men to be, he could never quite manage to leave people to their cruelest fate. He drew in a resigned breath, let it out again, and stood. His teabowl was empty. Digging into the seemingly endless folds of his moonlight white kaftan, Adoulla drew forth a copper fals and slapped it onto the table.

As if he'd been summoned by the sound, Yehyeh appeared. He exchanged God's peaces with Raseed, then cast a cross-eyed frown at Faisal's bloody clothes. But all he said as he and Adoulla embraced and kissed on both cheeks in the familiar parting gesture was, "Stay safe, Buzzard Beak."

"I will try, Six Teeth," Adoulla replied. He turned to Raseed and Faisal. "Come on, you two."

Raseed stepped silently out from where he leaned against the teahouse wall. It was like watching a shadow come to life and peel itself from the sandstone. They joined the flow of the Mainway, Adoulla and the dervish keeping the child between them.

At the corner Adoulla waved over Camelback, a porter he'd known for years. Camelback was nearly a foot shorter than Adoulla but had shoulders enough for two men.

The men exchanged God's peaces and cheek kisses.

Adoulla pressed a coin into the porter's palm. "Take Faisal here to Mistress Miri Almoussa's place in the Singers' Quarter." He had to speak loudly to be heard over a braying donkey half a block ahead.

The child panicked all over again. "But . . . but . . . don't you need me to come with you, Doctor? To show you the way?"

"No, child," Adoulla said, leaning down. "I will use my magic to track the ghuls. You would slow us down. And, besides, I will not put you in danger."

"I'm not afraid."

Looking into his eyes, Adoulla believed him. If Faisal came across the ghuls again, he would not run a second time. And that could only mean a little boy's death. Adoulla had seen such before. He had no desire to bear witness to it again.

"I promise you, Faisal, we will avenge your family. But your mother gave everything so that you could live. Do not throw that away so quickly. You will make her happiest by being a good boy and living a long life." Adoulla paused, letting the words sink in.

The child nodded, though he was clearly unconvinced. He went with Camelback, and they were soon swallowed by the crowd. Adoulla turned to Raseed only to find the dervish glaring at him.

"What? Why are you scowling so, boy?" Somewhere behind them on the street someone dropped something that broke loudly and gave off a vinegared scent.

Raseed glanced back, glanced at Adoulla, and sniffed. "You just sent a child barely ten back to a house of ill repute." He pursed his thin lips in disapproval.

The little holy man could be so thick sometimes. "I sent him to his *Auntie's* house. To one of the few places in the city where a penniless little orphan would be well-treated even were he not related to the proprietress. Miri and her girls always have need of an errand boy or two."

"'O believer! If a man asks you to chose between virtue and your brother, choose virtue!'" Raseed quoted from the Heavenly Chapters. "There are charitable orders where the boy would be better served. To grow up among such degenerate women is . . ."

Adoulla felt his fire rise at the boy's words. The last time he'd seen her—almost two years ago now—Miri Almoussa had made it clear that she wanted nothing more to do with him. Nonetheless, he'd be damned if he'd stand for her being insulted. He made his voice dangerous. "About whom exactly are you speaking, boy?"

The dervish clearly thought better of elaborating. His blue turban bobbed in a bow. "My apologies, Doctor. I meant only that a virtuous upbringing in one of the city's orphan halls, where the boy could learn a trade, would—"

"Would doom the boy to six nights a week of under-the-sheets *upbringing* by some drunken 'Godly servant of children.' They'd leave him alone on Prayersday. Hmph. He'd learn a trade all right."

"Doctor! I can't believe—" Raseed's words were cut off when a big bull of a woman shouldered her way between the pair, cursing them for standing idle in the

street. Adoulla started walking again, and the dervish
followed.

"Please, boy," Adoulla said, "spare me your solemn
protestations regarding that which you know nothing
of. He'd be more likely to become a whore in one of
those terror houses than he would if he'd been living at
Miri's from the day of his birth. In my orphan days, I
dodged such places for the dungeons they were. Nothing's changed. Now!" Adoulla half-shouted, clapping
his hands together in an effort to disperse the argument. "I need to go home to gather some spell supplies.
Then we head out of the city. Let's get moving. If we
linger too long, I'll end up thinking better of this."

They quickened their pace as much as the press of
people would allow. The sun shone clearly as they
stepped out of the street and its building-shadows
and crossed the open space of Angels' Square. Adoulla
did not stop and marvel yet again at the almost-living
expressions on the ancient statuary faces of the Ministering Angels. He did, however, push brusquely
through a knot of oddly dressed, gawking city-visitors
who stood staring crane necked at the lifelike marble
work. *Bumpkins!* Adoulla griped to himself, but he
didn't really blame them.

Even when civil war had wracked the city two hundred years earlier, Angels' Square had been a sanctuary
of sorts. All sides had agreed to shed no blood on its
stones. Though crowded cheek-by-jowl with refuge-
seekers, one could taste the peace of the place in the air,
or so the historians and passed-down stories said.

Today, aside from the pack of sightseekers, the square was largely quiet. If there weren't such grim work before him, Adoulla thought he might have felt some of the old peace. Instead, his thoughts were on tracking spells and a child's bloodied clothing.

He and Raseed left Angels' Square behind for grimy Gruel Lane. On the Khalif's maps, the narrow, dirty street that led from the Square to Adoulla's neighborhood bore the name of some long-dead ruler. But for centuries Dhamsawaatis had called it Gruel Lane for its poverty and its inhospitable inns. Avoiding the occasional puddle of piss, Adoulla made it to the corner that marked the border of his rough neighborhood, the ironically named Scholars' Quarter.

Pious old Munesh, with his wisps of white hair and his roasted-nut stall, stood on the corner agitating fire-heated trays of sugared almonds and salted pistachios. The aroma made Adoulla's mouth water. He stopped to buy a handful of roasted pistachios.

"Doctor!" Raseed had been silent for much of their walk home, and Adoulla had almost forgotten he was there. The dervish was clearly scandalized by the delay. Adoulla wished he were young enough to believe that zeal and an urge to combat monsters were enough to fill one's stomach. But the years had taught him otherwise, and he had a long day ahead of him.

"I've had only half a breakfast, boy. I need sustenance to think clearly, and a handful of moments here will matter little enough. The Heavenly Chapters say 'A starving man builds no palaces.'"

"They also say 'For the starving man, prayer is better than food.'"

Adoulla gave up. He grunted to Raseed, thanked Munesh and walked on, cracking shells and munching noisily.

His assistant was a true dervish of the Order, truer than most of the hypocritical peacocks who wore the blue silks. He had spent years hardening his diminutive body, his only purpose to be a fitter and fitter weapon of God. To Adoulla's mind, it was an unhealthy approach to life for a boy of seven and ten. True, God had granted Raseed more than human powers; armed with the forked sword of his order, he was nearly invincible. Even without the sword the boy could take on half a dozen men at once. Adoulla had seen him do it. But the fact that he had never so much as kissed a girl lessened Adoulla's respect for him considerably.

Still, it was Raseed's pious discipline that made him such a good battle companion. A man's character was most clearly displayed in the uses he put his gifts to. In his forty years as a ghul hunter, Adoulla had seen a man jump twenty feet into the air and had watched a girl turn water into fire. He had seen a warrior split himself into two warriors, then four. He had watched as an old lady made trees walk.

What he had seen people do with such powers varied as much, or as little, as people themselves. Their motivations covered the same range of reasons all men and women did things. Occasionally they helped other people and made sacrifices. More often, they acted selfishly and did wrong to their fellow children of God. Raseed, for his part, always went the first route.

A neighbor's child hollered Adoulla's name and waved in greeting from across the packed-dirt street. Clearing his mind of extraneous thoughts and slurping the last bits of salt and pistachio from his fingers, Adoulla waved back and stepped onto his own block.

He passed the small sandstone shop that belonged to his friends and ex-traveling companions, Dawoud and Litaz, a Soo couple who had lived in the city for decades. Apparently they were not home—the shop's cedar shutters were drawn tight. *Too bad*. Adoulla would never have asked his retired friends to accompany him on this ghul hunt, but Litaz had kept up with her alkhemy, and it would have been nice to borrow one of her remarkable freezing solutions or explosive preparations to aid in his work.

But it was Idesday, so Adoulla guessed that the couple would be spending the day and perhaps the night with friends at the Western Market, where traders from the Soo Republic swept in once a month with ivory, gold, and the yam candies that Litaz always had on hand to remind herself of home.

Finally, he and Raseed reached the pale stone townhouse that had been Adoulla's thin slice of Dhamsawaat for twenty-odd years. Adoulla opened the white-painted wood door of the townhouse and stepped through the gently arched doorway, the dervish following.

It was no palace. But it was much better than the hovels that were his origin and likely inheritance as an orphan on Dead Donkey Lane. That he'd been able to buy the building at all had been due to the vagaries of his calling, which for once had worked to his advantage. Many years ago he had, with Dawoud and Litaz, fought a golden snake forty feet long, with huge rubies for eyes—an ancient monster created in the days of the Faroes of Kem and awakened by a greedy man's digging. Just looking at the glittering serpent caused magical fear in even a stout heart, and it had already slain a squadron of the old Khalif's watchmen. But Adoulla and his friends had ambushed the creature and drained its animating magic.

The serpent had collapsed as they'd watched, crumbling into huge piles of gold dust. Near thirty years later, Adoulla could still smilingly recall the sound of those fist-sized rubies falling to the ground. *I am now a rich man,* he remembered thinking as he and his friends had gleefully scooped gold dust into their pouches and sacks, doing little dances of celebration all the while.

It had been a treasure to rival those of Dhamsawaat's great merchants. And though, over the past twenty-odd years, his calling had forced him to undertake several expensive journeys to distant places, he still had a respectable sum. He had no wife or children to keep, after all. His expenses had increased two years ago when Raseed, who had aided Adoulla admirably in a ghul hunt, had asked to stay on as an assistant. But even that had not cost him much, as the boy ate such simple fare.

Adoulla set to gathering his things. The marshes were less than a day's ride west by mule, so they'd need little in the way of traveling supplies. But there were preparations to be made for any ghul hunt. He slung a large, worn satchel of brown calfskin over his shoulder and moved about the townhouse's book-and box-cluttered rooms. As he went, he stuffed the bag with things collected from shelves, tabletops, and undusted corners. A punk of aloewood. A box of scripture-engraved needles. A vial of dried mint leaves. Pouches and packets, scraps of paper and bright little bottles wrapped in cloth.

In a quarter hour's time he was ready to go, and Raseed was already standing by the door, cleaning his sword. The dervish's own possessions were few: the sword, his blue silks, his turban made from a length of strong silk that could double for climbing or binding. He toted a square pack on his back that held their food-stuffs, a half-tent, and a small cookpot.

The boy ran his gaze up and down his sword's blade and slid it carefully into its ornate sheath of blue leather and lapis lazuli. Adoulla had watched him clean the blade just yesterday, and he doubted that the boy's sword had grown dirty since then. But he had come to understand that this ritual of Raseed's was about more than maintaining a cherished weapon. It was about focus. About reminding himself, each and every day, what truly mattered to him.

Taking a last long look around the bookshelves and bureaus of his townhouse, Adoulla himself felt something similar.

# Chapter 3

MEN AND WOMEN PACKED the stone Main-way and the sidestreets, inching along and shouting in competition for the few sedan chairs and mule rides available. From what Adoulla could see, those on foot were actually moving faster. Which meant that they would be walking to the stables at the edge of the city. *Wonderful.* He ought to have been born a Badawi tribesman, for all the walking he had done in his life. But on they walked, moving westward for half an hour.

"So here we are again," he grunted at Raseed, tired of the silence between them. "Leaving behind safety and comfort to kill monsters. Maybe to be killed. Almighty God knows I don't have much more of this left in me. You'll soon have to do this without a mentor, you know."

"You don't really mean that, Doctor." The boy crinkled his fine featured face in distaste as they passed a refuse cart, broken down in the middle of the street and stinking in the morning sun.

"I don't mean it? Hmph. Need I remind you of our last excursion? I was nearly beheaded, boy! This is how an old man should be living?"

"We saved lives, Doctor. Children's lives."

Adoulla managed to half-smile at the dervish. *I wish the knowledge of that still kept my feet from aching, the way it did when I was your age*, he thought. *I wish it could keep me from freezing up and accepting death.* But what he said was, "Yes, I suppose we did."

They kept walking, making their way past the gaudy storefronts that lined the Lane of Monkeys. Adoulla watched an ancient husband and wife sitting cross-legged on a long reed mat in front of a teahouse ahead of them. They were all dirty gray hair and wrinkled brown skin, playing a fierce game of bakgam. The man moved his token across the board's painted sword tips and, with a loud clack and a victorious smile, landed on the first sword. The old woman was about to lose. She scowled and spat, the glob nearly hitting Raseed as he and Adoulla walked by.

Just after they passed the old couple, Adoulla heard the rattle of triangle dice in the bakgam cup, the clatter as they hit the board, and a series of shouts. The old woman cackled and began a taunting, incomprehensible victory song as her husband cursed in disbelief. She'd rolled an eight!

*That should be Miri and me*, Adoulla couldn't help thinking. He should have married Miri a long time ago. He should have left the lunatic life of a ghul hunter.

Instead, year after year, he had foolishly decided that fighting fanged things and stopping the spells of wicked men was more important than happiness. Instead of a blissful marriage, he had monstrosities on his mind and a pile of "should haves" pressing down upon his soul.

He and Raseed finally neared the western gate which would take them out of the city. As they crossed a small alleyway, a doe-eyed girl of an age with Raseed smiled a none-too-shy smile at the dervish. Raseed made a choking noise and kept his eyes on the ground until the girl was a block away.

Though he knew it was a lost cause, Adoulla couldn't help himself. "What is wrong with you, boy? Did you not see the way that little flower looked at you? You could have at least smiled back!"

"Doctor, please!" The boy paused. "This attack. You spoke of the extraordinary powers of this ghul pack's master. Do you think one of the Thousand and One, rather than a man, made these ghuls?"

*So much focus on duty, so much neglect of what really matters. He doesn't know the painful end of this road . . . .*

Adoulla abandoned his avuncular attempt to get Raseed to act like a living, breathing young man. The dervish would rather think about monsters than smile at a girl. Very well. But he sounded too eager about the possibility of fighting a djenn. *If he'd ever actually faced one of the Thousand and One in battle, he'd feel differently.*

"It wasn't a djenn, boy. When one of the fire-born strikes, no one escapes, least of all a child."

The dervish nodded thoughtfully. Whatever else

Adoulla found irritating about Raseed, he was at least deferential to Adoulla's experience.

"I wonder—" Adoulla continued as they rounded a corner, but the words twisted into a shouted curse as he saw the massive crowd that lay before them.

"Ahhh, God's balls! The Horrible Halt!" Adoulla pronounced the Dhamsawaati term for the complete standstill of traffic with a familiar disgust. Before them, a wall of people seemed to rise up as the blocks-long tangle of carts, camels, and fools slowly pinched its way through the wide western gate. Adoulla collided with an unwashed little man who had been walking in front of him. He barely acknowledged the man's loud admonition to watch where he put his big feet.

"Some sort of gate inspection?" Raseed asked.

Adoulla snorted. " 'Gate inspection,' 'tariff-checks,' 'watchmen's business.' It's all the same monkeyshit. And there's more of it every day." At the rate the line was moving, it would be another hour before they were through.

A ghul pack was loose, which meant lives were at stake. But Dhamsawaat's hundred headaches hurried for no man. One did not walk through the gates of Dhamsawaat the way one walked through a town-house door. There was first the gray stone inner wall, then one passed through Inspector's Square, and then through the great main wall, a hundred feet thick. Then one crossed a house-lined lane past the last guardwall before taking the Bridge of Yellow Roses over a ditch. The process had never been a quick one, and due to the new Khalif's poor city management, it took longer than ever.

The duo cut through the throng as best they could without being truly rude. Adoulla did not want to start a fight, and fights were not uncommon in situations like these. Another quarter-hour and he and Raseed managed to get near the wide gate at the main wall. There the road rose slightly, and Adoulla saw that this was more than a simple traffic tangle.

*An execution!* The great gray paving stones of Inspector's Square had been cleared of carts. At its center lay a worn leather mat. A boy of no more than two and ten kneeled on the mat, his hands and feet bound and his eyes wide with terror. A huge, hooded man with a broad bladed sword stood over him.

Adoulla stopped walking, transfixed with horror. *Name of God! What could a child that age have possibly done to deserve such a fate?*

As if in answer, a high-pitched voice assaulted his ears. Turning toward the sound, he saw a liveried crier standing in an alcove carved in the stone archway above the gate. The man shouted shrilly through a metal cone.

"O fortunate subjects of God's Regent in the World, the Defender of Virtue, the Most Exalted of Men, His Majesty the Khalif, how God smiles upon you to provide you with such a ruler! See how your benevolent monarch, Jabbari akh-Khaddari, Khalif of Abassen and of all the Crescent Moon Kingdoms, protects you from the grasping hands of thieves! See how he punishes the wicked swiftly and terribly!"

Traffic still moved at an inchworm's pace, but most of the folk on the road were now gawking at the square. Adoulla stood still, wanting to stop this wickedness but knowing he could not. Someone behind him pushed past, trying to get forward in the press.

He looked back to the leather mat. *Almighty God, why do you allow this? Why do you send me to fight monsters outside of my city while such monsters live within it?*

God did not answer.

Raseed, who had also stopped, looked at him with concern. "Doctor, what do you—"

Without warning, something flew at the hooded executioner's face, covering it in an amber goop. Then the man's chest exploded in red.

*A crossbow bolt!* Men and women screamed. There was a sound like a thundercrack and a puff of orange smoke suddenly obscured the square. A moment later, the smoke cleared and Adoulla saw only the sprawled form of the dead executioner.

The bound boy was gone.

*What could—?*

There was another thundercrack, this one from the alcove above the gate. More orange smoke wreathed the recess where the crier had stood. It cleared almost instantly, and Adoulla made out the crier's liveried form slumped at the feet of a tall, broad-shouldered man. This man wore a costume of calfskin and black silk, emblazoned with falcons. His arms were as thick as some men's legs, but he moved like a dancer as he stepped to the alcove's lip.

*It's him!* thought Adoulla, who'd heard much of the man but never seen him. *Pharaad Az Hammaz, the—*

"The Falcon Prince!" The words left a dozen mouths around Adoulla.

*More trouble.* A confident grin split the famous thief's moustachioed face. Adoulla shouldn't have been able to read the man's facial expression quite so clearly at such a distance. An address-spell was at work, then— the kind that, supposedly, only the Khalif could afford. Every person in the crowd would have the same clear view of the Falcon Prince, would hear his words as if he stood beside them, and would find themselves . . . not *coerced* by the Prince's magic, but *open* to hearing what he had to say. It was likely the only reason they weren't panicking and fleeing.

Raseed growled. "The criminal!"

Well, *most* people would be open to hearing the man, Adoulla corrected himself. Technically, Adoulla could not dispute Raseed's epithet. Ten years ago, a string of flamboyant robberies of the city's wealthiest citizens were showily announced to be the work of a single brilliant bandit, who called himself the Falcon Prince. Pharaad Az Hammaz, as he had later revealed his name to be, never himself claimed to be true royalty, but the rumors persisted that he was the last heir of a kingly line from Abassen's dim past.

Royalty or not, the Falcon Prince was one of the most powerful men in Dhamsawaat. He and his small army of beggars and thieves had become an almost governmental force, the semiofficial voice of the poor.

And while the landowners and merchants who took up the cry of "share the wealth" were few and far between, Adoulla had heard from sound sources that a few of the Khalif's most powerful ministers, due to personal conviction or bribery, secretly backed the bandit.

"God's peace, good people of Dhamsawaat!" The thief boomed, his outstretched arms embracing the crowd. "Our time together is short! Hear the words of a Prince who loves you!" A small, cautious cheer went up from a few corners. "I've freed an innocent boy from the Khalif's headsman. His crime? Being fool enough to think he could pick coins from a watchman's purse and feed his ailing mother! Now, we grown folk know that watchmen are as attached to their purses as normal men are to their olive sacks." The bandit grabbed at his crotch and the crowd laughed hesitantly at his bawdiness. "But did the child deserve to *die*? Do we Dhamsawaatis care more for the ill-earned wealth of bullies than for the life of a child?"

The crowd grew bolder, and shouts of "No, no!" and "May God forbid it!" erupted from all corners.

The Falcon Prince stood, hands on hips, drinking it in. "I am guilty, good people! I freed the boy. I hit the headsman with a honey pie before I killed him! Only a hungry, hungry man would chop off a child's head for a few filthy coins. So I fed him! Honey and steel, good people!" The crowd laughed loudly now at the Falcon's cheerful, casual tone, and he went on.

"The old Khalif and I were enemies. He was no hero, but he spent fifty years watching over this city, which he loved. But for three years now, his fool of a son has bled Dhamsawaat. He has tried to find me and kill me. He! Has! Failed!" With the help of the address-spell, the Falcon boomed each word with a great drum's rumble.

The crowd sent up a boisterous cheer, and a small knot of men took up a chant:

*Fly, fly, O falcon!*
*Thy wing no dart can pierce!*
*Fly, fly, O falcon!*
*Thy heart and eye so fierce!*

The old-as-sand song—in which a noble falcon gouges out the eyes of a cruel king—had become associated with the Falcon Prince, and the new Khalif had made the singing of it punishable by flogging.

*There's going to be real trouble here*. A dozen watchmen in riveted jerkins shoved their way through the packed crowd toward the gate. They brandished slender steel maces and tried to keep their eyes on the alcove and the crowd at the same time.

As the Khalif's men moved toward the knot of singers the song died down. At once, though, a fresh round of "Fly, O Falcon" went up on the opposite side of the crowd. The watchmen's heads all whipped toward the sound in unison, but they let the singers be and tried to reach the Prince himself, who had stopped speechifying to caper to the tune as best he could in the small alcove. The bandit's jollity only caused the singers in the crowd to sing more boisterously. This time, men did not stop chanting when the knot of watchmen passed. And Adoulla saw the Khalif's men were scanning the crowd more anxiously as they made their way toward the gate. *A dozen against hundreds*.

Beside him, Adoulla sensed a sudden battle tension in his protégé. Raseed drew his sword soundlessly, and everyone around him took a step back. The blade was two-pronged, according to the Traditions of the Order, "in order to cleave right from wrong." Adoulla feared that Raseed was about to try to do so now.

"What are you doing?" Adoulla whispered.

"I'm going to help the watchmen, Doctor."

"The Falcon Prince is not our enemy, boy."

"With apologies, Doctor, he is *not* a prince. He uses magic to commit crimes. Exactly the sort of thing that we are obligated to fight!"

Raseed started to move again, but Adoulla grabbed his slender shoulder. He could hardly restrain Raseed if the dervish chose to interfere, but Adoulla hoped his age and authority would prevail.

"We are obligated to fight the servants of the Traitorous Angel. Pharaad Az Hammaz may be a criminal, but he feeds the poor and chastens the proud. Surely even your zealous eyes can see the virtue in that!"

The boy said nothing. He frowned hard at Adoulla. Then he sheathed his sword.

In the alcove, the Falcon Prince spread his huge hands wide as if welcoming the approaching watchmen to a banquet. "The Khalif's dogs come for me, my friends! If you hear their yappy mouths a-cursing, it is because some scoundrel has sabotaged their crossbows! But this is only the beginning, dear Dhamsawaatis! Stand ready! The day comes soon when we take back what is ours! There will be choices before us all, though some would have us believe that *they* are meant by God to do our choosing for us! But are we of Dhamsawaat bound by chains forged by the tyrants of past days? Does a man rule us without limit or wisdom just because his father ruled?"

A booming "NO!" went up from the crowd, and a dozen different voices shouted support.

"Let the Falcon rule!"

"God grant us a wise Khalif!"

"No chains here, O Falcon!"

Adoulla would wager money that the flamboyant thief had placed these men and women in the crowd himself. The watchmen were nearly at the gate now, but they had to push through an increasingly hostile crowd. The Prince continued.

"We of the Jewel of Abassen love a Khalif who does his duty. Who helps feed his people. Who steals not their coin. But a Khalif who dooms us with his greed and his cruelty? Well—" menace edged into the bandit's voice "— well, even a Khalif is but a man, and better a bad man should die than our good city!" Due to the address-spell everyone in the crowd saw the infectious gleam in the Falcon Prince's eye.

A clamor went up from the crowd. Some of it was outraged muttering. But a good number of folk were clearly emboldened by the Prince's regicidal words, and they made a lot of noise. At the edge of the crowd Adoulla noticed an extravagantly dressed merchant and a liveried civil servant making their way out of the crowd, frightened looks on their faces.

Raseed put a hand back to his sword hilt and shifted restlessly.

"When there is little food to buy and less work to be had, when half our sons have known the gaol and half our daughters have been shamed by watchmen, the people of Dhamsawaat have risen up before! It will happen again, my friends! Stand ready! Stand ready!"

The watchmen were now climbing to the crier's alcove. More of them were streaming in from the other side of the gate. But there was another thundercrack, another cloud of orange smoke, and the Prince was gone.

*Almighty God!*

The crowd quickly lost its boldness. Men and women went back to their business, giving the furious watchmen a wide berth. Beside Adoulla, Raseed cleared his throat, and Adoulla remembered the urgency of their task. Movement through the tight-packed crowd had been impossible during the Prince's appearance, and the crowd moved slowly now.

"Come, boy, this gate will be gummed up for hours now. Maybe we can cross over to the avenue and hire a sedan. With all the commotion here, the Chair-Bearer's Gate might actually be quicker than this mess." Adoulla tried not to dwell on how much time they'd lost already. Lost time meant more men dead beneath the fangs of ghuls.

They walked a half-dozen long blocks and turned the corner into an uncrowded alley. It felt like a different city. The alleyway was cooler, shaded as it was by tall buildings on either side. A hard-eyed woman sat on her doorstep, and she looked up suspiciously from the basket she was weaving when the pair walked by. She and a bone thin poppy-chewer, who lay sprawled on another doorstep, apparently talking to the clouds, were the only people in the alley. Adoulla's discerning nose detected stewed goat wafting from a window, and he greedily inhaled the smell.

"Watch your step, Doctor!" Even as the words left Raseed's mouth Adoulla felt his sandal sink into a warm pile of camel shit. Adoulla cursed and scraped his foot on the stone. He turned back to curse again at the brownish smear behind him.

And found himself face-to-face with the Falcon Prince.

*Name of God! Where did* he *come from?* The man was nearly six and a half feet tall. Taller even than Adoulla, and rippling with muscle where Adoulla jiggled with fat. His black moustaches were meticulously groomed, and his handsome brown face split in a grin.

Out of the corner of his eye Adoulla saw Raseed turn and draw his sword. The Falcon took a wary step back. The thief looked at Raseed as one might a dangerous animal. But he smiled again as he spoke.

"Well, this is something one doesn't see in every alley! A dervish of the Order and a ghul hunter—Doctor Adoulla Makhslood, I would guess." The Prince's manner was strangely casual, given the situation he had just fled.

Adoulla said nothing but let his face register surprise at being known outside of his home quarter.

"Yes, Doctor, I know of you. Had we time, I would

repeat all of the praises that I have heard sung of you among the poor of the Scholars' Quarter. But there are watchmen a few blocks behind me."

"Murderer!" Raseed spat the word and took a step forward, but Adoulla threw an arm across the boy's chest.

The Prince ignored the dervish and spoke to Adoulla. "Will you help me, Uncle? My next steps—and the lives of others—depend on whether the watchmen know my true path."

*So, a ghul-orphaned boy was not enough for old Adoulla Makhslood today, eh, God? No, You had to involve Your fat old servant in a mad usurper's plots as well! Wonderful.* Adoulla looked up at the Prince.

He could hem and haw, but there was only one choice here, and this was a matter of moments. "They will not know your true path," he muttered. Beside him, Raseed made an angry noise.

The Prince bowed his head. "The Falcon Prince thanks you, Uncle! Mayhap I will have the chance to return the favor someday." The bandit then leapt up, landing on a second-story balcony.

*Remarkable.* Adoulla had seen leaping-spells before, but the way the Prince's physical grace blended with the obviously magical enhancements was still impressive. With two more quick leaps he was on the building's roof and lost from sight. Beside Adoulla, the dervish let out what seemed an involuntary grunt of respect.

Adoulla heard the shout and clatter of approaching watchmen. "We saw him go the other way, yes?" he said tersely.

Fury filled the boy's tilted eyes. "I will not lie to protect that villain, Doctor!"

"Then conceal yourself, boy, and let me talk!" But the dervish did not move. "*Please!*" Adoulla urged.

The boy shook his turbaned head, but he stepped into the alley shadows, where he seemed to disappear.

Two watchmen rounded the corner running. *From the noise I'd have guessed it was a whole squadron. Belligerent fools.* Adoulla kept himself from darting his eyes about the alley's shadows. He prayed that the boy would stay hidden.

"You there, old man! Halt! Halt if you value your life!" The watchmen were both tall, fresh-faced young men. Again they shouted at Adoulla to halt, though he was standing still.

The pair thundered up and Adoulla could smell their sweat. "You! Did you see—"

"That way!" Adoulla shouted, pointing in the wrong direction. He put on his best irked-uncle face. "He ran down that turn-off! That dirty, damned-by-God bandit! He nearly knocked me over! What in God's name are you men doing to stop this, I ask? Why, when I was your age, the watchmen would never let—"

The two men shoved past Adoulla, running in the direction of his pointing finger. When they were out of sight, Raseed stepped from the shadows.

It was Adoulla's turn to shake his head. "We've lost a lot of time, boy. Looks like we'll be doing some night riding."

Raseed nodded with a grim relish. "Ghul hunting in the dark."

Adoulla smiled in spite of himself, feeling buoyed just a bit by his assistant's indefatigability. "Aye. And only a sword-for-brains little madman like yourself would be *excited* by the prospect."

Not quite wanting to know what Almighty God had in store for him next, Adoulla gestured to his assistant and walked on.

# Chapter 4

ON THE DUSTY WESTERN OUTSKIRTS of Dham
sawaat, Raseed bas Raseed watched the Doctor
huffing as he clambered down from the sedan chair
they had hired. Foul tannery smells pierced the air,
mixing strangely with birdsong. The buildings here
were fewer and farther between than they were within
the walls. Hut-like homes of sun-baked mud and small,
prosperous-looking houses of burnt brick lined the
road. Even here, where the crowds were much thinner,
a motley assortment of people filled the street. Some
part of Raseed, intensely aware of his surroundings, as
always, noticed all of this. But his uppermost thoughts
were on the brief encounter with the Falcon Prince, and
his own conduct during it.

*Hiding from men of authority to protect a miscreant! You
should have captured him,* the dervish chided himself.
*You should have insisted, no matter the Doctor's words.*
Pharaad Az Hammaz was a criminal, after all. And a

traitor to the Throne of the Crescent Moon, though the Doctor insisted that the bandit's cause was just.

*The Doctor*. Raseed had helped a seditious thief escape justice, and why? Because the Doctor had asked it. The wrongness of it struck him anew. It was true, Raseed had put himself into a sort of apprenticeship, and thus he owed the Doctor loyalty, but this business with the Falcon Prince . . . Raseed wondered what his Shaykhs at the Lodge of God would say if they could see him now. And he worried—as he did every day— that his actions had displeased Almighty God. How could he know, after all? Every night his meditation exercises helped him to settle his restless soul enough that he could sleep, but it was never easy.

A long-haired girl in a tight-fitting tunic walked by, and Raseed knew that Almighty God was testing him yet again. He averted his eyes and smothered the shameful ache that began to fill his body.

Life had been less confusing at the Lodge of God. But in the two years since High Shaykh Aalli—the most venerated and also the most permissive of his teachers—had sent him to train with the Doctor, Raseed had learned that the world was complex. *When you meet Adoulla Makhslood, little sparrow, you will see that there are truths greater than all you've learned in this Lodge. You will learn that virtue lives in strange places.*

Raseed had spent two years learning just how true his old master's words were. He thought back on the first ghul-hunt he had undertaken with the Doctor, when they had rescued the wife of Hafi the bookbinder from the magus Zoud and his water ghuls. Raseed had begun that hunt amazed that this impious, unkempt man was in fact the great and virtuous ghul hunter whom High Shaykh Aalli had praised so lavishly. But by the time the wicked Zoud lay dead, Raseed had been forced to see the truth of the Doctor's powers—and of his devotion to duty.

Even so, in his first days working with Adoulla Makhslood, Raseed had thought of leaving a dozen times, finding the Doctor oafish and irreverent. But High Shaykh Aalli had been clear in his orders, and a newmade dervish did not dare question the High Shaykh.

And, again and again over the past two years, Raseed had seen proof that somewhere amidst all of the Doctor's belching and cursing and laxity was a fierce foe of the Traitorous Angel. A man who served God with a soul-deep dedication that was not so terribly different from High Shaykh Aalli's. A man blessed by the All Merciful, and beloved unto Him.

Still, Raseed worried about what would happen when, someday, he returned to the Lodge to become a Shaykh himself. Each of his actions in the outside world would be judged, and when he thought on his own laxity in matters such as this business of the Falcon Prince, he feared the judgment would not be kind.

The Doctor turned from paying the chair-bearer and gave Raseed a piercing stare from beneath bushy gray eyebrows. "You're worrying about that business with the watchmen, eh?"

He did not ask the Doctor how he knew. "Yes, Doctor. It is just that—" Upset words burst forth, surprising himself with their intensity. "Whether or not he is a foolish man, we must respect our Khalif and his Heir! We must defend them! If that goes, what else will we lose respect for? The Ministering Angels? God himself?"

The Doctor rolled his eyes and scratched his big nose. He put his arm around Raseed's shoulder and steered their steps down a packed-dirt footlane that led to a pair of long, low buildings. "You know," the Doctor said as they headed for the stables, "there is nothing more upsetting than young people who sound like old people! Do you hear your own hysteria? Do you think that there have always been Khalifs, boy? God and man loved one another before there were palaces and puffed-up rulers. And if the Crescent Moon Palace crumbled tomorrow, God would love us still. 'For yea, they are the kings of men's bodies, but God is the King of Men's Souls.'"

The Doctor's quoting of the Heavenly Chapters was punctuated by the smell of animals—mule, horse, and camel—wafting toward them as they approached Sideways Sayeed's stables. The stablekeeper, an impeccably dressed but deformed man whose spine was bent nearly parallel to the ground, came out to greet them, his fine mother-of-pearl-worked cane thumping in the dirt. The Doctor made the arrangements, as Sideways Sayeed was one of his seemingly countless old friends.

Even were this not the case, Raseed knew, the Doctor would have insisted on doing the talking, as he considered Raseed too naïve to be trusted with certain tasks. A month after coming to live in Dhamsawaat, Raseed had gone supper-shopping. The Doctor had laughed at the scant bushel of wilted vegetables Raseed had brought home, asserting irritably that he'd have bought twice as much food with half the coins. Though two years had passed since then, Raseed knew his mentor still considered him to be "a genius of the sword but an idiot of the street," as the Doctor, quoting some poet, had once put it.

A few minutes later the Doctor cheek-kissed and God's-peaced Sideways Sayeed goodbye and handed Raseed the reins of a hardy looking mule. Leading his own mount back to the road, the Doctor looked anxious, scratching at his beard and glancing about him as if searching for something. Raseed guessed that it had to do with departing from Dhamsawaat. Leaving the city behind seemed to make the Doctor fidgety and melancholic by turns.

Raseed did not think he had ever met anyone so attached to a place. The ghul hunter complained about city life often, but Raseed knew that he loved it— perhaps *because* the King of Cities was a place that the Doctor could complain of familiarly, comfortably, endlessly. Raseed hoped it would please God to bring this good if flawed man back to his city soon. He pledged silently to use his sword arm and his virtue to make it so.

They reached the road, and the Doctor mounted his mule with a series of grunts and huffs from both him and the beast. Raseed eyed his own mule again. He'd had little need of steeds or pack animals in his solo travels. *The true dervish needs no horse,* said the Traditions. And his Shaykhs at the Lodge of God said that Raseed was the fastest dervish the Order had ever seen. He could run for miles without tiring. As far as pack animals went, the Traditions were equally clear: *The true dervish needs no more than he can carry on his back.* Still, the Doctor always traveled by beast, and called it "show-off-ish" when Raseed insisted upon walking beside him. Raseed had taken to hiring mules and sedan chairs along with the Doctor, just to keep from hearing him complain.

*Just for that? Or because you have grown lazy, and he gives you an excuse?* His own reprimanding voice echoed through his head. Next time he would walk, he resolved.

They spent hours riding, moving past suburbs and outlying farms until there were no signs that they had left the world's greatest city behind them. There were few people moving along the hard-packed road now, only one or two carts or camels at a time. Since leaving the Lodge, Raseed had spent little time outside of Dhamsawaat, and as he rode he marveled again at how the sky seemed to open up above them.

Finally, when the sun had sunk halfway to the horizon, and they were alone on the road, the Doctor brought his mule to a halt, struggling briefly with the beast. Raseed pulled up beside him. "Well," the Doctor half-shouted, "this is as good a place as any to cast the tracking spell. Come!" He gestured Raseed to the side of the road and dismounted with a loud grunt. The Doctor then reached into his satchel and hunched down to the ground with an even louder grunt.

*He is* always *making rude noises,* Raseed thought with

irritation. *Grunting, scratching, laughing too loudly. But it is my duty to keep him safe.* In one motion Raseed also dismounted, gathering the reins of both mules and standing over the Doctor protectively as he worked his spell.

The Doctor had pulled out a bit of paper, the bloody scrap of the child Faisal's clothing, a vial, and a long platinum needle. He wrote something on the paper, pricked his finger with the needle, and pinned cloth and paper both to the ground. Then he stood, closed his eyes, and recited from the Heavenly Chapters, sprinkling out a dark green powder—mint?—with each Name of God he spoke. " 'God is the Seer of the Unseen! God is the Knower of the Unknown! God is the Revealer of Things Hidden! God is the Teacher of Mysteries!' "

Nothing happened, so far as Raseed could see, but the Doctor, his brow sweaty now, opened his eyes and took his mule's reins from Raseed. He remounted and continued down the road. He said nothing, not even turning to see if Raseed was following. As Raseed mounted and trotted up beside the Doctor he realized why. *He's winded—the traveling, the spell—it's all taking its toll on him.* Raseed tried not to be worried by this.

Raseed gave the Doctor a few minutes to catch his breath before he spoke. "You have found the ghuls' trail, Doctor?"

"Aye," was all the Doctor said.

Mile after mile they rode the mules at a brisk walk, moving at a slant toward the sinking sun. As the road veered further west and closer to the River of Tigers,

the land swiftly sank and grew marshy. The air grew
more humid and more and more gnats filled it, irritating Raseed's eyes and nose. When the sun was touching the horizon with pink and purple, Raseed saw a
scrawny, bearded farmer walking toward them—the
only traveler they'd come across in an hour. The man
gave the mules a wide berth and mumbled "God's
peace" from the opposite side of the road as they
passed, avoiding eye contact. *Is he afraid of us? Or does
he have something to hide?*

*He is not why you are here,* Raseed chided himself.
*Stay focused.*

The landscape was dotted with large boulders that
might hide anything. Raseed watched for signs of
movement about them. The River of Tigers lay just out
of sight on their right, its presence indicated by a clean,
wet scent, by date palms and by the great patches of
steelreed that clacked in the evening breeze.

"Stop." The Doctor spoke the word loudly enough
to startle two marshbirds into flight. It was the first
time he'd spoken in a long while. "The trail veers off
here, but something is not quite right."

"What do you mean, Doctor?"

Raseed's mentor looked truly confused—a rare
sight. "I don't rightly know, boy. In all my years of casting tracking spells, nothing like this has happened.
Normally I feel—maybe better to say I *hear* within my
mind—God's prompts in the direction of my quarry.
And this is still the case. Our prey is close and in that
direction." The Doctor pointed off the road to the left,

toward a dense patch of boulders and a lone hill with a pointed top. "But I also hear His hints about other dangers. 'The jackal that eats souls.' 'The thing that slays the lion's pride.' I . . . I don't know what it means. In all my years I've never . . ." The Doctor let go of his reins and held his head in his hands. Raseed tried to hide his worry.

The Doctor took a deep breath and noisily exhaled. He looked up, shook his head, and ran a hand through his beard. "Gone. Whatever it was, it's gone." He looked around as if he'd been woken from a dream. Another deep breath and an exhalation loud enough to be a camel's. "Forget it, boy, never mind. I'm old and tired and haven't had enough to eat today." Raseed's mentor clearly did not believe this, but if the Doctor wished to say no more, Raseed could do little about it. "Let us continue," the Doctor said, turning his mule off the road and picking his way downward with the slight decline of the land.

Raseed followed.

After another quarter hour it was dark, save for the faint light of the stars and the moon, hidden behind a silvery shroud of cloud. They came to the base of the point-topped hill, and Raseed saw that it wasn't a hill at all, but a sloping rock formation that jutted up fifty feet from the ground at an angle, like a tiny mountain. The Doctor guided his mule's steps onto the rock, and its hooves clopped loudly against the stone. Behind, Raseed rode his own mount up the incline as it steepened sharply. The Doctor, following prompts that Raseed could neither hear nor see, then turned, to ride across the huge wedge of stone.

The precision of the rock's triangular shape and the smoothness of the stone made Raseed wonder whether the slope they were riding across had been shaped by men. *If so, what sort of men walked on it?*

"Doctor where does this stone come from? What building once stood here?" Raseed asked quietly. He prided himself that he did not feel fear easily, but there was something troubling about walking across the floorstones of the long-dead.

The Doctor spoke distractedly, looking all about him as he did. "It's from the Kem empire, that's for sure. Maybe the cornerstone of—"

The Doctor let the sentence die on his lips and drew his mule to a sharp halt, the animal objecting noisily. He narrowed his eyes and peered about. "Dismount!" he whispered, and clambered off his mule.

Raseed obeyed. He gathered both animals' reins, but let them fall as the Doctor whispered again.

"Let them go. No time to tie them." Again Raseed did as he was told, and the beasts trotted down the slope toward a patch of thornclover near the stone's base.

"Bone ghuls. More than one . . . nearby." the Doctor said, cocking his head. It looked as if he were listening to something inside his skull. He shot his big hand into his satchel. "Bottom of the slope!" he barked.

Raseed did not ask how the Doctor knew. He drew his sword and scanned the near-darkness below them.

Suddenly the mules began braying fearfully. Raseed's keen eyes made out their dark shapes, fleeing the stone slope.

Then he saw other shapes, man-like—one, two, three of them—stepping from behind boulders, moving up the incline. And he heard the hissing.

The hissing of ghuls was like no other sound in this world. A thousand serpents rasping with a man's hatred. Raseed had heard the sound more than once. But it still made his skin crawl.

The clouds blew across the sky and the scene below them was bathed in moonlight. Even the Doctor's old eyes would be able to see plainly now. Three bone ghuls, all claws and jaws and gray skin, were scrambling up the slope of the huge stone block.

"We have gone from hunters to prey, Doctor."

The Doctor grunted and pulled something from his satchel. Two of the three ghuls had closed to twenty yards. The Doctor regarded them coolly, held aloft a small stoppered vial and threw it to the ground. The glass shattered, the smell of vinegar and flowers filled the air, and the Doctor bellowed scripture.

"God is the Mercy That Kills Cruelty!" There was a sound like a landslide and the two closest ghuls, their false souls snuffed out, lost their man-like shape and collapsed into piles of turned earth and graveworms. *Two of the monsters at one stroke!* Not for the first time, Raseed marveled at the Doctor's powers. He felt reassured to be admiring his mentor and not fearing for him.

One of the ghuls still stood. The Doctor leaned forward with his hands on his knees, clearly worn out by his spell. "Your turn, boy!"

Even as the words left the Doctor's lips, Raseed sped toward the last creature, his sword flying out in search of ghul-flesh. The thing hissed with mindless malevolence and raked its long claws, but Raseed kept it at a double swordlength's distance.

He danced in two steps and slashed out, feeling his sword bite into the monster. There was a loud hiss and the ghul's severed claw went arcing through the air, maggots dripping forth like drops of blood. One of the maggots landed on Raseed's cheek. The ghul didn't even pause. It swung out with its mutilated stump and Raseed took a darting step back, not daring to brush away the itching insect.

The ghul pressed in, but Raseed had the advantage now. The creature didn't feel pain, and one-clawed it could still have easily killed most men. But Raseed was not most men. He snaked left, then right, always keeping the ghul's good claw at a distance. He waited for an opening and found it when the thing lunged at him with its snapping jaws.

Raseed shifted, brought his sword up, brought it down. The ghul's head flopped from its shoulders. Its body trembled and dissolved into a pile of maggots and grave soil.

Raseed brushed a maggot from his face and stepped back to the Doctor's side, finding him winded but unharmed. "Doctor! Where do you think—"

More hissing. The words died on Raseed's lips.

Two more bone ghuls clambered up from the ledge of the sheer far face of the stone block. *Merciful God!* Raseed had fought bone ghuls since joining the Doctor. But always one or two of them. He hadn't known a ghul pack of this size could be made. The Doctor still huffed beside him, likely unable to work another invocation so soon.

Raseed charged at the ghuls, his two-pronged sword out to his side as he slashed past them. His sword bit into one ghul's neck, was nearly wrenched from his hands. He drew the blade back and kept moving. He dodged claws, drew their attention away from the Doctor. The ghuls pressed him back until his heels were less than a yard from the cliff edge of the massive stone block. He tried to get a glimpse of the Doctor, but the creatures blocked his view.

Maggots dribbled from one ghul's neck-wound. That one staggered, its energy clearly unfocused. The other stared at Raseed with empty eyes. Some vicious unliving instinct within the monster was weighing when to strike.

The Doctor's big white kaftan-clad form shuffled forward, shouting. His voice was weak as he pronounced, "God is the Hope of the Hopeless!"

The wounded ghul collapsed. The other one flew at Raseed. The wind was knocked out of him as the monster slammed into him. He scrabbled back two steps.

The ground give way beneath Raseed's feet.

He and the ghul went plummeting in a tangle of limbs over the edge of the stone block.

Raseed tensed his body and focused his soul. He

twisted, letting his sword fly from his hand and kicking the ghul away as he fell. The rocky ground rushed toward him, but Raseed was calm within the slow-time sense of his training. His acrobatic skill was God-blessed, beyond that of any rope dancer or tumbler. This fall would not harm him.

He tucked himself into a ball and hit the ground rolling with only a hard grunt. He continued the roll for another twenty feet and stood, panting. His keen eyes caught the moon-glint of his sword a few feet away, and he scooped it up, reassured by the familiar feeling of its hilt in his hand.

*Where is the ghul?* Raseed looked around, bracing for another fight. He saw the bone ghul ten feet away, sprawled on the ground, twitching. The monster had landed head first, cracking its skull open upon a sharp, man-sized rock. The thing hissed feebly, twitched once more, and dissipated into a heap of dead vermin.

*Praise God!* Only then did Raseed allow himself to feel the stinging pain across his chest and ribs. The thing had raked him with its rancid claws, shredding his silk robes and grazing his flesh. *The wound will need herb-purging.* The Doctor had taught him some time ago that the old tale of ghul-wounds turning men into ghuls was nonsense, but the charnel monsters' dirty claws could still kill with any number of very real diseases.

Raseed heard the Doctor shouting from the top of the stone block. *Still more of the creatures?* He ran to the sheer face of the block and started climbing with the speed that ordinary men found so amazing. The Doctor had already been exhausted when he'd spoken his last invocation. In such shape he was a poor match for the minions of the Traitorous Angel. Raseed climbed faster. He ignored his wounds and the painful scrape of rock against his fingertips and hoped he wasn't too late.

# Chapter 5

ADOULLA HAD BEGUN THIS BATTLE feeling like a cocksure younger man—he'd sensed the ghuls early, dispatched several, watched his assistant sever another ghul's head. But that first burst of nostalgic bravado was gone now. Adoulla didn't doubt that Raseed had survived that fall, but he might need Adoulla's help. And there might be still more ghuls about. Adoulla was drop down tired, but professional pride and worry for his assistant kept him from collapsing. He turned toward where Raseed had fallen, digging into his satchel again and producing a small vellum envelope.

Something at the edge of his vision moved toward him. Adoulla spun away from whatever it was. Something heavy struck him across his back.

He went sprawling, the envelope and his satchel flying from his hands. A large form snaked between him and his bag. Stubbornly, he pushed away the pain in his back. He scuttled away from the creature, breathing heavily as he came to his feet.

Adoulla shouted out in shock. Another bone ghul. A *massive* bone ghul. The largest ghul he'd seen in forty years.

*Impossible! To make a creature of that size—along with all of these others!* The power involved was incalculable. The creature towered over him, and he was not a small man. Who could make and control this nine-foot monstrosity?

It took a step toward him. Adoulla looked from the thing's soulless eyes to its broad claws. One of those claws could crush his head like a melon. Indeed, only his half-conscious dodge had saved him from a broken back. And despite the world-weariness with which he faced each day, Adoulla was not ready to have his head crushed like a melon just yet. If nothing else, Raseed needed him.

He stared into the ghul's flat, pupil-less eyes. Softly, desperately, he began to whistle "Under the Pear Tree, My Sweet." As soon as the first notes left his lips, the monster froze in its tracks. A confident gaze and the ghul-soothing sound of a favorite song. It was an unreliable, old womanish charm, with none of the power or grace of scripture invocations. Sometimes it didn't work, and when it did it was effective for only a minute or so. But it had saved his life more than once.

The huge monster's claws were draped at its sides, and it swayed slowly with the tune. Adoulla tried to whistle, hold the ghul's eyes, and consider his options, all at the same time. The phrase *I am too old* kept getting in the way of his thoughts.

*Not now!* one part of him barked at the other. His satchel, with all of his components, lay on the ground just past the giant ghul. *It might as well be in Rughal-ba.* If he took a step toward it, he'd break the whistle charm. He kept whistling, but he was coming to the end of the song—and thus the end of the ghul-soothing.

Adoulla prayed that the ghul's claws would not catch him when he dove for his medicine bag. He didn't like his chances. *This is it, then*, Adoulla thought. *An ignoble death courtesy of a hissing abomination.* He couldn't say he was surprised. *What I wouldn't give for one last cup of cardamom tea, or one last meal in my townhouse.*

He weakly whistled the last note of the tune through dry lips and tensed his muscles. The creature squealed.

Then something leapt at the ghul.

It wasn't Raseed. Adoulla saw a flash of golden fur and a lashing tail. Some sort of animal had fastened itself to the giant ghul's back. The monster's milky white eyes widened and then contracted. It squealed again in pain.

Adoulla shoved melancholic thoughts to the side and tried to gather facts. What had hurt the ghul, and how could Adoulla use it to his advantage?

The gray-green monster twisted as it tried to shake this new attacker from its back. As the ghul turned, Adoulla got a better look at the extraordinary animal that had saved his life. A sleek she-lion with eyes like green fire and an impossibly shimmery gold coat.

Adoulla's mind raced with remembered lore. Not an animal at all. In fact, if the desert legends were to be believed, a creature such as this was an agent of the Angels' justice—and thus of God's. Adoulla said a quick, silent prayer of thanksgiving.

Still, *"God helpeth most the man who helpeth himself."* Adoulla risked grabbing for his satchel.

By the time he scooped it up and had his hand in it, though, he saw an invocation would not be needed. His rescuer had snuffed out the false soul within that monstrous mock human frame. As the thing died, it burbled in that manner that still, after all these years, turned Adoulla's stomach. Then, with a sound like the scrape of a great grave lid, the ghul crumbled, a carpet of cemetery soil and dead coffin-moths spilling forth.

A bright flare of sun-like light rippled out from the lioness' coat. When the flare subsided, a plain-faced brown girl of perhaps five and ten stood where the lioness had been. She was dressed in the simple sand-colored camel calf suede of the Badawi tribesmen. It was as if Adoulla had blinked and someone had replaced the razor-mawed creature of a moment ago with this green-eyed little girl.

It wasn't the first time he'd seen such a thing.

The rare, almost-forgotten gift of the lion-shape. He had known another tribesman thus gifted by God many years ago—a good man for a savage, but terrifying to witness when crossed. Adoulla would have to tread carefully here.

"Hello," he managed.

The girl stared at him with those emerald eyes, wary.

"God's peace," he tried.

The girl's expression softened almost imperceptibly, but she was still hard-faced. "God's peace," she said curtly, brushing her coarse, shoulder length hair from her eyes. A girl of her age speaking to a man of Adoulla's ought to have been more respectful in her tone—at the very least, she should have called him "Uncle." But the uncouth Badawi showed no decorum to any save their own. The girl followed her first two words with barked questions. "You were fighting these foul creatures? It was you who destroyed the others?"

"Indeed." Adoulla said, holding back the admonitions that were on the tip of his tongue. "Thank you for your help, child. It has been many years since I've been face-to-face with one who was gifted with the lion-shape."

The girl's mouth fell open. "You know of the gift? And you do not fear me?"

Adoulla shrugged. "You're used to dealing with your ignorant fellow tribesmen, no doubt. Feared you even while depending on your powers? Well, I am no ungrateful savage." The girl growled at the insult to her people, as if she were still a lioness inside.

Adoulla put both hands up placatingly. "I am a scholar of such phenomena and of their dark versions, girl. The lion-shape is a gift given to men by God through the Angels. '*You true Badawi watch for the Angel-boon—mane of golden sun, claws of silver moon.*' The shape is known to me, and is nothing to fear. Besides, after forty years of ghul hunting it takes more than a child wearing the shape of a lion to frighten me. Though I *am* surprised. It has been twenty years since I've met one of your kind. And I didn't know that the gift could be visited upon girls."

Adoulla heard the faintest whisper of noise as Raseed hoisted himself up from the sheer face of the stone. The girl turned at the sound.

"Well, boy, it's about time!" Adoulla said as the dervish came trotting up. "Leaving an old man to fend for himself up here! Though, as you can see, we are not alone."

The boy's sword was already in his hand, but his expression was more incredulous than battle ready. "Who is the girl, Doctor?"

"Well, among other things she was the instrument of God's Ministering Angels' preserving my life. But we've had no time for proper introductions." Adoulla turned to the girl, who was studying Raseed. "I am Doctor Adoulla Makhslood, young woman. My assistant is called Raseed." A cold wind picked up and Adoulla folded his hands beneath his armpits to stay warm.

The girl frowned again. "You are a ghul hunter? And this one is a dervish?" she asked brusquely, without taking her eyes off Raseed.

Adoulla arched a displeased eyebrow at the ill-mannered child, though he wasn't sure she saw it. "I am, and he is. But I thought that even the rudest of Badawi would have better manners than to nose into a stranger's business before even giving their name."

No hint of embarrassment crossed the girl's features. "I am Zamia Banu Laith Badawi, Protector of the Band of Nadir Banu Laith Badawi."

Adoulla glanced at his assistant. It was only then that Adoulla really saw the blood-stained slashes in Raseed's blue silks. The cuts didn't look deep, but Adoulla knew from experience how they burned. Of course, the stoic boy would show no sign of complaint. But herbs were needed there—ghulsbane and lavender. Adoulla was no healer, but his friends Dawoud and Litaz had taught him some little bits. "You're hurt," he said to his assistant, reaching into his satchel and producing a poultice pouch. He tossed it to the dervish, who sheathed his sword with clear reluctance and began mashing the pouch in his hands, preparing it for application.

Adoulla's nose twitched at the floral pungency of the herbs being crushed. He looked back to the girl. "Zamia here can take the lion-shape, boy. You do recall my lessons on the old powers of the Empty Kingdom's desert tribes? She just destroyed the largest ghul I've ever seen."

The dervish's eyes widened, and his hands stopped squeezing the pouch. He frowned slightly. "Impressive, Doctor. But the Traditions of the Order say 'Being my enemy's enemy does not make you my friend.'"

"Well, do a little dance, boy—for once those old hypocrites of yours had something wise to say. But I am not calling her a friend. I'm simply saying that she saved my life."

The girl spit. "Vile men! Do not speak of me as if I

weren't standing before you!" Tribesmen's speech had always sounded to Adoulla like rocks talking. This rough-looking girl sounded like a grating rain of pebbles. She focused her angry young glare on Adoulla. "What are you doing out here, old man?"

"*Doctor*, girl! You will call me *Doctor* or *Uncle* or *something* more respectful!" Angel-chosen or not, Adoulla had had enough of this rude little girl's tone.

"The Badawi owe no allegiance to city titles," she said sneeringly. Then, reluctantly, "But I will call you *Doctor* if you wish." An even more arrogant expression spread across the girl's homely features. "You say with your own tongue that I saved your life—this means that you owe me a debt of death."

Adoulla barked out a laugh. *Such notions these people have.* "Does it, now? I am a ghul hunter, girl. Do you know how many lives I have saved? How many men and women and children I have kept from the claws of monsters? Did they pledge their lives to me? Did they become my slaves? No. This is a relic from one of your people's ridiculous six-hour six-night story poems."

The girl growled again but said nothing.

Adoulla sighed. "Look. You asked in your mannerless way what we are doing here? Well, as it stands, this ghul pack slaughtered a marsh family a few days ago. My assistant and I—"

"I saw them," Zamia interrupted, and it was as if all of the arrogance had been bled from her voice. "I have been tracking these creatures for almost a week now, since they left the deep desert of the Empty Kingdom. I found the marshmen after they were killed, their ribcages cracked open, their hearts ripped from their chests. And their eyes . . . I've seen dead men before. I've *killed* men! Watched life's light die in their eyes. But this was . . . There was no brown or black or white in their eyes— only red! Not blood. A glowing red like . . . like nothing I've ever seen. If that is what it means to die beneath a ghul's claws . . . ." The girl shuddered, folded her arms around her boyish frame, and fell silent.

Adoulla, as well, found himself momentarily speechless. Eyes bright with the color of the Traitorous Angel—more evidence that there was something here even grimmer than the hunting of ghuls. His insides clenched in fear. "Bone ghul or water ghul, sand ghul or night ghul, the unholy monsters eat the still-warm hearts of men. But this . . . This business with the eyes is something still more horrible. A cruel kind of magic, a form that the old scrolls say has vanished from this world. A sign that not just the flesh, but the soul itself has been sucked away and swallowed like marrow."

The girl's green eyes widened with shock. "Such a thing is not possible!"

Raseed, whose hands had been moving beneath his tunic as he applied the poultice, spoke before Adoulla could answer her. "The girl is right. God would not allow such a thing! The Heavenly Chapters say 'Yea, though the flesh is scourged, the soul of the believer feels no—'"

"Please, boy, no scripture quoting! Your inadequate interpretations help nothing here, and my energies are needed for more important things than enlightening you through exegesis. Now—"

Zamia tilted her head and sniffed. "You're telling the truth," she said in a suddenly weak voice. "I smell no trace of deceit upon you." And tears began to well up in her eyes.

Adoulla was perplexed. "And I smell no deceit upon you, Zamia Banu Laith Badawi. Though, despite its prominence, I'm sure my nose is not quite so accurate as yours. But now it is my turn to ask questions. Why these tears now? And how is it that you came to be here alone, stalking these monsters? Where is your band?"

"That is none of your concern," Zamia said, her words wooden and heavy as she wiped a few tears from her plain face. The wind whipped up for a moment, the sound blending eerily with the harsh call of a hunting night-kite.

"We clearly share an enemy, girl. Surely even a tribesman can see that we should share information as well." The girl's eyes tightened, and Adoulla recalled a favorite saying of Miri's: *Bees and beetles alike love honey more than vinegar*. That Miri rarely followed this dictum herself meant little. Adoulla needed to try a different tack. "Zamia, I don't mean you any insult. I know what it is to lose your happiness to the ghuls. And I can help you, girl. If you let me."

When the girl spoke it was with the voice of a dead woman. "I lied. When I spoke of finding the marshmen's bodies, I said that I had never seen such a thing. I lied. I had seen it days before. It happened to my band."

*So that's it.* Adoulla reached out a comforting hand to the girl, but she stopped him with an angry look. She swallowed, wiped away another tear, and continued. "I was out scouting one night, far ahead of the rest of the band. The next morning, when I returned to where they'd set their tents . . . What I found . . ." The girl's matter-of-fact tone slid away. She fell silent, her eyes wide with remembered horrors. Then she smothered her pain again and went on.

"Bodies. All of their bodies. All seven and fifty of the Banu Laith Badawi—old Uncle Mahloud and spoiled little Wazzi. Faziza, who believed that she really ruled the band. My father. My beautiful young cousin, who would have been chieftain—his body had been burned. All of them, do you understand? I am the last."

It had the sound of something the girl had been repeating to herself. Adoulla did not speak, hoping the girl would go on.

"There were foul, puzzling smells everywhere," she said after a moment. "Jackal-scent where no hair could be found. Fresh spilled child-blood that smelled of ancient buildings. But these scents led nowhere. The only sign I could find was this." Reaching into her tunic the girl drew forth an ornate curved dagger. The blade was stained with what looked like dried blood.

"It was my father's. He had hidden it in the folds of his chieftain's robes. There is blood on it, but the scent is neither man nor animal. And if the stories are to be believed, ghuls bleed no blood."

Adoulla's mind raced, recalling the strange phrases that had come to him earlier when he'd sought God's help in finding the ghuls. *'The jackal that eats souls.' 'The thing that slays the lion's pride.'* He turned the lines over in his head but still came up with nothing. "Generally, the stories are *not* to be believed," he finally said to Zamia. "But that one at least is true. Which means that your father wounded something or someone else. God willing, that dagger may hold answers."

"God willing," the girl replied, though she didn't sound as if she held out much hope. "I have been trying to find the trail of the creatures for days now, seeking to avenge my band so that I may die with honor. I came upon them almost by accident just as they attacked you two." Zamia was quiet for a moment. She swallowed and then spoke again.

"This . . . this . . . soul-eating. This is what they did to my band." It wasn't a question. She looked straight ahead as she spoke, and her now dry eyes looked almost soul-eaten themselves. She held the dagger aloft. "This is all that I have of my father, though I will never wield it—for since I was given the lion-shape I foreswore other weapons. *'My claws, my fangs, the silver knives with which the Ministering Angels strike.'* This is the old saying."

*God save us from the poetry of barbarians!* But the words were as bitterly spoken as any Adoulla had ever heard. He had seen God-alone-remembered how many pained faces during his career, but looking at the pain on the face of this rough little girl who was a lion, was not made easier by that history. Still, he knew that, unlike most victims he had dealt with, this one would want and need hard truth more than coddling.

"Listen to me, Angel-touched one. Your family is dead, in body and soul. I can offer you nothing that will

change that. But I can offer you a chance at vengeance."
It was the only thing a tribesman could want right now,
Adoulla knew. "You may travel with us as an ally if
you wish, Zamia Banu Laith Badawi."

Beside him, Raseed made a choking noise. Adoulla
had almost forgotten he was there. "Doctor! We cannot
have her . . . . There is no reason to—"

"Hmph. You forget yourself, Raseed bas Raseed.
Who is the mentor and who is the assistant here, boy?
Besides, we need Zamia's knife to find the one that did
this. The ghul pack has been destroyed. Now we must
find out who made it. And we must kill him. Unfortunately my tracking spell has taken us as far as it is going to take us."

"Can you not work another spell, then?" The girl
was tense. If she were wearing her lion-shape, her tail
would be switching, Adoulla thought. He ran a hand
over his beard.

"My invocations have their limits, child, just as your
powers do. The Chapters say 'The mightiest of men is
but a slim splinter before the forest of God's power.'"
He pulled out the scarlet-spotted scrap of cloth that
he'd used in his tracking spell. "The blood on this was
spilled by the ghul pack we just destroyed. That is how
I was able to track them. But the pack's master—the
*true* murderer of those marshmen, and of your band as
well—well, God requires more from us to find him. The
blood on Nadir Banu Laith Badawi's dagger is a good
start. May I?" he asked, reaching gently for the weapon.

"You recalled his full name," the girl said, her angry
face showing what Adoulla supposed was a savage's

respect. She handed him the dagger with an anxious look in her eyes.

Adoulla had to nurture that respect if he wished to have the girl's help without her arrogance and second guessings. Besides, he found that he was desperate to offer her some sort of comfort. He held the blade aloft and squinted at it. "Your father wounded this creature, Zamia. With this weapon we can find the thing and its master and destroy them. Your father has served your band to the last."

He handed back the dagger, but the girl's face was blank now. She said nothing. *Hmph. And why am I trying to indulge her incomprehensible tribal foolishness, anyway?* He got back to the matter at hand, making his tone coolly professional. "A man with the power to make such a ghul pack—and to command these cruel old magics—will have powerful screening spells at his disposal. He knows I am looking for him now, and he will prepare counter measures. Even with this trace of blood, his trail will be impossible to find without the aid of an alkhemist. Praise God, I happen to know one of the best in Dhamsawaat. She does not work on the road anymore, but she'll help us nonetheless. We'll return to town tomorrow."

The girl's eyes flashed, and Adoulla saw all his progress fly away. "Tomorrow!? Why do we not return *now*? I am looking for the dog that murdered my band, you fat old fool!" The little Badawi's expression was petulant and murderous.

His temper's fire flared, and Adoulla had to remind himself what this savage girl had suffered. Still, he would not be told what to do by a child. Especially not a child with the gritty accent of a sand-behind-the-ears Badawi. She needed to be reminded of what was what.

"Listen to me, Zamia Banu Laith Badawi. These are deep, dark waters we are in here. We need help. But before that we need rest. You may eat with us now, if you wish. We will return to the city *tomorrow.*" Angel-touched or not, at bottom the girl was just another wounded child of God with a monster problem. Adoulla had learned over the years that those whom he helped needed as much as anything to be told what to do.

After a moment of silent seething, the girl seemed to come to the conclusion that she had little choice but to obey him. She ran a hand through her hair, drew herself up and put on a neutral face. She ignored the invitation to eat. "Very well, Doctor. Tomorrow," was all she said. She gave Raseed an unreadable look then trotted toward a large rock overhang.

Adoulla watched her disappear behind the rock. He turned to his assistant and caught the boy half-gaping. The dervish shot his eyes to the ground. Adoulla knew this was not the time for ribbing, so he restrained himself. Instead he simply said "You fought well today." He always felt awkward bestowing praise, but it did the self-doubting dervish good.

Raseed's yellow-brown cheeks reddened ever so slightly, and he bowed his head in acknowledgement. He was as uncomfortable receiving compliments as Adoulla was giving them. Perhaps, Adoulla mused, this had something to do with why they worked well together.

The boy cleared his throat. "I will go and retrieve the

mules, Doctor. They can't have gotten far." Tension was evident in his voice. *He's more troubled than usual.*

"What is it, boy?" Adoulla asked bluntly.

The dervish seemed to think for a moment before speaking. He adjusted his turban. "The Falcon Prince, a fierce ghul pack, an Angel-touched girl Badawi! Enough wonders and monstrosities for a lifetime. Does this day not trouble you, Doctor?"

Adoulla shrugged sleepily. "More than I can say. Still, I've seen worse, boy."

That was a lie, of course. But it earned a brief, impressed smile from Raseed. The dervish nodded once and, without making a sound, stole his way down the sloped stone.

He watched Raseed's swift steps and felt a stinging envy for the tirelessness of youth. For a few long moments Adoulla just stood there, listening to the insects of the night and wincing at the pain across his shoulder blades. There was a great stone-scrape across his shin, too, that he'd been too tired or too frightened to notice. He wondered if there was any inch of him that had not been slashed or bruised at some point in his life. Then he made his way carefully down the slope.

A few minutes later Raseed returned, silent as ever but betrayed by the noise the mules made as he led them. The beasts themselves seemed to be unharmed, praise God's small providences. Adoulla had always found mules to be admirable animals—intelligent and suspicious of authority, but maligned as obstinate and ill-tempered. *Not unlike me.*

The boy produced a small bronze cookpot and

prepared a simple soup over a sputtering fire. Out in the cold night, something small squealed as it died. *Perhaps the girl is out there hunting up supper*, Adoulla mused, not sure if he was joking.

Raseed was clearly preoccupied as they set to their bread and broth. There was more to it than the horrors and wonders they'd seen today. Adoulla knew the cause, though he doubted the boy had yet admitted it to himself.

*The girl.*

No doubt the dervish was twisting himself in knots trying to square the circle of his pious oaths with a young man's natural reactions, and only half aware he was doing so. When Adoulla was a young man, he would have told the girl that she had a lovely face and been done with it. Though this particular girl did not have a lovely face, exactly.

No, the girl was not what anyone would call pretty, but she had a rough, vital energy that clearly spoke to Raseed. But the boy was incapable of being honest with himself, let alone with a woman. Adoulla faulted the rigid Lodge of God, which had trained the boy into being a sword of a man.

Then again, Adoulla himself hadn't known a woman's touch in a while. He glanced and occasionally winked at young women but he felt awkward doing anything more. And among the older women, there was only one who mattered to him.

*Miri.*

Before he fell asleep, Adoulla let his thoughts linger for a while on Miri Almoussa. The great love of his life's warm, welcoming curves danced before his mind's eye, and he could almost hear her heavy, husky voice whispering loving taunts in his ear and offering him teacakes. His eyes fluttered shut, and he drifted toward sleep, already half-dreaming of swaying hips and sugar frosting.

And again a small animal cried a death-cry out in the darkness.

*The war is upon us. The slaughtered calf screams.*
*And thieves in the night have stolen my dreams.*

The line from Ismi Shihab's *Leaves of Palm* came to Adoulla unbidden. With a dejected snort he rolled over and resigned himself to sleeping alone on a pallet on the cold, hard ground.

# Chapter 6

ZAMIA BANU LAITH BADAWI stretched and flexed her muscles by the light of the still rising sun. She sipped from her waterskin, pulled on her gazelle-hide boots, and packed her bedroll.

Just as her thoughts went to last night's battle and to her new allies, she caught the approaching scent of the dervish Raseed. A half moment later, the lithe little holy man peeled himself from the shadows of a rock not ten feet away. She felt a flash of shame—no man or animal had ever gotten so close to her without her scenting them before! The last traces of the ghul pack's corrupt stench had blown away on the night wind, and she was better rested than she had been the night before. She had no excuse! But when she *did* get a clear scent on the dervish she was shocked out of her self-scolding.

*Ministering Angels help me!* She had never been in the presence of a scent that was so strong, yet so clean. Zamia found her shame deepening, but for new reasons.

It was all she could do to keep from staring at the pure-smelling, clean-shaven little man in blue. She made a small, surprised noise.

"God's peace," the holy man said by way of greeting, his angular face unreadable.

"God's peace," Zamia repeated. The morning air felt warm and thick in her lungs.

"I apologize if I startled you," the dervish said flatly. "We are packing up and will leave soon now."

She snorted. "You didn't startle me. And, as you can see, I am ready to leave already."

The dervish bowed his turbaned head. "Of course." Even standing at ease here, he had an air of war about him. Zamia would have known that the little man could fight even had she not seen his handiwork against the ghuls the night before. The dervish's confident grace as he moved, the hardness in his tilted eyes, the way his hand rested naturally on his sword-hilt— these were signs her father had taught her to recognize in an enemy or an ally.

Though she could not say why, Zamia found herself recalling the taunts that two of the boys in her band had made—never to her face—about her rough, ugly looks. They had been jealous of her power and renown, no doubt, but . . . . It had never mattered to her before whether their insults were rooted in truth.

The dervish was staring at her.

She scowled at the little man. "What is it?"

A tiny lizard darted across the rocky ground between them. Raseed eyed it for a moment but looked directly at her when he spoke. "I have been wondering about something, Zamia Banu Laith Badawi. From what the Doctor has told me, it is not your people's way to seek help from the outside. I know that you have lost your band, but why have you not sought out the help of the other bands in your tribe? Angel-touched or no, you are young to be on your own so."

"Young! I am five and ten! How much older are you, *little* man? Two years at most?" Zamia sucked her teeth in annoyance. *But he is straightforward, at least, not like the Doctor with all of his words and smiles.* The dervish held her eyes with his, and something powerful moved through her body.

"At our last tribal council my father's band was water-shunned by the other bands of the tribe," she said finally. "Because of me. Because he dared to name a girlchild Protector of the Band. And now—" she laughed bitterly, despite herself—"now I can't even avenge my band, for no Badawi will answer my rally. And so I have failed as Protector." Zamia finally stopped herself, not quite believing she had just spoken those words. *Why are you telling this stranger about this? Because his scent is clean? Because you will fight beside him? The tribe's business is the tribe's, the band's business is the band's!*

The dervish scratched beneath his blue turban. "But you—"

"We will speak no more of this," she said firmly. "What of you, Raseed bas Raseed? Where is *your* kin? Why have *you* no family name?" She found that she could not quite keep the scorn from her voice. "No kin?

No band? No tribe?" Her stomach clenched as she realized that the same could now be said about her.

The dervish sighed and then recited what seemed familiar words with a quiet intensity. "My name is Raseed bas Raseed—the old way of saying 'Raseed, only Raseed.' I am a dervish of the Order. I need no father among men, I need no brother among men, I need no son among men." He drew up to his full height, which somehow seemed taller now. "God is my father, the forked swords of the Order are my brothers, virtue is my son."

They were mad words, Zamia knew—for what was a person without family? Yet she found herself moved by them, and intrigued by their stern-faced speaker. Again shame crept up within her, wearing the bloody bodies of her kin. She had no right to be looking at a man so. She was the Protector of the Band, and she had failed. All that was left was giving up her life for vengeance. The road of wife and mother was not hers to walk.

But what if—God forgive her for daring to think it—what if she lived? She was the last of the Banu Laith Badawi and she bore the burden of keeping her band from dying out. She would need to marry and bear children for that to happen . . . .

The confusing, shameful thoughts fled as Zamia scented the Doctor's approach. A moment later she saw his big, white-clad bulk trundling under the rock overhang.

"All-Merciful God, is the holy man spitting pious

sayings at you already?" he asked. "The sun is barely up! Don't misunderstand me—his laconic little jewels are all inspiring enough the first couple of times you hear them. But after that they start to sound a bit pompous."

Raseed made a small, unhappy noise in his throat. "Doctor. Please." He sounded like a bullied boy.

The ghul hunter waved a conciliatory hand, and when he spoke Zamia heard annoyance and affection dance in his voice. "Oh, to be sure, Raseed is most useful to have around. The boy can cross a room in the space of a breath and—God is my witness!—I've even seen him kill a Cyklop!"

*A Cyklop? Truly?* Zamia's desert-bound people knew little of the one-eyed giants of the mountains, but she had heard tales of their legendary strength. She risked a brief, impressed glance at Raseed. The dervish stood stock still, saying nothing.

The Doctor went on. "But, you see, Raseed thinks he is 'wise beyond his years.' I will tell you this, girl: There is no such thing as being wise beyond your years. One can only know as much as one has lived to know, though it is certainly possible to learn a great deal less than this. The boy entered the Order at a young age and has had a hard dervish's life. He is more serious than most young men his age. How many of them, after all, learned to split rocks with their fists before they learned to shave? But rock-splitter or no, he is a *young* man who would do well to remember that fact more often."

Fifty different feelings filled her. She kept her eyes on the ground and said, "We should be going."

Seeming to speak to no one in particular, the dervish said quietly, "I am a young man, but as there is an elder amongst our number, one of us at least ought to act in a proper manner." Zamia looked up and saw a tiny smile on the dervish's pretty, birdlike face. Then he walked away, heading for the mules.

Clearly such retorts were rare, for the old man just stood there for a moment blinking in shocked silence, watching the dervish walk away. The ghul hunter turned to Zamia and let out a laugh that shook his broad shoulders and big gut. "Ha! 'One of us ought to!' Hee hee! 'Dignified and proper!'" He shouted at Raseed's back, "Indeed, boy, indeed! And since it clearly isn't going to be me, it might as well be you!" The Doctor waggled his bushy grey eyebrows and gave Zamia a conspiratorial wink. "He hates it that I call him 'boy,' you know."

"And I hate your calling me 'girl,'" Doctor.

The old man gave an offended sniff. "Bah. I'll tell you like I tell him—I call you youngsters as I like! I am, after all, old enough to be your grand-uncle, my dear."

Zamia felt anger flare inside her as they turned to follow Raseed. "Before he died, my grand-uncle called me Protector of the Band." Her mind's eye conjured an image of her gnarled gray grand-uncle Mahloud, whose age had not diminished his skill at water-finding. The ghuls had killed him, too.

Again the memories hit her like a hammer blow to

the stomach. Why could she not shut them out? She could not sit here and make herself sick with this mourning every few hours. Vengeance would never come from such weakness.

The old man said something, apparently repeating himself. The third time, Zamia actually heard him. "Are you all right, Zamia?"

She growled, low and long. She shoved weakness to the side. "I am fine, Doctor. Why are we standing here chattering? Were we not about to depart?"

The old man sighed a tired sigh and fell quiet. Zamia looked at him more closely.

She had watched as he destroyed three of the foul creatures which had so easily slain the fierce warriors of her band. She knew that he wielded great power. But as she looked at him now, a fat old man sweating heavily though the sun was hardly up, she saw none of the sorts of signs her father had taught her to watch for in a warrior. Being honest with herself, she knew she would not have been able to slay that massive ghul had its attention not been focused on the Doctor. But why had he seemed so helpless? Whistling and looking like he was half ready to die without caring whether he took his enemies with him. Having a ghul hunter on her side would improve her chances for revenge—she was not fool enough to think she needed no allies. But this old man . . . .

And then there was the dervish. The Badawi were not as coy as villagers about the truths of man and woman. Though Zamia was Protector of the Band, the older women had taught her, the same as they had the other girls, of the things she had to look forward to. The things she would feel when she looked at a man, and the things she would do when wed. When she looked at Raseed, though, what she felt was confusion. The dervish was a powerful ally but a distraction. Her mind spun with contradictions.

Over the course of the morning they made their way along a road of packed dirt that grew broader and smoother the farther they went. The dervish offered her his mule. He meant no insult, she supposed. How could he know that a Badawi would ride nothing but a pureblood horse? Walking on a road was compromise enough.

Zamia walked two steps behind her new allies, trying to train her feet to the hard earth of the road. And trying to keep her troubled mind from spinning. The little party walked in silence, and Zamia found herself almost missing the Doctor's inane, griping banter. Better than being alone with the painful pictures in her head.

They traveled for hours, the old man and Raseed occasionally exchanging a few words. Zamia largely ignored them as she dwelled on the knife in her pocket. She would never wield it herself, of course, but in a strange way it had become the most important thing on God's great earth.

It was just afternoon when a strong wind-shift brought Zamia out of her grim thoughts. They were coming upon a large mass of men's scents. A few minutes later the road—already the broadest Zamia had ever seen—passed between two large rocks to join

another road, twice as wide. And it was as if they had
stepped into a sandstorm of people. Zamia tried to look
everywhere at once, the threatening scents of a dozen
different strangers assaulting her. It was all she could
do not to take the lion-shape. *What is wrong with you?
Did you react this way when the trading caravans met up
with the band?* She was without her father's guidance
now, but that was no excuse. *Focus. You cannot panic at
every pack of men that passes.*

The three of them were absorbed into a dense but
quick moving line of travelers that snaked its way toward Dhamsawaat. Zamia could see that the road continued straight ahead for a long stretch, then rose at a
sharp angle with a massive, shrubby dune. The shrubs
more or less covered the dunes now, instead of dotting
them, which meant that they were coming close to water. A good deal of it, Zamia guessed from the increasingly dense web of brown-green. *The River of Tigers,* she
thought. *It must be nearby indeed.*

A moment later, she saw the thick green ribbon of it
in the distance. Zamia knew that outsiders thought the
Badawi dazzled by the smallest stream. The idiots
knew nothing of the beautiful brooks and springs that
nurtured the great oases of the Empty Kingdom. But
this big river, with its boats and the men fishing it . . .
Zamia *was* dazzled, though she did all she could to
hide it.

Across the river, were the farms and orchards that,
as her father had taught her, sent their yields year in
and year out to the hungry hordes of Dhamsawaat. Ol-
ives, dates, wheat, waxy earth-apples, small fields for

pasture. This was as close as Zamia had ever come to Dhamsawaat. The Banu Laith Badawi were—had been, she corrected herself painfully—fiercely independent even for Badawi. Her band had had little contact with townsmen. But even an independent band sometimes needed things from other peoples—tools, fruits and grains, and, when wild pasture was hard to find, grazing for their animals. The Protector of the Band was expected to advise on all aspects of the band's health, and she had accompanied her father several times to trade at the fairs that were sometimes held near here. But this close to Dhamsawaat, something was different. There was a . . . *life* that came from the city, and Zamia could already sense it.

They pressed on. The incline of the road was steep enough now, and the sun hot enough, that thick rivulets of sweat were pouring down the Doctor's face. Zamia wondered again about doing battle alongside this fat old man. *For the moment*, she reminded herself, *you have little choice—these two are the only allies you have in the world*. It was a disturbing thought, but it soon flew from her mind. For then, the road crested the dune, and Dhamsawaat, King of Cities, lay before her.

Zamia stopped dead in her tracks and, for several long moments, could not speak. *I see why this place is called the Jewel of Abassen*, she thought, seeing the gleaming domes of turquoise and gold and white that dotted the carpet of buildings. *I always thought father's stories were exaggerated, but now I see he did not do the horrible size of this place justice.*

It almost made her swoon. The buildings! She did

not know how to begin counting them—flat, peaked, and domed, in stone and tile, a dozen different shades. And rising up as high as mountains! Above it all, near what seemed to be the center of the jumble—if it *had* a center—rose a huge white dome. Zamia was not much used to buildings and had trouble gauging the dome's size, but she was certain that whatever building it topped must be bigger than some of the trade villages she had seen.

It had to be the legendary Crescent Moon Palace, the opulent home and stronghold of the Khalif and his family. Zamia's people knew little of, and cared little for, the supposed ruler of all Abassen. The Badawi limited their interactions with city men as much as possible, wary of becoming bakgam tokens at best, or slaves at worst. Yet even among the Badawi the magnificence of the palace was known, and the few who had seen Dhamsawaat had confirmed that the stories did not exaggerate the splendor of the palace. Even from this distance Zamia could see that they had spoken truly.

Outside the great city walls, they came to two long buildings that stank powerfully of horses. There the Doctor handed the mules over to a stooped man wearing ridiculous city clothes. They then proceeded on foot, making their way through the city's massive gates and into an even denser press of people. Zamia had to remind herself that this was not some feverish dream. *There is so much stone and brick. The very air is thick with it!* She forced herself to stop staring about like a sun-dazzled child.

More astonishing than the buildings were the people. If she had thought there was a great mass of them on the road into the city, she saw a hundred times more of them now as she passed through the streets. The densest gatherings of men Zamia had ever seen were the village and pilgrimage sites to the northeast. She'd been shocked when she saw those places, with their hundred roofs and buildings of two stories. But this—this was impossible. A riotous mix of clothing and complexions. It was terrifying. Men's and women's scents bled together with a thousand others, and countless people darted in and out of her peripheral vision.

How could she scent out enemies in a crowd like this?

"There are so many people here!" she said without meaning to.

"You should have seen it on our way out of here!" the old man bellowed. He turned to Raseed. "We'll get home twice as quick, I think."

Zamia had trouble imagining the streets being any more crowded. Veiled Rughali women lined the street, grinding sweet-smelling spice with pestles the size of war clubs. Girls in gemthread half-robes walked arm-in-arm with soft, wealthy-looking men. Two boys led small goats along the edge of the crowd. She even saw two men wearing the camel calf suede of Badawi tribesmen. She avoided their eyes, but they seemed more interested in the city itself than in the odd sight of a young tribeswoman alone in the Jewel of Abassen. Zamia tried to ignore all of the beast- and people-scents as best she could—the sights were confusing enough.

A hard-faced man jumped in her path. Zamia tensed

for a fight, weighing the risks of taking the shape in this unfamiliar place. The man, smelling of deceit, shook a leather cup and screamed about triangle dice. Before Zamia could do anything, the Doctor elbowed the man away, spitting something about rigged games of chance. The man bowed mockingly and turned to his next potential player.

Again she resisted the urge to turn on her heel and run at lion-speed back into the desert. But she thought of her father, who had been to Dhamsawaat once in his youth. This gave her strength—If Nadir Banu Laith Badawi had visited this monstrous place and lived to tell the tale, surely his daughter could honor his memory by doing the same. Thoughts of her father and of his fate filled her with increasing resolution. She reminded herself that the path to vengeance—the only thing she lived for now—moved through this sandstorm of a city and its colorful carpet of . . . hundreds of people? Thousands? She did not have words for the number of people who must live in such a place.

They continued down the street slowly, the press of the crowd preventing them from moving any faster. Every few moments she looked to her left to make sure the Doctor was still there. She'd fought against the fiercest warriors of rival tribes. She'd killed a ghul. But Zamia found herself as frightened now as she'd ever been in her life. What if she were to get separated from the old man? How would she find her way back to him? Amidst the trackless dunes of the desert, she could follow anyone or anything. But here? With all of these buildings and carts and smells and sounds and people? *This city could swallow me whole and no one would notice.* She stepped even closer to Adoulla Makhslood, and her voice came out as a whisper.

"How many people live in Dhamsawaat?"

The old man smiled in a way that made her feel like a fool, though she did not think that was his intention. "My dear," he began, "how many people were in your band?"

"Around fifty, most years."

"And how many bands make up your tribe?"

"Around one hundred. We have a tribal council once every three years." Her dry eyes stung with recalled tears of frustration as she thought of the last tribal council she'd attended, only one year ago. But despite the unjust treatment her band had received at the last council, Zamia swelled with pride remembering the huge masses at the gatherings of the Banu Laith. She raised her chin as she spoke. "The Banu Laith Badawi are a great tribe. Our numbers when we gather are fearsome. The gathered tents dot the dunes like . . ." She trailed off, realizing how ridiculous she was about to sound.

The old man cleared his throat, pretending not to notice her embarrassment. "Imagine your whole tribe gathered, then ninety-nine more tribes of the same size. Then, next to them, one hundred more tribes of the same size. Two hundred of your tribal gatherings next to each other and on top of one another. That is how many people are in the city before you." The pride in his voice was unmistakable.

For a moment she thought the old man was lying to

her. But why should he? Still, how could so many all live in the same place? How could they breathe? How could they move from place to place without going mad?

She asked the Doctor these questions, knowing she would sound naïve but not quite caring. The old man laughed and said, "Why, my dear, I go a bit more mad every time I step out my front door. That is the true test of a living city! Remind me to tell you about the time it took me two full days to get from the Lane of Monkeys to the Far Gardens!"

The crowd opened up a bit as the Doctor and the dervish led her through a great paved square lined with statues. Zamia was so focused on staying close to the Doctor that she took no real notice of the statues until she was right next to one. It was a depiction of one of the Angels, she realized. When she looked into its eyes, she froze in her tracks at the beauty she saw. The Banu Laith Badawi traded vigorously enough that small bits of the city carvers' fine stone craftwork sometimes came into tribesmen's hands, inevitably displayed with an untribesmanlike vanity and affectation that had always irritated Zamia. But the work here, on these statues—the way their eyes were full of life . . . .

The Doctor tugged at her arm. "I know, child. Even after all these years, I am sometimes awestruck by their beauty. But let us move on." Again he smiled with pride, as if he were a chieftain, and this city his band.

They walked a bit more, and the buildings they passed now were clearly the homes of poorer folk. People on the street called out greetings to the Doctor, eyeing Zamia curiously but asking no questions. They finally came to a stop before a tall building of whitish stone with two sad-looking clumps of thornclover sitting before it in earthen pots. Using a large iron key, the Doctor opened the front door. He stood there for a moment, then raised his palms skyward and smiled. "Thanks be to God that I am here to set foot on my doorstep again!" he bellowed.

As soon as they stepped inside, the old man sat down hard on a divan of dark wood and let out the loudest yawn Zamia had ever heard. He offered her a worn cushion that would have been a prized possession among the Banu Laith Badawi but was clearly not appreciated as such by a city man like the Doctor. The dervish disappeared into another room and returned with water in a cool jug and a plate of nuts and dried fruits. He lit a small olive oil lamp, and the mellow smell of it soothed Zamia. The trio nibbled and sipped for a few minutes before the dervish spoke.

"I fear I know already what your response will be, Doctor, but I would suggest that our next move should be to inform the Khalif's men of this threat."

The Doctor rolled his eyes. "If you know my response, boy, then there's no need for me to say that the Khalif's attentions on these matters would be more of a hindrance than a help."

Zamia was sure she wore the same cynical look as the Doctor. She made a noise in her throat. "Even the Badawi know that the Khalif's men are wicked, dervish! The dogs of Dhamsawaat care little for what has happened to the Banu Laith Badawi."

" 'Dogs of Dhamsawaat'," the Doctor repeated. "What is that, some savage scorn-name for city men? You do realize that *I* am a Dog of Dhamsawaat, do you not, girl? Yet you are ready enough to accept my help!"

Zamia kept herself from growling at the old man. "*Your* help, Doctor? Was it not I that saved you from that foul creature last night?"

"She has a point, Doctor," the dervish chimed in, apparently giving up on his suggestion regarding the authorities. For only the second time, Zamia saw that hard-but-pretty, fine-featured face register amusement. Again she thought bitterly that, not long ago, had she met this man, her thoughts might have gone quickly to courtship. To the pride with which her father would have entertained the notion of such a match, and the grudging admiration the band would have had for his battle skill. But now such thoughts were useless. The band—the band's memory—demanded the avenging lioness. The marriage-minded girl dishonored them.

The Doctor muttered about disrespectful children and ran a hand over the endless folds of his kaftan. Then he stood and began to pace. "Now. As I said last night, this business with the bloody knife is the purview of the alkhemists. My alkhemist friends are not home now, but we will call on them at first light. Then I will want you to meet another youngster who has lost kin to these same monsters. The two of you are the only ones to witness this threat, and it will help me to hear you speak again, side-by-side."

Zamia could not contain her anger. "More talking!?

We waste a day, old—Doctor! Surely there are others in this city with these skills."

The old man shrugged. "A handful. But they all charge *very* dearly indeed. And they aren't the types to take kindly to savage children who come barging into their shops telling them what they *must* do, as I've no doubt you would do."

Zamia growled.

The old man only smiled. "Besides, not one of them is as good at what they do as Litaz is. Whatever time we lose in waiting we will more than gain back due to her aptitude. Now do try to settle yourself. We've much to do tomorrow. And as soon as we have a quarry we will begin the hunt."

The Doctor's smile turned hard. "You think me a lazy old oaf. And when I look at you I see an impertinent savage of a girl. But in the Name of God, our meeting in battle together brings the Heavenly Chapters to my mind: 'O believer! Look to the accident that is no accident!' We were meant by God to fight this bloody cruelty together, Zamia Banu Laith Badawi. And so we shall."

The glint in the ghul hunter's eyes gave Zamia the first real hope she'd felt in days. It was a vicious, bitter sort of hope, but it was all she had. Nadir Banu Laith Badawi's band *would* be avenged.

For an hour or so Zamia lay half-dozing on a divan just inside the front door. It felt good, despite the dark thoughts that crept in at the edges of her ease. Then the Doctor announced that it was time to eat.

Zamia did not understand city people. A shriveled old woman who lived next door to the Doctor brought over plates of food. Though she looked nothing like him, Zamia assumed that she was his sister or his mother—why else would she live so close, and why would she feed him thus? But the woman did not stay to eat with them—and the Doctor gave her a coin before she left! It was as rude and shameless as anything Zamia had seen, but then, she had heard that city men paid coins for lovemaking as well.

The Doctor loaded his plate with thick slices of meat stuffed with a rich green dressing. "Pale wine and pistachio lamb! Thanks to All-Providing God that not *everything* He sends my way is a maddening trial!" The old man filled his cup, guzzled it down, refilled it. "Eat, girl!" he bellowed, bits of pistachio flying from his mouth as he gestured to the plates before him. "We'll be on the move again soon enough, I fear. You'll wish then that you had eaten!" He took another long gulp of pale wine.

Zamia tried to tell herself that she was not hungry—that she had no room in her for anything but revenge, though she knew it for a lie. The smells set her stomach growling as if the hungry, thirsty lioness within her were speaking up. With no further prompting from the Doctor, she sloshed back half her wine and began to stuff herself with mouthfuls of lamb. After a few bites, though, her stomach began to clench.

"This city food is too rich," she said, then drained her cup with a second and third gulp.

The dervish smiled a mesmerizing smile. "I couldn't agree more, Zamia Banu Laith Badawi. You will notice that I am eating only fruit and bread-and-beans. The diet of the pious."

She found herself speaking. "You may call me simply Zamia, Raseed." *Where did that come from!? This cursed wine is too strong!* The dervish mumbled something embarrassed-sounding and locked his eyes on his plate. *He is older than me, yet he seems so young.*

"Well," the old man bellowed, tipsily breaking the tension, "such bird food is suitable enough, perhaps, for little holy men's mouths. But not for a man of my . . ." he paused, hefting up his big belly with both hands, "a man of my . . . significance." The ghul hunter turned to Zamia, a note of solicitude entering his voice. "I have spent long decades as a servant of God, you know. I've traveled roads this presumptuous boy has never even heard of. Forty years' worth of days at war with the Traitorous Angel. Is it so wrong that I should wish to spend my nights like this?"

The old man took another big swallow of wine and turned back to Raseed with a troublemaker's smile. "You're as bad, sometimes, as those Humble Students you respect so much! Perhaps you should join their stupid little sect! Scandalized by ale and dancing and such!" He poked a reproving finger at Raseed. "Remember what the Chapters say: 'God speaks through these Chapters, not through the mouths of priests. His scriptures are not written upon papyrus, parchment or vellum. They are marked in men's memories, stamped on men's hearts, engraved in men's souls.' Yet your Order and the Humble Students act as if the Chapters were written on their lips."

He took another drink. "Before their glory faded from Abassen, the ghul hunters' ways were unbending in some things. But at least they never claimed to be holy men. God is the Most Beneficent Host, boy! When you've forgotten that, you've forgotten why we fight!" His tirade over, the ghul hunter threw his hands up in exaggerated exasperation.

For a while then there were only the sounds of eating and the old man's heavy breath. When the meal was done they sat there silently. Then the Doctor's too-loud voice shattered the silence.

"Speaking of fighting," he said as if ten minutes had not passed, "I have been wondering something, Zamia. If, God willing, we find this damned-by-God servant of the Traitorous Angel and we defeat him, what will you do then?" Zamia felt the pleasant haze of the wine burn away in an instant. *Why does he bring this up now?* It sounded to her as if the ghul hunter already knew what her answer would be, and disapproved of it.

"All that matters is that I kill whoever or whatever has done this. Likely I will die doing so. This is as it should be. Martyrdom for me, vengeance for my band."

The winey cheer was gone from his voice. "Martyrdom? Are you so eager to die, Zamia?"

She came to her feet and hissed at the old man. "Why should I wish to live? Everyone I know is dead! My band is dead! I can only pray that my fate is to avenge them before I die myself!"

The Doctor stared at her, and his gaze was hard. "Remember that even fate has its forking roads. Your father saw the touch of the Angels upon you and chose you to be Protector of the Band, though you are female. He understood the Chapter that reads 'Only so many fates for each man, but always a choice.'"

The Doctor poked idly at the single bean on his plate—the only bit of food that remained there. "But enough grim talk for now. We must see to what we city folk call your sleeping arrangements—and what the Badawi call 'some random patch of sandy dirt.' Oh, I am sorry, girl, I only jest. But of course we would not shame you by having you sleep in the house of a man not your husband or father. I don't doubt my neighbor—the old woman who brought our dinner— will set a pallet for you. For a young woman such as—"

Zamia growled. "I am not a girl, Doctor. My father *did* choose me for Protector of the Band, and that is what I am. The Protector sleeps where he must. If you would be so kind to set a pallet here at the foot of the stairs, that will be fine."

Beside her, the dervish made a strangled noise.

Zamia ignored him because she could not afford to lose control of herself. "What I want to know," she asked, "is whether we are truly safe here, Doctor. I do not wish to wake to the feeling of my ribcage being cracked open. The one whose ghul pack we fought— what is to stop him from striking us here?"

The Doctor yawned and smiled patronizingly. "Sneaking ghuls about within a city is no easy matter, child. And besides, my home is charmed so that no ghul can cross its threshold." The old man shoved his dirty plate rudely in Raseed's direction and got up from the table. His lazy expression grew urgent again. "Listen to me. *One* of the Banu Laith Badawi still lives. When *she* dies, *then* your band is dead. Until that day, girl, your band lives." He waggled a big finger at her and left the room.

She turned to where the dervish had sat, afraid but excited to be alone with him. But when she turned, the little man was gone. Something inside her twisted and untwisted in disappointment and relief.

A little while later, a great storm of things flew through Zamia's mind as she lay on her pallet seeking sleep. The sight of her brother with his heart torn out and his eyes shining red. Her father's hand, clutching a dagger. The sound of ghuls hissing. The smells of this strange city. Raseed's brief smiles.

And the Doctor's admonitions. *Your band lives*, he had said. She had already counted herself half-dead, she realized. She'd been acting as if the band of Nadir Banu Laith Badawi were gone from God's great earth forever. The ghul hunter, with his city man's love of this one building he called home, did not understand her people. He did not understand what she had lost. But he had started her thinking nonetheless.

*Home*, Zamia thought. For the nomadic Badawi, it was not a place. The strains of one of her people's most important songs forced its way into her head. It would start with the boys singing,

*Home is where my father is! I am a true Badawi!*

Then the men would take their turn, singing

*Home is where my sons are! I am a true Badawi!*

Then all would sing together:

*Home is where my band's tents are! I am a true Badawi!*

The song was a boastful one, intended to flaunt her people's superiority to the soft villagers and city folk. But now it took on a mournful irony. Her father had joined her mother in death. She had no sons or daughters. The isolation of her band meant that no other band would take her in. How could she ever know a home again?

The burning need for revenge had pushed her far. But her body felt as if it would melt from exhaustion. There was nothing more she could do tonight. Nothing that is, but mourn all she had lost. And so, sure that she was out of the hearing range of her new-found allies, and more tired than she'd ever been, Zamia Banu Laith Badawi, for the first time in years, very quietly cried herself to sleep.

# II.

THE GUARDSMAN DID NOT KNOW how many days he had been held in the red lacquered box.

The lid opened and the gaunt man's hard hands pulled him, naked and whimpering, from the box. The gaunt man threw him to the dirt floor. The guardsman lay there, his throat burning with thirst, trying to remember his name. All he could remember was that he was a guardsman, born in the Crescent Moon Palace and sworn to service there. That the other guardsmen served under him. The gaunt man and his shadow-creature would not let him forget that.

And he remembered the street thief and the beggar. The gaunt man had killed them both slowly, letting their blood spatter onto his already filthy kaftan. He had made the guardsman listen to their pleas. Made him smell their waste as they soiled themselves in fear.

He did not know where he was now. A room. Rafters and scrabbling rats. A cellar? A cell?

Then he heard the squealing in his mind, and the jackal-thing's voice was in his head again.

*Listen to Mouw Awa, once called Hadu Nawas, who speaketh for his blessed friend. Thou art an honored guardsman. Begat and born in the Crescent Moon Palace. Thou art sworn in the name of God to defend it. All of those beneath thee shall serve.*

*Listen to Mouw Awa, who is unseen and unheard by men until he doth strike! Who doth laugh away sword-blade and arrow! Who was remade by the Jackal God and freed from his prison by his blessed friend.*

*Listen to Mouw Awa and know no hope. Know that none shall save thee. Mouw Awa doth use his powers to sneak and smuggle and kill his blessed friend's enemies. The fat one, the clean one, the kitten.*

The shadow-jackal-man continued to whisper in the guardsman's mind of blood and bursting lungs. Again he felt hard hands under his armpits. The gaunt man dragged him to the other side of the dark room, where a great black kettle bubbled and hissed and smelled of brimstone, though there was no flame beneath it. The liquid within the kettle looked like molten rubies, and the red glow of it lit the gaunt man's black-bearded face.

He felt himself being lifted and plunged into the kettle. He felt his skin being scalded. And somewhere he heard the shameful screaming and pleading of a man who had once been strong.

# Chapter 7

ZAMIA BANU LAITH BADAWI breathed in the scent of her family's death again. She bolted awake, screaming and growling and reliving that horrible night when she'd found her band.

*No, it was just a dream. This is a new night.* She was not in the desert. She was lying on a pallet in Doctor Adoulla Makhslood's townhouse.

But that cruel crypt-scent was still there.

*Not just a dream!* Out of the corner of her eye, Zamia saw motion. Something lunged at her. Only her Angel-touched reflexes and the years of training with her father saved her. Something—something almost man-shaped—smashed into the pallet where she had lain a breathspace ago.

*No! Mouw Awa the manjackal is unseen and unheard by men until he doth strike. But the kitten hath scented him!*

The thing before her was shadow-black, save for glowing red eyes. Somehow she heard its words with both her ears and her mind. The creature held a vague shape—something like a jackal walking about on a man's two legs. But the edges of its outline whipped and wavered like tent flags in the wind.

The reek of her band's death wafted from the creature. The smell of burnt jackal-hair, and of ancient child-blood. Its eyes. They were a brighter version of what she had seen in her dead bandsmen. And looking at the abomination before her, Zamia knew that it was this thing that had eaten the souls of her band—of her father.

She screamed in fear. The thing lunged at her again, and she barely managed to dodge back from its shadow-wrapped fangs. She shouted.

"RASEED! DOCTOR! ENEMIES!" It came out lioness-loud, louder than any girl's shout could be, as she took the shape. When she was younger, she had needed to *try*, over and over again sometimes, to take the shape. But now it came without thinking, in the space of a breath. One moment she was a woman, the next a great golden lioness. One moment a girl's fear filled her, the next her veins raced with sunlight.

With the claws and fangs and gold coat came confidence. She dodged another lunge and growled at the creature. "Whatever you are, you have murdered the Banu Laith Badawi. I'll tear out your throat!"

The thing before her made a sickening whine, between a dog's and a vile man's. *Mouw Awa is alone no more. He hath been found by his blessed friend. And he shall slay the kitten and the fat one and the clean one for his blessed friend. Mouw Awa doth shiver, knowing how salty-sweet will be the kitten's soul-of-two-tastes!*

Hearing this thing's voice in her head was disturbing, but her father had taught her years ago to pay attention to an enemy's body rather than their words. Zamia roared again to rouse her allies. Then she leapt at the foul creature before her.

Even as she did so, she tried to understand what this monster was. Could her claws cut a shadow?

Zamia raked out a left paw and found her answer. The foul thing—*Mouw Awa*, it had called itself—spit and whined and danced back in pain.

*The kitten hath cut Mouw Awa! Savage as her father, the cruel cutter of Mouw Awa's blessed friend!*

The sheer speed of the creature as it leapt at her caught Zamia off guard. She managed to stay a half-step ahead of one snap of its maw, then another. But she was tiring already and all signs were that this creature was not. And she was not used to fighting in these cramped conditions.

She scrabbled back and tipped over a small bookstand, which pinned her rear paws. *God help me!* The creature closed, and its scent threatened to overwhelm her.

A streak of blue flew at the thing that called itself Mouw Awa. *Raseed!*

The dervish's sword was out, and he slashed at the creature, drawing its attention away from Zamia. Once, twice, and thrice Raseed's forked sword cleaved into the thing, but it made no mark.

"Be careful! This thing—it has the stink of my father's wounds!" Zamia growled. Then she flexed her back legs and shattered the wooden bookstand. Splinters bit into her flesh, but she ignored them.

She watched monster and dervish, looking for an opening. Again Raseed's sword slashed into Mouw Awa, but the thing just whined and sneered. Mouw Awa's fangs missed their mark once, then twice. The creature lashed a forearm across the dervish's chest. Raseed went flying as if he'd been kicked by a horse. Zamia's heart sank into her stomach.

Out of the corner of her eye, Zamia saw the old man appear on the stairs, shouting. She ignored the Doctor, though, and flew at Mouw Awa.

*Neither sword-blade nor prayer doth stop Mouw Awa. He hath smuggled in the spell-makings. He shall savor the twin tastes of lion and child while his blessed friend's creatures slay the clean one and the fat one.*

The creature dodged her strike and threw something at the ground. There was a sound like wind whipping, and suddenly two man-sized sandstorms were boiling in the middle of the room. Then the small storms took shape—arms, legs, fangs.

*Merciful God! If the desert dunes were made monsters, they would look like this!* The man-shaped things snapped their jaws, showing teeth like jagged rocks. One darted out a forked tongue. No, not a tongue. A pink rock viper. The desert's deadliest snake.

Zamia saw these creatures come between her and her allies, and that was all of the attention she could spare. The mad, murdering monster before her had earned death, and her only purpose on God's great earth was to kill it.

She slashed out again and again, but Mouw Awa always seemed a step ahead of her blows. That shadow-wreathed snout seemed to sneer. *The kitten doth hiss and spit, but she shall die in the mangling maw of Mouw Awa, once called Hadu Nawas.*

The other combatants were to her back now. Behind her she heard shouted scripture, Raseed's cries, and magical sounds like small thundercracks. It took all of her discipline not to turn from her foe. Something was on fire, and the smoke, along with the creature's cruel scent, made her gag.

She growled loudly. Her band's enemies had fled like children from that growl. But Mouw Awa just pressed the attack again, coming close enough that Zamia could feel a strange heat coming from its maw.

The creature lunged again and missed. She saw her chance. She sprang, seizing the opportunity the overconfident monster had given her.

*Given me!*

Too late, Zamia realized that it was *she* who was overconfident. Mouw Awa was not off balance. The thing had feigned and drawn her in. Her claws raked out, and dug deep into shadow-flesh. But the creature shifted position, and its black jaws snapped, digging into her ribs. Zamia screamed and hissed and clawed at the thing again. Mouw Awa stumbled away from her, grievously wounded.

But its fangs had done their damage. Now she was aware of nothing but her pain. The pain, and a burning red heat that made her whimper. Then there was only darkness.

*Merciful God help me!* Only half believing what he saw, Adoulla watched two sand ghuls come to false life in his library. Zamia was locked in battle with a creature like the shadow of a jackal come to life—the likes of which he'd never seen. Raseed was struggling to his feet.

Adoulla noticed these things, but the sand ghuls were what held his attention. The power involved in raising such creatures from a distance, in commanding them from some unseen place, in subverting the ward spells Adoulla had worked here, was incalculable. The number of men that would have had to be murdered and maimed to work these magics. . . . They faced a dire threat indeed.

One of the ghuls charged Adoulla, a snarl etched on its grotesque almost-human features. Adoulla's hands were already in the pockets of his kaftan. He drew forth a small vial and uncorked it with his thumb. The sand ghul's raking claws were now only inches from Adoulla's eyes, but he stood his ground calmly, sprinkling crushed ruby in the air before him and reciting.

"God is the Oasis in the Desert of the Soul!" The ruby dust turned to ash in midair. The ghul collapsed into a pile of loose sand and dead beetles. Adoulla felt grains of sand and less pleasant things blow across his face as the creature was drained of its animating magic. In a sort of reflection, he felt the drain of the invocation hit him hard—his chest tightened, and a stitch stung his side. After their battle the night before, he didn't have much left in him.

*Too old*, he thought. But even as he thought it he saw the lion-girl fighting desperately against that shadow-thing and watched Raseed trying hopelessly to slay a sand ghul with his sword.

*No, not too old*, he told himself. *These children will die if I am.* He summoned strength from God-alone-knew-where and fumbled in his satchel for some remedy against these creatures.

He thanked Beneficent God aloud when his fingers closed around three smooth stones the size of grapes. He gathered the lightning beads—each a swirl of mother-of-pearl—and looked up to see that Raseed had been knocked to the ground again. He was already getting to his feet, but the ghul he'd been battling now darted toward Adoulla.

Adoulla twisted as the thing hissed and swung at him. He somehow managed not to be torn open by those rocklike claws. But the flat of the ghul's great forearm caught him across the chest like an iron bar. He fell backward, landing on his ass with a grunt, the wind knocked out of him.

He started to throw the beads, then hesitated. They'd cause a fire, no doubt. His home . . .

But he had no choice. Adoulla threw.

The sand ghul hissed loudly as the tiny stones struck it. They were sucked immediately into the thing's abdomen, sand shifting away from sand to briefly reveal a writhing mass of scorpions and shiny black beetles. Adoulla spoke the invocation.

"God is the Lightning That Strikes Thrice!" It was slurred with pain and regret, but it was enough. There was a loud but muffled noise, like a peal of thunder wrapped in a wool blanket, and the sand ghul froze in its tracks. Then another muffled peal and another as the beads exploded inside the creature. Sheets of lightning-fire shot out from the sand ghul's midsection, scalding the arm Adoulla threw up to protect his face. Small fires caught in the room and spread with magical speed. Adoulla could smell paper burning and wondered in agony what books and scrolls he was losing. He saw his furniture catch fire, the very walls of his home aflame. Then the invocation's drain hit him and he collapsed, pain and smoke filling his mind.

Raseed watched one of the sand ghuls crumble from the Doctor's invocation and thanked God as he faced off against the second one. He had never fought sand ghuls before, though the Doctor had spoken of them. It was not like fighting bone ghuls or water ghuls. No matter how many times Raseed swung his sword, the blade found no flesh to bite. Every thrust slid into loose sand, and it took every bit of Raseed's skill just to dodge the ghul's blows as he freed his sword.

*Almighty God, what can I do against such a monster?* But his thoughts were dashed out of him as the creature slammed him to the ground with a great, grainy fist. He came to his feet quickly and saw the Doctor toss something at the ghul and speak an invocation before passing out. There was a thundercrack sound, and Raseed threw up an arm to shield himself from a sheet of fire. He turned his face from the blast and saw Zamia fighting that shadow-creature.

Raseed's skin and silks were singed, but he ignored the pain. When he turned back to the sand ghul, he saw that the Doctor's invocation had had a remarkable effect. At the sounds of the small explosions, the creature had stopped moving, incapacitated by whatever passed for pain in such a monster. The magical heat of the explosions had caused the palm-tree-thick midsection of the sand ghul to melt into glass! The melted remains of scorpions and centipedes clouded the glass with black. The sand ghul was stopped in its tracks.

Small fires burned about the room, catching and spreading with astonishing speed. But Raseed focused on his enemy. He knew an opportunity when he saw one. Glass could be broken.

He sheathed his sword, extended his right arm and pointed his fist at the sand ghul. With a loud shout that focused his soul, he flew forward, thrusting his fist into the thing's stomach. *If it* has *a stomach!*

There was an earsplitting crack. Then a thick tinkling sound like a thousand tiny bells. Raseed felt countless splinters of hot glass digging into his skin, from his knuckles all the way up his arm to his elbow. But he was focused, and not a glimmer of pain made it through his training. *Praise God.*

In a blur of movement he withdrew his arm from the monster's midsection. The sand ghul collapsed in a rain of sand, broken glass, and dead centipedes. Raseed turned from the waist high pile before him, scanning the room.

The whole house was filling with smoke and fast-spreading fire. The townhouse walls were blackening with flame. The Doctor lay moaning in pain but did not seem to be badly wounded. A golden lion—Zamia!—squatted in the corner, growling and whimpering as she bled. Raseed's breath caught in his throat.

The jackal-creature, clearly wounded, struggled to stand and make its way to the window. It whined as shadow-stuff whirled about it in tattery flags. Raseed heard it speak somehow in his mind even as he moved toward it.

*No! Mouw Awa hath been cut and bitten! Might this mean his death? No! His blessed friend shall heal him. His blessed friend shall sit on the Cobra Throne while Mouw Awa's howls doth hound the air!*

The thing clawed at the lattice window, splintering the dark wood and howling in pain. Before Raseed could reach it, it leapt from the second story window to the hard-packed dirt road below. *The fall will kill it*, Raseed half-hoped. But as the thing hit the ground it seemed to simply . . . melt away. He himself had a remarkable skill in stealth, but this was different. Mouw Awa did not hide . . . it *joined* with the lamp-shadows. The thing had fled but it was not dead—Raseed could sense that much.

It was Raseed's duty to pursue, but his eyes were drawn to the limp forms of Zamia and the Doctor. They needed him now. The tribeswoman had changed shape again in the space of a moment. He felt his heart would burst, seeing this girl of five and ten years with a grisly wound in her side. The Doctor moaned and sat up, coughing from the smoke around them. The flames blazed hotter, the wood of divan and bookshelf cracking and popping in the fires.

Zamia whimpered. Only her mouth moved, making pained, pleading sounds. His gaze returned to the street below. *O God, is it wicked to let such a monster flee just to save the lives of friends?* But even as his soul asked Almighty God for guidance, his body choked from smoke and moved to Zamia's side.

Suddenly a glowing green light filled the townhouse. As he reached Zamia, he saw a hundred tiny hands the color of seawater stamping at the flames and waving away smoke. *Magic.* But not the sort of spell the Doctor worked. Whatever it signified, Raseed didn't care. All that mattered was Zamia's wound, which was bubbling and hissing horribly, as if with an alkhemist's acids. Raseed felt tears filling his eyes and not only from the smoke.

He felt the Doctor's large hand on his shoulder and heard that gruff voice in his ear. "Come, boy. Help has arrived."

Raseed snarled at his mentor. "We should *not* have brought her here, Doctor! She's just a child!" An incoherent cry escaped from his throat. "We should *not* have brought her!" He was startled by the sudden impulse to strike the Doctor.

The Doctor winced from the smoke and the pain of his wounds. "Snap out of it, boy! I said there is help here!"

Raseed saw, more than felt, a bony, red-black hand on his forearm. Dawoud. Litaz. The Doctor's friends. The smoke filled his eyes and his mind. He let himself be guided out of the burning townhouse, only half-aware of what was happening.

The next thing he knew, he was standing in front of his ruined, soot-blackened home. The spell-fires were already dying, but they had done their damage. The Doctor sat on the street, his head in his hands. His Soo friends—the tall, bald magus Dawoud and his wiry little wife Litaz—stood beside him, gently setting Zamia's unmoving body onto a litter.

"The fire's been dealt with," Dawoud was saying to the dazed-looking Doctor. "We got to it before it could spread to the neighbors. My magics keep them from seeing or smelling what has happened here. But what in the Name of God *has* happened here, Adoulla? And who is *she*?"

The Doctor stuttered, obviously trying to regain his wits. Raseed heard himself doing the same thing.

"Questions for later," he heard Litaz's voice say from somewhere. "Whoever she is, she's dying here. We have to get her to our home, *now*. Raseed!"

He realized he'd been staring uselessly at Zamia's unmoving form, her soot-stained face, and her closed, long-lashed eyes. Again he tried to speak, but his throat burned from smoke and tears. Ash caked his silks. "Auntie?" he finally managed.

The little Soo alkhemist's voice was sharp, and her blue-black features were stern. "We've brought a litter," she said, the rings in her twistlocked hair clicking as she nodded toward the wood and leather frame. "Help me carry it."

His hands and feet moving without his seeming to

will it, Raseed obeyed her command. As they lifted the litter, Zamia shrieked once in pain. Raseed felt as if the sound were tearing out his insides. Zamia grimaced and then fell silent.

"There's hope here yet," Litaz said. "*Move*, boy!"

Raseed blinked away more tears, and he moved.

# Chapter 8

IN THE HOUR OR SO that was neither night nor morning, the Scholars' Quarter of the great city of Dhamsawaat was quiet. The most indefatigable of the street people had finally gone to bed, even if bed was merely a bit of dirt lane. The first of the cart-drivers, porters, and shopkeepers would not hit the street for another hour or so. Litaz Daughter-of-Likami stared out her cedar-framed window, rubbing her temples and thanking Merciful God for small blessings—the soothing quiet had made the first part of her work a bit easier.

The busy, rough Scholars' Quarter was usually so noisy that its name—a vestige of the city's long past, Adoulla had told her—seemed an intentional irony. But Litaz prided herself that she, her husband, and their old friend Adoulla kept the bookish appellation from becoming a total lie. Ages after the neighborhood's sages and students had been replaced by cheap shopmen and pimps, the three of them ensured that learning still lived in the Quarter. That their learning pertained to unnatural wounds and creatures made of grave-beetles made no difference.

Litaz turned from the window and considered the half-dead girl lying on the low couch before her, her coarse hair splayed across the cushions. The tribes-woman's labored breathing was the loudest sound in the room. A sharp contrast to a few hours ago, when they'd come charging in with a dying, Angel-touched girl on a litter.

The wound was like none Litaz had ever seen. The tribeswoman had been bitten, though not so badly as to be life-threatening. But within the wound, it was as if the girl's soul had been poisoned rather than her body. It didn't fit any of Litaz's formulae. Praise God that Dawoud—as he had in so many of their past healings—had intuited what to do. Her own tonics and wound poultices had stabilized the girl's health. But it had been Dawoud's powers—his mastery of the weird green glow that rose from within him as his hands snaked back and forth above the girl's heart—that had truly brought her from the brink of death.

The smell of brewing cardamom tea brought her out of her thoughts. She could hear Dawoud in the next room, clinking cup against saucer for her. Making each other's tea was half the reason they had such a happy marriage. It was one of the most important lessons of alkhemy, one that had stuck with her from the first days, when she'd left behind the stifling lifestyle of a

Lady of the Soo court to pursue her training: Simple things ought not be taken for granted. She'd seen a horned monster from another world kill a man because of a small error in a summoning circle. She'd seen a husband and a wife grow to hate each other because they'd forgotten each other's naming-days.

A shout came in the window from the street: a late drunk, or an early cartman. As if in response, the Badawi girl—*Zamia*, Adoulla had called her—made a pained noise. Litaz said a silent prayer for the girl and worried over the limits of her own healing-craft. She pulled a clay jar from one of the low visiting room shelves and scooped a handful of golden yam candies from it. The sweet, earthy flavor filled her mouth and calmed her. They were expensive, these tiny reminders of home, but there was nothing quite like them.

"You deserve the whole jar of them, hard as you have worked these past few hours. I think the girl will live because of it." Her husband came into the room bearing a tea tray in his bony, careworn hands. Concern for her was etched on his wizened red-black face.

"Where are Adoulla and Raseed?" she asked.

He jutted his hennaed goatee at the stairway. "Both upstairs. The boy is in some kind of self-recriminating meditation. Adoulla is mourning his home and wracking his brain regarding this attack."

Litaz had been doing the same since Adoulla had hurriedly explained that the girl was Angel-touched and described the creature that had attacked her. *It would not be madness enough,* some sliced-off, calloused part of her thought, *for our Adoulla to bring us a dying Badawi girl. She would have to be a shape-changer, too.* As though seized by her old friend's soul, Litaz snorted out a bitter laugh. She took a teacup from Dawoud and sipped as she sat by the girl's side.

The tribeswoman wore a pained grimace as she slept. Again Litaz found herself troubled by the strangeness of the girl's malignant wound. For decades she had traveled with her husband and their various companions, dealing with creatures and spells that most men thought unfathomable. But Litaz knew that everything in this world could be analyzed. The ghuls, the djenn, balls of fire, and bridges made from moon-rays. All of it made sense, if one understood the formulae. She had given up years ago on searching for liquors of agelessness and turning copper into gold that stays gold. Nor did she waste her talents on the stupid duties that employed the city's handful of other master alkhemists. Working for weeks at a time to separate alloys or encourage crops—and make rich men richer—was not a way to spend a life, no matter the wealth such work might bring.

But helping hurt people was different. Looking at the girl's wound again, Litaz once more set to work as an assessor-of-things. She had only ever read about soul-killing. It was new to her, though she knew it was an ancient magic. What mattered here, though, was that it had nearly killed a girl in the home of her and her husband's closest friend. That made it their problem, too.

She set down her teacup and put a hand to the carved wooden clip that held up her long twistlocks. Dawoud, her opposite in so many ways, had often teased her that it was a fussy, Eastern Soo hairstyle. Years ago he'd proposed that she shave her head, like one of his red-black countrywomen from the Western Republic! The thought still horrified her.

Her husband stepped wordlessly to her side and put his hand on her back. She felt the pressure of his long, strong fingers and thanked God, not for the first time, that someone so unlike her could be such an inseparable part of her.

Litaz heard a noise on the stairs and turned to see Adoulla wearily making his way down them. Dawoud's hand left her back, and he went over to embrace their friend. She didn't really see the pain in Adoulla's heavy-lidded eyes until she heard him speak in a voice not his own—the small voice of a weak man.

"My home. Dawoud, my home. It . . . it . . ."

He trailed off, his eyes shining with tears, and his big broad shoulders slumped. It troubled her to see Adoulla this way—he was not easily shaken. Her husband stepped back from embracing his friend and shook the ghul hunter by his shoulders.

"Listen to me. *Look* at me, Adoulla! God is the Most Merciful, do you hear me? It will take money to repair, and time, but six months from now you'll be back where you started, minus a few old books and scrolls."

Adoulla swallowed and shook his head. "Six months

from now, I'll probably be a crimson-eyed corpse whose soul has been severed from God."

With their main patient resting, Litaz and Dawoud tended to Adoulla's bruises and tender ribs. Their friend sat with vacant eyes as they worked, flinching in pain, but saying nothing. Afterwards he fell into a deep, snoring sleep on a pile of cushions in the greeting-room corner. Then, with Adoulla's hard-eyed young assistant insistently keeping watch, she and Dawoud slept as well.

Upon waking a few hours later, Litaz made more tea and Adoulla thanked her for it as if she had saved his mother's life. He was a bit less inconsolable after his rest, grim planning clearly giving him purpose.

"That jackal-thing that calls itself Mouw Awa, and its mysterious 'blessed friend'—they must be stopped. Somewhere out there is a ghul-maker more powerful than any I've ever faced. I fear for our city," Adoulla said. He took a long, messy slurp of tea and wiped the excess from his beard.

Your *city, my friend, not ours,* some resentful part of her protested. She'd lived in and loved Dhamsawaat for decades now, but the older she grew the more she pined to return to the Soo Republic. This city had given her meaningful work and more exciting experiences than she could count. But it was in this dirty city that her child had died. It was in this too-crowded city that her husband had grown older than his years. She did not want to die saving this place—not without having seen home again.

She spoke none of this, of course. And she sat complacently as Dawoud said, "Whatever help you need from us is yours, brother-of-mine. Whatever this is you are facing, you will not face it alone."

For a long while, the three of them sat sipping tea. Then Dawoud spoke again, a hard smile on his face as he poked a long finger at Adoulla. "You know, despite the dangers facing you, you should thank Beneficent God. Thank Him that we live two doors down. That we came home late at night rather than in the morning. That we were walking home when we saw the smoke from your house."

At the word 'house,' Adoulla sighed, his eyes wet and shining. He thanked Litaz again for the tea, stood, and walked forlornly out the front door.

Dawoud stood with a grunt and followed Adoulla. She heard the men walk slowly away from the shop, talking however men talked when they were alone with one another.

Litaz set sad thoughts aside and went to check on Zamia. The girl's teeth had unclenched, and she slept untroubled now. It was time to apply the second poultice. Litaz placed a small pot of mixed herbs over the hearth.

A few minutes later they began to boil, leaving behind a sticky residue. She removed the girl's bandage and cleaned the wound again. Then, with a small wooden paddle, she applied the still-hot muck from the pot. She watched her poultice burn magically away from the wound, absorbing the girl's pain. Wisps of smoke curled into the air, leaving half-healed flesh in their wake. Using her other hand, she pushed pressure points on the girl's palms.

As if struck by lightning, Zamia sat up and screamed until she was out of breath. Then she sucked in a great gulp of air and screamed again. Litaz felt badly for the neighbors, but they were used to the cries of the afflicted that sought relief in her skills.

Raseed jumped up from the pile of cushions where he'd been sleeping. "Auntie! Wh-what?" he said, blinking sleep from his tilted eyes and going for his sword.

"Go back to sleep, Raseed. All is well here—the screaming is a good sign. Evidence that the girl's soul is still strong." Even as Litaz spoke, Zamia lay back again, falling into a deep sleep.

Dawoud and Adoulla entered the room, drawn by the screams. Just as well. It was now Dawoud's turn to treat the more metaphysical pain that consumed the girl.

He looked a question at Litaz, and she nodded. He crouched before Zamia's sleeping form, his hands moving in slow, serpentine circles as they hovered an inch from the girl's boyish body. He closed his eyes and winced as if he were in pain. A slight glow of green surrounded his hands. He kept his eyes closed tight and his hands danced until the glow faded and her husband collapsed onto a stool, clutching at his chest.

*It's been a long time since he's strained his powers so. It's aging him almost before my eyes!* Litaz thought again of their homeland and prayed that her husband would

live to see it once more before the body-costs of his calling claimed him. She ran to him and placed an arm
around his bony shoulders.

He spoke through clenched teeth, clearly exhausted.
"It is time to wake her."

"Wake her?" The dervish frowned at them. "Forgive
me, Auntie, Uncle—but she has been grievously
wounded. We must let her rest, yes?"

The boy nosed in where he didn't belong, and there
was something behind it. *Does he think he loves her?*
Litaz wondered. "The girl was too close to death, Raseed. She must be awakened—if she *can* be awakened—in
order to remember that she is still alive. There will be
time to let her rest later."

She turned to her juniper wood case and removed a
vial full of big pinkish salt grains. Bringing the vial
over to the Badawi girl and placing it under her nose,
Litaz pulled out the stopper and turned her own nose
away from it.

Zamia jerked upright. She began to cough and moan
in pain. As she coughed, blood stained her mouth and
nostrils.

*Thank Almighty God.* Though Raseed looked terrified, Litaz knew the blood was a sign of further recovery. *She just might make it through this all right.*

Raseed was now close at the girl's side, clearly
wanting to do something but not knowing what that
something was. "What is happening to her?" he
shouted.

Litaz rubbed her temples and forced patience. She
pushed the boy back and dabbed away the girl's blood.

"It is hard to explain, Raseed. We have, for a few moments, fooled her soul into thinking it is in an unwounded body. Her soul will be forced into remembering this attachment. She will wake, in shock but aware and able to speak. *Then* she will need rest before we complete our treatment. If God wills it, the bonds that He has tied between body and soul will reattach."

Litaz stood back, and a moment later the girl opened her bright green eyes.

"Did . . . did I kill it?" were her first words. There was no need to ask what she meant.

To Litaz's surprise—and, she would swear, his own as well—Raseed stepped forward to answer her. "You gave me an opening, but I failed, Zamia Banu Laith Badawi." He bowed deeply, shame etched on his face. "I beg you, accept my apologies. But know that it was your valor that drove the creature off." The boy fell silent and took a step back, looking ashamed to have spoken.

*Ah*, Litaz thought, thinking on the beautiful, foolish ways of young people. *He doesn't* think *he loves her. He* worries *he loves her!*

The girl spoke strongly in response to the dervish's words, as if she'd been awake half the day and had not been sitting between death's teeth mere moments ago—another good sign. "What did you expect?" she said, "I was trained by my father." Then she closed her eyes and fell asleep again.

When afternoon came, Litaz sat with Dawoud and Adoulla in the kitchen over small bowls of goat's milk and cherryfruit, discussing their next moves. Raseed, as usual, stood.

"So what now?" her husband asked.

Adoulla's whiskers were tinted with burgundy. He wiped his face on his sleeve, and the stain slid sorcerously away as he spoke. "In the past day and a half I've fought bone ghuls and sand ghuls and some half-mad thing I've no name for. The man who commands these creatures must be found. I took this from the girl—it belonged to her father," Adoulla said, producing an ornate curved dagger and laying it on the table before him. "We were, in fact, planning to visit you before . . ." he stopped, swallowed, and went on weakly, "before these monsters attacked us. I'd hoped that your scrying spells might—"

A wordless cry—Zamia's—broke in from the sitting room.

They all rushed to her. The tribeswoman was awake, but she ignored their hails. She lay there squinting and craning her neck, as if concentrating fiercely on something unseen. *Ah. She is trying to take the lion-shape,* Litaz realized. And she was apparently unable to do so.

Zamia's eyes grew wide and wild, and she started to thrash about. It was Dawoud who finally stepped forward and laid a calming hand on the girl's forehead.

"Settle down, now, child. I said settle down! Thank Merciful God that you still live. We have brought you back before death could quite snap its jaws on you. But my wife is tired, and you have no idea the costs of a magus's magics. Lay still and don't waste our work." It was as close to tender as he ever got with a patient.

But the girl jerked back. "A magus? You worked your wicked magics on me? O God protect me! The shape has been taken from me! Better to have died!" A lionlike growl came from somewhere within her.

Not two and ten hours ago, the child had been dead in most of the ways that matter, and now she was well enough to be fiercely displaying Badawi prejudices. Litaz couldn't take all of the credit here. The girl's Angel-touched healing powers were truly wondrous.

Adoulla ran a hand over his beard and fumed at the bedridden girl. "Better to have died, eh? Damn you, girl! Asking no questions and taking no coin, my friends have exhausted themselves to heal you. Worked wonders with spell supplies that cost a year of work-man's wages! Not to mention the deeper costs. And you repay them with this savage superstition?"

With each exasperated word, Adoulla's color deep-ened. Litaz wondered whether Adoulla knew what he was doing here—a bit of provocation like this could be good for rousing the girl's spirits to a temporary rally before she passed back into a deeper, recuperative sleep—or if he was just taking out anger on a barely living child. She stepped over to him and laid a hand on his arm, but he went on.

"If Dawoud had let you die, *girl*, your band would go unavenged. Isn't vengeance what you live for? Kill-ing and codes of honor and all that?" He turned to Ras-eed. "God save us from obsessed, ungrateful children. No wonder your eyes go so googly when you look at her, boy! You've found your mate-of-the-soul!"

Zamia scowled at Adoulla, and Raseed mumbled

some outraged denial. Adoulla went on. "He won't so much as smile at pretty city girls. But put a plain-faced savage who kills in the name of the Angels before him, and his soul's all aflame! Oh, stop your sputtering protests, boy! So insistent on denying the obvious. Yes to head-chopping, no to kissing!" He looked to the sky. "How in the Name of God did I become a part of such a world?"

He turned back to Zamia. "Listen to me! This was the only way to save you. You owe Dawoud and his wife thanks. Indeed, were they living by your barbarous Badawi codes, you would owe them some sort of ridiculous life-debt, no?"

Zamia growled a sulky little lion growl. *How does she make lion noises with a girl's throat?* the scholar in Litaz wanted to know.

The girl nodded once at Dawoud and pushed words out as if each one wounded her. "The Doctor is right. You did save my life, and I . . . I owe you a debt." Dawoud patted the girl's shoulder with a dark, bony hand, but Zamia looked at it as if a rock-snake had dropped onto her.

Her husband spoke bemusedly. "Where does this fear come from, young one? Stories you heard round the campfire? Where the magi are all dressed in red robes, cackling amidst mountains of skulls? Drinking blood from a chalice, while the newborn babe cries on the altar? Hmph! Such dark assumptions from a girl who grows golden fur and rips out throats with her teeth!"

Zamia lifted her chin, her scraggy hair falling back.

"The shape is a gift from the Angels! Where does *your* foul power come from?"

Litaz was thankful her husband was being patient with the child—he could be a hard man with anyone but Litaz. When he spoke, though, he still wore the same bitter smile. "God gave me my gifts. I draw my power, girl, from my own lifeblood. From the days that I have left in this world. Now. You still owe my wife thanks, do you not?" At this, he turned and walked out of the room.

Zamia said nothing for a moment, then dipped her head. "I have been remiss with rightful gratitude, Auntie. I thank you for your aid and beseech God's blessings upon you."

*So there are some doorways in that wall of tribal pride and distrust. Good.* "'God's blessings fall on he who helps others,'" Litaz quoted. "Just remember that the next time you are in a position to do so."

The tribeswoman started to ask a question, but Litaz cut her off. "You've done too much talking already, child, and you are not in the clear yet. If Almighty God wills it, your shape-changing powers will return to you in time. But now is the time for rest." Litaz filled a mug from the pot of hemlock tonic that had been steeping on the stove and gave it to the girl. "You will wake every few hours now, and that is best—it will keep your body from forgetting that you live. Each time you wake, you must force yourself to look around and talk a bit. Then you must take one long draw from this mug before you fall back asleep—no more than that, if you wish to wake again! Do you understand?"

The girl, already growing tired, nodded sleepily.

"Good, now take that first draw."

The girl did, and a moment later she sat up energetically in bed and started fidgeting impatiently. Good. The other herbs in the tonic needed to overstimulate her for a few minutes before the hemlock could force her into a restful sleep.

At that moment, Adoulla trundled down the stairs, bellowing. " 'Hadu Nawas'—that is what the foul creature said of itself. I know that name, Litaz! I've read it somewhere. A history? An old romance?" He looked at her beseechingly, but she was quite sure she'd never read whatever book Adoulla had half-recalled.

Her friend cracked his bumpy knuckles irritably, then slumped his shoulders. "Of course, whichever book it was is a heap of wet ashes now."

Litaz saw Zamia trying to stand and laid a restraining arm across the girl's flat chest. Zamia slurred angrily. "You had knowledge of this murdering thing, and you don't *remember?*" The girl's voice was scornful but weaker, drug-heavy. Good. She would be asleep in moments.

Adoulla showed what passed for patience with the wounded child. "Well, if I'd memorized every book in my library, my dear, I'd have had no *need* for a library!"

"City men and their books!" Despite the drugs and the wound, the girl's savage haughtiness seemed to animate her. "If this knowledge had belonged to my people," the girl hissed with surprising strength, "it would be passed down in song and story, so that ten men would know—"

Litaz saw the patience flee her old friend's eyes. "And, tell me, where is all of that knowledge now, Zamia Banu Laith Badawi?"

The tribeswoman wore the memory of dead family on her face. Adoulla's words were cruel. But Litaz knew her friend well enough to know where they came from. He mourned his books as much as the girl did her tribesmen, and he no doubt found it hard to stand by while this supposedly ignorant savage of a girl made mock of his life of word-gathering.

Still, this was too much excitement. A line was being crossed that could hurt the girl's recovery. Litaz placed a hand on Adoulla's arm. It was enough. The ghul hunter threw his hands up and looked disgusted with himself. "Aaagh. I need to think. Some fresh air," he blurted and bolted for the door, slamming it behind him.

The girl narrowed her emerald eyes in her own apparent self-disgust. As if she were willing the lioness within her to kill the weak little girl. She mumbled something about revenge, then closed her eyes and fell asleep.

Raseed started after Adoulla, but Litaz dissuaded him. The ghul hunter needed to be alone with his thoughts, not preached at by a boy a fraction of his age.

Litaz looked at Zamia and allowed herself a moment to celebrate her own skill. Because of her efforts, Zamia just might live. Then she looked at her front door, which Adoulla had just slammed. He would live, too, despite his pain.

She took a deep breath. Dhamsawaat was already half-mad with the tension between the Falcon Prince and the new Khalif. Now there was this threat. She hated being dragged back into this bleak world of cruel magics and monster-hunting. But somehow this would work out, she told herself. Somehow God would guide them through this, and then perhaps she and Dawoud would finally return home and leave this thrilling, beautiful, damned-by-God city behind them.

# Chapter 9

ADOULLA SLAMMED the heavy wooden door to his friends' shop behind him. How low he had sunk, shouting at a half-dead child! Though he called her "girl," he had begun to think of Zamia as a lioness, or a desert stone. He reminded himself that she *was* a child, even if she was also more than that.

Dawoud stood a few yards away from the shop, his arms folded, staring out at the street. The magus turned at the noise Adoulla made and arched a white eyebrow at him. Adoulla was in no mood for more talking. He tried to stride past his friend, but Dawoud's talon of a hand grabbed Adoulla's arm.

"Are you all right?"

Adoulla laughed mirthlessly. "All right?! The love of my life wants nothing to do with me except to avenge her dead niece. I have a savage girl's near-death on my soul. I'm old and ready to die, and God is testing me with monsters fouler than I've ever faced. My home—"

and here, Adoulla knew, his voice cracked "—my home is charred and smoking and every book I've ever owned is gone. On top of all of this, my dreams are of rivers of blood in the streets."

Dawoud stroked his hennaed goatee and frowned. "Rivers of blood? I had almost the same dream. But it was in the Republic."

That news did not help Adoulla's mood. "Well, it seems that we dream-prophets are a dirham a dozen. May it please God to make us both *false* prophets."

Dawoud nodded grimly. "Walk with me," he said, and they began a slow stroll up the block.

Adoulla filled his lungs and emptied them, calming himself. "It's just too much, brother-of-mine. God has given me more than I can carry."

A man with a camel plodded by, mumbling happily to his animal. The magus put a thin hand on Adoulla's shoulder, gripping fat and muscle. "Not alone, do you understand? You will not carry it alone."

Dawoud was talking about taking on these creatures with him, as they had done in years past. Adoulla couldn't let this happen. "I can't ask that of you two. Name of God, I'm sorry to have involved you as much as I have."

"This thing that tried to kill your little lion-girl, Adoulla. It frightens me. You know how much it takes to frighten me. You know the things I have seen, because you have seen them too. But soul-touching that wound! The creature that bit Zamia is like cruelty . . . cowardice . . . treachery, given form. I could feel it. But twisted up inside all of that was something even worse . . . a grisly kind of loyalty. Loyalty to a very powerful man. There is something wicked at work here that I cannot ignore. Something that would never let my wife and me sleep quietly in our beds. I know you feel it, too."

A stream of screaming children shot down the street, playing some chase-game. Adoulla wiped a hand across his beard, feeling spent though it was barely afternoon. "Aye. I hate to think of what sort of man that thing calls 'friend.'" He shook himself and stole a sidelong look at Dawoud. Perhaps he felt like talking after all. "How are *you*? Those healing magics you worked. . . . Well, we're none of us as young we used to be."

Dawoud smiled sadly. "And, you are thinking, some of us are growing old more quickly than others, eh? *How am I*? Worn out, Adoulla. Three-quarters dead, the same as your fat old ass, or worse. But it would not matter to me if my wife did not seem younger and younger than me each year."

They'd had this discussion many times before. Dawoud was not quite five and ten years older than his wife. But her vitality made her seem younger, while the physical toll of Dawoud's sort of spells made him seem older. Most folk would guess there was thirty years separating them. Over the decades, Adoulla had had friends with grim diseases or horrible old injuries. Such catastrophes came to fill a certain place in people's lives, like a second spouse or an extra-demanding child. So it was with Dawoud and the withering costs of a magus's magics.

A pleasing breeze cut between the buildings, and Dawoud breathed it in. "There were times," the magus chuckled ruefully, "that I thought I wanted such a thing—a so-much-younger wife. What man does not? But now . . . I do not know. Part of me just wants to let her go . . . to make her go home to the Republic."

"How many times are we going to have this conversation, brother-of-mine? We both know you couldn't live without her. Besides, you act as if it were your choice! As if Litaz would ever let you go! And 'make her go?' Ha! I would like to see that!"

Adoulla felt a familiar small sting of jealousy. He had always admired Litaz. She was brilliant, even-handed, and simply one of the prettiest women Adoulla had ever known. More than once he had had lovemaking dreams of her, had woken half-wishing she was his. Once every few years, over a chance meal together when Dawoud happened not to be around, Adoulla found himself wishing it again for an evening. But he took such moments for the fancies they were. Adoulla was happy for his friends. Their two lives had long ago become one—of that there could be no doubt.

Adoulla had never known such a love. He did not hold Miri Almoussa any less dear than Dawoud held Litaz, but a twenty-years' flame was different than a wife, as Miri had reminded him, tearfully and testily, over the years. Before she had told him never to visit her again.

He shook off his morose heart's musings. There was work to be done. But he had little to go on. If he knew the name of the ghul-maker—the man this thing Mouw

Awa called "blessed friend"—he could cast a tracking spell. Sadly, the names the jackal-creature had called itself—Mouw Awa, Hadu Nawas—would not serve for such a spell. But they might still be of use—if only Adoulla could recall where he'd heard them before.

Again, he tried to force open his memory. And again he drew a blank. Somewhere buried in his brain was a clue that could help save his city. But this was not the place to dig it up. He said goodbye and God's peace to his best friend in the world and then went to think.

Adoulla didn't know if it was his imagination or if there was really still a charred stink to the air of the block from the night before. He started to turn back to his townhouse—to make himself see the smoking shell of it. But he found he couldn't quite force his feet eastward. To face that sight right now. . . . He thought it might finally break him.

It was just as well. He could do nothing there, and maudlin wallowing wasn't going to stop the monsters that were loose in his city.

Adoulla turned his steps to Gruel Lane. As he walked, he gingerly touched his chest where the sand ghul had slammed its ironlike arm into him. But the flesh there was no longer tender. Compared to the girl's wound, his own bruises had been easy enough for his friends to heal. Adoulla shook his head, impressed yet again by his own poor fate. No matter how many times his extraordinary friends managed to patch him up, he ruminated, he always managed to show up again with a fresh wound.

He made his way to the great public garden and

found a tiny hillock on which to sit, his bright white kaftan splayed around him. He loved this place that came to life at this late afternoon hour. It was nothing like the Khalif's delicate gardens, where quietly chirping birds selected for their song dotted the branches of the orange and pomegranate trees that suffused the air with their soft scents. In the Khalif's gardens, rippling brooks flowed magically upwards and filled the gardens with their lulling babble. No one there spoke above a whisper.

It was supposed to be soothing—the perfect place for princes, poets, and philosophers to be alone with their thoughts. But Adoulla, whose calling had more than once brought him to gardens that his station should have barred him from, thought he would go mad in such a place. For one, the tranquility was got by keeping the city's rabble away at swordpoint. But there was more to it than that: He simply could not *think* in the Khalif's gardens. He felt as if doing so might break something delicate.

The public garden of the Scholars' Quarter, on the other hand, hosted some of the most riotous smells and sounds in all Dhamsawaat. Uppermost were piss, porters unwashed after a day of lifting in the sun, and a thousand kinds of garbage. But beneath these were layered the smells that said "home" to Adoulla—if anything in this unwelcoming world did.

As an orphan-boy, as a ghul hunter's apprentice, as a young rascal and sometime hero, and now, as an old fart, he needed to breathe these scents. The brewing cinnamon-paint of the fortune tellers, the shared wine barrels of gamblers and thieves forgetting their troubles, the skewers of meat that dripped sizzling juices onto open fire pits and, here and there, a few flowers that seemed to be struggling to prove that this was a public garden and not a seedy tavern . . . Adoulla took it all in. *Home.*

Then there were the sounds. His calling had taken him many places, but Adoulla had yet to find a people as loud as those of his home quarter. The children and the mothers scolding the children. The roving storytellers and those who applauded and heckled them. The whores who offered warm arms for the night, and the men who haggled shamelessly with them. All of them going about their business in the loudest voices they could find. For cruel fate or kind, Adoulla thought, these were his people. He had been born among them, and he hoped very much to die quietly among them.

*Bah. With your luck, old man, you'll be slaughtered by monsters in some cold cavern, alone and unlamented.*

For what seemed the hundredth time that week, Adoulla silenced the discouraging voice within and tried to focus on the problem before him. He sat and breathed and thought.

"Hadu Nawas," the creature had said. The meaning of it was at the edge of his thoughts, but the harder he tried to grasp it, the more he felt like a man with oiled fingers clutching at a soapcake.

Baheem, an aging footpad who tried to rob Adoulla twenty years ago and, ten years ago, saved him from a robbery, walked past. He gave a friendly nod and pulled at his moustache, not bothering to speak, understanding that Adoulla was in meditation. Adoulla was known here, and that was why, of all places in the city, he could do what must be done here. Familiarity. It put him at ease, and when he was at ease he noticed things, put things together in their proper place.

Adoulla beckoned to Baheem, gesturing at a flat grassy spot beside him. His thoughts were not going where he needed them to, and trying to force them would only give him a headache. He knew from experience that distraction and idle chatter could help.

Baheem and he said God's peaces and Baheem sat. The thick-necked man then produced a flintbox and a thin stick of hashi. "If you don't mind, Uncle?"

Adoulla smiled negligently and quoted Ismi Shihab. "'Hashi or wine or music in measure, God piss on the man who bars other men's pleasure.'"

Stinky sweet, pungent smoke soon surrounded the pair as they sat talking about nothing and everything—the weather, neighborhood gossip, the succulent shapes of girls going by. Baheem offered the hashi stick to him more than once, and though Adoulla refused each time, he could feel the slightest hint of haze begin to creep in at the corners of his mind just from sitting beside Baheem.

It was pleasant, and Adoulla happily let his thoughts get lost in the rhythm of Baheem's complaints. For a few moments he managed to almost forget all of the grisly madness that filled his life.

"I've heard a pack of the Falcon Prince's men were found dead in an ambush," Baheem said. "Word is, their hearts were torn from their chests! It has to have been the Khalif's agents, though you think they'd have gone for the public beheadings they love so much."

Adoulla's distracted half-cheer evaporated. *Hearts torn from their chests?* He struggled to think through his secondhand hashi haze. It sounded as if the Falcon Prince faced the same foe as Adoulla and his friends. *And Pharaad Az Hammaz could prove a powerful ally in this.* Adoulla started to ask about this, but Baheem was on a hashi-talkative roll now, his complaining uninterruptable.

"And then there's the damned-by-God watchmen and this dog-screwing new Khalif!" the thief said quietly but forcefully, punctuating each word with a pull of his moustache. "These rules they have! Take the other day. I'm trying to move goods through Trader's Gate for my sick old Auntie—" he smiled shamelessly "—and two watchmen stop me, asking for a tax pass. Now, of course, I *have* a tax pass. An almost legitimate one! But these sons-of-whores start talking about new taxes and tariffs on this gate and that gate, at this rate and that rate, and pretty soon I'm headspun and copperless. Their rules and regulations are all hidden script to me, Uncle, but I know well enough when someone wants to starve my children to death. I—"

*Hidden script and dead children! That's it! God forgive me, why didn't I think of it before?* All his other thoughts fell away as Adoulla realized that Beneficent God had at last handed him a clue. "Of course! Curse my fuzzy-headedness, of course! That's it!" Adoulla leapt up and grunted with the exertion of it. It was so sudden that Baheem actually stopped talking.

Baheem came to his feet more easily, clearly ready to fight despite the hashi-haze. "What is it, Uncle?"

"Baheem, my beloved, right now I am on a hunt that could kill me. And if that happens, many others in our city will die. But if it doesn't happen, I owe you a night of feasting on the silver pavilion!"

Baheem had the good street sense to ignore the more dire part of Adoulla's pronouncement. "The silver pavilion! I'd rather you just pay my rent for a month! If I knew I had information that valuable, Uncle, I would have sold it!"

"Not information, Baheem, just the gift of your company. God's peace be with you."

"And with you, Uncle."

Adoulla cheek-kissed the thief and left the gardens, fragile hope finding a home in his heart.

# Chapter 10

RASEED BAS RASEED WATCHED the Doctor storm out of the shop and slam the front door. He was used to his mentor's irascible temper, but had never seen him quite so furious. Raseed had felt his own cheeks flush with anger at the Doctor for scolding Zamia Banu Laith Badawi so. She was not responsible for the Doctor's loss, and did not deserve to be mocked. But Raseed supposed her words had been the bushel that proved the camel's bad back. The Doctor was old, and seemed to grow more worn and weary with each passing day.

*For the weary man, virtue is the strongest tonic,* Raseed recited in his mind. The Doctor merely needed to be reminded of the good works he had done to further God's glory, Raseed realized. He started for the door, intent on consoling his mentor.

But Litaz's small hand gripped his bicep and pulled him back. "Adoulla needs to be alone now, Raseed.

Trust one who knows the ways of old men. He will be fine."

Raseed started to protest. But when he thought on it honestly, he doubted that his pious advisements would mean much to the Doctor. He sighed and nodded and sat on an ebonwood stool. With effort, he kept his gaze on the ground, and away from Zamia Banu Laith Badawi's sleeping form.

"You *can* look at her, Raseed," Litaz said. "She will not be violated by your eyes, you know." Instead of doing so, though, Raseed looked at the alkhemist.

She had taken down a small, nearly empty vial from a shelf. She held the vial aloft, eyed its blue glass suspiciously, and sucked her teeth in annoyance. "I was afraid of this," she said more to herself than to Raseed.

"What is the matter, Auntie?"

She stared at the stoppered vial for another moment, shook her head, her hair-rings clinking, and looked at Raseed. "A small setback. The tribeswoman's healing is going well. Remarkably well, thanks to her angel-touched powers. But we have hit a hitch here. I am all out of crimson quicksilver. It is a powerful solution that causes blood to flow more freely. We need it for two purposes: it is necessary for completing the healing spells we have worked on the girl, but it will also help to distill the blood on the girl's dagger so that we can try to use it to learn more of our enemies. I'll need you to go fetch me another vial."

Annoyance rose in him—he was a holy warrior, not

an errand boy! But he smothered his irritation, knowing that an unacceptable pride was at the root of it.

"Of course, Auntie. Where can crimson quicksilver be had?"

Litaz set down the vial, and her dark, heart-shaped face grew grim. "The jungles of Rughal-ba. There is a powerful monster there called the Red Khimera whose horn must be cut from its—"

Raseed's blood began to race, but he quickly felt the fool as Litaz's sober instructions slid into a snicker.

"Hee! Oh, forgive me, Raseed! I am only teasing you. No, no, do not be angry with me. It is just that there are so few occasions for jest in my life these days. But God's truth be told, the determination I saw in the set of your jaw is a tribute to your valor."

Raseed accepted this compliment without comment and set aside his annoyance at being teased.

"In fact," Litaz went on, taking up charcoal and paper and writing as she spoke, "you need only go six streets over to the Quarter of Stalls. Just past the Inspector's stall you will see the shop of Doctor Zarqaw-layari on the left. You will know it by the green-painted door. Give him this. He will fill my order and charge me later." The alkhemist handed him the note and ushered him out the door and into the warm afternoon air.

As he walked, Raseed thought he heard the voices of the Doctor and Dawoud coming from around the corner behind him. But he figured that they would wish to be left alone, so he headed on without stopping. The late afternoon sun half-dazzled his eyes as he walked.

He passed a man making water against the stone wall of a shop, and another man who was healthy enough to work begging for alms. He noted each of them with contempt and walked on.

The tempting scent of frying earth-apples welcomed him to the Quarter of Stalls. Raseed passed the row of rough-hewn food stalls, ignoring his stomach-rumbling hunger. A few minutes later he reached the green painted door Litaz had described.

It sat half-open, and he stepped inside, knocking once to let the shopkeeper know of his arrival. The room was unfurnished, save for a shelf of neatly sorted bottles and boxes against the far wall and a worktable not unlike the one in Dawoud and Litaz's shop.

A middle-aged Rughali man in a tight-fitting turban—Doctor Zarqawlayari, no doubt—looked up from the worktable in distracted annoyance. As he took in Raseed's blue silk habit with a surprised look, however, he straightened and then bowed formally.

"God's peace, Master Dervish. Well, this is an honor! One does not see many men of the Order in this city. I . . . what may this humble and unworthy shopkeeper do for you?"

Though the praise or scorn of mere men should mean nothing to a true servant of God, Raseed found himself quite thrilled to be treated with such respect. The people of Rughal-ba were less lax in such matters than the Abassenese. Not for the first time in his life, Raseed wondered whether he'd been born in the wrong realm.

*You were born exactly where Almighty God decreed—*

*now keep to your business,* the reprimanding voice within him scolded.

"God's peace to you, sir," Raseed said. "I have been sent here by Lady Litaz Daughter-of-Likami." He handed the man Litaz's note.

The shopkeeper read the note slowly in silence, then looked up with an apologetic grimace. "Ah, yes, Lady Litaz. A good woman, and one of my best customers, even if she is sometimes late in paying her accounts. But I regret that I must disappoint you both, Master Dervish."

Raseed arched an eyebrow in inquiry.

Again Doctor Zarqawlayari grimaced in real-seeming regret. He scratched at his goatee nervously. "Left and right, men are preparing for the worst, and thus crimson quicksilver is in even greater demand than normal these days. It is a rare solution in the best of times, and these are not the best of times. I've but the one vial left. And a Tax of Goods has just been announced in the name of the Defender of Virtue himself. The Inspector of Shops will be visiting tomorrow morning to collect his levy, and I must save this vial for him."

For a moment Raseed found himself struck dumb. Finding and defeating a vicious ghul-maker. Saving Zamia Banu Laith Badawi's life. Surely these were crucial things in God's eyes. That something so simple, so profane, as the vagaries of trade and politics could interfere seemed impossible.

"But . . . but we need that vial!" he finally managed to say. "There are lives at stake!"

The shopkeeper spread his hands in a gesture of helplessness. "I *am* sorry, Master Dervish. Truly I am. But there are lives at stake on my end of the stick as well. If I don't hold the required portion of my goods for the Khalif's requisition, they'll throw me in the gaol. My family would starve. What am I to do?"

*But without crimson quicksilver, Zamia will die. And we will be no closer to finding the foul killers we hunt.* Raseed pictured walking back into Dawoud and Litaz's home empty-handed, and something within him snapped.

*I could simply take what we need here.* The thought pierced his heart like a poisoned arrow. He felt sick just thinking it. *Our need is great, and our cause is just. Would God—*

Behind him, the shop door slammed shut, rattling the bottles on shelf and table. Even before he turned, Raseed sensed the presence of other men. He spun around and saw three rough-looking figures fill the other end of the room.

A small man with a face like a rat's brandished a long knife. He was flanked by a burly man with one eye wearing a brass punching glove and a tall red river Soo with a fighting staff. "Ahh, God's peace again, Doctor Z!" the rat-faced man said. "You know why we—eh? Who's this fool?"

The shopkeeper spoke in frightened tones. "Damned-by-God extorters! This is the second time this month they've come for my goods. Please, Master Dervish, help me!"

Raseed felt uncertainty fly mercifully from his heart. This was thievery, and he knew what he had to do. He drew himself up and faced the trio. "If you are here to take that which God has not given you, this will not go well for you. I suggest you leave now, wicked ones."

The one-eyed man spoke, his voice like a blacksmith's bellows. "'Master Dervish,' huh? Look, we got no bones to pick with the Order, boy. This business is between this greedy son-of-a-whore and our Prince. So why don't you just make your scrawny ass scarce before we grown men have to spank it, eh?"

The Soo man spit once, smiled, and thumped the steel tip of his staff against the stone floor.

*At last, something that makes sense again. A clear path of action.* "Defend yourselves," Raseed said softly.

Then he leapt.

There was too little room in the confines of the small shop to draw his sword. Instead, Raseed lunged at the rat-faced man first, palm-punching him in the face and breaking his nose. In the same motion, he grabbed the man by his throat and tossed him at the one-eyed man, sending both of them down in a heap.

Raseed spun just in time to dodge a staff-blow from the third thug, who was having a hard time wielding his weapon in such tight quarters. With a chop of his hand, Raseed split the astonished man's staff in two, then sent him flying into the wall with a spinning kick.

One-eye was back on his feet now, and he stood back warily, looking for an opening. The man threw out a punch but found only air. Raseed drove his elbow up, shattering the man's jaw, and he collapsed.

Rat-face, who was still on the ground nursing his

broken nose, tried to stab Raseed's leg. Raseed snaked back and stomped on the man's wrist, which broke with a satisfying crunch. The little man dropped his knife and curled into a ball, whimpering in half conscious pain.

The Soo threw his staff halves at Raseed, yanked the shop door open, and ran. Raseed started to pursue, but first turned back to make sure the shopkeeper was safe.

The man's mouth hung open, a gratifying look of awe on his flushed face. "Oh, thank you, Master Dervish, thank you! And God's blessings upon you! Those thugs were—"

Raseed heard a noise. Without warning, his feet were swept out from beneath him. He fell hard onto his back, the wind knocked out of him. Above him a light flashed in his eyes, and he felt suddenly nauseated and disoriented.

*Sorcery of some sort. These villains had accomplices outside the shop,* he realized and cursed himself for being ambushed so easily by common criminals.

He fought past the sickness in his stomach and the after-light still dancing in his vision and started to rise to his feet.

And suddenly a sword was at his throat.

Raseed looked up past the light motes swirling in his eyes to see the suede- and silk-clad Falcon Prince, holding a small mirror in one hand and a saber in another. The edge of the blade grazed Raseed's neck.

"We meet again, friend of Adoulla Makhslood! And you've damn near killed two of my men!"

Raseed said nothing, but waited for his dizziness to

fade and watched for a moment's inattention in order to knock away the thief's blade.

"Boys!" the impossibly tall bandit said to his men, his eyes and his sword alike still glued to Raseed. "No shame in getting whipped by this one—he fights as well as any man I've ever seen, save perhaps myself. But stop your groaning and moaning. Grab that jar of blue powder there and get out of here! A thousand apologies, O noble shopkeeper, but we must, in the name of the good people of Dhamsawaat, confiscate your supply of nightpetal essence. Worry not, though—I swear to you in God's name that it will find a loving home in the hands of my master alkhemist, who will make good use of it."

*Thievery, mockery, and vain Name-taking all in one swoop of his tongue!* It was disgusting, and Raseed's blood burned at not being able to do anything to stop it.

"Oh, come now," Pharaad Az Hammaz said, speaking again to Raseed as his men made their escape. "Don't look so upset, young man. You're only on your back now because I resorted to dirty tricks. When I saw how well you fought, I wasn't about to take a chance on face-to-face foolishness. I had to use all my stealth and my very last dazzle-glass." He tossed the small mirror to the stone floor, where it shattered.

"Your sight and stomach will return to normal in an hour's time. Just lay there for a moment and catch your breath. As for me, well, I must be elsewhere. But perhaps our paths will cross again." The bandit backed away and toward the shop door quickly, keeping his sword pointed in Raseed's direction until he was out the door and out of sight.

The moment the sword edge left his throat, Raseed tried to stand. He was still disoriented from the effects of the thief's magic mirror and, as he came to his feet, he barely managed to keep himself from being sick.

An hour to recover, the bandit had said, and Raseed did not doubt that was the case for normal men. But Raseed was a weapon of God, not some hapless watchman. Ignoring the whimpers of the still-shocked shopkeeper, he forced himself to take step after step and moved, as fast as he could, out the green-painted door and after the bandit.

Stepping out onto the street Raseed scanned the crowd and saw a knot of gawkers staring and pointing at the side of a townhouse. There he saw Pharaad Az Hammaz climbing to the building's roof, obviously aided by the same remarkable leaping magic he'd used after thwarting the execution in Inspector's Square.

Shoving his way through the crowd, Raseed grit his teeth against his rioting stomach, took a few soul-focusing breaths, and leapt up to a second story window box. His feet and fingers found holds in the wood latticework of the building's window-screens, and he climbed as quickly as he could. For a moment his head swam in dizziness, and he thought he would fall. But he called on all the strength he had, kept climbing, and finally hoisted himself over the edge of the rooftop.

He stood and, on the other side of the flat roof, saw

the Falcon Prince, his brawny arms crossed and an impudent grin on his moustachioed face.

Raseed drew his sword.

"*Most* impressive, young man!" the bandit boomed. "God's balls, I've never seen a man recover from the dazzle-glass's magic so swiftly!" Suddenly the man's saber was in his hand.

Despite his dizziness, Raseed sped at the thief, swinging his sword. Pharaad Az Hammaz parried one blow, then another, and another.

Steel sang out loudly each time their weapons met, and with the impact of each blow Raseed thought he would vomit. But he grit his teeth and fought on, pressing the attack, looking for an opening in the thief's defenses.

There was none. The Falcon Prince was sweating now, but the smile never left his face. "Do you know, I think you might have had my head by now, if you weren't still sick and dizzy," he shouted. "But you are. And so —"

The bandit darted back, dodging yet another of Raseed's blows. Then, with a speed Raseed would have thought impossible, Pharaad Az Hammaz kicked a booted foot into Raseed's midsection. Raseed fell backwards, his stomach emptying, and his sword flying from his hand.

*This is it, then*, the voice within him spit. *Death at the hands of a common criminal. And you dared to call yourself a weapon of God!*

But, instead of closing in for the kill, Pharaad Az

Hammaz reached into his tunic and produced a small object, tossing it at Raseed.

"I've no more time for this," the thief bellowed, "but I leave you with a gift. Catch!"

Acting purely on reflex, Raseed caught the small glass bottle the thief tossed at him. *What new trick is this?* he wondered, seeing the bright red liquid that sloshed and sparkled in the late afternoon sun.

"Doctor Zarqawlayari's last vial of crimson quicksilver, young man! It's yours, now—take it with my blessings. I heard your plea to the shopkeeper before my men made their presence known. The Falcon Prince is in the business of saving lives when he can. Better that you and yours should have it than that tyrant the Khalif."

As the man babbled, Raseed started to go for his sword, which lay a few feet away.

"The seal on the vial has been broken, though," the thief continued, edging back toward the opposite side of the rooftop. "Open air is slowly creeping in now, which means you have less than an hour to get it to Lady Litaz. We can do our little sword dance up here all day, if you wish. Or you can save whomever's life it is you came here to save." The bandit kept backing away as he spoke, making his escape.

Raseed came to his feet and looked toward his sword.

"You can thank me later!" the Falcon Prince shouted mockingly, and he leapt effortlessly—sorcerously, no doubt—to another rooftop, leaving Raseed staring stupidly at the vial in his hand.

His stomach cramped in agony, and his throat burned with bile. His head still swam, and for a moment he stood motionless. The scales of his soul weighed stolen goods against the life of an angel-touched girl.

Then Raseed silenced the outraged voice within him and began to make his way back to the Scholars' Quarter.

# Chapter 11

ZAMIA BANU LAITH BADAWI found herself amidst a confusing rush of sounds and sights and smells. The keening winds of the Empty Kingdom. The sweet smell of dried dung burning in the air. The tanned tents of her people. The happy cries of those she knew to be dead.

*A dream.*

She floated just above the tents, as if sitting in a tree that was not there, and watched the Banu Laith Badawi go about their work—cooking, cleaning hides, grooming camels, mending clothes. She tried to call out to them. Her throat grew sore with the trying, but no words came. She growled, she tried to approach them, but nothing happened.

Her father stepped into view, speaking to someone she couldn't see.

*I am a Badawi chieftain, not some slavish townsman! Laith Banu Laith Badawi decides what is best for his tribe!*

*God took your mother, Protector, with the same hand he used to give you to me. And the Angels gave you this gift. I will not reject what God, and the Ministering Angels, and the woman who was my night air, gave to the band because of the idiocies of the Banu Khad or the Banu Fiq Badawi. They are fat, weak bands full of hypocrites. Let them say what they wish among their own damned-by-God tents about my choice for Protector of the Band. But they will deal with you at council with the same respect that we show their Protectors or there will be blood feud!*

These words. Zamia knew these words. Her father had spoken them to her not a year past. It had not come to blood feud, but instead to the water-shunning of her band. And then something had struck the Banu Laith Badawi, something more foul than any feud. She had known, when she had come across the heart-robbed corpses of her tribesmen, that it had not been the Banu Fiq or the Banu Khad.

Suddenly her father was gone, and the desert with him. Zamia woke and slept and woke and slept and it was all as one. Once, a cloud seemed to lift from her eyes and mind. She saw, for a few clear moments, that she lay in the Soo couple's shop. Then the cloud of sleep lowered again.

She was back in the desert, far from any tents, deep among the dunes. She watched a green-eyed girl a bit younger than herself pick her way quickly across the sand. The girl was dressed in Badawi camel-calf suede, but she traveled alone, with no other tribesmen in sight. Suddenly the girl stopped and turned and looked at Zamia. Then, before Zamia's eyes the child began to grow taller, her mouth growing hard and her eyes going cold. Aging.

And Zamia screamed as she saw that the girl was her. She watched herself, bandless, tribeless, and alone, growing old and then shriveling into a skeleton. Then bones turned to dust and blew away in a howling wind.

She woke with a scream and sucked in air. Then she vomited, tears filling her eyes. She felt weak and wasted, like the old woman she had become in her dream. Suddenly there was a loud banging, and she heard shouted words that made half of her want to flee and half of her want to kill.

"Mouw Awa! Mouw Awa!"

The Doctor's voice. It took a befuddled moment for Zamia to realize that these were real sounds, not dream-echoes. *The monster strikes again!* Fear filled her. She tried to take the shape. Her body burned with the effort, like trying to draw breath in a sandstorm. But the shape did not come. She was helpless. She tried feebly to gather her strength.

But after a moment she realized that there was no attack, praise be to God. She was in the Soo couple's home. The Doctor was stomping about the shop shouting, and Zamia realized the banging noise had simply been the heavy door slamming as he'd entered.

"Mouw Awa! Mouw Awa!" the ghul hunter shouted again. "It's Kemeti hidden script—Name of God, why didn't I recall right away? The 'Child Scythe'—now I know where I've read that name! Litaz! Litaz Daughter-of-Likami! Where are you, woman? Dawoud! Where is your wife?"

Both of the Doctor's friends appeared on the stairway. Litaz's expression was one of stern irritation. "Name of God, Adoulla, I told you the girl needs quiet in order to rest. Have you lost your mind? What is all this shouting?"

Zamia was fully awake now, and she managed to sit up on the cushioned divan. She was pleased to note that where her wound had burned before there was only a light stinging.

To her left, Raseed leaned against the white-painted wall, looking even more uneasy than usual. His silks were dusty, and he looked pale, almost as if he'd been sick.

Not wanting to look at the dervish too long, she turned back to the Doctor. His smile was broad as he boomed words at Litaz.

"Litaz! My dear, please tell me you recall my lending you a book—"

"You've lent me many books, Adoulla. Which one?"

"Written by the court poet Ismi Shihab. A rare copy of his private memoirs from just before the civil war— remember? It took Hafi five years to find me this book! Remember?"

Litaz rolled her eyes. "Right. I remember you forcing it on me. You were so excited to have found it. Boring stuff, nothing like his poetry. I read a few pages of meaningless royal intrigue and set it aside. It's still upstairs somewhere."

"Thank All-Provident God that you are such a poor returner of things, my dear! Praise God!" The Doctor leapt up the steps, positively beaming. The Soo couple followed. Zamia heard the sounds of frantic rummaging upstairs, and more shouted conversation between the Doctor and Litaz about books.

Zamia longed to fight someone. She was uneasy with the poking around and reading that the Doctor seemed to find so necessary. The urge to leave these dawdling old people nearly overtook her, and again she forced herself to face rock-hard reality. A Badawi warrior always found the most effective way to deal with enemies. And trying alone to find her enemies and stage a suicidal ambush was not the most effective way. She had no one else to turn to. She could expect no help from her people, even in fighting creatures such as these. In fact, Zamia knew, there would be those who would blame the appearance of such monsters on her band's supposed corruption.

She was again overcome with a terrible sense of all she had lost. She thought of home—of spiced yoghourt and fresh flatbread. She wished, with tears forming in her eyes, that she could see her father, or her cousin, or any of her band, one more time.

*With my father against my band! With my band against my tribe! With my tribe against the world!* The old Badawi saying echoed mockingly through her head. She was the last of the Banu Laith Badawi, and she had no children. What was band now? What was tribe?

Her thoughts were interrupted by the Doctor's shouts from above "A-ha! It *is* here, praise God!" The ghul hunter came running downstairs, the others behind him. He sat at the low table beside her divan and opened a small black book.

"You have more right to hear this than anyone, Zamia."

She nodded appreciatively, still feeling weak.

When they were all gathered around, the Doctor jabbed a thick finger at the book before him and bellowed, "This book! This is where I know the names Hadu Nawas and Mouw Awa. Ismi Shihab's memoirs. Listen to this, all of you.

*"Hadu Nawas was the last living member of a once great family. He was wealthy and kept a fine mansion near the Far Gardens, on the outskirts of the city. Once, twice, thrice did dark rumors arise among the poor people of that neighborhood about children disappearing into Hadu Nawas's mansion. The Khalif knew of the man's warped ways, but Hadu Nawas was a political ally, so the Khalif did nothing.*

*"The winds of politics shift quickly, though. A series of events—intricate as puzzlecloth, quick as lightning, made Hadu Nawas an enemy of the court. And suddenly the pious Khalif was outraged by Hadu Nawas's child butchery."*

Here the ghul hunter looked up at Litaz. "And you say you found this book *boring*, my dear?"

Litaz shrugged. "I did not read that far."

The Doctor turned back to the book and kept reading.

*"I was there—sent as a recorder of crimes—when the watchmen burst in on that man-shaped monster. He had made an unspeakable little lair for himself beneath his mansion. There were indecent drawings on the walls and child-sized*

cages. We found Hadu Nawas with a hatchet in his hand and a gratified snarl on his face, standing over a little girl's body.

"I cannot lie to God, so why lie to the page? We bound that man and beat him. Tore out his nails, stabbed at his olive sack and tortured him right up to his trial. Some wished to put the fiend on display but the Khalif forbade speaking of the crimes to the common people.

"The web of influence was woven such that the Khalif wished to purge the perished Nawas family's name of this last-of-the-line madman. So Hadu Nawas's name was stripped from him. It was decreed that he would be sealed in one of the tainted tombs of the Kem—destined to die of thirst or madness in the deep desert ruins.

"As a part of this punishment, the murderer was given a new name, a name tainted by the corrupt old Kem, to mark him for his imprisonment. It was not Hadu Nawas that was sealed in that tomb. It was Mouw Awa, the Child Scythe."

The Doctor closed the book and scratched his big nose. "That is all the poet has to say."

Zamia shuddered, and not only from her weakness. More than once, her band had spotted the imposing ruins of an ancient Kemeti pyramid or obelisk. But no Badawi in his right mind would go anywhere near these places, which were known to be tainted by the foulest sorts of magic. To be imprisoned in such a place. . . .

"Cast into a ruined pyramid to die," the old magus said. "Well, something obviously found him there. Something that would not let him die. That had a use for the soul of a killer of children."

"The Dead Gods," Litaz said, her voice eerily flat.

The Doctor scratched his balding pate in thought. "Well, my dear, you Soo know more about the heathens of old than we Abassenese do, but there *are* books that say that the Faroes of Kem ruled with soul-eating magics from their gods."

Raseed, who had been long silent, narrowed his tilted eyes. He drew his sword and began to clean it. "With apologies, books and history are not our concern. This creature Mouw Awa is murdering men and women. Worse. If the Doctor speaks true, it keeps their souls from God's presence. It—and whoever set it to killing—must be found and slain *now*."

The way the dervish stood and spoke made Zamia want to be nearer to him. Were she not lying down, she feared she would have taken a step toward him against her will.

"So how can we hope to kill this foul thing?" Raseed continued. "My sword made no mark on it. My boldest blade-strokes did nothing."

Dawoud's brow furrowed in thought. He pulled at his hennaed goatee. "I am not surprised by that," he said. "This Mouw Awa was apparently born of ancient Kem magics—twisted spells that your steel and even my own powers and Adoulla's invocations could well be useless against. What say you, beloved?" Dawoud turned to his wife, not looking hopeful.

The alkhemist shook her head, her hair-rings clinking. "Given God's help and months of study, perhaps I could try and devise some substance to fight such a thing, but we don't have months."

Zamia found herself speaking the words almost before she thought them. "It fled from my claws. I wounded it badly. Sense says I am the only one who can kill it." She was very aware of what her next words were, and speaking them filled her with nausea. "Except that I am, myself, wounded and half dead. And I cannot take the shape."

Litaz sniffed at her. "Don't insult our craft, child. You're not half dead. The way you heal, you'll be back on your feet in a couple of days."

Zamia turned her head and found the Doctor looking at her so hard that she felt certain he could see through her.

"Indeed," the ghul hunter said. "And may it please God that it be so. For the child may be right about her claws." He stopped staring at her and seemed now to stare hard at nothing. "Do you know, I've read translated accounts by barbarian priests in the Warlands? The land of Braxony was once tormented by creatures half wolf, half man. The heroes of that land were able to slay the monsters with silver swords—swords that they claimed were touched by Angels, as I recall. Of course those were just *books* and *histories*, and thus not our concern," he said, sparing a droll look for Raseed.

Raseed made a noise in his throat. "The Angels would never visit blessings on those heathenish lands! Their favors are not for thieves and blasphemers! They—" he fell silent and looked at the floor. For the first time since she'd met him, Zamia scented something impure wafting from the dervish's body. Something almost like deception. *Impossible*, she told herself. Perhaps her senses had been a bit confounded by injury and healing drugs.

The Doctor shrugged his big shoulders at his assistant. "I don't know about that. But this is similar to what *your* people say of the lion-shape, is it not, Zamia? When you told me you carry no weapon, what was that bombastic bit of verse you spoke?"

It disturbed Zamia that she was growing so used to the Doctor's insults to her people that she had begun ignoring them. "I am a Badawi, not a timid townsman. Bombast is not an insult to a true tribesman."

"Fine, fine. The *saying*, child, what is it?"

"*My claws, my fangs, the silver knives with which the Ministering Angels strike.*"

Then without warning, she felt tears begin to well up in her eyes. She wiped them away. "I am the only one who can avenge the Banu Laith Badawi, and I cannot take the shape!"

"You will avenge your band, Zamia. Rest easy in that," the Doctor said, and Zamia thanked God for the confidence in his eyes and scent.

The ghul hunter went on, his voice growing softer. "Child . . . you should know     That is . . . well, your pain is the freshest here, Zamia, but it is not unique. God's truth be told, girl, we're a veritable orphan hall here! The boy's kin left all claim to him behind at the gates of the Lodge of God. My friends are a thousand miles and twenty years away from anyone they called family. And they've lost . . ." the Doctor stopped himself from saying something. "They've lost much more

than you could know to this half-secret war we fight
against the Traitorous Angel."

Zamia looked over at Litaz. The alkhemist's normally warm smile was nowhere to be seen. She gave
Adoulla a sad look and stood up. In her small blue-
black hands she held Zamia's father's dagger.

Zamia reached out weakly, wanting to hold the
weapon in her own hands. "That dagger. My
band's . . ." she started to say.

"Don't worry," Litaz said, "I will return it. But—
thanks to Raseed—we now have a solution that will
distill the strange blood that blackens it to an analyz-
able essence. It will take me a little while to prepare it,
though."

The alkhemist darted another look at the Doctor—
irritated rather than sad. "Adoulla, since you are so set
on sharing secret pains today, maybe you should speak
to the girl about your own family." She left the room.
Dawoud followed her out, throwing the Doctor an
apologetic glance as he did so.

"And what, Doctor, was that about?" Zamia asked.

"Ask Litaz some time, and she will tell you, child.
She is right, though, that I owe you a bit of my own
story—for there should be a balance, between allies, in
what we know of each other's pain."

Raseed, looking disgusted with himself and still
smelling atypically of deception, stepped out of the
room, giving her and the Doctor a bit of privacy. She
watched the dervish go, puzzled, then forced her attention back to the ghul hunter. "Litaz mentioned
your family," she said.

"Aye. She means my parents, really. I only have the dimmest memories of them alive. Mostly I recall finding their bodies. As a boy, I told myself stories about them every day: they were killed because they were really a Khalif and queen in disguise and I, like a story hero, was a secret prince.

"But they weren't royalty," the Doctor went on. "They were a porter and his wife, ordinary people of the Scholars' Quarter, who left me, through no choice of their own, to a cruel fate with no kin and no money."

The Doctor paused to fetch Zamia a clay cup of cool water. She took a long drink from it, felt the sweet pain of her parched throat coming to life again. She didn't know what to say to the Doctor's words. "How did they die?" she asked, realizing too late that to these too-subtle city men, such a question might be taken as rude.

But the Doctor only sighed. "Pointlessly, my dear. They died pointlessly. No grand prophecy, no dark mission of the servants of the Traitorous Angel. Just a pathetic, desperate piece of shit with a knife, who was drunk or stupid enough to think he could somehow get a few coins out of my completely coinless father." Vacantly, the ghul hunter plucked up a bit of brown cloth from a Soo sewing tray sitting on the cushion beside him. As he spoke he began to twist the cloth in his hands, apparently unaware of what he was doing.

"When I was barely a man I managed to track their killer down. He had ended up a one-legged gutter-sitter, obliterated by wormwood wine. I had started to study my craft then, but in truth I was still the street tough that had led the other young troublemakers of Dead Donkey Lane. But when I found that man, I was more vicious than I'd ever been in any brawl. I killed him with a knife. Stabbed him ten times. It takes a man a long time to die from a short-bladed knife. Long enough for me to wake from my rage. Long enough to find myself holding a bloody blade, hovering over the body of a still-begging cripple."

The Doctor shook himself. "I still can't explain what I felt at that moment. But you and I have more than one thing in common. To this day I keep my hand free of the feel of killing-steel. I've seen enough knives and swords. Now, instead of killing, I do all that I can to keep men from dying."

"When we met, I wondered why you were traveling on such dangerous errands unarmed."

"Aye. I am not a soft man, Zamia. I travel with those willing to kill. I flatter myself that I can still throw a punch as good as a man half my age. But . . . well, there is a difference between cold-blooded guttings and giving a cruel man a bloody nose once in a rare while."

Dawoud appeared in the doorway and snorted. " 'Once in a rare while'? Do not let him fool you, girl. Adoulla Makhslood has handed out cracked ribs and swollen skulls a good bit more often than 'once in a rare while'!" The magus walked over and patted the ghul hunter on his shoulder. "This one's as much a savage as any Badawi, make no mistake!"

Zamia was about to take the magus to task for thus characterizing her people, but a sudden stink—so strong that to Zamia's keen senses it was almost a physical object—filled the room. At first she was sure one of the old men had broken wind. They kept pointing accusing fingers at each other and snickering like children. But it was a different sort of stink, a scent her senses didn't recognize. And it was streaming in from the small shop's cedar windows. "What is that smell?" she asked, gagging around the words.

The Doctor stopped snickering and, as he spoke, his voice dripped with disdain. "That is the smell of the dyers and the tanners. The new Khalif, in his infinite wisdom, had the wafting-spells reroute the stink through the Scholars' Quarter last year. Now one evening each week that damned-by-God smell gets dumped upon us and lingers for an hour. Were it any more than that, I swear to you the Khalif would have a riot on his hands."

Dawoud grumbled something, walked over to a large knit pouch that hung on the wall, and produced from it two pieces of folded cloth. He handed them to Zamia and the Doctor. "Sad to say, I'm almost growing used to it. But Litaz has taken to keeping these around."

"Praise God for your wife's wisdom, brother-of-mine." The Doctor held the cloth over his mouth and nose. As Zamia followed suit, she was surprised by the pungent but pleasant smells of mint oil and cinnamon and under these the stinging scent of vinegar.

The magus's eyes tightened, and his voice grew firm. "I won't let her be hurt," he said. He spoke to the Doctor as if Zamia were not right there. "We are with you, my old friend, you know that. But this isn't like the old days. I will not let Litaz be hurt. Now it is that before anything else."

Zamia felt words rising up within her but she kept them down.

The Doctor set down his scented cloth. He put a big brown hand on his friend's shoulder. "*I* will not let her be hurt either, brother-of-mine."

Zamia believed him. In that moment, the Doctor seemed frighteningly alert to her. His face looked less round, somehow. Hard and haggard. She wished her will alone could heal her wounds and return her powers. To be lying in a sickbed while brave old men—yes, Doctor Adoulla Makhslood was brave, Zamia had to confess it—did the work of avenging her tribe. . . . It twisted her stomach.

Zamia vomited over the edge of the divan. Thin yellow bile splashed onto the Doctor's kaftan, then slid away.

Zamia was mortified. Her stomach twisted into further knots from pain and drugs, stink and embarrassment, and the taste of bile. She vomited again, this time at least finding the copper pail Litaz had placed beside the couch.

At that moment, the alkhemist swept into the room and began shooing out the men. "Out, you two! Out! This child is a chieftain's daughter, and she has just emptied her guts before you. Do you think she needs two old goats hovering over her? No! Leave this between us women of high station. I said go! Name of

God, can you men not make yourselves useful elsewhere?"

Zamia was as thankful for the alkhemist's presence as for any rescue by an armed ally. She felt better now that her stomach was empty and, when the men had left, she smiled weakly at Litaz. But the little woman looked heartbroken as she sat beside Zamia.

"Do you know, only a day ago I was dreading the drudgery of drawing up accounts after Idesday? I thought that was going to be the great pain of my week. Now? I have a houseful of pain and loss."

Shame flooded Zamia's heart. "I am sorry, Auntie, to have brought my troubles to your door."

Litaz waved away the words. "I'm not speaking only of you. Adoulla Makhslood lost a lifetime's worth of books and talismans in that fire, Zamia. He is doing things only a young man should do in order to re-arm himself: sleep-stealing spells, self-bleedings, and such. We fought side by side for many years, dear, and I'm not sure I've ever seen him more determined."

Zamia found comfort in this. She felt her respect for Doctor Adoulla Makhslood deepen almost physically. Litaz continued as she cleaned up the mess Zamia had made.

"You must understand what he has lost, Zamia. That townhouse . . . it was a sign of something. A sign that this man without wife or child or high station held something in this world." The alkhemist shook her head. "But I suppose these things would make little sense to a tribeswoman, especially to one as young as you. *'With my father against my band! With my band against my tribe! With my tribe against the world!'* You think us all quite strange—this little family of not-blood—do you not?"

Zamia thought for a moment before speaking. "Strange? Perhaps. But also admirable. So different from one another, yet so dedicated to each other. God's truth be told, I've never seen such a way of being before. My own band feared me, even as they were happy enough to call me Protector." She stopped herself before saying any more. How dare she speak ill of her band—her *dead* band!—to this woman who was practically a stranger!

She changed the subject. "You and your husband, Auntie. You have been married to him a long time, yes? And you sleep with him despite his tainted powers?" Only after she'd spoken did she realize that, to a townsman, this was inappropriate talk.

But Litaz just laughed. "Ha! Do you think he's grown hooves or something? He has all the same elements that make a man. We may not be the hot-blooded couple we once were, but yes, of course I sleep with him!"

"And yet you two have no children?"

Litaz smiled a small, sad smile and said nothing.

"Forgive me Auntie, I should not have—"

"No, no, there's no need for forgiveness, child. We had a son, Dawoud and I. It was a long, long time ago. He was a beautiful boy, and in his beaming little face was everything that was handsome of the Red River Soo and the Blue."

The air was thick with the sadness in the woman's words. "He . . . he has gone to join God, Auntie?"

A tiny, graceful nod. "Yes. Twenty years dead. He would be older than you, had he lived." She looked at Zamia as if trying to decide how to say something. "Dawoud and I were taught hard lessons when we were young, Zamia Banu Laith Badawi. Lessons about the wrath of the Traitorous Angel. And about . . . vulnerabilities." For a few long moments the alkhemist seemed to stare at something far away.

"Well," Litaz finally said, standing up. "My scrying solutions should be boiling by now. I must attend to them. You should eat something and sleep a bit more now. And take this tea, which will complete your healing." The alkhemist fed her pocketbread filled with chick peas and olive oil, then gave her a too-sweet medicinal tea. Zamia had barely set down the cup before her eyelids began to droop and she slid into a dreamless sleep.

She half-woke several times from her feverish healing sleep. Each time she caught the Doctor's scent, awake and active. More than once she looked around and saw him there in the sitting room, pounding out some herb or filing some metal into a vial, mumbling some invocation as he did so. Once she saw him slash his own forearm and drip blood onto a piece of vellum. Litaz's words about the Doctor's determination floated through her head as Zamia drifted in and out of sleep.

When she finally, truly woke she was alone. The wound in her side still ached painfully, but the nausea was gone, and she felt a renewed strength in her limbs.

It was hard to tell time by the city's sun and moonlight—buildings warped it in weird ways—but from the dark outside the windows, Zamia guessed that it was very late at night.

Again she tried to take the shape and again felt as if she were trying to breathe sand. She stifled her tears, though, and shakily brought herself to her feet. From another room she heard voices—the Doctor's, Litaz's, Dawoud's. Zamia's steps were slow and awkward. She followed the sound of the voices to the room adjoining the sitting room.

The room was crowded with things and people. A shelf of books, racks of bottles, and strange tubes made of glass. The only relatively clear surface was a large table made of some strange metal. The Doctor's white-kaftaned bulk was perched on a low stool, and Raseed leaned against the wall beside him. Litaz sat in a tall chair before this table, her husband hovering over her shoulder, both of them looking at a massive wood-bound book that lay open there. Beside the book was a bizarre brass and glass apparatus. One part of the thing looked like a small claw, and Zamia saw that this claw clutched her father's knife. Litaz was looking into another part of the device—shaped like a huge eye—and evidently comparing what she saw to the figures and words in the book.

Study, the memorization of plants, the intricacies of the stars. For years, her father had tried to teach her that these were a part of being Protector of the Band. "Patience, little moon, is a warrior's virtue," he would say. "Your strength alone is not enough. You must have knowledge, too, little rose. And judgment. And, as I say, little emerald, patience." Though she was always 'Protector' when there were others to overhear, in private her father had perhaps a dozen "little" nicknames for her. She loved the way he'd peppered his speech with them, even as he had raised her to be a warrior.

Her father's greatest worry had been that Zamia was too lion-like. "You'd do well to spend more time learning the townsmen's letters and less time stalking sandfoxes! There are many ways in which the Protector must defend the band," he'd said just a fortnight ago, looking so disappointed that it hurt Zamia inside. Just to make her father happy, she had tried to pay attention to the book full of meaningless marks as he tried to teach them to her. Had tried hard. But try as she might, she was not made for such things.

Her new allies all looked up as they heard her approach. Raseed stopped leaning on the wall and took a step toward her before he seemed to stop himself. The Doctor's eyes were wide, perhaps surprised that she was on her feet. Litaz looked at her with the same puzzled face that she'd worn when looking through that glass eye.

The old magus, though, was the first to speak. "Name of God, child, you should be resting! How is it that you're on your feet? God's balls, how is it that you're *awake*? You should be heal-sleeping for another two or three days!"

Litaz bit her lip, looking as if she were still puzzling something out. "The touch of the Angels," the alkhemist said. "Amazing. Clearly, the power God's ministers granted you goes beyond your lion-shape. Even with our healing magics helping, you should not have been able to walk for a week."

Zamia raised her chin just a bit. "Perhaps we 'savages' are more resilient than the soft townsmen you are used to treating, Auntie."

The Doctor made a farting noise with his mouth and laughed. "Yes, yes, surely it is the innate bravery of the Badawi at work here, girl."

Before Zamia could respond, Raseed was at her side. "'God's mercy is greater than any cruelty,'" he quoted from the Heavenly Chapters. "You were grievously wounded, Zamia. Praise God that you are recovering swiftly, but still you ought to be resting now, for—"

Litaz made an irked noise. "Please," she said to Raseed, "don't give advice when you know not of what you speak. The best thing for Zamia now is *not* to sleep. The crimson quicksilver is reawakening her blood, just as it is the blood on this knife. If she can walk, let her. And speaking of blood, she has a right to see whatever answers we may glean here." The Soo woman turned to Zamia and gestured to the only other stool in the room. "Sit. I was just making the final adjustments to my scrying solution. I was asking the men, but you'd know better than they—when you wounded this Mouw Awa creature, did it bleed?"

Zamia forced herself to think of those few moments that had nearly killed her. Of her fangs digging into that monster's foul flank. It had been both like and unlike tearing into flesh. There was shadow and pain but. . . . "No, Auntie. No, it did not bleed."

"As I told you," the Doctor said, stroking his beard in thought. "The girl also said that to her remarkable senses, the blood on this knife smelled of neither man nor animal, whereas this Mouw Awa smelled of both. As I'd suspected, this must be the blood of the one who *made* those ghuls. The one whom that monster called 'blessed friend.'"

"Well, whatever its source, it is the strangest blood I have ever seen. Full of life and lifeless. All of the eight elements are here, but they are . . . negated somehow. Sand and lightning, water and wind, wood and metal, orange fire and blue fire! How could they all be in one drop of blood, and yet *not* be there?" The little woman turned to her husband. "Stranger still, within the clots there are creeping things moving about. It is as if this blood came from some mix of man and ghul. It makes no sense. Still, my love, you should work your magics here. God willing, they may give us better answers."

Using a tiny silver spoon, the alkhemist scooped a bit of white powder from a jar into a glass vial filled with red liquid. The liquid began to bubble and froth and turned bright green. Litaz then took this liquid and poured it over the bloodied knife that had been Zamia's father's.

A bright green light began to shimmer off of the knife. The light grew brighter and brighter until it filled the room.

"You can begin," the Soo woman said to her husband. "Stand back," she said to the others, doing so herself as she spoke.

The magus stepped forward, placing his gnarled

hands a hairsbreadth above the knife. An eerie green light began to glimmer about his fingers as they weaved back and forth around the blood-stained blade. The old Soo's eyes rolled back, and he chanted a wordless chant in an oddly echoed voice. *Wicked magics*, Zamia thought. Instinctively, she started to take the shape . . .

And of course found that she couldn't. Panic rose in her again—she could feel the shape just beyond her reach, and feel the pain of her wound keeping her from her lion-self. *Almighty God, I beg you, help me!*

But then the magus was speaking, and she *had* to heed his words, for that was the path to vengeance for the Banu Laith Badawi. Tears burned in her eyes, but again she shoved thoughts of the shape aside and listened.

"This blood is like . . . like the cancellation of life," Dawoud said as his long dark fingers darted back and forth above her father's knife. "More than that, the cancellation of existence. Like the essence of a ghul, whose false soul is made of creeping things. But with will. Cruel, powerful will."

The Doctor spoke quietly to Litaz, as if Zamia and Raseed were not there. "This all makes a horrible sort of sense, when I think on it. There's an old tale of a man called the ghul of ghuls—a man who was like a ghul raised by the Traitorous Angel himself. A man who'd cut out his own tongue to better let the Traitorous Angel speak through him. Who had his soul emptied, then filled with the will of the Traitorous Angel. He is supposed to wear a kaftan that can never be clean and—"

The Doctor fell silent as Dawoud's head tilted back

and the magus grimaced as if in great pain. The old Soo was touching the knife now with his fingertips, and he screamed.

It was a wordless screaming chant at first, but the pain-laced sounds resolved into words: "THE BLOOD OF ORSHADO! THE BLOOD OF ORSHADO!" The magus's body jerked about strangely as he screamed, but he kept his hands on the knife. "THE BLOOD OF ORSHADO!"

Litaz leapt up and pried her husband's fingers from the blade. Dawoud stumbled into the corner and collapsed onto a cushion with a pitiful moan. He held his head in his hands and sat there, shuddering.

The Doctor wore worry for his friend on his face. "Your magic takes its toll on your body. For that, brother-of-mine, the world owes you." He clasped a hand on the magus's shoulder. "But magic can also take its toll on the mind. Praise be to God that the girl's would-be assassin was unhinged enough to rattle on so. Clearly, this Orshado is the one who that monster called 'blessed friend.' I've long said that my order was misnamed. For in realty it is men, not ghuls, that I hunt. And now we have a quarry. With a tracking spell and a name we "

The Doctor's eyes flashed, almost as if he would cry, Zamia thought.

"I've forgotten," he said softly. "I've no scripture-engraved needles. They were ruined in that fire, like everything else. Soiled beyond use if not destroyed."

Zamia wanted to insist that there must be another way, but she found that gathering her thoughts and words was an effort. She was weaker than she had admitted to the others. Her heart swelled when Raseed seemed to speak her thoughts for her.

"Are there no other spells you might work, Doctor? Is there nowhere else you might buy such needles?"

The Doctor shook his head. "It's more complicated than that, boy. Those needles take weeks to make. If we were in a remote location, or facing a novice magus, I might try a cruder invocation. But the city is full of life-energy that will confuse a tracking spell, and this Orshado no doubt commands powerful screening magics. Only flawless components and impeccable invocations would have even a chance of finding our foes."

The Doctor looked around at each of them and seemed to force a smile. "But let's not all look so hopeless, eh? We've a couple of names to aid us now, at least. Almighty God willing, even without a tracking spell, we will find this damned-by-God monster and its 'blessed friend.'"

In the corner of the workshop, Raseed shifted uneasily. His sharp features drew down in a frown. "That phrase bothers me, Doctor. How could such a creature have friends?"

The Doctor raised a bushy eyebrow. "You know, boy, I've heard people ask the same about Raseed bas Raseed! 'His face is so sour,' they say!"

*He is always making mock, even of matters of life and death,* Zamia thought, noting the Doctor's oafish smile as he poked the dervish in the ribs.

As if he were thinking her thoughts, Raseed frowned.

"Apologies, Doctor," the dervish said, "but there is little cause for jesting here."

The ghul hunter smiled a frustrated smile. "Wherever on God's great earth a man tries to make light of his troubles, trust a damned-by-God holy man to open his mouth and put a stop to it! And here I thought this one—" he jabbed a fat finger again at Raseed "—had been learning to loosen up a bit."

Though Zamia could not say why, Raseed reacted as if struck. "Loosen up? May God forbid it. If anything, this is a time for redoubling virtue and vigilance. The Traitorous Angel's foulest servants stalk the city," the dervish said forcefully. "May it please All-Merciful God to protect us all!"

"May it please God," all present echoed ritually. When Zamia looked back at the Doctor, he was no longer smiling.

# Chapter 12

"MAY IT PLEASE GOD," Dawoud Son-of-Wajeed said, and heard his words spoken simultaneously by the others. "So now we know some of what we face," he said. "What do we do about it?"

For a long few moments there was nothing but silence. His words hung in the air, and the group's grim expressions reflected the enormity of the situation. Dawoud scanned the faces that filled his sitting room. His wife's eyes carried the impression of having seen too much, and Adoulla's features displayed a weariness that Dawoud knew was reflected in his own. The young warriors' expressions were different, though, Dawoud thought. The emerald-eyed girl and clean-shaven boy were more determined than resigned. The older trio's stances were set by weary habit, but Raseed and Zamia's were set by will.

Adoulla's assistant was the first to speak, and he did

so heatedly. "We *must* warn the watchmen, Doctor. Or perhaps the Khalif himself. Someone in authority needs—"

The ghul hunter snorted in disbelief. "You still think this is where our energies should go, boy? After two years in this city even a slave-to-titles such as yourself must recognize that the Khalif isn't going to believe such as us. And even if he *did* believe there was a threat to Dhamsawaat, his greatest concern would be how it affects his coin purse. It is a waste of time trying to convince a selfish man to care about what lies beyond his nose. No. The Khalif will be as helpful as a hole to a pail. But I have learned that the Falcon Prince may share some of our troubles. He could—"

*He cannot be serious!* Dawoud cut his friend off, putting a hand on Adoulla's big shoulder and wagging a finger in his face. "How can one man be so wide-eyed and so damned-by-God cynical at the same time, brother of mine? Even if we could find Pharaad Az Hammaz, linking our fates to his would bring more trouble than aid. Half this city is hunting him! And besides, there *are* a few good guardsmen out there, you know. Most notably their captain."

He turned to Raseed, who looked desperate to kill something. "Your idea is sound, Raseed. And the Captain of the Guard, Roun Hedaad, is known to me. Indeed, Litaz and I once saved his life. Tomorrow morning I will go to the Crescent Moon Palace and try to speak to him about what we've turned up. It is a vague warning I'll be bringing him, but he will be thankful for it nonetheless. It cannot hurt to have the guard aware that this threat is out there. And it just might help."

Adoulla stroked his beard. "Hm. Roun Hedaad is a good man as guardsmen go. A *very* good man. But everyone knows he is a holdover from another era and wields little power these days. The Captain of the Watch holds the real power. Still, it's not a bad idea, I suppose. If anyone in the palace is going to look past his self-interest long enough to wonder about the slaughter of poor people, it will be Captain Hedaad. So perhaps someone *should* speak to him." Adoulla turned to Raseed. "Are you satisfied, boy?"

The dervish inclined his turbaned head in acknowledgement, then turned to Dawoud. "And thank you, Uncle."

Beside him, Litaz stood and spoke softly. "Roun Hedaad *will* make a good ally in this. I wish I could accompany you, my love. But the girl's healing is still incomplete. Come tomorrow morning she'll need crimson quicksilver, and I'll need to be here with her in order to apply it. Speaking of which," she turned her beautiful eyes to the tribeswoman, "it is about time to apply a sleeping salve. Come with me, Zamia. This is a private matter between women—let us leave these oafs to themselves."

To Dawoud, the girl seemed about to protest—no doubt she fumed at the idea of being left out of battle planning—but her head drooped and her body was clearly putting the lie to her will's stubborn resilience. With weak steps, she followed his wife out of the room.

Dawoud turned to Adoulla and Raseed and shrugged. "So I will go alone. Litaz must stay here, and the Khalif has little respect for your order, Adoulla."

Adoulla rolled his eyes. "Aye, and the feeling couldn't be more mutual. We're best off dividing tasks, anyway. As for myself," he started, then looked hesitant, embarrassed even, to speak his next words.

*What is this?* Dawoud wondered. His old friend was rarely embarrassed by anything.

"As for myself," the ghul hunter continued, "come morning I will go to the Singers' Quarter to speak again to the boy Faisal, whose family was slain."

*So that's it.* Adoulla was ashamed of his own weakness. Afraid he was making selfish choices. Anxious that Dawoud would judge him harshly for it. Well, Dawoud could never pass judgment on this man whom he'd been friends with for a long lifetime. But neither would he let Adoulla lie to himself.

He smiled as he spoke. "Aye, speak again to the boy. And while you are about it—what do you know?—you will be at the house of the only woman that you have ever really loved. It is funny how All-Provident God arranges these things, eh?"

He'd meant only to tease his friend, but Adoulla's expression was dark and troubled. "Miri Almoussa knows a great deal about the history of this city—she may have more information on our enemies."

At this the dervish, who Dawoud had nearly forgotten was there, chirped up. "With apologies Doctor, I hope you will excuse me from accompanying you tomorrow, for—"

"For a holy man ought not be seen traipsing about a whorehouse, eh? And ought not associate with certain types, eh?" Adoulla's tone spoke of the weariness of an old argument. "I grow truly tired of this, boy. You cannot call a man 'partner' and insult his friends at every turn."

The boy's tilted eyes went wide, and Dawoud thought his own might have, too. Adoulla seemed unaware of his surprising choice of words.

"I . . . I have never dared call myself your *partner*, Doctor. I am merely your assistant."

Adoulla shrugged. "You're my assistant in ghul hunting, true. But you and that forked sword of yours are near as good at it as I was in my prime."

The boy looked profoundly embarrassed, and pink points tinted his golden cheeks. "I thank you, Doctor. But in any case I do not ask to be excused for the reason you named. Rather, I ask to remain here and act as a guard for the women." Now it was the boy's turn to look ashamed of himself and stammer. "The monster may return. I've . . . I've failed once to protect Za—er, the tribeswoman. Due to my lack of diligence, she was attacked, and if I am to—"

Dawoud could not listen to this. Adoulla teased the dervish but essentially coddled the boy's rigid nonsense. Dawoud would not. If the dervish wished to judge himself guilty on the basis of nothing, that was his business. But Dawoud and his wife were being drawn back into grim matters that they'd left behind long ago. They had little choice—as foul a force as Dawoud had ever sensed threatened their best friend. But he'd be damned by God if he was going to go into battle with confused warriors at his side.

He wheeled on Raseed. "Do you have jackal fangs, boy? Not so far as I can see. So how in the name of Merciful God is it your fault the girl was wounded? The life you have chosen is war, young dervish. A war against the Traitorous Angel. The sort of thing your Order *talks* about in all of their oaths and Traditions. Well, this is the reality. The girl ought to praise God that she's still alive. People—people we care for—die in wars. You seem unprepared for this. And perhaps unprepared to do the duty you left the Lodge for."

Raseed lowered his head, his blue turban bobbing "You are correct, of course, Uncle." The boy's look said that each word was pulling a sword blade through his guts. "I must put 'the sun of God's good before the candleflame of one life.' I just . . . I . . . it was my fault that—"

Litaz reappeared in the doorway, apparently having put the tribeswoman to bed. "What with the enemies that are after Adoulla, I *would* feel better if I could work without worrying that a ghul pack is going to knock down the door. Let the boy stay here with me and act as a guard."

Dawoud nodded. "Anything to keep you safe, beloved."

He and Litaz spent half that night lying beside each other, too anxious to sleep and not secluded enough to make love. Dawoud held Litaz's small hand in his, but they said little. Finally, they drifted into sleep.

When he woke at dawn he did not wake Litaz. Instead

he said silent goodbyes to her and a loudly snoring Adoulla, and stepped quietly out the door into the still half-dark morning.

Soon the nights would be growing shorter. The Feast of Providence, the night before the shortest day of the year, was almost upon them—though he'd do no celebrating until this Orshado and the things that served him were destroyed.

Dawoud started walking and soon left the Scholars' Quarter behind him. He breathed deeply of the early morning air, trying to drive from his body the taint he'd felt when he'd worked his scrying spell last night. The power behind that taint . . . there was more to this than a handful of killings, Dawoud felt certain. That sort of power aimed at bigger things.

For the first time since he and Litaz had seen the smoke rising from Adoulla's townhouse, Dawoud really turned over events in his head. He was angry to have been dragged into this business. For decades, his and his wife's work had drawn them away from all that was normal and happy. Dawoud's body wrecked by magic. Their baby boy murdered by monsters. When they had fought and traveled beside Adoulla and others, the hypnotic song of responsibility had called them onto paths of danger and madness, like the snake-tailed dune maids that lured desert travelers to their doom. But they'd left that all behind. Dawoud's greatest worries these past few years had to do with ministering to the poor without going broke, and with his wife's increasing desire to leave this city he had made his home. But now. . . .

He passed a shuttered storefront, then stopped walking as his chest suddenly tightened and blazed into pain. In the course of his calling Dawoud had been both stabbed and poisoned, and this felt like both at once. He began to cough and nearly collapsed from it.

It was several minutes before the coughing fit passed. Standing frozen there on the street, he panted painfully, feeling his body taking on more age than was its due. The healing and scrying magics he had worked over the past day—it had been many months since he'd done such. He felt the toll with every labored breath. Loudmouthed Adoulla liked to complain about his old man's aches, but he knew nothing of pain. Of weakness. When Dawoud worked his magic—Name of God, when he simply walked down a dusty Dhamsawaat street too fast!—it felt as if God's great fingers were pinching his lungs shut.

With this Orshado and his monstrous servants out there, Dawoud, his wife, and his oldest friend were needed more than ever before, but he did not know how long he could last back in this life. Not for the first time, his head was filled with visions of himself as a doddering invalid who needed his wife to spoonfeed him.

He tried unsuccessfully to keep his face from betraying his pain to the porters and cartmen passing by. But, he saw, he needn't have bothered—for the busy people of Dhamsawaat didn't give three shits for a dying old man's agony. The only looks he received were looks of disgust. After a moment his breathing began to return to normal, and he gave the self-centered people around him his own look of disgust. *Perhaps Litaz is right. Perhaps it is time at long last for us to leave this cold-hearted city.*

He leaned heavily against a stone wall and allowed himself one deep shudder. Then he focused his soul and drew himself up. There was a task at hand. And if he was going to be there for Litaz, he had to be strong. He clenched his fists and pressed on, trying not to feel the ache that was building in his back.

He stepped out onto the Mainway, ignoring the hawkers' shouts. For half a moment he toyed with the idea of hiring a sedan chair. But it was only toying. In all his years in Dhamsawaat, Dawoud had only ridden in one a handful of times. As with other things, his wife had been able to move from the Soo way to the Abassenese with more ease. When she was not with him she often hired chairs. *Being a rich Blue River girl prepared her for having men carry her on their backs,* he supposed with a snort, dodging past a bowlegged pistachio seller.

For an honest Red River Soo like himself, such a way of moving through crowds was simply wrong. Not doing so on the way to the palace, though, meant a long, hard walk. At least the day promised to be a cool one.

He walked for an hour and a half down broad roads before turning down Poulterer's Row, which was packed with people preparing for the Feast of Providence. Every neighborhood in the city had a chicken seller, of course, but on Poulterer's Row one could peruse the rare delicacies of the great master merchants: purple partridge, sun-dove, heron-stuffed swan. It was also the only place in all of Dhamsawaat that one could buy a pickled ostrich egg from the Republic. The smells of death and feather were thick here, and Dawoud was seized by a dry retching. He sat for a moment and gave a copper fals to a water seller who poured from his skin a cup of water so welcome it made Dawoud thank God aloud.

After yet another hour of his sandals slapping stone and packed dirt, Dawoud made it to the western gates of the Crescent Moon Palace. It had been a couple of years since he had been down this way, and he found himself newly dazzled by the building's brilliance. Rising from the great white dome on a thin spire of gold was a sculpture of a man on horseback wielding a long lance. The head of the statue was changed to resemble each new Khalif. Dawoud realized he'd not been to the Palace since the new Khalif had taken the Throne of the Crescent Moon.

The statue gleamed, showing the lean-featured Khalif's martial prowess against God's enemies. Of course, everyone in Dhamsawaat knew that the new Khalif, like his father, had never once been in battle in his pampered life. It was the kind of hypocrisy that made Adoulla choke on his breakfast, but Dawoud wasn't much bothered by it. Matters of state were about hypocrisy as much as anything else. The Soo people understood this as a simple fact that needn't be condemned—a thing that simply was.

Dawoud approached the squat stone guardhouse that stood beside the gate. Calling on Roun Hedaad meant getting word to him by way of a helpful watchman. Dawoud did not have Adoulla's total scorn for the Khalif's men, but he did know that most of them could not be truthfully described as helpful. A pair of them exited the guardhouse and walked by, wearing steel-studded leather jerkins and displaying the slim maces that were their weapon of office. They eyed Dawoud as they did everyone they passed—with a vaguely menacing squint, ready, almost eager, for trouble. Dawoud gave these two a deferential old-mannish nod and sought out the least hostile looking watchman he could find: a lanky boy with soft eyes.

"God's peace, young man. I must get in touch with Captain Hedaad immediately regarding an urgent matter."

The boy said, more politely than Dawoud expected from a watchman, "If you've got a complaint about the watch, Uncle, I'm afraid you'll need to take it to the eastern gates office. They'll get you an audience with a vice captain and in a few days perhaps—"

"Forgive me, young man, but this is not a matter that can wait. My name is Dawoud Son-of-Wajeed, and I am well-known to Roun. I promise you that if you give him my name he will want to see me right away."

The boy fixed those soft eyes on Dawoud, trying to somehow spy out ill intent. He put an idle hand on his mace and scratched his nose. "Well-known, huh?" Another long look. "Fine. But you'd better not be jerking me about here, Uncle."

Dawoud inclined his head graciously.

Half an hour later a different watchman led Dawoud into a small chamber just inside the palace proper. The room was crowded with grain sacks and coils of chain, but there was a small divan in the corner. The watchman gestured to it gruffly, then left. No sooner had Dawoud settled gratefully down onto the dark wood than Roun Hedaad's wide frame filled the doorway.

Dawoud started to stand, but the Captain of the Guard kept him from doing so. He bent down to embrace Dawoud and they exchanged greetings. Then Roun sat beside him.

The squat man had always seemed to Dawoud to be cut from a block of brown stone. There was the slightest bit of gray in his thick black moustache now and a few tiny lines at his eyes. But he looked as hard as ever, as did the masterwork four-bladed mace at his side.

"Thank you for making time to see me, Captain."

The man scratched his club-shaped nose. "I can always make time for a man who saved my life."

Dawoud waved a dismissive hand. "Well, my wife's tonics had as much to do with that as anything. Besides, we were paid a good price for our work then."

"Fair enough. So what is it you have come here to ask then, Uncle?"

*If it were Litaz here, she'd have planned all of the words to use here.* But that was not how he did things. "You know some of the strange, cruel magics my wife and I once made a life of fighting," he said to the Captain of the Guard. "I've come to you because such a threat is loose in Dhamsawaat now."

Dawoud told what little they knew of Mouw Awa and his master Orshado. The names. The killing they had done. As he told his tale, the captain's unsubtle face was easy for Dawoud to read—shifting from annoyed disbelief to deeper consideration to half-skeptical fear. But the captain was respectful enough not to interrupt.

"All I ask," Dawoud began, then fell silent when a richly-dressed page came darting in. The page ignored Dawoud and whispered something to the captain. Dawoud's old ears could only make out the words *he wants, your turn*, and Roun's protests, before the boy left the room.

Roun grimaced at him. "Well, Uncle, you're in luck—His Holiness asks me on occasion to bring before him whatever security matter I am dealing with at a given time. He does the same with his ministers of treasury and his under-governors. He does it to show his active interest and to let the many arms of his government benefit from his wisdom." There was no irony in Roun's voice—indeed, the Captain made an admirable effort to infuse the words with sincerity, but Dawoud needed no magic to tell the man's true feelings.

*Still, this may be for the best. Perhaps the Khalif will actually listen.*

Dawoud was shown not into the Court of the Crescent Moon, but into a small audience chamber. "Small" for the Crescent Moon Palace, of course, meant that the room was larger than Dawoud's whole house, but it felt different from the publicly visible parts of the palace Dawoud had seen. Here the auras of opulence and command did not exactly diminish, but they took on a kind of intimacy. This was a place for a powerful man to pretend he was lending his ear. *Almighty God willing, he will lend it in truth.*

Dawoud was announced with a string of the tepid pleasantries spent on common people. The court-speaker boomed in his baritone that the guests were honored to be in the presence of "God's Regent in the World, the Defender of Virtue, the Most Exalted of Men, His Majesty the Jabbari akh-Khaddari, Khalif of Abassen and of all the Crescent Moon Kingdoms." Then, in unison with Roun, Dawoud knelt and bowed as deeply as his weak limbs would let him.

High windows displayed Names of God in glass ground with emerald and opal. No noise from the palace bustle outside came through the plush brocade drapes. Off to one side, court musicians played reed pipes and two-stringed fiddles, all plated in platinum. Thick carpets of puzzlecloth, worked over and over again with the Khalific seal, muffled the sound of footfalls. At the far side of the room, just below the ceiling, a strange gold lattice box, the size of a small carriage, protruded from the wall just above head height. *The Khalif's speaking-box.* Designed so that Abassen's ruler could hold court without enduring the profane gazes of his subjects. And within sat the Defender of Virtue.

The small, rose marble archway below the box was flanked by two cowled, black-robed men who gave off, to Dawoud's sorcerous senses, a heady waft of magical power. *Court magi.* Legally, no one in Dhamsawaat worked spells without the permission of the Khalif's own enchanters. In reality, a number of minor spells, invocations, and ghul-raisings went on without this handful of men being able to stop them. The true purpose of the court magi was preventing the practice of any magics that might harm the Khalif or his wealth. Dawoud knew little of their ways, though—they spent their time cloistered in their own minaret behind the palace proper. What went on within that thin spire of silvery stone, God alone knew. Dawoud knew only the scorn with which this sort regarded the vulgar magics of a man like himself.

Dawoud saw vague movement behind the golden grillwork of the speaking box. *Does he always hold court from within that stifling cage?* The idea made Dawoud ill, but it lent a sudden sense to some of the Khalif's more ruthless acts. Ruling from such confinement could make a man mad. *This is what Adoulla—and that mad Falcon Prince he admires so much—do not see: that* every-one *pays a price for the way the world works, even the so-called powerful. That power is a trap as well.* The effects of magery on his own body had long given Dawoud a keen—not to say, brutal—awareness of such facts.

The sun shone through the jewel-tinted windows and the Khalif's box seemed to be wreathed in rainbows. Cage or no, for a moment Dawoud almost believed the man *was* God's Regent in the World.

The court musicians stopped playing. A long-faced man dressed in rich silks, clearly a senior minister of some sort, asked Roun what matters of guardsmanship he brought before the court.

Only then did Roun seem to recognize the wispiness of what he knew. His face flashed confusion, but he spoke steadily. "This man beside me, O Defender of Virtue, is Dawoud Son-of-Wajeed. He is a true servant of God who once saved my life when a poisoner tried to kill me to stop me from serving your father. More to the point, your Majesty, this man has spent many years hunting the minions of the Traitorous Angel. He was in the midst of telling me about a potential threat to Your city, majesty, when you summoned me here. It is, perhaps, best if I let him tell the court."

"O Most Exalted of Men, I am here to ask you—" Dawoud began, trying in his rough Red River way to use court phrasings the way Litaz had taught him long ago.

The long-faced minister's scandalized eyes bulged. "You are neither minister nor captain! You must speak to the *court*, sir! You shall not speak directly to His Majesty!"

He'd miscalculated. Despite her having forsaken her family, Litaz was a Pasha's niece. She had taught him an etiquette appropriate to a man of much higher station. She'd warned him of this when she'd tried to train him years ago, of course. Why did he only ever seem to recall his wife's warnings in the moments after failing to heed them?

Within the golden box Dawoud heard a man clear his throat. The court fell completely silent.

"He is a streetman, Jawdi. He cannot be expected to speak like a man of Our court. Continue, O venerable subject, and know that We hear you."

*Perhaps he is not so bad as the city's wagging tongues claim.* Dawoud didn't fool himself that the Khalif had anything but scorn for him. But showing polite respect to the scorned was as sure a measure of character as Dawoud knew. He dragged a labored breath deep into his chest and chose his words carefully.

"I am as honored as a man can be to be permitted to speak before you, O Defender of Virtue. As Captain Hedaad says, I have made a life of fighting the influence of the Traitorous Angel. The Captain can tell your Majesty that I am no madman. Of the lives I have saved . . ." He paused, searching for his next words.

The long-faced minister broke in here. "I hope, sir, you have not come into the radiant presence of the Defender of Virtue merely to boast of your back-alley accomplishments. His Majesty's every moment is worth your weight in gold. To waste them is a crime worse than murder! Speak, sir, if you've something of import to say!"

"Of course, your Eminence." The man looked slightly mollified. Good, he'd got that title right. No doubt it pleased these men to see a common man like Dawoud try nobly to match their ways of speaking—so long as he wasn't too good at it. Not that they needed to worry about that.

"I will come to the point. A strange threat is looming over your Majesty's city. One as learned as His Majesty knows better than I that before the Great Flood of Fire, the Kem ruled this land. We know that God punished them, and that they were wiped from the slate of the world. Some things from their age—a bit of statuary here, a buried wall there—remain, perhaps left to us by God as a warning against wickedness. Yet other foul things from God-scoured Kem have survived, O Defender of Virtue. Or at least, the influence of their cruel magics has."

"You speak of the Dead Gods?" one of the court magi asked scornfully, the first words that either of the black-robed figures had spoken. The man's voice said he did not take the threat seriously. The memory of the tainted soul he'd touched with his scrying spell filled Dawoud. He had to *make* these men take him seriously.

"Yes, your Eminence. One of the Dead Gods of Kem—or the potent shadow of their power—has taken hold of a man who was already a vicious killer. It has given him power and freed him from fear of swords and fire. Their magic has mingled with this dark soul, and the creature born of this union calls itself Mouw Awa the Manjackal. This thing is loose in His Majesty's city. It has killed dozens already. What's worse, its master is—"

"Why, sirrah, have we of the court heard nothing of these murders, then?" the long-faced minister interrupted scornfully. "Where is—"

The second court magus silenced the man with an upraised hand. *So that's how the whipping order goes here.* "This man's ramblings are not fit for the blessed ears of the Defender of the Faithful. At most perhaps one of his fellow streetmen with a few trick-spells has murdered a few other streetmen." That black-cowled head turned to Dawoud. "The court commands you to return to your home. Speak to the first watchman you see there, and he will address this matter in the manner already ordained by His Majesty's Law."

Dawoud dared to speak when he should have kept

his mouth shut. When would he again have the ear of the Khalif? "Ten thousand apologies, your Eminence, but this Mouw Awa and its master—he is called Orshado, though we know little more than that—are no streetmen. They *will* kill again. And they will not be satisfied with killing tribesmen and street-people. Powerful villains aim their arrows at the powerful. The danger to the palace is—" Too late, Dawoud fell silent, realizing his mistake. *Idiot! Tossing threats at the most powerful man in the world!*

The golden grille of the opulent box swung up with a sudden bang. Dawoud felt his old heart seize up at the sound. *Please God, do not let him be angry with me. I want to see my wife again.* The might such a man commanded. This was what Adoulla did not understand. That all the scorn in the world could not protect one from such power. Dawoud still could not see within the box—there was a more than natural darkness at work there, unless he missed his magus's guess—but a thin, pale hand shot out from the shadows. The Khalif jabbed two fingers, ablaze with huge rubies, out angrily at Dawoud. Courtiers and servants alike gasped and shot their eyes downward.

"After Captain Hedaad's introduction, We were inclined to be kind toward Our Venerable Subject. But after this nonsense We are displeased. You should thank Almighty God that We have not had you thrown in the gaol."

Dawoud had faced death a hundred times. He had not survived to die at an annoyed ruler's whim. He deepened his bow, punishing his old limbs and holding in his grunts. "God grant you ten thousand blessings for your mercy, Majesty."

God's Regent in the World must have sensed some insincerity in Dawoud's words, for the Khalif broke from the formalized language of the court sovereign. "Shut up, you old fool! You come in here, making threats to Our city and Our Palace!? You tell nail-biting tales of a phantom killer as if We were some merchant's boy and you were Our fright-mongering nurse? And, no doubt, this threat's shadow would lift from Our Court if only We were to buy some trinket or spell from you, eh? Bah! My father would have had your head, old man!"

*Your father would have pulled* his *head from out of his backside and taken such a threat seriously.* Dawoud kept the words to himself.

Beside Dawoud, Roun bowed deeply. "I beg your Majesty to forgive this old fool for bothering you. I swear by God that Dawoud Son-of-Wajeed would never dream of offering your eminence any harm or threat of harm. His feeble old Soo mind is rattled with imaginary threats, is all."

The Khalif was silent for a moment, and the court seemed to hold its breath. When he spoke again, his intonation was unabashedly rude. "Bah! Captain, We should have *you* flogged for wasting Our sacred moments with this idiocy. Name of God, you are both fortunate that We are known for Our mercy. If We are ever made to look at your ugly face again, magus, We shall part your head from your shoulders. The same goes for you, Captain, if you do not bring matters of *real* urgency to Us next time We ask. Now begone, both of you!"

Dawoud bowed deeply three times, backing away as he did so. *The fool! Name of God, if one uncouth old Soo is enough to make the man drop his court-phrasing, maybe Adoulla's right.*

Roun escorted Dawoud to the palace gates in silence. He led Dawoud to a small, secluded courtyard with a tiny fountain and waved away a solitary guardsman. When they were alone, the square-shaped man let out a breath and threw up his hands.

"You see how things stand, Uncle," the captain said. "Truth be told, this sort of recklessness is rampant now. The watchmen . . ." The man trailed off, clearly aching to relieve himself of his thought-burden but reluctant to do so.

Dawoud encouraged him. "With apologies for knowing that which I ought not, Captain, I have heard that there is . . . tension between the guard and the watch."

Roun spoke half to himself. "Look, in every city there will be watchmen who harass blacksmiths' daughters and knock down old men for a few coins or a laugh. But there is cruelty and there is *cruelty*. There is corruption and there is *corruption*. People can no longer afford to pay the taxes we're asking. Too many are finding their way into the gaol. Far too many. And every debtor imprisoned, even for a fortnight, is a recruit for that preening traitor Pharaad Az Hammaz!"

"Indeed," Dawoud agreed.

"And then there is the thief-purging. Here in the palace matters legal and martial fall to me. But in the streets the captain of the watch rules, and he was appointed because he has never in his life balked at a chance to bully. This new drive to wipe out pickpocketry is madness. There will be a lot more one-handed men in Dhamsawaat before it's through. The last amputation I saw was of a boy of ten years. But at least the boy only lost his hand! Too many men have been made to kneel on the executioner's leather mat of late."

"Aye," Dawoud said. "I'd heard about the boy who was to be executed before the Falcon Prince—"

Roun's expression turned dangerous. "The bastard's name is Pharaad Az Hammaz, Uncle! He's *not* a Prince! Anyway, incidents like that are driving good men away from the guard and the watch. A fortnight ago my second-in-command, Hami Samad—a man born and raised in this palace, and as steadfast a man as I've ever met—left the guard, abandoning his duties without saying a word to anyone." Roun knuckled his moustache and sighed, fatigue overtaking his features.

"Well, I am sorry to have added to your troubles. The Khalif was not happy with you for bringing me before him."

Roun waved a dismissing hand at Dawoud's apology, but there was real worry in the captain's eyes. He frowned, and his brow knitted even tighter. "What *is* going on, Dawoud? Whatever the Khalif's flatterers think, I know you would not be here if there was not dire reason."

"And there is, my friend. The servants of the Traitorous Angel are at work. But I don't know much more than the little I've told you. As soon as I learn more I will let you know, Captain, I swear it."

Roun gave him a long look. "Very well, Uncle. Just be sure that you do. And I'll set my street spies a-digging at these names and crimes you've told me of. I am always here at the Palace, so when you wish to speak to me again, just have a guardsman summon me."

Dawoud exchanged cheek-kisses with the Captain, then made his way back to the street. Pain raged in his muscles and bones. Too much bowing and walking. He needed rest and, more than anything on God's great earth, he needed to see his wife again. *I could have died in there on a fool's whim.*

Dawoud thanked Almighty God aloud that he lived. Then he achingly made his way home.

# Chapter 13

WALKING DOWN BREADBAKERS' BYWAY, Adoulla passed a public fountain of once-white marble. Children played in its basin, and their shrill shouts shoved their way into his ears. "Brats," he huffed to himself, though he knew he'd been twice as loud and obnoxious when he was a street child.

*To save one child from the ghuls is to save the whole world.* The professional adage came to Adoulla for the thousandth time. But what would it cost to save the whole world? His life? *O God, does not a fat old man's happiness matter, too?*

This fight had already cost him his home. The place that he had loved so for so long was ruined. Vials of powdered silver and blocks of ebonwood. The Soo sand-painting he'd bought in the Republic, and the Rughali divan that fit his backside so comfortably. But most of all, the books! Scroll and codex, new folio and old manuscript. Even a few books in tongues he'd once hoped to learn—leatherbound volumes in the boxy script of the Warlands to the far west. He'd only ever managed to learn to read a few of their strange, barking words. Now he'd never learn more.

He moved against the onrushing flow of foot traffic, making his way over the smooth, worn stones of the Mainway. He was comfortable moving against the crowd. How many times had a mob of sensible men been running away from some foul monster while foolish Adoulla and his friends ran toward the thing? Irritated anew at the thought of the things his calling made him do, he pushed his big body grumpily up the downstream of people.

Another pack of children chased each other through the crowd of walkers and pack animals. The little gang threatened to career into Adoulla, but the group split before him like a wave, half the brats flowing to either side. He reminded himself that, if he didn't do his duty, more little faces like these could soon be smeared with blood, their eyes aflame and their souls stolen. In his practiced way, he kept panic from rising at the thought of the threats that were out there, unseen.

Adoulla passed men from Rughal-ba, with their neatly trimmed goatees and tight-fitting turbans. He saw Red River and Blue River Soo. He heard the false promises of a hundred hawkers, the single-stringed fiddle of a roving musician, the argument a feral-eyed, twitching man was having with himself. Unlike most sons of Dead Donkey Lane, Adoulla had seen many towns. Those folk he'd grown up around would leave the city only a handful of times in their lives—even going to another quarter was an occasion for some of them. Adoulla, on the other hand, had seen the villages of the Soo Republic with their low, bleached-clay houses of hidden luxury. He had seen the strange mountain-hole homes of the far north, where rain froze. He'd been to the edge of Rughal-ba, where, instead of being a character from lewd shadow-puppet plays, the ghul hunter was respected by powerful men as an earthly agent of God, and was considered a slave of the Rughali High Sultaan—if a rich and powerful slave.

But this city of his—his for some sixty years—well, there was nothing to compare with its streets. The crowds had annoyed Adoulla all his life. But of all the places in the Crescent Moon Kingdoms he had been, Dhamsawaat alone was *his*. And somewhere in his city, murderous monsters were preying on people.

*And so, you old fart, Dhamsawaat needs you.* Rotating this truth proudly in his mind made Adoulla feel just a little bit less tired. But as his sandaled feet brought him closer and closer to the house of Miri Almoussa, his fatigue returned twofold.

True to the code of the ghul hunter, Adoulla had never married. *When one is married to the ghuls, one has three wives already,* was another of the adages of his order. He didn't know much about the old order—a few adages and invocations passed down many years ago by his teacher, old Doctor Boujali, and learned from old books. The ghul hunters had never been as cohesive a fraternity as the Dervishes' Order—and any man could wear white and claim to chase monsters. Still, over the years, Adoulla had tried to adhere to what he had learned of the ways of his ancient order. He was a permissive man in many ways—no less with himself than with others, he had to admit. But in some things rigidity was the only way. Saying marriage vows before God would cause a ghul hunter's kaftan to soil, and it would cost him the power of his invocations. As with so many of God's painful ways, Adoulla did not know why it was so, only that it *was*.

The crowd thinned and Adoulla strode through Little Square, his kaftan billowing in the breeze. Little Square was not little at all—in fact, in all the city it was second only to Angels' Square in size. But the name was old, from the days when Dhamsawaat had first been built on the ruins of a Kemeti city, and had only had two squares. Long rows of brown, thorny shrubbery framed its eastern and western sides. These low, desert bushes served as a back wall for the stall-less, beggarish sellers who lined the square to Adoulla's left and his right.

Little Square was a haven for the less prosperous merchants and tradesmen of the city—those too poor or too unreliable to have earned, through honest work or bribery, a real shop or stall in one of the better markets. The square was flanked by these men and women, sitting on rugs or standing beside sorry piles of goods. Adoulla's eyes moved up the column of half-rate cobblers and rotten-vegetable sellers to his right.

He cursed as he caught sight, a dozen yards ahead, of a skinny man in the white kaftan of his order. He strode over and made the noise in his throat that he made when genuinely offended. Litaz had once said that it sounded like he was being pleasured by a poorly trained whore.

For all that he mocked Raseed's dervishhood, Adoulla had also pledged his life to an antiquated order that Dhamsawaatis knew mostly from great-grandparents' tales and bawdy shadow-puppet plays. Adoulla had learned long ago that most men professing his life-calling were charlatans who had bits and pieces of the proper knowledge but had never been face-to-face with a ghul. They used cheap magic to make their robes appear moonlight white and took the hard-earned money of the poor, mumbling a few bogus spells and promising protection from monsters.

The hairy young man with an oily smile who stood before him wore such cheap robes. He was the sort who claimed to hunt the "hidden spirits" supposedly behind working peoples' every trouble. The sort who claimed to tell the future. *The rotten-vegetable sellers of my order.*

When he was a younger man, and more defensive of the honor of his order, Adoulla had thought it his duty to root out such hucksters and send them packing with their robes dirtied and their noses and false charms broken. But the decades since had taught him resignation. Other charlatans would always pop up, and the people—the desperate, desperate people—would always go to them. Still, Adoulla took enough time now to give the fraud a long, scornful glance. They knew Adoulla, these men, knew him to be the last of the real thing—was it wrong that he took some pride in that? This one, at least, had the decency to lower his eyes in shame.

That such thieves thrived was sad, but it was the way of the world. Adoulla passed the fraud by, spitting at the man's feet instead of throwing a punch as he once would have. The fool made an offended noise, but that was all.

By the time he reached Miri's tidy storefront it was past midday. The brassbound door was open and, standing in the doorway, Adoulla smelled sweet incense from iron burners and camelthorn from the hearth. For a long moment he just stood there at the threshold, wondering why in the world he'd been away from this lovely place so long.

A corded forearm blocked his way, and a man's shadow fell over him. A muscular man even taller than Adoulla stood scowling before him, a long scar splitting his face into gruesome halves. He placed a broad palm on Adoulla's chest and grabbed a fistful of white kaftan.

"Ho-ho! Who's this forsaker-of-friends, slinking back in here so shamelessly?"

Despite all his dark feelings, Adoulla smiled. "Just another foolish child of God who doesn't know to stay put, Axeface." He embraced Miri's trusted doorman, and the two men kissed on both cheeks.

"How are you these days, Uncle?" the frighteningly big man asked.

"Horrible, my friend. Horrible, miserable, and terrible, but we praise God anyway, eh? Will you announce me to Miri, please?"

Axeface looked uncomfortable, as if he was considering saying something he didn't want to say.

"What is it?" Adoulla asked.

"I'll announce you, Uncle, and there's not a man in the world I'm happier to see pay the Mistress a visit. But *she* isn't gonna be happy to see you. You're lucky her new boyfriend isn't here."

Adoulla felt his insides wither. For a moment he had no words. "Her . . . her . . . *what*?" he finally managed. "Her *who*?" He felt as if he'd suddenly been struck half-witted.

"Her new man," Axeface said with a sympathetic shake of the head. "You know him, Uncle. Handsome Malnsoor, they call him. Short fella, thin moustache, always smells nicer than a man should."

Adoulla did know the man, or at least knew of him. A preening weasel that twisted others into doing his work for him. Adoulla's numbness burned away in a flame of outrage.

"*That* one!? He's too young for her! Name of God, he's clearly after her money!" He gestured with one hand to the greeting room behind Axeface. "The son of a whore just wants to get his overwashed little hands on this place. Surely, man, you must see that!"

Axeface put up his leg-of-lamb-sized hands as if frightened of Adoulla. "Hey, hey, Uncle, between you and me, you know I love you. You'd make a great husband for the mistress. But you've made some damned-by-God stupid choices far as that goes. Surely, man, *you* must see *that*, huh?" Axeface poked him playfully, but Adoulla wasn't in the mood.

At all.

Seeming to sense this, Axeface straightened to his full, monstrous height. "Look, Doctor, the bottom line is, I don't see nothin' Mistress Miri don't want me to see. That's how I stay well-paid, well-fed, and smiley as a child. But if you want to see the Mistress, hold on."

Adoulla was announced and ushered into the large greeting room. Scant sunlight made its way through high windows. Tall couches lined the wall opposite the door, and a few well-dressed men sat on them, each speaking to a woman.

Then she was there. Miri Almoussa, Seller of Silks and Sweets. Miri of the Hundred Ears. Miri. Her thick curves jiggled as she moved, and her worn hands were ablaze with henna.

"What do *you* want?" she asked him, a cold wind blowing beneath her words.

Adoulla's irritation briefly eclipsed his longing. "You may recall, woman, that *you* asked for *my* help, even after your having asked me to 'walk my big feet out of your life and never come back.' But this is not the place for us to speak."

Miri arched an eyebrow and said nothing, but she led him to the house's tiny rear courtyard, sat him down at a small table, and brought him a tray with fruit nectar, little salt fish, and pickles. She sat down beside him and waited for him to speak. But for a moment Adoulla just sat there, listening to the birds chirping in the courtyard's twin pear trees and avoiding Miri's eyes.

He didn't break the silence until Miri began to tap her silk-slippered foot impatiently. "I'm here, Miri, because I have learned something of your niece's killers. But not enough yet to stop them from killing others. I would like to speak to your grandnephew again, as he may have recalled something new."

"Faisal is not here. Some of the girls went on a work-break trip to see the new menagerie the Khalif has set up outside the city, and I thought it a good idea for him to try and forget his pains, so I sent him with them. He won't be back for a day or so."

Adoulla plucked up a pickle and smiled to himself at the thought of a whores' holiday to see strange beasts—surely Miri was the only proprietor in the city who would allow such a thing.

As happened so often, Miri seemed to read his thoughts. She did not seem amused. "All people who work deserve days away from their labor, Doullie," she said flatly. "And whores are people, even if my business depends on letting *men* forget that fact."

He would not rise to the bait. "Of course. In any case, I did not come only to speak to Faisal. I came also because Miri's Hundred Ears are always open, sometimes to songs the rest of us don't hear. For instance, does the name 'Mouw Awa' mean anything to you? Or the name 'Orshado'? And what do you know of the case of Hadu Nawas?"

Her offended expression melted away, and she took on the look of Miri, knower-of-many-things, narrowing her smoky eyes and crinkling her nose. Miri's face when she was trying to recall something was the same as when she was rifling through her cabinets for a particular blouse. " 'Orshado' . . . it sounds like a northern name, perhaps? I couldn't say for sure. But Hadu Nawas . . . he was an enemy of the throne, yes? One of the many conspirators killed in the civil war?"

"Not quite killed, it seems," Adoulla muttered.

Miri gave him a perplexed look but continued. "If I recall correctly, he was also rumored to be a child-killer. Now, 'Mouw Awa' . . . Hm. All I could tell you is that it sounds like . . . like Kemeti hidden script?"

Adoulla snorted. "Indeed. Though it took *me* a full day to have that lock click open in my mind. Sometimes, my sweet, your erudition makes me sick with jealousy."

"Well, even leaving aside our difference in age, I've been hit on the head far fewer times than you, Doullie." She deigned to smile at him, and he felt his soul warm.

Adoulla winced theatrically, as if he'd been punched in the gut. This response to Miri's jibes had always made her laugh in the past. But instead when she met his eyes, she let her smile slip and turned away from him.

There were a thousand things he wanted to say to her when he saw that, but none of them would do any good.

"How is your grandnephew faring?" he asked.

"How is he faring?" Her thick braid with its streak of silver whipped as she spun to give him an incredulous glare. "How is he *faring*!? He's broken! How *else* could he be after what happened to him? You see so much of this horror that you don't even see it for horror anymore! He is a boy, Doullie! A boy of eight! Not one of your suicidal, fanatical friends! Not some 'foe of the Traitorous Angel'!" She bit off her next words quietly. "This—it's this madness that drove us apart."

This time Adoulla's wince was not feigned. Miri had always had unhappy words for the life he led, and for the friends who shared it, but those words had never been this sharp, this scornful.

She wasn't stopped by his pained face. "Look at the world around you, Doullie! Forty years you've spent in this hunting. All that death. Why? What has come of it? Is the world a safe place now? A happier place?" She sank into her chair and put her face in her hands. "Merciful God, I'm sorry. Now you've upset me. What I meant to say was—" But she said nothing more.

"Your niece's killers are still out there, Miri. They . . . they burned my house down."

"I heard." Of course Miri of the Hundred Ears had heard. Yet still she had all these hard words for him. "God protect you," she said now.

Miri and he had been closer in the days when the townhouse was new, he reflected. Much closer. She had helped him choose it. Adoulla said nothing for a long time. Then he started to speak, though he didn't know what he was going to say. "Miri, I—"

Miri held up a silencing hand and, with her other, wiped away the beginnings of tears. She took a deep breath and looked at Adoulla. Her eyes were weary but filled with love, and she spoke softly. "I'm sorry, Doullie. I didn't mean the things I said."

Adoulla had never been more tired in his life, and he tried to keep the pain out of his words. "Yes, you did."

Miri's voice was steadier now, and she twined the end of her long braid around her hand—a habit Adoulla had noticed long ago, a sign that she was steeling herself. "Well, yes, I did, but . . . I do know why you do what you do, Doullie. You—" A smile spread across her face, and she started laughing, at the same time that Adoulla did.

" 'Why you do what you do Doullie, you'?" he said, imitating the funny sound of her words. They both laughed. And Adoulla hurt again, knowing that it would end very soon.

Why had this been his fate? Why could he not have been one of the men he often walked past in the early morning light of the markets? Selling lemonjelly cubes and going home every evening to a deliciously fat wife who drenched herself in rose oil. Laughing at stupid things and keeping one another warm when the night wind whipped through the windows. Taking the day off to be with her and losing only a few coins in his pocket. But his job—his calling—was different. When Adoulla neglected his duties, gruesome things happened in the sleep-rooms of children. It wasn't fair. It wasn't.

His eyes burned, and he realized that they were beginning to tear up. *What is wrong with me? I'm a breath away from crying like a woman!*

Mistress Miri Almoussa of the Hundred Ears

showed the secret, defenseless self that she only ever showed late at night to him. "I . . . I am sorry, Doullie. So often I have had such hard words for what you do. And yet I am here like all the rest, begging your help for my family."

Miri's kohl-lined eyes were furious and on the verge of tears. When the first few fell, Adoulla placed an arm around her broad shoulders and wiped them away. Being seen crying would hurt her reputation.

"How long have we known each other, woman? Thirty years, now? Don't you worry about such things. My help is always yours. Why these tears, huh? Everything will be fine, God willing."

She sniffed once again, wiped away another tear and set her jaw. "Fine? O Merciful God! My niece is dead! Everything will not be fine, Doullie. Everything is going down to the Lake of Flame and the Traitorous Angel. But you're right . . . there's no point in crying. Not where men can see, anyway." With one last sniffle, she was all calmness again. "So. Have you any more clues as to who or what is behind her murder?"

Adoulla struggled to recall all that the mad creature Mouw Awa had revealed. "There *was* one thing more," Adoulla said at last. "The monster I am hunting . . . it spoke of its master sitting on 'the Cobra Throne.' Have you ever heard of such a thing? Do you know where it might be?"

Miri bit her lip and looked troubled. "I have," she said. She took a breath, then a sip of nectar, and went on. "It was years ago—after one of the Falcon Prince's first raids. All of the city's talk was on the gold and weapons he'd stolen from the old Khalif's treasure house. But my sources told me that the Prince himself was most interested in a dusty old scroll he'd found."

Adoulla was as impressed as always with the things Miri knew, and it must have shown on his face.

Miri shrugged "Of course I was interested. I am the font of all knowledge in this city. No one in Dhamsawaat would know anything if not for my spies. And books are like spies' reports frozen in amber. If the Falcon Prince wanted to know something that bad, it must have been valuable, I figured. So I had one of my Ears within his organization act as eye and pen, copying as much as he could of the stolen scroll. Those were different days, of course. Pharaad Az Hammaz's operation was not quite so airtight then. In any case, my spy had to use a *very* expensive scrivening-spell, but the scroll proved useless to me. It cost an obscene amount to copy it, but the jest was on me—all but the title of the thing was in a thrice-ciphered version of hidden script. The characters were there, but pricey, pricey magics which might not have even worked were required to break the cipher-spells. Wealthy as I am, I still didn't have enough to waste on trying to translate it."

Adoulla, growing impatient, spoke around a mouth of saltfish. "Forgive me, my sweet, but I asked you about—"

"'The Cobra Throne.' That was the title of the scroll. It was about ancient Kem. But as I say, not worth the price of translating. For all I knew it was about some old buried hoard of the Faroes somewhere, which may or may not have ever existed and may or may not have already been hit by graverobbers. And I'm not the sort to go funding a grave-digging. Then there was the possibility that the Falcon Prince had stolen it only because the *original* was valuable. I didn't know, and it wasn't worth wagering further funds to find out. God's truth be told, I don't think that the gold-grubbing Khalif had ever bothered to translate it, either. At least, my spies at the time had heard the Falcon Prince mock this fact."

Adoulla snorted. "Aye, that sounds like the work of Khalifs—locking away knowledge and words without even reading them."

"Why is this important, Doullie? What is going on?"

Adoulla ignored her questions. "Please, my sweet, tell me that you still have a copy of this scroll."

Miri's offended sniff cut through her worried expression.

"Have you ever known me to throw away something of potential value? Name of God, for thirty years I didn't throw *you* away!" Weariness overtook her smoky eyes. "Be careful here, Doullie. If the Falcon Prince is involved in this. . . . I know you admire him, but he's a dangerous madman. And from what my Ears tell me, he is furious right now about the murder of a beggar family who was under his protection—mother, father, and daughter all found with their hearts carved out. Apparently the same fate struck a squad of his men as well."

Adoulla had nearly forgotten Baheem's giving him that last bit of interesting and troubling news. But he only half-analyzed it now as he was overcome with thankfulness. Whatever else was wrong in the world,

God had seen fit to keep this woman in Adoulla's life, worrying over him. This funny, strong, bedchamber-skilled woman who loved him. Manjackals and ghuls could not change that fact.

Still, this news increased Adoulla's sense that Pharaad Az Hammaz might make a useful ally. "Can you put me in touch with him, Miri? It may help me put an end to these murders."

She squinted in thought for a moment, then shook her head. "Perhaps . . . perhaps I could. But I'm sorry, Doullie, I won't. That would require my making more contact with his people, and after he killed this last headsman. . . . No, it's just too dangerous. The man has lots of right-sounding ideas," Miri continued, "and I must admit, he is remarkably handsome. I'd wager you didn't know that I once saw those calves *very* close up. *Did* you know? Never you mind where or when."

She was trying to make Adoulla jealous. To upset him. It was working. He felt—not in a pleasant way—that he was a boy of five and ten again.

"But despite these things," she went on, "he is, beneath all his pretty words, talking about civil war. Wars are bad for business. And a war inside the gates of the city? Almighty God forbid it. Do you know what happens to whores in a war, Doullie? Of course you do. I've got arson and rape on the one hand and a clinking coin purse on the other, Doullie. For me and mine, it's an easy choice. I've got a house full of innocent girls to protect here."

Adoulla smiled despite his frustration. "Innocent? A funny word, all things considered."

Miri did not smile back. "Yes, you damned-by-God oaf. Innocent. My new girl Khareese fled her father not three weeks ago. What does she know of war?"

Adoulla sighed. "Well, Pretty Eyes, I know well enough that you won't be budged when you won't be budged. But at least tell me what your Ears have heard of these murders."

Miri shrugged. "Not much. The watchmen marked it up to street folk killing street folk. The family did their alms-seeking outside of Yehyeh's teahouse, and they were found dead there, along with old Yehyeh himself. They—"

"What? Yehyeh? When did . . . ? Who . . . ?" Words failed him and his stomach sank as he watched Miri's eyes widen.

She took his hands in hers. "Oh. Oh, Name of God, Doullie, I'm so sorry. I'd forgotten what friends the two of you were."

Adoulla felt a sob begin to rise within him. He smothered it, and something within him went cold. "Yehyeh . . . Minstering Angels . . . Yehyeh." He spoke absently. "Oh, Miri, don't you see? Things can't stay safe forever, no matter who rules. You with your Hundred Ears know that better than most."

She sighed and nodded. "I know. But maybe they can be bearable for another few years. That's all I dare ask of God."

He ran his hand through his beard. "And then what, my sweet?"

"Then I'll climb warm and sleepy into my grave, God willing."

She rose and kissed his forehead. Then she went in search of the scroll she had mentioned, leaving Adoulla alone with birdsong, the scent of pear trees, and thoughts of his dead friend.

*Dead. May God shelter your soul, you cross-eyed old rascal.* He recalled Yehyeh's words of a few days ago—before Faisal, before the giant ghul, before Zamia, before Mouw Awa. Before he was killed. *"May All-Merciful God put old men like us quietly in our graves."*

The teahouse owner had no family that Adoulla knew of. Likely the watchmen had already tossed his body in the charnel commons. Adoulla thought about going to his own grave alone. And then he thought, as he had not allowed himself to while Miri was before him, of the words Axeface had said just an hour ago. *Her new man.*

When she returned a few minutes later, handing him a scroll-case, he found he couldn't quite keep his thoughts to himself. "So what's this I hear about Handsome Mahnsoor spending his time around here? Everyone on the street knows the fool is too cheap to be an honest customer to you."

She stared at him then, and her face took on the angriest look Adoulla had ever seen her wear. "May God damn you, Doullie," she said in a near whisper. "May God damn you for daring to be jealous." Something cruel grew in her eyes. "Do you want to know the truth? Do you? Well, I will tell you. Yes, Mahnsoor has been spending his time with me, Praise be to God. And, praise be to God, last night he asked me to marry him."

*Last night. When I was busy learning about a living-dead killer and his master.*

"And what did you say?" Adoulla heard some man somewhere ask with a weak voice like his.

"That is none of your damned-by-God business. Unless you are prepared to compete for my hand?"

Adoulla felt the familiar pain of having no good answers for the person on God's great earth he cared most about. "Oh, Pretty Eyes. I know you don't want to hear this, but there are . . . ways other than a formal marriage before God. We could live—"

"Lake of Flame! Do you think, because of what I do for a living, that I am completely bereft of virtue?" Miri's eyes tightened. "Well, I'm not. And what is a woman's greatest chance at showing her virtue? In marriage."

"I know that you possess a thousand virtues, Miri." Adoulla meant every word. But Miri just threw up her hennaed hands in exasperation.

"Oh, no. No more of that damned-by-God sugar talk. It's been many years since I could keep myself warm at night remembering your words while you were nowhere to be found. My niece is *dead*, Doullie. It is a reminder from Almighty God. I've got a good twenty years left in this world if God wills it. Thousands of days, thousands of nights. I'm not going to spend them all alone. I'm *not*."

She fell silent, gazing up into the tree branches. When he looked at the line of her broad neck, the sandbrown skin smooth despite her near fifty years, he felt like he would weep.

Adoulla kneaded the flesh of his forehead with his knuckles, trying to somehow rouse the right words. He kept picturing Yehyeh, who had always said that marriage was a fool's move. *Dead*. Yehyeh was dead. Perhaps Miri was right. Perhaps there *was* some message from God to be found in these murders. About priorities. About what was left of his own life.

Adoulla stared at his hands. If he and his friends found this Orshado—this ghul of ghuls—and defeated him, then what? Would God's great earth be purged of all danger? Would the Traitorous Angel's servants all just go away? No. When would Adoulla's work be done? He'd asked himself the question many times, but today he faced the honest answer for perhaps the first time in forty years. His work would end only when he was dead. Or when *he* ended it.

He swallowed hard and looked up from his hands. "Miri."

"Yes?" she said, her voice flat.

"This is it, my sweet. I . . . I cannot let a man who has murdered my friend—and your niece—stalk this city any longer. But if I live through this. . . . That's it for me, then. I'm done. Men can find someone else to save them from the ghuls."

Miri rolled her eyes, the hardness he knew so well returning to her voice. "Do you want me to do a little dance? I mean, I've only heard *that* ten times before, Doullie! Don't you think I know by now that such declarations are just words on the air? They'll be blown away by the first strong breeze that comes along."

Adoulla swallowed again and took hold of Miri's

shoulders, giving her the most level look he could. "Not this time." He found himself speaking formal words that he'd never said, not in thirty years of half-meant promises. "I swear this to you, O Miri Almoussa. In the name of God the All-Hearing, who Witnesses all Oaths. In the name of God the Most Honest, who loves truth and not lies. I *swear* to you that when this is done I will return here and, if my fate is so kind that you haven't yet married this money-grubbing fop, I swear in the name of God the Great Father that I will touch my forehead to the ground before you and beg you to marry me."

He knew that she understood what such an oath meant to him, but Adoulla also knew that Miri lived in a world of oath-shatterers. He expected more scornful skepticism. But Miri Almoussa just stood there, eyes shining, lip trembling, looking as lovely as the day Adoulla had met her.

And she said not a word.

Hours later, he found himself walking wearily back into Dawoud and Litaz's greeting room. The Soo couple sat on a divan speaking quietly. Raseed sat cross-legged on the floor, engaging in one of his breathing exercises, but the pallet where Zamia had been recuperating was empty. A good sign.

His friends looked up as he entered.

"What news?" Dawoud asked. "Did the boy have anything new to tell?"

"The boy?" Adoulla asked, confused for a moment. "Oh, him. Little Faisal. He was not there, as it happens. But," he said, brandishing the scroll Miri had given him, "Miri Almoussa gave me this, which may hold some answers for us. What of you, brother of mine? How went your meeting with Roun Hedaad?"

Litaz answered for her husband. "Dawoud managed not to get himself killed by the Defender of Virtue himself. And to give a vague warning, but that is about all. But tell us, how *is* Miri?"

Adoulla frowned, sensing the subtle edge beneath the alkhemist's words. "Please, my dear, none of your snobbish scorn for the whoremistress, eh? Of all days, not today."

Dawoud snorted. "You forget that my beloved wife is, even after decades in Dhamsawaat, a slightly prudish Blue River girl at heart."

Litaz's eyes filled with half-serious lividity. "Prudish?! You of all people, husband, know that—"

"He said *slightly* prudish," Adoulla pointed out with a smile, feeling buoyed a bit by the presence of his bantering friends.

Litaz rolled her eyes. "You know it has nothing to do with that, my friend. We just want better for you. It's all we've ever wanted. I have no problem with . . . with what Miri *is*, but she won't let you be what you are! So I've been squawking this tune for near twenty years, so what? It's as true today as it was a dozen years ago: There are women—younger women, pretty women— who would be able to live realistically with the white kaftan you wear."

Adoulla plopped down onto a brocaded stool and let out a loud sigh. "Even if that were true, my dear, it wouldn't matter." For a long while the room was silent, save for the soft sounds of Raseed's inhalations and ex-halations. Then Adoulla heard himself say, "She is go-ing to marry another. At least, another man has asked for her hand. A younger man."

Dawoud gave him a look of loving sympathy. Litaz stood, walked over, and took his big hands in her tiny ones. She squeezed, smiled sadly, said nothing.

Raseed, finally looking up from his exercises, spoke confusedly. "Doctor, I don't understand—"

"You and your understanding can go down to the Lake of Flame, boy! Now shut up—we've more impor-tant things to discuss! Where is the tribeswoman, any-way? Off stalking the city for gazelles?"

"I'm here, Doctor," Zamia said, emerging from the back of the house where she'd no doubt been making water. Adoulla noted that she walked more or less steadily on her feet and that much of the weakness he'd seen in her only last night was gone. "Did you learn anything that will help me avenge my band?"

To his surprise, Adoulla found that he could not speak of Yehyeh's murder. It was foolish, he knew—these were his closest friends in the world, and allies who needed all of the information they could get. But Adoulla thought of Litaz trying to find drops of Yehyeh's blood or some such, or trying to analyze the angle at which his heart had been ripped out. And he felt that his own soul would somehow snap if he did not keep this one bit of grimness to himself for now. So, as his friends and allies listened, Adoulla instead recounted what little else Miri had known, and told them about the thrice-ciphered, hidden script scroll that spoke of the Cobra Throne. "Though All-Merciful God alone knows how we're going to unravel these cipher-spells. The costs and the expertise involved . . ." he trailed off, exhausted and daunted by just about everything in his life.

Litaz shot a worried look in her husband's direction. "Actually, I do know of one man who might have the skill and inclination to help us with this. And he would do it quickly if I asked."

Dawoud's expression was perplexed, then bitter. "Him. Well, I have no doubt that *that* one will be all too ready to help. He will be falling all over himself to give you what you need. At a price."

Adoulla smiled. "Yaseer the spell-seller. Of course. It seems, then, that I am not the only one fated by God to get help from an old heart's-flame."

Litaz sighed. "He will gouge us but will do so less severely than others would. And he'll do honest and discreet work. If I send a messenger now, I should be able to see him by tomorrow."

"By all means, send a messenger. And you should take the boy with you tomorrow."

Both Litaz and Raseed started to speak, but Adoulla cut them both off. "I know, I know. *You* can take care of yourself," he said, gesturing with one hand toward Litaz. "And *your* place is protecting me, or Zamia, or whomever you've decided duty dictates today," he continued, gesturing with his other hand toward Raseed. "But between Dawoud and Zamia and myself we can, Almighty God willing, handle any threat that might strike here. You'll be carrying a great deal of coin, Litaz—and even aside from that, the more I think on it, the less comfortable I am with any of us being alone out there. Indulge me, eh?"

With that Adoulla walked off and made water before dragging himself to the makeshift bed his friends had set for him. He was exhausted, but he could not stop thinking about Yehyeh. And about Miri. The choice she had made. The oath Adoulla himself had made. Miri's words, *thousands of days, thousands of nights,* echoed in his head, as did Yehyeh's words about old men and graves.

Sleep was a long time in coming.

# Chapter 14

THERE WAS A CLEAN TANG to the late morning air, and Raseed bas Raseed breathed it in deeply as he made his way toward the North Inner Gate. Litaz Daughter-of-Likami walked a half step in front of him, dressed more richly than Raseed had ever seen. Her long dress was embroidered with amethyst gemthread. She wore rings of gold and coral in her twistlocks, and a jewel-pommeled dagger sheathed in dyed kidskin on her belt. *Is she expecting a fight?* Raseed resolved to be even more watchful than usual.

The inn where they were meeting Litaz's contact was in the Round City, the innermost part of Dhamsawaat. A sixty-foot wall of massive, sun-dried bricks surrounded the Round City, with great gates of iron in its northern and southern sections. The pair joined a line of people making their way through the North Inner Gate and, in a short time, reached the gate itself. As they walked through, Litaz smiled and nodded at one of the watchmen on duty. The man eyed Raseed's habit and sword but said nothing.

As soon as they passed through the gate they turned from the huge gray paving stones of the Mainway. Litaz led the way confidently and Raseed followed. They rounded a corner and stepped onto Goldsmith's Row, a paved lane that was narrower than the Mainway but still quite broad. Leaving behind the press of pedestrians and shouting porters already building up, the pair joined a traffic flow that was decidedly quieter and less crowded.

Litaz bit her lower lip and mumbled to herself, obviously deep in thought. So Raseed remained silent and took in his surroundings. He had been in Dhamsawaat for nearly two years now, but he'd never been down Goldsmith's Row. He looked about with interest.

Tidy storefronts and splendid houses lined the street here, the crude, open, stone windows of the Scholars' Quarter replaced by fine sandalwood screens and, in the more opulent shops, leaded glass. Though one could walk here from the Scholars' Quarter in less than an hour, the two neighborhoods were a world apart.

Here were the homes and shops of Abassen's wealthiest merchants and most distinguished craftsmen—elite importers and perfumers, gemcutters and jewelers, bookbinders and glassblowers. Here also, in decadently furnished mansions, lived the courtiers and viziers and their families—those who did not live at the palace itself. Raseed marveled at how few people there were, and what little noise they made.

No doubt many of them were home preparing meals

for the Feast of Providence, which was this evening. But there was more to it than that, Raseed thought. This was the sort of place where one could be alone with one's meditations. The streets of the Scholars' Quarter were never this quiet, or this empty, or this clean. Raseed envied the residents the solemnity of their surroundings. *No great stinking puddles. No loud donkey-whipping. No hashi smoke drifting in the window. No muttering madmen. Would that I had a place like this to meditate and train.* He tried to smother this unacceptable covetousness. *O Believer! Worship God wherever fate finds thee—whether prison, prairie, or Prayersday table*, the Heavenly Chapters say.

His service with the Doctor did not bring him into contact with the overfed inhabitants of the Round City. It was probably just as well. The denizens of the Doctor's home quarter disgusted Raseed with their degeneracy and lewdness. But while the hashi-smokers and whores of the Scholars' Quarter were foul, the men and women here were perhaps even more foul. Here was wealth, as much wealth as anywhere in the Crescent Moon Kingdoms. Here was every opportunity for virtue and learning, with none of the dire incitements to vice that poverty brought. But the Doctor claimed that the people of Goldsmith's Row ignored such opportunity, using their incalculable riches only to devise new and more luxuriant vices.

*Partner*, he had called Raseed the other night. But Raseed was unworthy. He'd said nothing to the Doctor or the others about his encounter with Pharaad Az Hammaz. About taking the stolen goods the thief had given him. He hadn't gone so far as to utter a falsehood—when he'd returned to the Soo couple's shop and Litaz had asked after his dusty silks and disheveled appearance, he'd put off her questions, and she hadn't pressed him. The wrongness of it burned his soul, like a foretaste of the Lake of Flame.

*Partner*. Again he turned the word over in his mind. Unworthy though he was to speak prayers to God, he prayed now that the Doctor was safe. There was no telling when that Mouw Awa creature would strike again.

"Raseed?" Litaz's voice intruded on his thoughts.

"Yes, Auntie?" He scanned the thin crowd about them as he answered.

"Zamia Banu Laith Badawi—she is interested in you. Do you see this? Do you understand how careful you must be with this?"

He felt as if she had slapped him. Without meaning to, he stopped walking. He closed his hand around his swordhilt, said nothing, and started walking again.

Litaz's heart-shaped face split in a patronizing smile as she walked beside him. "And you have taken an interest in her, too. Anyone with eyes can see that plainly enough," she said, sounding amused.

He began to dispute the alkhemist's words but found that he could not quite do so without speaking a falsehood, which was forbidden by the Traditions of the Order. He tried to find something to say. But all that he could come up with were questions. "With most humble apologies, Auntie, you should not say such things," he said at last.

"She's a Badawi, Raseed. Even as she is fixed on revenge, she will be thinking about keeping her band from dying out." Litaz's smile deepened. It was the smile of one who knew more than Raseed did about certain matters, and he found that it upset him. He kept walking, keeping his gaze straight ahead, hoping to force an end to the conversation.

But Litaz continued. "It's all right, you know. What you feel when you look at her. You've been holding a sword so long that you've known little else. But there is *nothing* wrong with what you feel when you look at her."

The Soo people had a frankness in speaking of things inappropriate—it was not surprising that the Doctor was so comfortable among them. Raseed felt his face flush, and he bit off his words. "You speak of such things too openly!" he said. And surely none could blame him if he was more curt than one ought to be with an elder.

But if annoyance was edging into his voice, it was annoyance with himself as much as anything. He *wanted* to be comforted, despicably weak as he was. He wanted to reach out to Litaz and talk to her about these things. But that was simply unacceptable. He fell silent.

She smiled gently. "If you want to talk, young man, I swear before God that I'll say not a word to anyone. Not even to Adoulla or my husband."

They moved on, turning off of Goldsmith's Row to enter a neat but narrow cobblestone alleyway. Something in his soul clenched and then relaxed. He felt the words come without his bidding them.

"I don't have any *secrets*, Auntie. It is just that . . . she has been chosen by the Angels themselves! I wish that. . . . It . . . it is so . . . *difficult* sometimes. When I went to seek the crimson quicksilver I—"

"You would do best to answer quickly, harlot, and truthfully!" The harsh voice came to Raseed's ears at the same time that the speaker—a robed man with a whip—came into his field of vision. The man was lean and gray-haired, and two big men with short, thin clubs stood with him. These other two might have been twins—both young, huge, and hook-nosed. All three men were clean-shaven and wore plain turbans and heavy robes of brown sackcloth belted with coarse rope. They had a girl trapped in the alley.

*The Humble Students!* Wandering mendicants that scoured wickedness from the streets and taverns of the Crescent Moon Kingdoms. Raseed felt even worse than he had a moment before. He glanced at Litaz. Her smile had twisted into a hard line; she looked more the old warrior than the kind grandmother now.

The Humble Students were charged with chastising those who needed to be chastised, helping men and women to walk the path of God. But Raseed had learned that some Humble Students did this more out of greed or cruelty than righteousness. Praised in Rughal-ba, mocked in the Soo Republic, in Dhamsawaat the Students were few in number—tolerated by the Khalifs, disliked by the people.

Unsurprisingly, Raseed's mentor was among their despisers. "*I don't trust anyone who claims to serve God by beating up dancers and drunks,*" the Doctor had growled once.

The trio stood shoulder-to-shoulder twenty yards down the cobbled alley. They were facing in Raseed and Litaz's direction. Their gazes, however, were set on a girl wearing a gauzy blouse and tight leggings with pale laces. Raseed picked up the cloying smell of cheap oil of violet from the slender girl, far away though she was. *Trouble,* the dervish knew. As he stood surveying the scene, Litaz shot forward. The Students and the girl all locked their eyes on her.

"What is the matter here?" Litaz's voice was bold, and it instantly agitated the Students.

The gray-haired leader frowned. "The matter? An unclean girl is to be shown the way of God. Do you wish to watch and learn from her example, outlander? The Republic is a decadent place. The Soo more than most would benefit from our lessons." There was no emotion but scorn in the man's voice.

Litaz flashed a caustic smile. "I've seen the Students' lessons before, brother. I'm afraid I can't say that I always approve of them."

The man arched an eyebrow. "Watch yourself, woman. We do not need the *approval* of outlanders. We found the tramp going about her foul business in plain view. The whorehouses of this city have been left to fester, and now their rotted fruit spills onto respectable streets. But if the watchmen will not do their duty, we

will do it for them. Ten lashes is the punishment."
Leather creaked as the man flexed his whip.

The girl jumped in, sensing her chance. "I . . . I
wasn't working on the street, Auntie, I swear it! I . . . I
wouldn't do that. I was just coming from . . . coming
from a . . . from a friend's house." The girl lowered her
eyes in shame. *She can't be more than four and ten*, Raseed
thought, disgusted. But he felt something shameful—
painfully shameful—race through his body as he
looked at her.

"What is your name, girl?" Litaz asked.

The girl looked at the alkhemist with hunted-gazelle
eyes.

"Suri."

A look of surprise crossed Litaz's face. "Suri? Truly?
That is one you don't hear every day."

The girl made a noise in her throat and ducked her
head.

"Suri," Litaz repeated. "A beautiful name. And a
very, very old one." She turned to the Students with a
clearly forced smile. "Surely you brothers see the sign
from Almighty God here? The Heavenly Chapters'
story of Suri says 'O Headsman, drop your sword and
serve His mercy! O Flogger, drop your whip and serve
His mercy!'"

The gray-haired Student spread a conciliatory hand,
but he sneered as he did so. "The Chapters also say
'And yea, proper punishment is the sweetest mercy,' do
they not? A new era is coming, outlander! An era when
only those who walk the path prescribed will prosper."

The two big men were tensed for a fight. Raseed found that he was as well. He took a step toward Litaz.

"The 'path prescribed'? And the Students will be the ones to judge what that is?" The alkhemist's eyes narrowed as she spoke. "Please, let the girl go. I ask you to indulge an old woman." When this earned no response, Litaz's pleading slid into threat. "Look, we're not on the riverdocks, brothers. Do you think the respectable people of this neighborhood—who you know can't stand your order anyway—do you think they will sit idly by while you beat a girl in their streets?"

The eldest Student's sneer deepened. He ran a hand over his smooth brown jaw. "Listen to me, woman. Leave now. Please. Do you see? I say *please*. Go back to one of your perverted outlander neighborhoods. I will not ask you again." He turned his head toward Raseed. "And you, Master Dervish?" The man's brittle-sounding voice made the title a mockery, but for the first time he looked unsure of himself. "Are you *truly* keeping company with this trash?" Raseed parted his lips, but no sound came out. Words flew into his head.

*I am here in company with her, but—*
*Please forgive her, brother, she—*
*I am afraid that I must—*

But none of them made it through his suddenly dry and cracked throat. Raseed had faced and killed highwayman, Cyklop, and ghul, but he now found himself paralyzed and unable to speak.

The gray-haired man's uncertain expression evaporated, replaced by a cold scowl. "I take it by your silence that you *are* here with this mad old degenetress! Where is your virtue? Have you stopped serving God already, young man?" The two big hook-nosed men began to shift, clearly itching for a fight.

There was the incongruous sound of laughter as two young couples entered the alley, took one look at the scene before them, and swiftly turned back.

Litaz drew her dagger from the kidskin sheath at her waist. *What is she doing?* Long and broad-bladed, in her little hand it was a small sword. "Leave, Suri," the alkhemist said with a deadly calm in her voice. When the girl didn't move, Litaz shouted "Leave! Now!"

The girl ran before the men could grab her. The two big Students started to follow, but their leader held up a hand and they froze. Suri flew from the alley without a word or a backward glance.

"This old whore's vice is greater than the other's was," the lead Student spoke to his men with an eerie calm. "She will take the girl's punishment." He focused his words on Litaz. "And who *are* you, whore-with-a-knife, to think you can interfere in God's work with impunity?" The man seemed genuinely curious.

Litaz gave no answer.

The veins in the man's neck bulged. "Whoever you are, you will find that you are sorely mistaken!" Raseed did not approve of the man's tone—there was an unvirtuous anticipation there at the thought of proving Litaz mistaken in some brutal manner.

Raseed's hand went to the hilt of his sword before he thought about who his opponents were. The Order held ties with the Humble Students. These men might be unpleasant and overbearing, but they were Raseed's allies as far as duty was concerned.

*But.* Litaz Daughter-of-Likami was a true servant of God who had doubtless fought more real battles than all three of these men combined. And she was one of the Doctor's dearest friends. Raseed's mind raced, and his hand flexed on his pommel.

Litaz broke the silent moment. "The Father of the Universe does not tell us to beat frightened girls, *brother!* Can your kind can find no other way in which to spread virtue?"

One of the big men began to slap his club against his open palm. He moved two steps closer to Litaz. The men were nearly in swinging range now, and Raseed took two long strides closer. The gray-haired man shot Raseed a warning look then spoke more calmly to Litaz. "Such rude words. Come, woman. *Old and withered or young and hale, all must live by His words.* Come and be chastised. It will be quick and feather light for one so small as you, I swear in the name of God."

Litaz laughed a bitter little laugh. "Come try and *chastise* me, brother. You'll end up lying in the street."

Everything happened at once.

The two hook-nosed Students lurched at Litaz. They were not fighting men. That was clear enough to Raseed. No need for his sword. He blocked the assailant closest to Litaz and thrust a fist out.

Raseed didn't realize he'd decided his loyalties until the man was lying bloody-nosed and unconscious on the ground.

For what seemed the thousandth time that week, Raseed's stomach lurched with the wrongness of his actions, but he looked up, ready to do the same to the other two Students. Litaz stood between him and them. He froze as he saw the alkhemist was offering up the jeweled pommel of her dagger to the men. *She's surrendering her weapon?*

The leader hesitated, confusion and rage battling on his beardless face. "What—?" he said.

The dagger's pommel-stone hissed. A jet of bright green vapor shot forth, a small cloud of it seeming to wrap around each man's head. Litaz sprly jumped back a few steps, dodging a few clumsy club swings. On the edges of the cloud, Raseed felt the vapors sting his eyes and nostrils.

The Students reacted more dramatically. They slid coughing to the cobblestones, the bigger man's wooden club clattering as he fell. A moment later, all three men fell still as corpses. They were breathing, though barely, Raseed's keen senses told him.

Litaz coughed a hacking cough a few times, and Raseed echoed it, wincing at the acrid green smoke that was already dissipating on the clear morning air. The alkhemist brushed some sort of residue from her dagger-hand onto the skirt of her dress. It left a little green-black stain. Litaz looked down at the unconscious Students with grim satisfaction, and there was no mistaking her pride in her handiwork. She carefully sheathed her dagger, looked at Raseed and shrugged her shoulders.

"'Lying in the street.' I warned them, did I not?"

"Auntie! How? What?"

"A rare solution called the Breath of Dargon Loong."

"Like the monster from the stories?"

Litaz shrugged again. "Yes. Though, to hear Adoulla tell it, the Dargon Loong is real enough, even if most think him a mere story."

Only then did Raseed notice the several onlookers who now darted away from the scene. Raseed began to warn Litaz of the danger she had gotten herself into but thought better of it. *She has pulled you into it, too,* his doubting voice told him. He looked down at the immobilized Students. *I am on the right side of this,* he told himself. *I am!*

"Let us keep moving, Auntie," was all he said.

Her confident grin slipped, and for a moment she looked every bit an old woman. "Listen, Raseed. I am playing brave about this because I have just assaulted the Humble Students. This is going to bring trouble to my already troubled house." A sadness entered her eyes. "O God, please let them be safe!" She clearly was not speaking of the Students. "Raseed, if that creature, that manjackal, strikes again . . ." She left the thought unfinished and gestured to Raseed that they should walk on.

Eventually, Litaz brought them to a halt at the threshold of an elegant two-story inn of green glazed brick. Huge lattice screens hid the inn's courtyard from the eyes of passersby. They stepped through a small open section of the screen into that courtyard, which was decorated with twin fountains of almost translucent marble. Two big, well-dressed men ushered them into the inn itself. *Guards*, Raseed guessed, though they acted more like hosts and wore no visible weapons. They respectfully took his sword from him, promising to return it upon his departure. He noted approvingly that they handled the weapon with a proper reverence.

The greeting room of the inn was massive, almost as open and airy as the courtyard. A dozen parties sat at low tables of white wood worked with tortoise shell. Litaz smiled and waved to a fat man at a round table, hard against the far wall. The wall was dominated by a jade and emerald gemthread tapestry depicting a verdant grove of olive trees. The fat man, alone at the table, waved back, smiling cheerfully at Litaz as they approached. He looked as if *he* were an olive. The almost greenish sheen of his complexion matched the tapestry, and he was little, as short as Raseed, but egg-shaped and strangely sleek skinned despite being of an age with Litaz. To top off the effect, he wore rich, dark green silks.

"Lady Litaz Daughter-of-Likami!" As they approached, the olive man leered at them, stood, and bowed, making fussy noises all the while. Raseed gave a slight but respectful nod. Litaz embraced the man warmly. "You've kept me waiting, wonderful one. But the Ministering Angels know any wait would be worth it."

Litaz's smile was bright. Raseed found that he was not cunning enough to determine whether or not it was a false smile. "Beloved Yaseer," she said, and grazed the man's forearm with her small hand. "I am very sorry we are late, old friend. We ran into a little trouble on the way here."

Yaseer waved away an invisible trifle. "Not at all, my dear, not at all. I will refrain from asking you what sort of trouble. No doubt it's best that I don't know. No doubt."

Raseed did not like this too-smiling fool with his shifty movements and shifty words. But he kept silent, forcing his features to neutrality.

Yaseer did not return the favor. The man's smile dropped as he looked Raseed over, and he frowned a puzzled frown. "Who have you brought with you, Lady? I've never known you to need a bodyguard, excepting that sour-faced husband of yours." Yaseer stared rudely at Raseed but still spoke to Litaz. "Is he *truly* a holy man? You are a friend of the dervishes now? You who once told me they were the pompous peacocks of the—"

"That is enough, Yaseer!" the alkhemist broke in. She flashed an apologetic glance at Raseed.

The olive man spread his soft-looking hands, the picture of openness. "As you will, my dear, but you know I don't discuss business with strangers. Especially not the clean-shaven sort that use forked swords 'to cleave the right from the wrong in men.' You will have to tell your virtuous bodyguard to leave."

Raseed took an angry half-step forward before he remembered himself. Somehow he kept his voice level. "I will not leave her alone if—" he began.

Litaz put her blue-black hand on his shoulder and squeezed gently. "Raseed, please."

*There is too much at stake to be stiff-necked now.* He bowed his head in acquiescence and found himself wishing for some reason that the Doctor were there right then. "I will wait by the door, Auntie," Raseed said.

"Thank you, dear."

Raseed moved to the inn's entrance. He grasped for a swordhilt that wasn't there. Then he waited, his thoughts still racing, his soul still uneasy.

# Chapter 15

LITAZ REMAINED STANDING and watched Raseed move to the corner of the inn's greeting room.
She was agitated. She could not stop thinking about the
encounter with the Students and the trouble it might
bring. She had not killed anyone today. She had not
even really harmed anyone—the Breath of Dargon
Loong was essentially harmless and only rendered its
victims unconscious for a few hours at most. Still, she
had made dangerous enemies. Given the chance, Litaz
knew, the Students would be brutal in their retribution.
The fact that it was only their pride that was wounded
would not make them go lightly on her. But what had
her options been, after all? To let the girl be whipped
like an animal?

She turned to Yaseer and forced herself back into
tranquility. The encounter with the Humble Students
had been an hour ago. And there was work to be done
in the present. *Best to get this over with.*

She made her tone businesslike but gracious as she spoke. "I am pleased the messenger got my note to you. And that you were able to fulfill such an unusual request so quickly."

Yaseer was listening to her but was not-so-subtly watching Raseed, craning his neck to get a better look at the dervish. The spell-seller's smooth features crinkled in troubled scrutiny, then returned to Litaz with a warm, and she was fairly certain, unfeigned, smile.

"Hm. I'm glad to see you are still in one delicious piece, O-Eyes-of-Starlight! Your message made me think you were in mortal danger. 'Emergency,' 'Most crucial,' 'Our city threatened'—these sorts of words filled your little letter. You had me up all damned-by-God night, O Breath-of-Roses! And it was *remarkably* expensive scribing this spell—powdered emeralds, those damned-by-God ink mushrooms that only the Banu Kassim Badawi-trained camels can sniff out! Such things are far from trifles, even to one with as much coin as the eternally heartbroken spell-seller before you. 'What could be so crucial about some dusty old scroll in thrice-ciphered hidden script that she would need my cipher-spells so damned-by-God quickly?' I asked myself. 'And why should I do this, when I know I won't even be able to bring myself to charge her what I ought to?' For love?"

The wounded lover was a half-serious role that Yaseer had always played around her. She couldn't help but smile. For a sweetly painful moment, she thought about what life with such a robust man would be like.

She was glad that Dawoud had not come. *He would be furiously jealous right now.* As she thought of her husband, Litaz's smile faded, and the weariness returned.

"But you have never been a woman to scream 'ghul' when no monster is about," Yaseer continued, " 'There must be something to it,' I said to myself, 'if she is in such a lather over this.' You have always been a woman of sense, save for your refusal to marry me."

She thought of that years-ago time, just after the one trip home she and Dawoud had ever taken. Of finding the cologned letter with Yaseer's scandalous proposal to her—her, a woman already betrothed. She had barely kept Dawoud from killing the man. "I was already married when you asked me, Yaseer."

Again the plump man waved away something invisible and unimportant. The long-bearded owner of the inn directed his servants in setting out an array of plates, and he bowed obsequiously to Yaseer the whole while. When the host withdrew, Yaseer shook himself as if waking up from a bad dream.

"Oh, my dear, forgive me. Breakfast is served. Will you join me?"

Spread before the spell-seller was a breakfast that would have made Adoulla whimper in joy. Medallions of clove-and-mint mutton, poached pigeon eggs, honey-fried colocasia roots, fine grain date porridge, hundredflake teacakes, dark and light teas, and two-fruit nectar. Litaz was not the eater Adoulla was, but the fight earlier had made her ravenous, and the dozen layered aromas made her stomach rumble. But she would not share a full meal with Yaseer. Too many invisible snares.

She measured the proper response as if she were in her workshop, filling a notched bottle. "I am afraid I have little time, my friend. I am in a great hurry." She bobbed her head deferentially, and the rings in her twistlocks clinked lightly. "But I will take a teacake, if you do not mind?" She could not be utterly rude if she was doing business with the man. She sat at the white wood table, plucked up a hundredflake cake, and nibbled at it. It was delicious, and she had to resist devouring it as ravenously as her body told her to. "Thank you."

Yaseer shrugged his fleshy shoulders, the green silk of his shirt rippling. He smiled naughtily and gestured toward the corner of the room where Raseed now stood. His tone was conspiratorial. "So. A dervish, is it? And young enough to be your baby boy. Is it true what they say? That they shave *everywhere*?" Again the olive oil smile. "No, no, don't answer, don't deny. I'm just happy to see that you *do* have some scandal left in you, my dear. I am so very glad to know that you are enjoying life despite your muck-and-hovel, care-for-the-poor lifestyle. A lithe little baby boy of the Order, forked sword and all! Name of God! It's so decadent I'm almost inclined not to be jealous. Ahh, but I can see I'm embarrassing you. How are you, anyway?"

Finally, Yaseer had to stop for breath. Litaz refused to be drawn in to the banter, and she jumped into the brief silence with the most polite directness she could muster. "As I said, Yaseer, I am in a hurry. I *am* sorry. I am doing just fine, though, praise be to God. Speaking of enjoying life, you seem to be doing quite well for yourself. That brooch alone could feed a family for a year. Who have *you* been working for?"

The soft man's eyes crinkled again, this time in a mild taunt. "Oh, pretty one, you know that I can't tell you that. Let's just say that those rare individuals like you and I—we who know certain secrets and crafts— are in great demand these days." He sipped a leisurely spoonful of porridge before continuing. He was clearly not concerned with Litaz's hurry. "Talk of rebellion and chaos has men and women of means preparing for all contingencies. Such preparations are very good for business, praise be to God."

The diplomatic thing then would have been to be quiet. But Litaz found she couldn't help herself. "And it is all still just trade to you, Yaseer? These gifts that have been given to us by God? A way to make coin, with no thought to those who cannot pay?"

Yaseer smiled without a trace of guilt. "Not all those with knowledge disdain it so much as I sometimes think you do, O Lips-of-Lavender, giving your skills and your time away to flea-ridden idiots who don't ap- preciate it anyway, who throw stones at people like you and I. If I'm going to be praised sycophantically when my skill succeeds and called 'charlatan' or 'witch' when it fails, I'll at least have some coin in the bargain, thank you very much. Should I bother telling you yet again that there are much handsomer places in the world for you than in that filthy alley with that gnarled husband of yours? Places where your unmatched skills and your more-vital-than-its-years body would receive all the appreciation they deserve?"

As in years past, Yaseer was so ridiculously earnest that some part of her did want him. Still, it was not too difficult to assume her most off-putting smirk and get back to business. "No, Yaseer, you should not bother. But do be careful, will you? There are dangerous days coming, and there is more than talk on the horizon." She took a deep breath. "Now . . ."

Yaseer bowed his head slightly. "I thank you for your concern, O Voice-of-Birdsong. As to your commission, I have the scroll right here." The shiny man attempted a reprimanding glare. "As I said, it kept me up all damned-by-God night. You will pay steeply for that rush and for my lost sleep. Now, increasing the cost of the scroll is the obscurity of the words that—"

Litaz grit her teeth. She did not have time for this. "What's the bottom line, Yaseer?"

There was nothing soft or oily about Yaseer now. He looked around for unwished observers and, finding none, produced a small piece of paper and a stick of charcoal. He jotted down a number and slid the paper to Litaz. "This is the total cost. It is not negotiable, since your note commanded that I start work right away, and stated that you would pay 'any price.' " The spell-seller melodramatically drew from beneath the table a thin, foot-long, ebonwood cylinder. The dark scroll case was etched with gold and jade.

"That's a fortune!" She quickly ran tallies in her

head. Things had changed so much since she'd left the Republic. Years ago, her husband had teased her for being a rich Blue River girl who knew not the value of money. And it had in fact taken years for Lady Litaz a-Likami of the High Line of Illuminated Pashas to become simply Litaz Daughter-of-Likami. Now it was she—with her numbers-and-measures way of seeing the world—who managed the money matters of their shop and household. She thanked all-Merciful God that she was good enough at it that Dawoud didn't know how close in circumstances they'd grown to the poor folk they ministered to.

She was ready to pay Yaseer's price if she had to. Still, haggling was always worth trying. She put on a courtly smile and toyed with her twistlocks. "You speak of the appreciation I deserve—but does this price reflect it, my dear?"

Yaseer shook his shiny head sadly. "I *am* sorry, Eyes-of-Starlight, but we both know that appreciation only goes one way between us. Since you think me a contemptible mercenary, I'll be getting no kisses any time soon, I know. Therefore I am forced to treat you as a simple customer, I'm afraid."

She gave him a wry smile. "And am I paying extra for the scroll case?"

He smiled back. "My work cannot be carried around folded up in one's pocket—not even your paradisiacal pocket, my dear."

*Enough of this bantering,* Litaz thought. She was tired and she was worried about her husband and her friends. And, she admitted to herself, the longer she sat there the more she felt jealous of Yaseer's wealth. This sort of high-living—this and more—had been her inheritance once. And she'd thrown it away to follow her heart and to learn arts that she'd never have been allowed to pursue had she remained a respectable Lady of the Court of Three Pashas. She'd never truly regretted her life choices. But she did sometimes find herself wishing that God, From Whom all Fortunes Flow, had not forced her to make such choices in the first place.

*But He did, whatever your wishes,* she told herself. *Now focus!* "Very well," she said to Yaseer. "I do hope, though, that I can trust you to be discreet about this transaction?"

"Hmmm. Yes. *Discretion.* Why *are* you suddenly interested in thrice-ciphered hidden script, anyway? It's as obscure as it gets, cipher-spell-wise. What dusty old thing *are* you deciphering with this spell, anyway? No, no, I know you won't answer. Well, discretion is a commodity like anything else. But *that* is a commodity that I *will* grant you in honor of my *appreciation* for you. Now, the fees please." Again Yaseer had to stop for breath.

Litaz reached into the folds of her embroidered robe and withdrew from a secret bosom pocket a parcel of coins, tied up in a piece of lavender cloth. "There are a few extra dinar in there. Keep them, my friend."

She could admit to herself, if to no one else, that she enjoyed the look on Yaseer's face as he nuzzled the bag with his lips. "Gold was never drawn from a sweeter mine, my dear. I thank you, I thank you, I thank you."

And, at last, after a few more polite gestures and words, Litaz was finally able to say goodbye and God's peace to the spell-seller and make her way toward the inn's exit. It seemed that her fate was growing kinder. With the spell in hand, she and her friends could stop stumbling about in the dark. She hoped.

Litaz allowed herself to feel a small sense of victory. It was a lot of coin to part with—a good part of the little she and Dawoud had—but then, she'd known Yaseer's help would not be cheap.

With a glance, she collected Raseed from his anxious guard duty at the gilded doorway. He reclaimed his precious blade, and they stepped from the inn into the courtyard. She said nothing to the boy until they reached the street.

"Well, dear," she said when they'd left the courtyard, "despite our earlier troubles I think we can tell the old men that we—"

"Halt!" The word was shouted at them by a handsome young watchleader with an ugly look in his eyes. Beside him stood the gray-haired Humble Student whom they'd encountered earlier. Behind him were four other watchmen. The two big Students were nowhere to be seen—*probably still sleeping on the street*, Litaz guessed—but every man had a weapon in his hand.

"Do you think that God sleeps while you wicked folk live your unrepentant lives?" the gray-haired man asked. If a man could kill with his eyes, she and Raseed would be dead right now. "As I told you, outlander witch, you will be chastised! And, praise God, his merciful fury demands that your punishment reflect the enormity of your sins."

The watchleader cut annoyed eyes at the man, but his look for Litaz was even less friendly. "You will come with us, woman. And you, too, dervish."

*This man is no zealot,* Litaz guessed at a glance. *The Students found some greedy, demand-a-dinar thug of a watchleader.* The analyzer-of-things in her went to work: *What can be done here?*

"Sirrahs, I most humbly beg—" she began, just as she heard Raseed beside her say something about his authority and the Traditions of the Order.

"Shut up, both of you!" the Student shouted. "No more words!"

The watchleader sighed. "Oh damn you all, by God!" he said, taking in the Humble Student as well. He pointed at Litaz, however. "Just come with us. Now. And we'll take your weapons."

"What is this?" She hadn't realized that Yaseer was in the courtyard archway behind her until she heard his voice, quiet and forceful and with none of the play that had been in it moments before.

"What concern, Sirrah, is this of yours?" the watchleader asked. The barest hint of fear entered his voice, fueled no doubt by the obviousness of Yaseer's privileged position.

"My concerns are those which I declare mine, man." The spell-seller fumbled for something in his silken belt pouch. When he brandished it—a four-finger ring set with a purple stone that shone with engraved lines representing the sands, seas, and cities of the Crescent Moon Kingdoms—Litaz heard herself gasp out loud. *The Khalific seal!? So* that *is who he's been working for!* She'd known only that he'd been living in the Palace Quarter.

The Humble Student barely seemed to notice. "Watch yourself! You have wealth and some token of state, man, but Almighty God, who—"

The watchleader turned to the gray-haired man. "Be quiet, damn you by God! I know the Khalif's Seal when I see it, and as I think on it, this man's face is familiar to me from the Palace Quarter. Still. . . . " He weighed something on the scales of thought. "Forgive me, Your Eminence, but you have not announced yourself aloud in the Defender of Virtue's name. Because . . ." Doubt became certainty as the man's eyes locked on Yaseer's. "Because, perhaps, you—ah, forgive me—perhaps Your Eminence is engaged in that which the other ministers would question, eh? Again, I humbly beg His Eminence's forgiveness."

"You presume much," Yaseer said in a cold voice.

The watchleader bowed low, and there was genuine apology—the sort fueled by fear—in his voice. His men looked terrified. And even the Student seemed to doubt himself. But Litaz could sense Yaseer's nervousness as well. This was no dim-witted watchman they were dealing with. The man was a watchleader in the Round City and would know as well as Yaseer that news of the misuse of the seal could bring great trouble.

"A thousand apologies to Your Eminence," the man said at last. "But tonight is the Feast of Providence and my thoughts are on feeding my family. It would take the merest of gestures—the merest of pittances—to destroy my presumption."

*Money.* Without a second thought, Litaz dug out a handful of dirham and offered them to the man—far more than she could afford, but she could not think now of next year's expenses.

The man looked as if he wished to spit on her, but he took the coins just the same. "Leave," he said, clearly feeling daring. "Leave now. Take your filthy poisons back to the Scholars' Quarter. If I see you in this neighborhood again, I won't be responsible for what my men do." The man spared a long, despising look for Raseed, then turned and walked off, his men trotting down the block after him.

The gray-haired Humble Student lingered long enough to give a last glare. "This is not over for you, Soo witch. Or for you, false dervish. You two will be easy enough to find." Raseed winced at the word *false*, but Litaz just stared at the Student until the watch-leader shouted at him to follow, and he stalked off.

Then she turned to Yaseer. "Thank you," she said, feeling, against her every wish, her heart half in her throat. "Thank you, Yaseer! I could kiss you!"

"But you won't." The spell-seller's soft face was not jovial or playful now. His eyes were as hard as Litaz had ever seen them. "You owe me a great debt. A great debt." He shot a poisonous look at Raseed and turned and walked away coldly.

Some part of Litaz started to reach out to Yaseer, to stop him from going. But it was only a part of her. What the whole of her wanted was to see Dawoud. It was long past time to go home.

# Chapter 16

AS THE SUN WAS JUST BEGINNING TO SET,
Raseed followed Litaz into the Soo couple's
home. He was pleased to see that Dawoud Son–of–
Wajeed, the Doctor, and Zamia Banu Laith Badawi
were all there in the greeting room, safe.

"We would have been here sooner," Litaz said upon
entering, "but we ran into some . . . complications with
a group of the Humble Students."

"What?" the ghul hunter and the magus shouted at
the same time.

"Complications? What are you talking about?" Dawoud asked.

Zamia said nothing, Raseed noted. But she looked
healthier than she had even the night before. "Praise
God." He whispered the words without meaning to,
and Zamia looked at him quizzically. He lowered his
eyes in shame.

"I had to put a couple of them in their place, but that

is not what is important right now. This is," the alkhemist said. She placed the ornate scroll case on a low tea table. Then she collapsed onto a cushion. "Name of God! It will feel good to rest tonight."

Raseed had to speak up. "And you have earned rest, Auntie. But I cannot allow myself to rest now. If this scroll will help us learn more of the fiend Orshado's plans, I must—with apologies—I must have that information as quickly as possible."

Dawoud came to stand between his wife and Raseed. "These things don't happen in the blink of an eye, boy. The cipher-spell takes as long to work as a careful spell-scrivener's hand. We'll have whatever answers this scroll may hold, but we'll have to wait until morning to do so."

"We have some time for the luxury of rest, then," the Doctor said.

Raseed tried to speak in further protest, to insist that they had no such luxury, but Litaz cut him off with an upraised hand. "Indeed, and furthermore," she continued, flashing an annoyed glance in Raseed's direction, "we have *need* of rest."

"Zamia Banu Laith Badawi certainly does, whether she knows it or not." Dawoud added. He looked at Zamia, and Raseed was impressed to see how little she seemed to still fear Dawoud—or at least how little she now showed.

Litaz went on. "And we shall not just rest, but celebrate! For sunset marks the Feast of Providence."

The magus arched a white eyebrow. "So it does! You know, I had almost forgotten."

"As had I," the Doctor admitted.

Litaz rested a hand on her husband's shoulder but spoke to the group. "We must never forget our feasts. Tonight is dedicated to thanksgiving for the bounty that God provides us. On such a day it is our *duty* to celebrate life through food and drink. The Heavenly Chapters say 'O believer, thou shalt smile for God's Providence at festival and at funeral.'" The alkhemist turned to him. "Am I wrong, Raseed?"

He bowed his head. "An obscure verse, Auntie, but . . . but you are not wrong."

Dawoud and Litaz went into their workshop, the magus carrying Miri Almoussa's scroll, the alkhemist carrying Yaseer's.

Minutes later they emerged. Then Raseed heard the unmistakable sound of a pen on paper begin to scratch away in the workshop, though there was no longer anyone in there.

"The cipher-spell has been set to work," Dawoud announced. "Now, Almighty God knows, it is well past time to eat!"

Somewhere in the past few days, Litaz had managed to request the feast foods ahead of time. An old man and his son arrived, whisking in with half a dozen copper-covered dishes from a high-priced hire-kitchen off of Angels' Square before whisking back out. They all sat down, and Raseed's stomach growled. A white block of creamed cheese glowed with magenta turnip slices. Steam wafted from risebread with roasted chickpeas. Sour-and-sweet pickles, mutton cubes with peppers and nuts, garlicky greens, fruit, and salty almond pudding.

*And when did you come to have such gluttonous eyes?* a reprimanding voice within him asked.

At Litaz's request, Raseed said a simple prayer over the food. Then they ate.

Raseed pushed his teacup away, and declined each plate passed to him. He sipped his water, and took a few bits of turnip and bread. As happened so often, the Doctor's loud voice boomed in on his thoughts.

"Well!" said the Doctor, standing up a bit stumblingly as he spoke. *He is getting drunk,* Raseed worried. "Well!" the Doctor repeated, "I have learned, over the years, to trust my soul's senses. I'd guess I'm not the only one who believes that this blood-storm that's been gathering about us will soon thunder down. But I thank you, All Provident God, for giving me this meal with beloved friends beforehand." The Doctor rubbed his big hands together and looked out on the array of plates before him. "Name of God," he half-shouted. "Litaz, you know how to set a table!"

Zamia spoke softly, brushing her hair from her eyes. "The Doctor speaks truth, Auntie. You and your husband's hospitality is generous enough to make a Badawi jealous!"

Dawoud chuckled gently. "Heh. It doesn't come cheaply, let me tell you. Now you see why I married a rich Blue River girl!"

The alkhemist looked worried at this. Raseed could not say why, and truly it was none of his affair.

The old people ate and drank and talked. They regaled Zamia with tales, which Raseed had already heard more than once, of the foes they had vanquished over the years. Of the Invisible Robbers and the Golden Serpent, of the Four-Faced Man and a dozen minor magi.

Raseed only half-listened, sipping his water, until he heard Zamia speak.

"The Lady of Thorns! My father told me of her famous crimes! It was said that her father was a wicked djenn."

The Doctor snorted scornfully as he poured himself more wine. "The uninformed *always* say that when they meet someone who can do things that they think impossible. 'The blood of the djenn!' Idiocy! The Thousand and One can bear no children, any more than a man can give a child to a bear!"

Dawoud reached rudely across the table and poked the Doctor in the gut. "Do you mean to tell me, you old fart, that I have been wrong all these years? That your father was *not* a bear?"

The Doctor laughed. "Well, at least a bear is a noble animal! At least my father never begat a child upon a damned-by-God *goat*." The Doctor reached over and pulled on the magus' hennaed goatee and the old men laughed tipsily.

They finished with the dishes, and the table fell quiet for some time. After a while the Doctor let out a loud breath. "Yes, well, all of this talk has made me hungry for sweets." Dawoud brought his wife's cup, then Adoulla's, then his own, to the lip of the large pitcher of palm wine, tipping the golden liquid into each glass carefully.

Zamia declined a second cup, Raseed was pleased to

see. She took only one small morsel when Litaz passed around a plate with varied teacakes and preserved fruit.

Yet this was not out of caution. Raseed saw that, if Zamia seemed to be less afraid of Dawoud Son-of-Wajeed, she'd apparently quickly grown most warm and at her ease around his wife. Litaz explained to the tribeswoman, "The rug is from my husband's part of the Republic. Where I come from, we didn't eat on rugs—we sat in tall chairs—at a waist-high table. It's taken me many years to get used to the squatting. When I first—"

The alkhemist was interrupted by the Doctor's snickering. He was entertaining himself and the magus with his juvenile antics. On his plate, he'd built a face from teacakes of various shapes. He commenced to perform a little show in which the face's spice cookie "lips" begged, in a high-pitched puppet-show voice, "No, Doctor! Pleeease don't eeeat me! In the Name of Merciful God, I beg of you don't eeeat meee!"

"But in the Name of Beneficent God," the Doctor said to the teacake in his own voice, "I was made to devour you, little cakes, and my fate cannot be changed!" Litaz and Dawoud guffawed.

*They are worse than children sometimes*, Raseed thought. He was pleased to note that Zamia seemed unamused. *She is serious about life, as a young woman should be. Chosen by God's own Angels.*

But then, as she continued to watch Adoulla's bizarre little show, Raseed saw a smile creep across the tribeswoman's full lips. Then a small, modest giggle.

Raseed found that he was not disappointed. He found, in fact, to his shame, that he could not look away from that smile. He found that Zamia's little laugh cut through him like a sword poisoned with pure happiness. He tried to force his disciplined eyes to look away, but he could not. Zamia turned and looked directly at him. As her green-eyed gaze met his, and she saw him staring at her, a look of pure terror replaced the smile on her face.

She covered her mouth with her hand and bowed her head again. He followed suit, casting his eyes to the neatly swept stone floor. *You were staring at her! You were staring at her, and you've shamed her. Have you no shame? Do you serve God or the Traitorous Angel?*

He needed to be alone with his meditations—or as alone as he could be in this crowded house. He finished his bit of food and water, then begged to be excused.

"Go on, then," the Doctor said. "I'll be going to sleep soon myself."

"Perhaps at this very table, big nose down in the teacakes, if precedent is any indication," Dawoud said with a wicked smile.

The Doctor harrumphed, and the two old men started going at each other again. Raseed stood and headed down to find a quiet cellar corner.

"Don't stay up all night praying and protecting, you hear me, boy?" the Doctor called after him. "You take a turn at watch, but get some sleep, too. On a hunt this dangerous, if you don't stay alert you end up dead. Even you."

Raseed made ablutions and meditated until he had

pushed fear and the soft sound of Zamia's laughter out of his thoughts. He'd thought he was too fired with duty to sleep, but sleep came.

The next thing he knew, Dawoud was waking him to take the last two hours of watch. As thin slivers of pink and orange light began to be visible through the window, he heard the strange magical pen-scratching sound of the cipher-spell at work, just as he'd heard it when going to sleep.

An hour later, as he sat on a stool by the front door, a loud voice suddenly boomed through the shop. Raseed leapt up in shock, his sword in his hand.

THE BROKEN WORDS ARE NOW MADE WHOLE! THEIR TRUTH FOR EVERY EYE AND SOUL!

It was the voice of Yaseer the spell-seller, coming from the workshop. Raseed cursed his own incompetence. How could the man have entered the house without Raseed seeing him?

But when he shot into the workshop, ready to kill if need be, there was no fat spell-seller there. The Doctor and Dawoud both followed him in, looking sleepy-eyed and unalarmed.

"Doctor, I heard an intruder's voice!"

The Doctor looked at him sleepily, as if wondering who Raseed was.

"There's no intruder, Raseed," Litaz told him as she, too, entered the workshop, Zamia trailing behind her. The alkhemist wore her houserobe, but Zamia was already clad in her Badawi camel-calf suede. "That's just Yaseer's signature. A reminder, when the spell has done its work, of the man who crafted it."

Raseed kept his eyes from meeting Zamia's. He looked to the workshop table and saw that the scroll the Doctor had brought from Miri Almoussa's was now glowing faintly. Beside it, atop a pile of what looked like burnt parchment, was the scroll case Litaz had been carrying.

Dawoud picked up the intact scroll and unfurled it, whistling an impressed whistle. "That Yaseer may be a sack of unprincipled scum, but he does good work, there is no denying. The scroll has been deciphered."

"Now let us see if it's got anything worth telling us," the Doctor said.

They all settled into seats as Dawoud read aloud.

*"No one knows how the Throne of the Crescent Moon was made. And few know that it was once called the Cobra Throne. Its great curved-moon back, which was once carved in the shape of the Cobra God's spread hood, takes no mark or burn. The Kemeti Books of Brass, lost to us now, claimed that the Faroes, called also the Cobra Kings of Kem, sat upon it for their coronations, just as the Khalifs would come to do. But though the Khalifs have sat on it in coronation for centuries, there are those who say they know not its true power. That the throne was ensorcelled with unseen death-diagrams; bewitched by the Dead Gods, who loved treachery. That this power could be called only by spilling the blood of a ruler's eldest heir upon it on the shortest day of the year. The Books of Brass claimed that he who managed to drink blood so spilled would be granted command of the most terrible death*

*magics the world has ever known—master of the
captive souls of untold numbers of long-dead slaves.
The dark arts of the Cobra Kings, scoured from the
world by God, would return."*

"It ends there." The magus rolled the scroll and set
it down.

The Doctor buried his face in his hands and let out a
low groan. "Litaz, my dear, tell me, in the Name of Almighty God, who is Our Only Refuge, that you have
some good, strong cardamom tea."

A quarter hour later, they all sat planning in the
greeting room, the elders drinking tea and smoking,
the smell of apple tobacco wafting up from a water
pipe.

"I do not want to do this," the Doctor said. "We had
a fine feast last night, and to open the morning with
this dark talk.. . . But, I've been beaten and bruised, and
my home lies burnt and ruined. I have lost my one true
beloved and the promise of a peaceful life. I won't lose
my whole city as well. I *won't*."

He gestured with the pipe's long mouthpiece at Dawoud. "But perhaps it won't even come to that," he
said, sounding to Raseed as if he were trying to convince himself. "Do you think this Orshado is even capable of this? To break into the palace, let alone to wrest
control of it from the watchmen and murder the Khalif's son? Even to one such as I, who has seen his share
of impossibilities, these seem near-impossible tasks. He
would need allies within the palace, a dozen age-old
incantations to get past its ward-spells—not to mention

that there must be a thousand men guarding the Khalif." The Doctor passed the pipe's mouthpiece to Litaz.

Dawoud looked at the Doctor. "You don't understand, brother-of-mine. You didn't *feel* this ghul of ghuls. His cruelty. His power. How much these enable him to do when the Traitorous Angel works through him."

"But even with war spells and death-diagrams," Litaz broke in, exhaling smoke, "a throne is but a symbol. Without an army, without watchmen, his bloody design will only get him an angry mob storming the palace."

"No," the Doctor said, and Raseed saw the reluctant resolve rise in his eyes. "No, my dear, your husband is right. It's not that simple. These are not dinar-grade magics we are dealing with here—no spells to rob houses or to make a murder look like an accident. These are the sorts of death spells the old books speak of—cruel magics through which every child, woman, and man in Dhamsawaat—aye, even the birds and the beasts—would wake one day to find themselves drowning on air, their lungs bursting like rotted fruit. The sorts of war spells that would allow one man to slay a horde, that would make an attacking army's blood turn to boiling venom, that would turn a whole mob's intestines into cobras. But it is even more than that. Such magics work as a . . . a focus. A man who knows how to use that magic could kill thousands in the space of a day. And then he would cull the foul power from *those* unwilling sacrifices to kill more men."

Litaz's expression was one of pure horror, and

Raseed had no doubt that his own face wore the same look. "Madness," she said at last. "Madness! Even if—God forbid it—even if he murdered all of Dhamsawaat, every other realm would rise against him. The Soo would send our mercenary legions, the Heavenly Army of Rughal-ba would—"

The Doctor's eyes were cold as stone now. The water pipe's flaming coal fizzled and died. "If he seizes the throne, he will not have to worry about these things. He will become the Traitorous Angel's Regent-in-the-World. Armies will not be able to stop him."

"But *why*?" Zamia asked. "Why would any man—even a cruel man—do these things? What could he possibly gain?"

"Power," the Doctor answered without hesitation. "The same thing that a man gains when he murders one of his fellow men. The same thing that a ruler gains when he sends his armies to kill and die. Power and the promise of a name that will live forever. What the Traitorous Angel offers his servants is no different. Though this man's ambition is as a sea next to the puddles and ponds of earthly killers."

Raseed spoke quietly "Praise be to God that the Khalifs of Abassen have been secure enough in their majesty that they have never used these foul powers."

The Doctor farted loudly. "Oh! Pardon me! But perhaps my body responded of its own accord to your foolish suggestion." He wagged a finger at Raseed. "Do you really believe, boy, that the Khalifs have never used this power because they have righteously *chosen* not to? No. Men do not pass up power, least of all Khalifs. No doubt the powers of the throne were never known to them. The Court magi have always been puffed-up thugs, confident in the simple brute force of their own magery. They have never been great readers or researchers. The coronation likely lives on as an ignorant inheritance, a reason for royal pomp and ostentation in which power is nominally passed from one generation to the next. But my guess is—and for this I *do* praise All-Merciful God—my guess is that this scroll hasn't been read in hundreds of years."

Litaz kneaded her forehead with a knuckle. "Until now," she said. "Until now, when it has been read not only by a half-cracked would-be usurper but by a powerful servant of the Traitorous Angel—more than that, a man who carries a true shard of the Traitorous Angel within his soul."

Zamia took a sip of tea. "But if this scroll's knowledge has been so secret, how is it this Orshado knows of it?"

Raseed was impressed to see a look of calm enemy-assessment rather than fear on her face.

"That one has ways of learning things," the Doctor said, and *his* expression was as close to fear as Raseed had ever seen. "Ways that no man who values his soul can even fathom. The Traitorous Angel grants powers that God will not. He demands the sort of thing he has always demanded. Fear. The entrails of innocent old women. Pain. The eyelids of children. No books or clumsy rumors for the servants of the Traitorous Angel."

Dawoud spoke with a hollow voice. "Orshado.

When I touched that blood. . . . I swear that none of you know the depths of the cruelty we face. With this one in command of such magics, the whole world will drown in blood within a week."

*"Six days thine to make man's world, six days mine to unmake it,"* Raseed recited. "The Traitorous Angel's taunt to God upon his expulsion." He had always hoped to be part of a battle that mattered this much. But he found now, to his shame, that he wished otherwise.

"We must stop him, then," Litaz said matter of factly. "For reasons heavenly and earthly both. The new Khalif is a fool and a murderer, but his son . . . it was the boy's idea to build those new poorhouses last year on the other side of Archer's Yard. To put a hospice house there for the street people. Small gestures but more than his father makes. It is said he is a sweet-tempered boy, full of love for the common folk."

The Doctor snorted "Give him another decade of life in the palace, and that will change! I can't claim to be pleased with the notion of rushing to rescue the Khalif *or* his little shit of a son."

Litaz rolled her eyes. "We don't do this for their sakes, Adoulla. You know that. But we have little choice here."

Dawoud lifted his teacup and drained its dregs. "So we go to the palace," the magus said, "though we'll not have an easy time getting an audience, no matter how many wild-eyed warnings we bring. Especially after my last visit. We'll be lucky not to be taken for assassins ourselves. Roun Hedaad is a good man, but his guardsmen will be happy enough to fill us with crossbow bolts with little provocation. And even if we get past them, the Khalif will not see us."

Adoulla wore a dark scowl as he spoke. "And what if the Khalif *does* listen? What if we somehow stop this Orshado? Then this foul power will be the Khalif's to seize. Do any here truly doubt that he would slay his own son in order to do so?"

Raseed started to say that such a thing was not possible, but he knew the Doctor would mock him. And, as he thought on it, he was not sure that he could speak such words without uttering a falsehood.

For a long moment, none of the others answered the Doctor either. Then Dawoud stood. "It matters not. We can only do what we know we must do and leave the rest to the merciful hand of Almighty God."

"Yes, it is all cut-and-dried," the Doctor said sarcastically. "We need only defeat the most powerful ghulmaker we've ever faced. And somehow slay his unkillable creature while we're at it."

"The monster Mouw Awa is not unkillable, Doctor," Zamia said, her voice half growl. "God willing, I will be the one to prove this." Raseed's heart beat faster, hearing such brave words.

The Doctor stroked his beard. "Aye, Zamia Banu Laith Badawi, may it please God to make it so. It has been only few days since the creature left you lying on a litter, all but dead. Your healing, praise God, goes miraculously well. Do you think—" the Doctor's voice grew as gentle as Raseed had ever heard "—do you think you can take the lion-shape again?"

Tears filled Zamia's emerald eyes, but they did not fall. Raseed felt sick with knowing that he wanted—wickedly!—to go to her and to hold her as he had sometimes seen men hold women on Dhamsawaat's streets.

A rueful scowl spread across Zamia's face. "I don't know, Doctor. Each month for several days, when I am—when women's business is upon me—I am unable to take the shape. Yesterday was the last of those days. Even were I unwounded I would not be able to take the shape until the sun is at its highest point today. Come noon, though, I will try. If, may Almighty God forbid it, I fail, I will at least die trying."

Raseed was incredulous—to make the tribeswoman speak of such shameful things, and then to ask this sacrifice of her! "Doctor, she was nearly killed the last time we faced this creature! We cannot ask her to—"

The girl's growl was louder than any she'd made before. "No one is *asking* anything of me, Raseed bas Raseed. Things are as they are. I know the murderer of my band. Through my own carelessness he . . . it . . . escaped once. It will not happen again."

The Doctor nodded. "Sometimes even a blind man can see the hand of God working. This thing Mouw Awa must be destroyed. Of that there can be no doubt. And God's Angels have very clearly given us the proper weapon to do so. *'To break down a wall when God grants a door is the work of fools.'*"

Dawoud broke in, his words sounding hard and dry. "It is as it is, then. Zamia, you shall travel with us to the palace, and if we cross paths with this Mouw Awa, it falls to you to kill it."

The old people went to prepare themselves, and Raseed found himself alone with Zamia. As soon as they were gone, she stepped close to him, and he fought furiously with himself to keep from breathing in her scent too deeply. When she spoke, he jumped, startled.

"Raseed bas Raseed," she said quietly, "before we go to face our deaths, I would ask a question of you."

"Yes?"

"Do you understand that, with my father dead, you must ask me directly if you wish for my hand in marriage?"

Raseed felt as if a sword had been slid into his guts. "I . . . I . . . Why would you ask . . ." He found he could not form words from his thoughts.

But the tribeswoman simply shrugged her slender shoulders. "The Heavenly Chapters tell us, *O woman! Ask a hundred questions of your suitor and a hundred questions of yourself.*"

"Suitor!?" Raseed had never before felt so lost within his own soul. Ten different men warred within him. "May God forgive me, Zamia Banu Laith Badawi, if I have behaved in a manner that . . . if I have shamed you by . . ."

"Shamed?" She looked baffled, which only confused him more. "How does shame come into this? I have simply seen the way you look at me. The only shame here would be born of deception. Can—?" she broke off at the sound of the Doctor's heavy footsteps approaching from another room.

"If God grants us our lives beyond this day, we will speak of this again," she said quickly. Then she nodded formally to him, ending the conversation.

Raseed went into his deep-breathing exercises, feeling more need for the calm they brought than he ever had. He stretched and prepared his mind and his body for battle, wondering whether he would die this day or live on with a soul full of shameful desires—and not knowing which would please God more.

# III.

THE WORLD WAS MADE OF pain and the guardsman's soul was formed from fear. How long had he sat unmoving in this cauldron, with only his head above the roiling red glow? He recalled, like dreams, slight sips of water and gruel. Some small, still-thinking part of him said that he was being kept alive while his body macerated slowly in the sparkling ruby oil.

The gaunt man in the filthy kaftan was there, holding open a sack of rich red silk. The shadow-jackal was beside him. The gaunt man upended the sack into the cauldron. Bones and skulls—men's, but too small for men's—spilled out with a ghastly clatter. Fragile looking skulls, tiny ribcages and fingerbones. . . .

The shadow thing's voice squealed again in his mind. *Listen to Mouw Awa, who speaketh for his blessed friend. Thou art an honored guardsman. Begat and born in the Crescent Moon Palace. Thou art sworn in the name of God to defend it. All of those beneath ye shall serve.*

*Thou doth see the baby-bones. Infants fed and fed and then bled dry. All for the fear that doth now waft from thee.*

*Listen to Mouw Awa. His blessed friend hath waited so long for the Cobra Throne. Shortest days hath come and gone and gone and come. Never one quite right. Mouw Awa the manjackal knoweth well the pain of waiting. He helpeth to deliver his blessed friend from waiting, as his blessed friend did for Mouw Awa.*

The gaunt man burned things before him. His eyes burned with smoke as the jackal-man droned on.

*Thou smelleth the smoke of red mandrake and doth recall fear. Thou smelleth the smoke of black poppy and doth recall pain.*

And suddenly, a whole piece of the guardsman's mind slid back into place. He was Hami Samad, Vice Captain of the Guard, and there was nothing he could do but beg for his life through a cracked throat. "Please, sire! I will tell you whatever you wish! About the Khalif, about the palace!" He began to weep wildly. "Ministering Angels preserve me! God shelter me!"

The gaunt man stared at Hami Samad with black-ice eyes. The guardsman felt the gaunt man's spindly fingers dig roughly into his scalp. The gaunt man's eyes rolled backward, showing only whites. Horrible noises filled the room, as if a thousand men and animals were screaming at once.

There was a tearing noise, and there was pain a thousand times more searing than anything he had yet felt. Impossibly, he felt his head come away from his body. Impossibly, he heard himself speak.

"I AM THE FIRSTBORN ANGEL'S SEED, SOWN WITH GLORIOUS PAIN AND BLESSED FEAR. REAPED BY THE HAND OF HIS SERVANT OR-

SHADO. THE SKINS OF THOSE-WHO-WERE-BELOW-ME SHALL MOVE AT THE MUSIC OF MY WORD. ALL OF THOSE BENEATH SHALL SERVE."

The last thing he saw was Hami Samad's headless body in a great iron kettle, spurting blood that mixed with a molten red glow of boiling oil.

# Chapter 17

THE SUN WAS HALFWAY UP IN THE SKY, and its heat was already making itself known. Dawoud sweated and huffed to keep up with the two young warriors and his indefatigable wife. He and Adoulla walked several strides behind the others, the ghul hunter's breath coming nearly as heavily as Dawoud's own. Ahead of them, Litaz spoke softly to Zamia and Raseed, but Dawoud and his old friend kept silent as they strode, saving their breath for breathing.

An hour passed, and the sun climbed a bit higher. They made their way through the large paved caravanserai that marked the entrance to the Palace Quarter. Ahead of them, a group of merchants argued heatedly with one of the Khalif's coin collectors.

"Do you see this, brother-of-mine?" Adoulla asked quietly. "It's not just the poor that the Falcon Prince speaks to. The Khalif has made his own bed of scorpions. He has even alienated the minor merchants with his taxes and his half-day-long tariff lines. The small timers are just waiting for an excuse to join the Prince's supporters."

Dawoud laughed. "That would be some alliance! Like a bad prophecy: 'O watch for the day when the thief and the shopkeepers lie down together!'"

Adoulla gave him a sidelong glance. "It's not so impossible. The Prince has always been daring. His targets have always been those with the biggest purses, men that most stall-keepers and middling merchants are happy to see get robbed."

The road followed the new canal that had been diverted from the River of Tigers. Dawoud poked Adoulla and gestured to the tiny boats that moved along the canal, knowing that his friend had not yet seen this newly made marvel. The swift, magically moving water that the little boats bobbed on fed into a massive waterwheel. "Follow a twisty route of wafting spells and copper pipe, and this is the other end of the stink that now haunts our neighborhood every month. This thing can grind as much grain as ten normal mill wheels, you know."

Adoulla snorted. "Yes, the end of the stick with no shit on it. Of course all the money from this monstrosity goes into the Khalif's coffers. And now we're off to save the son-of-a-whore's dynasty."

"Quiet!" Dawoud hissed as a watchman stepped out of a side alley, rudely crossing their path without so much as a glance at them.

The party stood and waited for the man to pass.

They approached the wheel. The noise it made—

creaking wood, splashing water, groaning chains—was deafening. It *was* monstrous, Dawoud had to admit. One could scarce believe it was made by men.

Then they passed through a marble arch, and a path of smooth white paving-stones, wide enough for six riders, stretched ahead of them for a hundred yards. At the end of the great path, which was grander than the Mainway itself, lay the Crescent Moon Palace, behind a high wall. As always it forced Dawoud's attention, though he'd been here just the other day.

Yet this time he found his eye drawn even more forcefully to the thin silvery spindle that was the minaret of the Court magi. *So much space for seven men when seventy could live there.* The Khalifs of Abassen had apparently never learned of the foul power that, for generations, had literally sat untapped beneath them. But what did the court Magi know? How would they fit into this mad sequence of magical events? He felt his tired mind spinning with too many damned-by-God complications.

As they made the long walk to the gates of the palace, Dawoud shifted his attention to Raseed. The boy's eyes kept darting to the tribeswoman and then to the paving stones before him. *He is worrying about protecting her. Wondering how to fulfill his duties and keep the girl safe at the same time.* This worried Dawoud. Not the dervish's cloaked devotion to Zamia—Dawoud accepted his wife's claims that the obvious feelings between the two young ones would not be an impediment; that in fact "love was what made everything else matter," despite the fact that young people's love was a thing of foolishness and first sights. No, it wasn't Raseed's interest in the girl that worried Dawoud. It was the dervish's obvious struggle with that interest, and the second-guessing that came with it. They were hunting monsters in the Crescent Moon Palace. In a situation like this, second-guessing could mean the death of the world.

They were about a dozen yards from the gate to the palace courtyards when a gray-eyed young officer of the guard stopped them.

"Hold! Who are you that you dare approach the palace of the Defender of Virtue wearing weapons?" The man's hand rested easily on the pommel of his sword.

"God's peace, guardsman. I am Dawoud Son-of-Wajeed, a friend of Captain Hedaad's. I must speak to the captain at once. He is expecting me to call upon him." It was true enough that he could say it with authority.

"Captain Hedaad?" The man looked uncertain but not unfriendly. "Well, I can't leave my post, Uncle. But if you truly have business with the captain, I will send for him."

"That will be fine. The matter is urgent, though, so please hurry."

"As you say."

Dawoud had been prepared to press silver into someone's palm in order to get his message up to Roun. But apparently his and his friends' fates were kind. In their hour of need, they had met with an honest guardsman. It was gratifying, while on this mad quest in a land not even his, to see Abassen's agents acting as they ought.

The young officer called a slender guardsman over. "Kassin! Send word to Captain Hedaad that—"

"Why, now, are we disturbing the captain?" a vaguely familiar voice broke in.

*Name of God, no!*

The long-faced minister from the Khalif's court came walking up surrounded by a retinue of a half-dozen guardsmen. *What on God's great earth is* he *doing here?* "What do we have here?" he said. The gray-eyed officer started to explain, but the minster waved the young man back to the guardhouse. Then he turned to Dawoud.

"You were warned to stay away from the palace, old man. And instead you have returned with armed friends! You are either mad or the foulest of traitors."

Dawoud knew better than to try and speak to this man of the threat that loomed over the throne. "A thousand apologies, your eminence. I am here only because I need to see Roun Hedaad." He heard his friends shuffling nervously around him.

The man's eyes narrowed. "The captain is busy. And you have disregarded most traitorously the express wishes of his Majesty. Your friendship with the captain does not change that. Men! Seize them!"

Dawoud heard Raseed mumble a prayer. The Badawi girl growled. Dawoud looked a question at his wife and Adoulla in the wordless near-language that the three had developed over decades of fighting together. *What do we do now?*

But neither his wife nor Adoulla seemed to have any answers. And really, there was nothing they could do. Even if they were somehow able to kill a squad of guardsmen, more would show, and they would die before ever getting inside the palace. Their only hope was going along for now and waiting for an opportunity—or creating an opportunity—to get word to Roun Hedaad. And to hope that he could actually do something to help them. The guardsmen took his wife's knife and Raseed's sword, and marched them at spearpoint away from the gate.

Dawoud cursed the slow roll of this own thoughts and saw his frustration reflected in his wife's and Adoulla's eyes. There was a way out of this—the three of them had destroyed the Kemeti Golden Serpent and bested a whole band of invisible robbers. These were just men with weapons. They had only to puzzle out . . .

His train of thought broke as he realized the minister and his men were leading them *away* from the palace. *This can't be good.* After a few minutes they were well away from the gates, in a secluded alley of the Palace Quarter. They came to a small, windowless house with a barred iron door. The minister opened this door himself with a set of three small keys. Once they were inside, the guardsmen closed the door behind them.

Adoulla was the first to finally find his tongue. "Why on God's great earth have you brought us here?"

A big guardsman casually shoved the ghul hunter with his spear-butt and told him to shut up. The minister, still not saying a word to them, went to the center of the house's one room and lifted up a dusty old rug.

Beneath the rug was a metal grille, which the minister opened with yet another key. Though it was rusty, the grille made no noise when the minister swung it up. There was a stairway—wide enough for two men— carved into the stone floor beneath the grille, leading down to God-alone-knew-where. *Some dank hole where we can be slain without the Captain of the Guard knowing about it, no doubt.*

"No more of this!" Zamia shouted suddenly, her thoughts clearly going down the same road. She drew herself up fiercely and, Dawoud noticed, tried to hide the pain still in her side. "I can smell the deceit on you! A Banu Laith Badawi is not marched into murder quietly like some docile townsman!"

"I said, be QUIET!" the same guardsmen who'd jabbed Adoulla said, accentuating the last word with a much crueler jab of his spear into the small of the tribeswoman's back. Zamia cried out and buckled but did not fall.

Dawoud didn't even see Raseed move. But the next thing he knew the little dervish was, with one hand, holding the big guardsman aloft by the throat. If Dawoud had ever doubted Adoulla's tales of the boy's more-than-human prowess, he couldn't doubt them now!

There was a sudden clatter of weapons, and another group of armed men came pouring out of the hole in the floor like ants from an anthill. They and the guardsmen formed a circle around Dawoud and his friends.

The new men were armed with daggers and cudgels. They wore the simple clothes of laborers or apprentices, though here and there Dawoud saw a bit of incongruous ornament: a silk scarf around the neck of the lanky man in front of him, an embroidered vest on a short but hard-looking boy to his right. At equidistant points of the circle of plainly dressed toughs were figures wearing some sort of livery. One of these was an ugly woman, tall and stout as a man. They were dressed identically, in tight-fitting linen breeches and thigh length overshirts the color of wet sand. The image of a swooping black falcon was dyed across the front of each shirt. These were better armed than the others. Each held a well-made cutlass and wore a small buckler made of steel-reed.

A bombastic voice boomed forth from the new group. "Leave the man be, Master Dervish! He has brought you here to speak with me, so let us start speaking!"

Pharaad Az Hammaz, the Falcon Prince, stepped into the center of the room. He moved like liquid in a man's shape, though he was well over six feet tall and had the thick, sinewy arms of a blacksmith. His hand was on the black-and-gold handguard of his saber. Raseed let go of the big guard who had struck Zamia and the man collapsed, clutching his neck and desperately sucking in breath.

Dawoud found himself fumbling for his thoughts like a boy playing Beat the Blind Man. "You . . . you . . ." he turned to the long-faced minister, "*you* work for *him*?"

The minister scowled and said nothing, but the Prince sketched a half-bow to Dawoud and his friends.

He put one of his massive hands on Adoulla's shoulder. "What are the chances, Uncle, that we should meet again like this?" the bandit asked. "That, in surveying the crooked gatekeepers of the palace, my men should see your bright white kaftan cutting through the crowd? And with such a strange assortment of friends about you? 'Az,' I said to myself, 'What are the chances? There must be something to this. Let's have a talk with the Doctor and find out what that something is.'"

One of the men wearing the falcon livery—a burly fellow with only one ear—spoke up. "Aye, sire, there be little enough chance of it. Little enough chance that it's a-makin' me suspicious. Something here be smelling of the Khalif's shitty finger, and this ain't a day for surprises. All of your work, sire, for all of them years, leadin' to today. They've already harmed one of ours." He gestured at the still half-choking guardsman. "Ask me, the only safe thing now would be to kill 'em." The matter-of-factness in the man's voice chilled Dawoud.

For a long, moustache-stroking moment, the Falcon Prince seemed to consider his lieutenant's suggestion. But the Prince's brown face split in a broad smile as he spoke. "No. No, Headknocker, that would be a dreadfully poor repayment to the Doctor here, who, mere days ago, nobly misdirected the watch to save my hide. And it would be a rotten foundation for our new order. Besides, this man earned his own throttling. Striking an unarmed girl like that!" The Prince tsk-tsked at the big guardsman even as he helped the man to his feet.

*Misdirected? What is he talking about?* Dawoud wondered. He could not imagine his old friend had become an agent of the Falcon Prince without his knowing it. And though he'd half expect Adoulla's assistant to leap at the chance to confront the most wanted criminal in the city, the boy was strangely still—as if paralyzed by some internal anguish.

"I'm afraid, however," the Prince continued, "that you *are* all my prisoners. And if you *are* agents of the new Khalif, that no-good son of a half-good man, I must warn you: I am not foolish enough to underestimate you. Even you, girl," he said, turning to Zamia and eyeing her rudely from head to toe, "are perhaps more than you seem, eh?" The Prince turned back to Adoulla. "So why *are* you here?"

*What do we do now?* Dawoud found himself wondering again. *What to tell, and what not to?*

"We are here," Adoulla said, "because we have read the same scroll as you. Because we know, as you do, that the Throne of the Crescent Moon was once the Cobra Throne."

*Well, that decides that.*

The Falcon Prince's dark eyes went wide. "Remarkable. I am not often surprised, Uncle, but you have managed to surprise me. Yet this knowledge is all the more reason that I must detain you until this business is done with." The bandit spread his empty hands before him and grimaced apologetically.

Adoulla's look was dark enough that even the imperturbable Prince took a step back. "Pharaad Az Hammaz, listen to me. We are not the only ones who know of the throne's powers. You have heard the people speak of me and of the dangers I have saved them from over the decades. I tell you now that there is another after the throne's power. Another who will strike the palace on this shortest day of the year. A man who is both more and less than a man. A man whose powers are greater and crueler than any of the magi and ghul-makers I have ever faced. He is called Orshado, and if he and his creatures beat you to the throne, I swear be-fore God that the bat-winged shadow of the Traitorous Angel shall fall over all of us for all our days, and for all days to come."

For a moment, the Prince looked genuinely con-cerned. But the smile swiftly returned. "The Traitorous Angel, eh, Uncle? I am sorry, but I have little time for such grandiose mysteries! I am a foe of the traitorous man! Of the traitorous Khalif!"

"And are you not troubled by the strange deaths of your men and of the beggars you have sworn to pro-tect?" Adoulla asked.

Suddenly the Prince's sword was out of its scabbard. "What had you to do with that, old man? If you had a hand in those foul murders, we will not go easy on you."

"I swear before God that I did not. In fact, we seek to slay the foul beings who did."

The master thief stared hard at Adoulla then sheathed his sword. "Well, then, Uncle, we must speak." He looked around the windowless house cau-tiously. "But not here. You and your group will accom-pany us."

The Prince's men marched them down the stairway in the center of the room. They entered a stone cellar, and here the long-faced minister again stepped to the center of the room. The man produced a thin wand from his sleeve and traced a series of symbols in the dust on the floor. Dawoud recognized magic at work, and he was only half-surprised when, without a sound, the seemingly solid stone of the floor slid open to reveal a tunnel that sloped sharply downward. The minister then said a familiar-seeming farewell to the Prince and went back up the stairs, two of the guardsmen following.

Dawoud and his friends were, in turn, marched wordlessly down through the tunnel, which quickly leveled off. A few minutes later they found themselves in a chamber the size of a small tavern's greeting room, with another tunnel leading out of its opposite end. The Prince's men produced clean-burning torches—the expensive sort treated by alkhemists—and took up positions along the walls.

"Here our words will not be heard by any ears above," the Prince said, bringing the group to a halt at last. "We shall wait here for word from my men in the palace. And you, Uncle, will tell me a story."

As they waited for some signal from the Prince's agents, Adoulla and Litaz told the bandit the little they had learned of Mouw Awa and Orshado. Dawoud stayed to the back of the group with Zamia and a still strangely silent Raseed, and he did not catch all of their urgent-sounding words, but he heard his wife ask, "Do you understand what a true servant of the Traitorous Angel could do with the same power you seek?"

He had never been able to effect the shifts in manner

that Litaz could—from steel to honey and back again, as the occasion called for it. In this strange life they shared, she tended to do the talking unless what was called for was to frighten someone with dire prognostications. In those cases, Dawoud would screw his face up into an ominous scowl and roll his eyes back

"You'll need our help," Adoulla said finally. "Hunting ghuls is not your province, Pharaad Az Hammaz."

Figuring that the pleading and sugar talk was done, Dawoud stepped to the front of the group. The Prince spared him a glance, but spoke to Adoulla. "You speak to me of ghuls, Uncle. But truth be told, such things are no scarier than watching your children die slowly on a dirty pallet from rat bites. No more frightening than having to smother your old Da-Da in his sleep to end the pain of a disease that could be cured, if only you had the coin. No worse than having your hand chopped off for filching a loaf of bread because the hunger was making you stark raving mad."

"Your theatrics are not—" Dawoud began.

"Not theatrics!" the big man boomed. "The truth! Life in Dhamsawaat! I could take you to meet the boy right now! Ten years old and he has one hand. The wound would have killed him, had my people not treated it. The stinking watchmen didn't even let him keep the heel of bread!"

A vicious gleam lit the man's ebonwood eyes. "It took some work to find the names of the watchmen that did it, but find them, we did."

Dawoud shuddered at the bandit's smile.

"*These* villains," the Falcon Prince continued, "*these*

monsters are before you every day. But unless it hisses and has fangs made of vermin, it is not worth fighting, eh? Pain-magic, death-magic—these cull power from torture and fear, yes? Starvation. Beatings. Making men live in little boxes. How is the Khalif different? Because he takes his time in sacrificing lives for his power? Because the workers' boxes by the tannery are a little bit bigger?"

Adoulla made an annoyed noise. "Don't pretend to be as thick-headed as that son-of-a-whore Khalif who you claim is a fool! The same servant of the Traitorous Angel that murdered your people is seeking that which you seek. He may be here already. And only my friends and I can stop him."

"Well, you know of things I don't, Uncle. Very well, do a little dance. But your spies—whoever they may be, and we shall have to discuss *that* one day—have not told you everything. The power of the Cobra Throne is terrible. But there is another way here. Just as the blood of a throne-coronated man's heir can grant great but cruel powers, the same heir can, of his own power, pass on the mastery of the throne's *kind* magics willingly. And those magics are just as great. The power to heal hundreds of lepers in a heartbeat's time. To feed a thousand men with bread and fishes. Some sources say the throne can even raise the dead. The Heir need only sit upon the throne, clasp another man's hand, and say that he wishes to pass on the throne's powers. Now imagine what a man with this power in his hands, and an honorable and wise group of ministers at his side, might do for our city. He could—"

Dawoud could not listen to any more of this. "Even if what you say is true, this is madness. No doubt you have agents within the palace ready to act on your command. But while the guardsmen are fighting with your men, Orshado and his creature will make their move—and all quarrels between men will become meaningless."

Adoulla ran a hand over his beard and stared at the bandit. He was actually weighing the Falcon Prince's traitorous plot!

"Adoulla—" Dawoud started to say, but his old friend cut him off with an upraised hand.

"Dawoud Son-of-Wajeed is right," Adoulla said. "This is the life of the world you play with here, Pharaad Az Hammaz. When I helped you dodge the watch the other day, you said you owed me. Now I ask—"

The big bandit let out a booming laugh. "Uncle, do you truly believe that I needed you to save me? I could have fled from those men were I asleep and one-legged! I saw you in that alley, knowing who you were, and decided to take a moment to test which way the wind blew with you."

"The wind blows out of my ass, man! But unlike you I am not deluded enough to call it perfume. This plan of yours *is* mad, and you are risking this city you claim to love for it. I ask you to call it off."

"I owe you a debt for your intentions if not your assistance, Uncle. But I'm not so foolish as to repay a dirham with a dinar! Besides, as your assistant will attest, I have repaid that debt already—or has this paragon of honesty withheld that fact from you?" He made a tsk-tsk-ing sound at the dervish, though Dawoud had no idea what the man was alluding to. "Well, 'pride can pickle even an honest man's tongue,' so no matter. But even if what *you* say is true, Uncle—and one-half my heart thinks it so—there's no damned-by-God way you'd be able to get into the throne room without my aid."

"So it would seem that we have need of one another," Dawoud heard his friend say. He opened his own mouth again to object but found that he had no better course of action to offer.

Adoulla turned to him, his bushy gray brows drawn down with his frown. "It is either this or we allow these men to bind or kill us. Need I remind you the price if we fail?"

"So we go to rescue the Khalif, only to help his greatest enemy," Raseed interjected, finally breaking his silence.

Adoulla waved away the boy's words. "I was never here to save the Khalif, boy. He can choke on bones for all I care! I am here to save my city and the world it sits in."

"Well, then." The Prince clapped his hands together and smiled pleasantly at Adoulla, as if they had agreed on a tea date. "It shall be so: you and yours may join us—for if this Orshado proves to be real, your powers may indeed be useful. But I warn you now that if you cross me, I will kill you all."

The steel in Raseed's gaze could cut a man. "And if you try to harm these people, thief, I will kill *you*."

Around them Dawoud heard the clatter and grumble of the Prince's men making their displeasure known. But the Falcon Prince himself seemed more offended than afraid.

"No one has harmed anyone yet, young man," the Prince said. "We are merely conversing. But threatening to kill me just might be enough to bring *you* to harm, if you are not more careful."

The dervish cast a long look at the armed men surrounding them. "I would duel you, then," he said at last to the Prince, "in single combat before God the Judge of All Things, for the fates of—"

"*Duel* me?" the Prince broke in. "You can't be serious? What fireside tale did you crawl out of, boy?"

*This from a man who calls himself the "Falcon Prince!"* Dawoud thought.

"You refuse?" the boy fumed. "But a duel is the right of all–"

Thankfully, Adoulla calmed his protégé, rolling his eyes behind the boy's back. He stepped between the two swordsmen and addressed the Falcon Prince. "Forgive him, Pharaad Az Hammaz, for he is young."

"'A genius of the sword, but an idiot of the street,' eh, Uncle? I'd sensed as much."

Adoulla barked a laugh, only belatedly seeming to realize that he was joining a stranger in insulting a friend. The ghul hunter lowered his head and then stepped toward Raseed, placing a hand on the boy's shoulder and mumbling something apologetic.

"I am impressed by your eyes as you watch over these dangerous young ones, Uncle," the Prince said. "As though they were your children, even though you bring them into battle. I understand it. Indeed all of these men you see with me are like my sons!" Dawoud was tired of the man's big mouth, but his gravity as he spoke seemed sincere, if practiced.

A pock-marked man old enough to be the bandit's father said dryly, "Well, Da-Da, if you ain't gonna take Headknocker's advice and kill these people, what's the plan?"

"We have new allies to aid us, Ramzi, but our plans are unchanged. Speaking of which, I hear—though no doubt none of you can—our man calling me with a silent signal. I must go speak to him. Watch over our new friends with love, now, eh?"

Moving faster than a man ought to be able to move, the Prince disappeared through the room's far exit. As soon as he did, the old tough called Ramzi stepped up to Dawoud and Adoulla and whispered menacingly, "You'd best learn to watch how you speak to our Prince!"

"Or *what*?" Dawoud gave the man his best *just try it* scowl. "You'll kill an old man for speaking his mind?" He was tired of being ordered about by thugs. If Dhamsawaat was trapped between men like the Khalif and men like this, perhaps Litaz was right. Perhaps, if they lived through this, they should leave this damned-by-God city.

The man gave him a long, hard look, but then his expression softened. "Let me tell you a story, outlander. Five years ago. I'm a one-copper-fals-from-starving rockbreaker. Never gave a God's peace for Khalifs and Princes and all that. One night I come home from the teahouse to find my youngest girl Shahnta dying of the three-day greenfever. No medicine for it but the tonics made by the Khalif's physicians, and you know how that goes. I pass two days and nights with my thoughts in the Lake of Flame, working to feed my half-starved unsick child when I should be home helpin' the wife tend to the dyin' one.

"Then there's a rap at our door, and the Prince is there with a handful of silver—not copper, mind you, *silver*, and one of the palace physicians! And the Khalif's man is stumbling over himself to take care of our girl! I'll never forget the look on that man's face. He wanted to help us so badly. Almost—" here Ramzi smiled wickedly "— almost as if his life depended on it. He wouldn't have bothered to brush flies from Shahnta's dead face before the Prince spoke to him, though. Now my clan is the Prince's clan."

Dawoud realized the man was a villager originally, by his accent. Villagers took such ties more seriously than city folk.

The Prince reemerged from the tunnel and headed back over to them. Dawoud cleared his throat loudly. "Kidnapping men and forcing them to do your work at swordpoint. Wringing one man's gain from another's terror. And what if one of the palace boys had died while this physician was away? He would have deserved it for being the child of a rich man? You are truly a hero, O Falcon Prince!"

Ramzi put his hand on his heavy club. "I told you to watch your tone, outlander!"

The Prince flashed the man a disappointed look.

"No, Ramzi. I thank you for your loyalty, but this is not our way. We are not fighting for the strongest or for he with the most armed men on his side. We are fighting for the man with right reason on his side. I have never asked that you follow me because of who I am, but because of what I stand for."

"Aye, sire, you've told me. Principles. I'm a man of principles, myself. But him . . ." The man flashed a threatening smile and pointed to his club. "He's an old-fashioned son-of-a-whore. *He* only cares about his clan."

The Prince smiled and clapped the man on the back. "You're a hopeless one, Ramzi. In any case, stand ready—you too, Headknocker—our people say it's nearly time for us to move."

Beside Dawoud, Litaz sniffed. "Headknocker! Camelback! Such names you Quarter boys give yourselves!"

Dawoud squeezed her arm. *This is not the time for your Niece-of-a-Pasha snoot, my love!* he said with his eyes. But she ignored him.

"Really! Are these the names your mothers gave you?" She clucked her tongue.

The thugs took it in stride. Headknocker bowed half-jestingly. "If you really want to know, Auntie, my mother named me Fayyaz."

"What do you know? Your mother named *me* 'The Bedchamber Stallion!'," one of Headknocker's fellows broke in, snorting a laugh.

In spite of her snoot Litaz laughed, too. *"O believer! When you meet a man on the road, know that God, who makes broken things whole, has cobbled your kindest fates together,*" she recited, turning to the Prince. "I needed that laugh. May it please God to make us friends rather than enemies, Pharaad Az Hammaz."

*She's still a spoiled Blue River girl at heart,* Dawoud thought. *Charmed by cold-blooded killers whom she thinks are loveable rogues.* Not for the first time in his life, Dawoud felt a burning hatred of men with able bodies and too-quick smiles.

The Falcon Prince inclined his head in agreement with Litaz. "May it indeed be so, Auntie, but I will not bother to ask it of God, who has left man to fight and scramble over bits of food and land. Who lets flesh-burning diseases kill children!"

Raseed snarled, and it was as bestial as any growl from the tribeswoman.

"Be as angry as you like, dervish," the Prince said. "God hasn't given three shits for His children in six thousand years! Do you really believe that He sits in the sky, smiling upon us? Look around you! Look at this mad, bloody, muddy world of ours. He made the world, He made us, and then he left us to fend for ourselves. And so far, my friends, we've made it a pile of monkeyshit." The bandit's eyes lit again. "But even shit has its uses. Fertilizer. Fuel. Oh, yes. But to serve these purposes it must be ground to bits. Or burned."

"Madman! Blasphemer!" Raseed took a long, threatening stride toward Az.

The bandit held up a hand to restrain his men and leveled a steely gaze at the dervish. "Watch yourself, young man. This is the real world, not a dueling circle. As you know, I fight dirty."

The dervish's hand darted to his swordhilt before he seemed to recall that he had no weapon.

Then Litaz jumped between them. *My wife, the peacemaker, Dawoud thought.* She drew herself up to her full height, which made her nearly as tall as Raseed but still left the top of her head well below the Prince's shoulders.

"Are you two mad? Are you thoroughly mad? There are God alone knows how many lives at stake right now and you buffoons are thumping your chests at each other? We don't have time for this! Idiots!"

*Well, maybe not "peacemaker," exactly.*

The Prince smiled. "You remind me of my mother, Auntie. And my mother was not a kind woman. But I will stand down if your yapping little holy man will."

"I will not allow blasphemy to pass unanswered," the dervish said coldly.

Litaz wagged a finger in Raseed's face, though her voice softened. "Answer me this, dear: Is this *truly* what you think God would have of us? Fighting one another over careless words while the world is carved into bloody pieces by the Traitorous Angel? We have precious little time. Are you serving the All-Merciful by wasting it here, shouting about how devout you are?"

Suddenly there was a series of frantic footfalls from the far tunnel. A man in the Falcon livery came trotting out, and the Prince went to confer with him. Then the master thief spoke to all assembled in the cave chamber. "The Soo woman is right, my friends—time is precious, and all is finally in readiness! Our time is at hand! We could have started a second civil war in this

city years ago. But the Falcon knows when to strike and
when not to. Have we screeched at the people about
the injustice they face? No! We have stabbed fat jewelers in their asses and stolen their rubies for the poor!
And now we stab the fattest jeweler of them all and
toss the world's greatest ruby to the crowd! Many of
our friends have paid great costs to make this day possible. Will we let their sacrifices be wasted?"

"NO!" the master thief's men shouted in unison.

"Our timing must be exact!" the Prince boomed.
"We've but one chance to suddenly appear in the midst
of the palace, weapons whirling, bold plans flying into
glorious motion as—" The man was lost in his own sto-
rytelling, and the rest of his words were lost as he led
the way out the far tunnel.

When they'd marched for a few minutes through
another twisting tunnel, the Prince trotted back again
to Dawoud and his friends. He spoke in low tones
quite unlike his bombastic bluster of moments before.

"I can see the words 'Where are we?' etched on your
faces," he said. "I'll tell you. We are in an underground
passage to the palace. There are several such tunnels,
some even the Khalifs never learned of. Older than the
Khalifate itself, dating back to the days of the Kemeti
Underground City. Known only to one who's spent
half a lifetime learning this lore. One tunnel in particular leads directly to the ruined Kem temple that the
heart of the Palace was built upon. Unfortunately, the
tunnel follows a rather circuitous route, snaking back
and forth until ten minutes' walk becomes an hour's.
Sound carries in here, so from here forward silence is

required of us. And I don't like to threaten newfound friends, but I must warn you that silence will be *enforced* if necessary. Oh, and I'd nearly forgotten—you may have your weapons back." The master thief gestured to one of his men, who handed back Raseed's sword and Litaz's dagger, then he scampered back to the front of the line.

They walked for an hour, back and forth, upslope and downslope, through tunnels and rooms of pale stone and packed earth. As they walked, Dawoud's feet ached and a thousand grim thoughts filled his head. But not a word escaped his lips.

# Chapter 18

NEARLY AN HOUR after Adoulla and his friends were hushed by the Falcon Prince, the tunnel sloped sharply upward, steep enough that Adoulla found himself breathing heavily. The tunnel then opened into a massive . . . cave? Room? Whether the space itself was made by man or nature, the great stone-walled expanse about him was dank, a series of huge pools intersected by thin walkways and tall columns of shaped stone. Water gurgled all around him, and he had to keep himself from cursing aloud from the shock of what he was looking at. *A cistern! Older than the Crescent Moon Palace and sitting smack dab beneath it! How long has it been since men walked down here?*

He felt as if the city he knew were transforming beneath his feet. His head spun such that it took him a moment to process the fact that there were already men there when the party entered the cistern—it was their low, clean-burning torchlight he saw by.

Two muscular young men stood in the center of the great space, making adjustments to a long ladder-like contraption of poles and ropes. This ladder climbed to the ceiling, where it was almost lost to his old eyes. But as he stared up into the darkness, he made out a small hole in the ceiling which the ladder was somehow lashed to.

*A well*, Adoulla realized, *a well that opens up within the palace.* The city *was* shifting beneath his feet! The simple existence of that little hole of stone was astonishing— would the ages-ago civil war have gone differently, had the Holy Usurper's forces known of this chink in the Khalifs' armor? How might the last—?

His thoughts were interrupted as the Prince turned to them and raised a finger to his lips, again demanding silence. The Prince strode forward and, using a series of hand signals Adoulla could not begin to follow in the half-dark, consulted with the two men at the ladder. A moment later, the bandit gestured for the group to gather around the ladder. A few of his men were already climbing it.

The Prince gestured for Adoulla and his friends to climb. Adoulla heard Dawoud curse softly beside him. But as the magus climbed, he seemed to have an easier time than he'd expected. As Adoulla began to climb he could feel why—there was something ingenious about the ladder's construction that made moving up it less arduous than it ought to have been. As the well-hole above him slowly drew closer, Adoulla sensed more than heard another group of the Prince's men enter the cistern below him and head for the ladder. *Of course.*

The Prince had had some special climbing-device rigged here because he intended for a good number of armed men to quickly make their way up it and into the palace.

Adoulla's palms burned a bit from gripping rope, and he was sweating beneath his kaftan. A few feet above him he heard Dawoud breathing hard. Ingenious device or no, he was thankful when they finally reached the top, climbed out of the well-hole . . .

And emerged right in the midst of a knot of tense-looking guardsmen brandishing weapons. Adoulla nearly dropped back down the rope-and-pole ladder in fear. Then he saw that these men were exchanging hand signals with those of the Prince's men who had climbed up before him. *More infiltrators*. He didn't know if he was pleased or disturbed by how pervasive the Prince's influence seemed to be within the palace.

The room they'd reached was two dozen feet on a side and made of gray stone. It smelled of the well water below. The Prince gestured Adoulla and his friends over to a small, arched doorway in the far wall. Dervish and magus, alkhemist and Badawi gathered around the Prince, as did a half-dozen of his men. Glancing behind them, Adoulla saw that the room was already filling with armed men, a steady stream of whom were quietly making their way out of the well.

The Prince led them through the doorway into a huge kitchen filled with low stone ovens. Two other doorways led from the kitchen to other rooms, and each of these was flanked by two guardsmen. Their lack of alarm at the Prince's entrance meant that they, too, were his agents. The smell of baking bread filled the room, but beneath it was another scent that Adoulla knew—blood.

In the center of the kitchen stood a massive dark brown woman, as big as Adoulla, wearing a cook's apron and holding a big, bloody cleaver. A dead guardsman lay slumped at her feet, his head opened by a nasty gash. The Prince dashed to the woman and exchanged a few quick hand signals. Then, with that more-than-human speed, he ran in a circle about the kitchen, sprinkling some sort of powder on the ground until it surrounded the whole room. He produced a flintbox, and lit the powder, which didn't burn with a visible flame, but surrounded them with a low blue glow. *Alkhemy*, Adoulla knew, but he knew little more than that. He looked a question at Litaz, but she only shrugged. It was a rare compound indeed that could baffle her. For what felt like the hundredth time that day, he was impressed by the Prince's resources.

"Well!" Pharaad Az Hammaz boomed, breaking the silence. "We can speak now, and the powder of the panthers will keep our words from being heard outside this room. My friends, meet Mother Midnight, Queen of the Khalif's Kitchens. For years now, she and the minister you met earlier have been helping me arrange this little festival of ours. If we survive this day, we will owe it all to her." The Prince turned to the big woman. "I presume, from the lack of shouts and bell-ringing, that we remain undetected?"

"Aye, Pharaad," Mother Midnight said, her voice sounding like a rockslide. "The few fools who stuck their noses in the wrong place at the wrong time have been dealt with, but we won't be able to keep these bodies hidden forever." She gestured with her crimson-stained cleaver to the dozen great ovens that dominated the room. Here and there, sticking out of the ovens, Adoulla saw a man's hand or booted foot.

He felt sick. *The dice have fallen from the cup, then. We are a part of this mad usurpation whether or not we wish to be.*

Beside him, Raseed and Zamia started to speak outraged words, but he turned to them with his hardest glare. "Orshado. Mouw Awa," he whispered harshly. "There is no other way to stop them now. That matters more than anything." Praise God, neither warrior-child said anything more.

"He's two rooms down, Pharaad. In the Velvet Chamber, about to take his private Thirdday Noonmeal. The Defender of Virtue is never truly alone, but this is the closest he gets to it all week. Everything is as you planned—this is the moment we've waited for."

Raseed broke his brief silence. "And do you feel no shame, woman? No shame at all in betraying your Khalif and master in this way?"

The Falcon Prince turned an angry eye on the boy, and Mother Midnight scowled and sucked her teeth. "Ask the Defender of Virtue about my daughter and his . . . appetites, holy man. Ask him about Mother Midnight, who loyally served him and his father before him, and was repaid with the rape and rejection of an only child who killed herself. Then speak to me of shame and betrayal."

To Adoulla's surprise, that shut the boy up. Behind them, more of the Prince's men filed quietly into the kitchen.

The Falcon Prince put a big hand on Mother Midnight's shoulder. "Auntie, I swear by my soul that in half a day's time you'll be able to ask the sack of scum yourself. Though I fear the only answer you'll get will be the sound of his head hitting the executioner's leather mat!"

He turned to Adoulla. "I don't see that there are any monsters here, save the one I've come a-hunting, Uncle. But two rooms from this one lies the man who is strangling our city. I give you and yours one more chance to choose. Follow me into that room and live with the consequences, or go back down that well—under my men's guard, of course—and sit this adventure out, despite your wild warnings of ghuls. Either way, the dervish's words make me wary. I will have your oaths before God that you will not betray me," he said, looking pointedly at Raseed, "or you will go no further with us."

*The heretic who asks for oaths,* Adoulla thought bitterly, and saw his wry expression reflected on his friends' faces as they each said "I swear it before Almighty God." All except Raseed, whose face may as well have been carved from marble for all that it revealed. *He knows, as I do, that this Orshado will show himself, and that it is his holy duty to help me stop such a man.*

*And no doubt another part of him wishes to watch over the tribeswoman.*

The boy said nothing. Adoulla cleared his throat. Mother Midnight, who'd been busy stuffing the guardsman's split-skulled corpse into an oven, tapped her foot and said, "We haven't time for this, Pharaad."

Adoulla gripped the dervish's elbow and squeezed. He saw Raseed's gaze dart once in Zamia's direction before the boy whispered, "I swear it before Almighty God."

Following the master thief, they moved from the kitchen into a room with intricately engraved white walls. The light scent of pleasant perfumes—more subtle than incense and no doubt disbursed by wafting-spells—filled the space. An ebonwood door in the opposite wall was the only dark mark in the room. Before Adoulla could begin to think about what a monumental moment he was partaking in, the Prince and a knot of his men had crossed the room and slit the throats of two guardsmen. The Prince kicked in the big doors with a seemingly impossible strength and flew into the far room. There was nothing Adoulla and his friends could do now but follow.

The Velvet Chamber, Mother Midnight had called it, and it was obvious why, ceiling, walls, floor, and a great canopied couch were dripping with the plush purple material. And in the center of it sat a lean, youngish man dripping with jewelry and resplendent robes, staring in stupefaction at one of his guardsman who had just cracked open the skull of another.

By the time Jabbari akh-Khaddari, God's Regent-in-the-World, found voice enough to scream, the Falcon Prince had already dashed about the room again with that glowing blue powder of his. Clearly, the sound of the screams was reaching no one.

"You . . . you're . . . how did . . . ?" the Khalif stammered without one whit of court-phrasing in his speech. "No intruder could have made it into . . ." He fell silent, clearly at a loss. He looked at Dawoud, and his kohl-lined eyes grew even wider. "You! Where did—?"

"No questions, tyrant!" the Prince shouted, his mad eyes ablaze with crazed purpose. "But *I* have a question for *you*! How does it feel to—"

The Prince's words were cut off as the Khalif touched one of his rings and a flash of light filled the room. Adoulla, sensing danger in that way that had become second nature over the decades, dashed toward the Khalif, and he saw Pharaad Az Hammaz do the same. Something slid into place behind him, and before him, he saw a thick panel of wood slide down from the ceiling, cutting him off from the Khalif. *False walls*, he realized, and they had cut him off from his friends as well.

The Falcon Prince stood beside him, pounding on the panels with the pommel of his sword. "God's balls!" the thief shouted, "These are made of ensorcelled wood. That sneaky son of a whore! Though in truth, I suppose it's no great matter. Dispatching him first would have helped, but he is not my true quarry anyway. In a sense, this makes things easier for us—he is cut off from the Heir."

"Easier for *you* perhaps, you damned-by-God madman!" Adoulla fumed. "My *friends* are on the other side of this thing! I won't leave them." Adoulla pounded on the wooden wall and shouted for his friends, not caring whether he was drawing down the attention of the guardsmen. He knew Dawoud and the others would be doing the same on the other side of the panel. But he heard no shouts, felt no pounding from the other side of the thin wood. *More magic at work.*

Genuine sympathy lit the Prince's eyes, but his tone was practical. "Do as you must, Uncle. But unless I miss my guess, breaking this wall down would be a whole day's work even for a master alkhemist such as the Lady Litaz Daughter-of-Likami."

Some part of Adoulla's mind noted that the Prince knew his friends' reputations as well as he'd known Adoulla's.

"Your most guaranteed gamble," the thief continued, "is to follow me. Without me by your side, you'll have trouble with both the guardsmen and my people, not to mention with finding your way through this monstrous maze of a palace."

The man was right, of course.

In frustration, Adoulla kicked the wooden wall that separated him from his friends, getting a stubbed toe for his trouble. He looked up in time to see Pharaad Az Hammaz tear down a velvet curtain and dart through a stone passageway that was hidden behind it.

The master thief had clearly memorized the layout of the palace, for he strode through confidently, making left and right turns down passageways and through rooms so quickly that Adoulla could not keep up. Adoulla huffed out, "I'll catch up," but the Falcon Prince was wild-eyed with purpose and paid Adoulla little mind anyway.

Adoulla followed through another long hall, dashing past a pack of skirmishing men in livery. The combatants looked up at him in surprise but were too busy trying to kill each other to bother with trying to kill him. He caught a glimpse of the Prince darting through a set of great ornate doors, thrown open. He followed.

He stepped into a huge room lit by perpetually burning magical lamps. In the uncanny glow of the flames he could see, lining the left and right walls, dozens of great cases of gold-lined glass. Each of them held a huge turban. *The Hall of the Heavenly Defenders*! The legendary symbolic resting place of the dead Khalifs, each of which was represented by a resplendent turban. Purple silversilk, peacock feathers, pearls the size of a child's fist. Adoulla forced himself not to gawk and strode on.

Another grand room near as big as a city block. The ceiling was worked with pearl, platinum, and gold. Brilliant tapestries depicting the Ministering Angels hung from the walls. Adoulla huffed his way past columns of rose marble, cunningly carved so that the waves and veins spelled out the Names of God. *These Khalifs really do believe they are God's Regents-in-the-World! Everywhere this palace calls out His Names,* Adoulla thought, *yet His work is nowhere to be found.*

From somewhere in the palace men were now shouting, and a loud bell was clanging an alarm. Much closer by, he heard the clash of weapons. Adoulla rounded a corner just in time to see Pharaad Az Hammaz exchange a brief series of sword strokes with two men who were guarding a small bronze door.

His broad-bladed saber feinted and parried like a masterfully made rapier. It glowed golden as it stabbed at the guardsmen. *Weapon magic.* The kind that cost a fortune. Again Adoulla marveled at the depth of Pharaad Az Hammaz's coin purse. The guards were dead within seconds, and the Prince flung open the door. Adoulla followed him in.

The room was smaller and daintier than most of those he'd seen in the palace, as if in reflection of its occupant: a frail-looking boy of nine years, wearing optical glasses and gemthread robes that must have cost as much as Adoulla's townhouse. He looked up and blinked as they entered.

The boy had the same face-shape as the Khalif. *The Heir.* Little Sammari akh-Jabbari akh-Khaddari sat cross-legged on a cushion in the center of the room, a huge illuminated book open before him. His mild expression was replaced with shock as he seemed to suddenly notice the mad racket filling the palace. Adoulla guessed that there had been a silencing spell cast on the brass door. *So much money and magic wasted on sheltering these fools from unpleasantness.*

"You— You are— You are *him*," the boy stammered with a bit more grace than his father had. "The Falcon Prince!"

"INDEED I AM, O TYRANT-IN-TRAINING!" the Prince boomed, advancing with his sword still drawn on the timid-seeming boy, who was practically bowled over by the sound. "I am the Falcon Prince, and my wrath is terrible! I have come to—"

"You are my hero," the boy said quietly, brushing a strand of long black hair from his face.

"I warn, you, spawn of a—eh?" Pharaad Az Hammaz blinked, his bombast dropping away. It was the first time Adoulla had seen the thief look unsure of himself. "What did you say?"

The boy looked ashamed that he had spoken, but he repeated himself. "I said 'you are my hero.'" The Heir looked at Adoulla, but only seemed to half-see him. An alarm bell clanged again.

It was quite a thing, Adoulla thought, to see the loudmouthed Falcon Prince speechless. It only lasted for a moment, though. The Prince turned and closed the brass door behind them, cutting off the sounds of chaos. With an effortless strength he dragged a heavy ebonwood couch over to bar the door.

"Hero?" The Prince asked at last.

"Yes!" the Heir said, closing his book and growing more excited. *The Thousand Tales of the Pirate Pasha*, Adoulla noted. Probably the most expensive edition of the cheap, tawdry book that had ever been scribed. The Heir stood up. "Yes! A hero like those in the books! Feeding the poor. Vanquishing villains with a sword and a smile. My advisors say there are no such men, but I know better. Almighty God willing, someday I will do the same!"

Adoulla thought that, if the Prince had been a pious man, he would have dropped to his knees right there and thanked Beneficent God for this bit of kind fate.

As it was, the master thief smiled from ear to ear and clapped a big hand on the boy's shoulder. "Well! It would appear my spies don't know everything about what goes on in the palace after all. *You* are certainly a better fruit than the rotten tree you fell from, boy. Not nearly the insufferable, power mad little shit I expected you to be."

The Heir smiled the smile of a child that had never been allowed to be naughty. "You don't call me Young Defender! I like that. Do you know that even my play-mates called me that when I was a little child?"

"When you *were* a little child?" Adoulla sputtered. "You *are* "

The Prince cut him off. "Well, *you* don't call *me* Pretender or Madman. We shall get on splendidly, boy!"

The Heir's glowing smile slipped. "But, uh, what is going on here, O Prince? Do you mean to kill me? Have you killed my father already?" To his credit, the boy did not sound frightened.

Pharaad Az Hammaz gave the boy a long look. "I will not lie to you, child. I am here to seize the Throne of the Crescent Moon. It holds grand magics locked within its marble, magics with which I can help the good people of Dhamsawaat. And I mean to seize the palace, too. There are sick people who need the medicines kept here. Starving people that might feast on the palace granaries."

The boy smiled sadly. "When I speak of such things

to my tutors they say it is the will of Almighty God that some have and some have not. And that I should not admire you because you are not a prince at all, but a murderer and a bringer-of-terror."

Pharaad Az Hammaz took a deep breath, and then his voice took on a booming tenor again. "*I* am a murderer? And what of your father, who dares call himself 'Defender,' but has others do the fighting and bleeding and killing and dying for him? Beggars and street-widows starve to death while your father's grain-houses are bursting, but that is the 'will of God,' eh? Cartmen and porters waste away from fevers that your father's physicians could cure! But *I* am the violent one! The bringer of terror! I have felt both hunger and the sword, my young friend! I would rather die of the sword. It is kinder. Faster. I've killed men, yes, but with my own hands, looking them in the eye. Your father, though, is the weak and lazy sort of killer. The kind who pretends he is not a killer. Is that what *you* wish to become?"

"No," the boy said, strong and clear as one of the alarm-bells that was still ringing away outside the room. "But what of my father, O Prince? What of me?"

"Your father has the blood of many men and women on his hands, Sammari akh-Jabbari akh-Khaddari. But if you aid me in this, I will let you and him go peacefully into exile, perhaps to—"

"No," the boy interrupted with an air of easy command that belied his bookish appearance. "If you want my help with this, O Prince, you must kill my father. I have sworn an oath before God that I would see him dead."

Adoulla watched the Prince gape at the boy and didn't doubt that he was gaping also.

"I . . . but. . . . Why . . . ?" Pharaad Az Hammaz stammered.

"You are wrong about my father's laziness in killing, O Prince. Perhaps you have heard that my mother, God shelter her soul, died from a fever. She did not. I watched my father strangle her because he thought he had seen her make sugar-eyes at one of his aides. When I tried to stop him, he beat me. He said I would understand when I grew older. This was five years ago, before he became the Khalif. All I have come to understand in that time is that it is my sacred duty to see him slain."

Behind them, the couch blocking the door creaked and began to split as someone tried to force their way in. The familiar bloodlust lit Pharaad Az Hammaz's eyes. His saber was at the ready.

*This boy's storybook notions will fly out the window if he sees the Prince slaughter his protectors before his eyes.* Adoulla put up a hand to the Prince. "Please. There is another way here—if, Young Defender, you will follow my lead." The Prince considered him and seemed to understand. The Heir said nothing.

The door behind them burst open in a shower of ebonwood splinters, and three armed guardsmen flew into the room.

"Young Defender!" the foremost of them shouted,

his body starting to bow before his mind recalled the circumstances. "Who are these men? Is that . . . ? Almighty God, stand back, Young Defender! We'll save you from this thug!"

Adoulla stepped forward. "Are you men mad? If this were truly Pharaad Az Hammaz, do you think the Young Defender would still be alive? Would we be here chatting? We are agents of the Defender of Virtue, assigned to protect the Young Defender in a time like this, and disguised to sow confusion in the Defender's enemies!"

The man looked skeptical, but he and his men did not advance. "Who are you, old man? What is your name? Why have I never—?"

The Heir's voice took on a powerful tone of command. "You have never seen these men because you are a mere guardsman and not privy to the Defender of Virtue's plans! Our father has assigned these two to protect me until the *real* thief has been found and killed! Half of your order has betrayed Us—indeed these two men tried to slay Us," the Heir said, gesturing to the corpses of the two door-guards the Prince had dispatched. "Go, now, and do your duty to Us! Now!" *Perhaps he is not so soft after all.*

"I . . . but. . . ." The guardsman said nothing more but waved his men on and trotted off in search of other enemies.

When they were gone, the Heir looked down at the corpses and let his sadness show. "Ayyabi was a good man," he said simply.

"Listen, child, we must—" Adoulla began, but he

may as well not have been there for all the attention the boy paid him.

"Good man or not, my friend, he was your gaol-keeper," said the Prince. "I know the life you live here. Under your father's stifling wraps for nine years now, unable to befriend whom you wish. Unable to leave the palace without two days' preparation. Forced to study things that couldn't matter less to you. Do I call it true or not, boy? Think of the kind and carefree fates that could be yours if you were not entombed in the Crescent Moon Palace."

The man was a master lutist, playing on the heart-strings of a child. The idea-seed of the freedom that would come with giving up the throne had been planted in the boy's head, and its fruit was already blossoming in the boy's eyes. A thousand possibilities that he had thought impossibilities were arrayed before him. Adoulla could see it in the boy's smile. Pharaad Az Hammaz didn't lie. He simply laid out the truth, in brash and dramatic ways. Adoulla supposed it was what people wanted to hear.

Perhaps he himself had been taken in a bit by it.

"And how could I escape this, O Prince?" the Heir asked, still staring at the corpses.

"Follow me to the throne room, boy, and I will show you." As the three of them walked, Pharaad Az Hammaz explained about the simple ritual that would allow the Heir to pass mastery of the throne's beneficent magics and rulership on to the thief. He said nothing of the death-magics the throne held, or of the blood-magic version of the spell.

"But what about recognition from the other realms?" the boy asked. "Rughal-ba? The Soo Republic?"

The Prince shrugged his large shoulders. "Let me worry about that. I have diplomats and clerks-of-law working for me as well as thieves and sell-swords." He winked at the boy incongruously. "Believe me, the clerks-of-law are scarier than the thieves! So. What say you, Sammari?"

"I'll give you the throne, O Prince. If you swear before God that you will use its power as a hero ought, and if you will kill the Defender of Virtue for what he did to my mother."

"I swear it before Almighty God, who witnesses all oaths." Pharaad Az Hammaz took the Heir's small hand in his huge one. Adoulla followed as the thief guided the boy through a series of opulent rooms that Adoulla had no time to stop and gawk at. Twice they dashed past men fighting, but the Prince kept the Heir moving.

And then they entered the throne room.

It was empty of men, as big as any of the rooms Adoulla had yet seen, and as rich in decoration. Carved wood that glowed with alkhemists' magic, puzzlecloth carpets woven from gold, perfumes and incenses wafting through the air in a dozen lovely scents. There were few pieces of furniture, however, save for the throne at the center of the room.

The Throne of the Crescent Moon sat atop a small dais. It was a cold, glowing white, as spotless as Adoulla's kaftan. The back of the throne was a ten-foot-tall slab of strange pearlescent stone, carved into a vague, delicate shape that might have been a crescent moon—or a hooded cobra.

Pharaad Az Hammaz let out a low whistle. "At last," he whispered.

They approached the throne. They'd almost reached it when a knot of men stormed into the room from the opposite archway. The Khalif, his sumptuous silk robes disheveled, was accompanied by a half-dozen armed guardsmen and a black-robed man who could only be a court magus.

For an instant they all stared at each other across the huge room.

"Kill them!" the Khalif shouted. "They have abducted your Young Defender! Kill them!"

Pharaad Az Hammaz's saber was out of its scabbard and glowing golden, but the Heir jumped in front of him. "They have *not* abducted me, Defender of Virtue! The good Prince has shown me the magic of the throne—a way to grant him dominion over the palace. And vengeance for my mother!"

The guardsmen halted, unsure what to do.

"Good Prince?" the Khalif sputtered. "Your head has been turned by idiot tales of noble robbers!" He turned to his magus. "What is he talking about? Magic of the throne?"

The cowled man shook his head. "Defender of Virtue, I do not—" Words died on the man's lips as a jackal-shaped shadow shot at him from the doorway behind.

Everyone in the room froze, hearing the hideous sounds of Mouw Awa savaging the magus. Before a single word of magic could pass the man's lips, he had been reduced to a crimson-eyed corpse. In the stunned silence that followed, soft footsteps drew all eyes to the archway.

*Orshado.* He was tall but reed thin, and his flesh was jaundiced. A patchy black beard covered his face, and his kaftan was the same cut and color as Adoulla's, but soiled with waste and blood. In his hands he held a red silk sack.

Adoulla suddenly recalled his nightmare from a week ago, before all of this horror had happened. The rivers of blood. His own kaftan stained with gore. It was said of the ghul of ghuls that his kaftan could never come clean. This, then, was the man that God had whispered of in the strange language of dreams. The foul man Adoulla was hunting. The man who had killed Miri's niece and slaughtered the Banu Laith Badawi. Who had murdered Yehyeh and burned down Adoulla's house and all of the precious memories it held.

Adoulla heard the manjackal's voice in his head as he had on that night. *The fat one doth preen in his unstained raiment. He hath tasted only the first of this burning world's ashes. He knoweth not the sweet fires of the Lake of Flame, which shall soon wash over all of this.* As Mouw Awa's voice echoed in Adoulla's head, Orshado waved a bony arm in a dismissive arc that somehow took in palace, city, and God's great earth all at once.

Mouw Awa leapt upon the Khalif, its shadowy jaws snapping. As Adoulla heard the Defender of Virtue's whimpering turn to screams, he was reminded that the murderous tyrant of his city was, after all, only a man. All of the Khalif's pomp and power, and all of Adoulla's grand hatred of him, were ripped away in an instant. Jabbari akh-Khaddari screamed again and was silent.

Adoulla was paralyzed with shock and fear, and he saw that even Pharaad Az Hammaz was, too.

Orshado withdrew a human head from the sack he held. In an unearthly voice, the head jabbered, "ALL OF THOSE BENEATH SHALL SERVE. ALL OF THOSE BENEATH SHALL SERVE."

All around Adoulla, the guardsmen's eyes rolled back, their skin shriveled, and their mouths echoed these words. As one they turned on Adoulla, the Prince, and the Heir.

In that instant, Adoulla knew, they had become something more and less than men.

*Skin ghuls.* Monsters made by twisting a living man's soul inside out. Even amidst all of the shocks he had seen in the past week, this was a shock to Adoulla. He had only ever read about them—had thought the foul art of their raising was thankfully lost to the world. Neither spell nor sword could destroy a skin ghul. The old books said that tainted flesh would rejoin tainted flesh and corrupt bones would reknit with corrupt bones until the death of the skin ghuls' maker drove the malign false life from their stolen bodies.

Mouw Awa crouched over the dead, red-eyed Khalif, blood and something half-tangible dripping from its jaws. Behind Adoulla, the Heir was whimpering.

The skin ghuls began to shamble toward Adoulla. Beside him, the Heir and the Falcon Prince still stood frozen with fear.

*So this is how it ends.* His befuddled old mind fumbled for thoughts. Tea and poetry. His friends and his city.

Miri, whom he wished to Almighty God he had wed.

*No. No, it* cannot *end here. I will not* let *it.*

Skin ghuls could not be slain, but they could be hindered. He could buy the Prince time to take the throne, or kill Orshado, or get the Heir to safety, or . . . something.

He dashed forward. His satchel had held little when he'd saved it from his burning townhouse. But it held what he needed now. He withdrew a small tortoise shell and shook it above his head, the three sapphires sealed inside making a rattling sound.

"Beneficent God is the Last Breath in our Lungs!" he shouted. It was an old invocation, one that would raise a wall that no ghul could cross. But it would do little against the even older magics of the Dead Gods. He would be at the jackal-thing's mercy.

A sheet of iridescent light rose up before him just as the ghuls neared him. Their blows did not touch him, though with each of their strikes the wall-of-light shimmered. Behind him, he heard the Prince finally snap out of his fear trance and trot forward.

Again Adoulla heard Mouw Awa's words in his mind. *The flippant one hath told thee soothing stories of medicant magics? Ha! His quest is doomed! The Cobra God doth not love life and kindness!*

Then the creature was upon him, and Adoulla felt his soul being slowly torn from his body.

# Chapter 19

ALL WAS CHAOS. Everywhere Litaz heard the thunder of boots and the clanging of weapons. Horns and bells blasted alarms, and from somewhere, the cry of "To arms, to arms!" rang out. Guardsmen hacked at one another with swords as those loyal to the Prince revealed themselves. Many gurgled from slit throats and died before they even realized what their turncoat fellows were doing.

Adoulla, Pharaad Az Hammaz, and the Khalif had been separated from them by extraordinary false walls that no amount of bashing could break. The walls had even blocked her scrying solutions. They were wandering rooms at random now, looking for their friend, but that was their only choice.

"We've got to find Adoulla!" she shouted to her husband as they followed Raseed down a hallway, blessedly empty.

Dawoud gave only a curt nod in response. His teeth

were gritted in that way that told her he was holding some unbearable energy at bay within himself, a spell that would rot him from within until he released it upon some unfortunate enemy.

They dashed into a roofless room of blue marble. The sun stood high in the sky above them, a great golden ball of light. Raseed led the way, his sword out and his blue silks blending with the walls in a way that made him nearly invisible.

They were in the middle of the blue room when two groups of a dozen men—half wearing the falcon livery and half apparently loyal guardsmen—charged in from opposite doorways. They shouted, brandished weapons, and flew at one another.

And Litaz and her companions stood between them.

She lifted her spraying dagger, letting her thumb float over the several buttons concealed in its handle. Raseed took a step toward the tribeswoman and assumed a defensive stance.

Then there was a strange shift in the energy of the air, a dazzling golden light, and both groups of men stopped charging. A loud growl rent the air beside her.

And suddenly Zamia Banu Laith Badawi stood beside her in the lion shape, her golden coat glowing. A more-than-animal fury lit those emerald eyes, and her tail switched in the air. And the girl had been so worried that she'd be unable to take the shape!

The Prince's men whispered sharply among themselves, then the whole knot of them turned about and ran. Half of the Khalif's men did the same, but six idiots with spears and swords stepped forward.

The lioness—Zamia—slashed at two of them with lightning quick claws, and they fell bleeding. A spearman tried to stab her but found that his weapon couldn't pierce that golden hide. Zamia crushed the man's arms in her fanged maw and whipped him away like a doll.

His companions fled just as Raseed reached them, ready to offer the lioness aid she didn't need.

"I Praise Almighty God and give thanks to his Ministering Angels!" Zamia said when their group was alone again. Litaz didn't know if she'd ever heard more sincere thanks. "All of your distillations and diagrams will not find the Doctor, Auntie. But I have scented the Doctor already. He's this way."

Despite her training and experience, Litaz found it a bit disconcerting to watch a lion face speak these words and lope off. *And where have her clothes gone?* the scholar in her wondered. But there was little to do but follow the lion-girl, who took the lead, following some scent that no human could find and padding swiftly past Raseed. The dervish's gaze followed Zamia for a long moment before he, too, followed. *The holy man who loved a lioness—it would make a good shadow-puppet show if—*

A man lunged at her from a wall-niche.

One of the Khalif's loyalists, but he'd apparently lost his weapon. Clearly, he saw her as an easy target. Before she could get her dagger up, the man punched her in the face. Stars of red light and burning tears filled her eyes, and blood flowed from her nose. She was a woman. God had not made her body for this.

But she had been making herself do this for years. She backed up a few steps and caught the man in the face with a spray of burning pepper-powder. He rubbed at his eyes, screaming. It was an easy enough thing to stab him in the gut after that.

Beside her, Raseed used his forked blade to wrest another guardsman's sword away. The dervish's sword slashed again and cut the man down. A third guardsman screamed and ran, ablaze in magical flames conjured by her husband. Then they were once again alone. Three lay at Raseed's feet, Khalif's men and Falcon Prince's alike. The dervish would kill anyone armed and foolish enough to look threatening, she knew. And she was ashamed to be pleased by it. Around a corner up ahead she heard Zamia growl at them to hurry.

They came to another open room—a vast courtyard lush with small steaming pools and potted plants and trees that would have been more at home in the jungles of the Republic. There was mighty water magic at work here, of that there could be no doubt. And the place was alive with animal sounds.

"The Green of Beasts," her husband's wheezing voice declared. "The Khalif's private garden menagerie—I've heard tell of this place."

"SQUAAWK! Even the Angels sing the praises of the Defender of Virtue! SQUAAWK!" A gray and green talking-bird, its voice magically altered into the most human Litaz had ever heard, flew to a higher tree branch in alarm as yet more men burst through the foliage, overturning palms and pink poisonflower bushes.

A squat, square-shaped man in an embellished livery stood amidst six well-armed guardsmen. "Dawoud Son-of-Wajeed!" the man yelled, brandishing his steel mace, which was already black with blood. Roun Hedaad. It had been years since she had helped save his life, but his was not a face to forget.

The compact man's furrowed brow made the deep grooves in his face seem even deeper. "And I see Lady Litaz, Daughter-of-Likami. So you two are with this lot of traitors? I owe you both my life, but it would seem you have arranged things so that I must kill you and pay for my ungratefulness in the Lake of Flame—for I cannot allow you to pass here."

Two monkeys scrambled past, chattering angrily. Dawoud stepped past the dervish and the tribeswoman, showing his empty hands and eyeing the guardsmen's crossbows warily. He spoke in a strained voice, an indication that he was still holding magical energies at readiness within him.

"Captain Hedaad, we are no traitors. We are here in the hopes that—"

Dawoud's explanation was drowned out by the sudden moaning of a half-dozen mouths. All around Roun Hedaad, his men shuddered strangely, their skins shriveling up and their eyes simultaneously rolling back until only whites showed.

In unison, each of those now-monstrous mouths chanted "ALL OF THOSE BENEATH SHALL SERVE. ALL OF THOSE BENEATH SHALL SERVE," as if reciting after some unseen tutor. Then, as one, they turned on their captain.

These were not mere turncoats, and this was not Pharaad Az Hammaz's doing. That much she knew at once. There was something in the air here that was unmistakably related to the tainted blood she'd touched in her workshop days before. But beyond that she knew not what she was watching now.

"Skin ghuls," her husband whispered in awe.

*Skin ghuls. But they are just a legend.* If she was not quite so old as Dawoud or Adoulla, she still had spent more than a score of years fighting foul magics. But nothing in her training had quite prepared her for this. She had seen things and done things that ordinary folk considered the stuff of stories. Now Litaz knew how those people felt when they saw her work.

Despite his age and his broad bulk, Roun Hedaad moved cat-quick, dodging the skin ghuls' swordswings. He lashed out with his mace, caving in one of the things' skulls. But that barely seemed to slow it.

The dervish and the lioness shook off their shock at the same time and shot forward. Raseed leapt, his sword whistling out in a slanted arc and slicing clean through the neck of the closest skin ghul. Its head fell to the floor and its body stumbled a step before collapsing. Then the head began to hiss, and the sprawled body began grasping around blindly in search of it. Raseed, his tilted eyes wide with shock, kicked the gibbering head away like one of the wooden balls Soo children played with.

Zamia had already pounced onto one of the things, and the silver flash of her claws was too swift for the eye to follow. She leapt away and on to her next target, leaving a bloody mass of mangled body in her wake.

But already the skin ghul's shredded flesh was, before Litaz's astonished eyes, weaving itself back together. By the time the girl had disemboweled another foe, her first victim stood again, not a mark marring its body.

Groaning, one of the things shambled toward Litaz and her husband, still brandishing the sword it had wielded as a natural man. As it splashed through one of the larger pools dotting the room, a green-brown blur leapt up and attacked it. A crocodile, the most fearsome animal of her homeland. The thing was tiny— either young or magically stunted in growth—but even a half-sized crocodile was fearsome. With three snaps of its jaws it bit the skin ghul in half. But as the ghul reassembled itself, one of its arms clawing its way out of the crocodile's mouth, the leathery beast dashed away in primal fear.

Zamia darted back and forth, harrying the monsters and dodging their fists and blades. Raseed's sword sliced through a skin ghul's wrist, severing its hand. Even as it hit the ground, though, the hand began to walk on its fingers back toward its body, looking like some sort of hideous spider. The dervish was back-to-back with Roun Hedaad now, and both men were bleeding. Both clearly wondering how to kill a foe that couldn't die.

From the doorway leading back to the blue room, there was groaning and hissing. More of the things were stumbling in. *Almighty God help us.*

"This isn't working. You have to do something," she said to her husband. She felt his long-fingered hand on the small of her back and some part of her was less afraid.

Then she heard him mumbling sonorously in that magical nonlanguage that she'd never come any closer to understanding in their thirty years together. He was preparing to release the energies he'd been holding at bay.

"All of you, get behind Dawoud!" she screamed at her companions.

Raseed and Zamia obeyed. But she saw sadly that Roun Hedaad could not—he lay dead, half his head cleaved off. Two of the skin ghuls were tearing at the dead captain's chest, trying to get at his heart. *Trying to feed.*

She stepped behind her husband, whose chanting had grown unnaturally loud. His sweet, gravelly voice never sounded so strong as when he spoke a spell, she thought. It was in the instant that a spell left his lips that he seemed most a man to her.

He fell silent and pointed his palms at the advancing horde of monsters—there were near a dozen of them in the Green of Beasts now.

A great blast of light—a glowing, golden beam as bright as the midday sun above them—shot forth from her husband's hands and slammed unerringly into the skin ghuls. She'd once seen that beam reduce a standing man to ashes. And for a moment, as the beam bowled over the whole pack of creatures, Litaz dared to hope her husband's magic had prevailed. Every single one of the skin ghuls lay still, smoke rising from their bodies.

She heard Dawoud draw in an exhausted, rattling breath, watched two new wrinkles suddenly seam his face.

Then she saw movement among the skin ghuls' bodies. Her heart dropped. The creatures had simply been slowed—already, they were starting to scrabble back to their feet.

"What now?" Dawoud asked, panting such that she thought he might die.

*Only ten years ago, he'd have been standing tall after casting that spell*, she worried.

"I don't know," she said. "We can't fight these things, though. We've got to get out of here."

Dawoud's spell bought them enough time to race through a great archway, out of the Green of Beasts and into a roofed room—a small stone antechamber.

Raseed and Zamia followed, but the dervish made an annoyed noise. "Auntie! Retreat is not the way of the Order—"

"Nor of the Badawi," Zamia's half-lion voice broke in.

Through the archway she saw the skin ghuls gather themselves into a mockery of a guard-squad and march slowly toward them. They had no time for this.

"Stupid children!" Dawoud bit off between breaths, echoing her thoughts. "Those are skin ghuls! Lion-claws, spells and solutions, forked swords—they are all of them useless against those monsters, if the old books are to be believed. Only Adoulla would know how to kill these things. And if we can't—"

He stopped speaking as a blood-curdling scream

rent the air—a scream Litaz recognized. It was coming from the next room. *Adoulla! Hold on, old friend, we're coming! At the very least, we'll all die together!*

Zamia and her companions stood in a small antechamber off of the Green of Beasts.

"Only Adoulla would know how to kill these things." Dawoud Son-of-Wajeed said. "And if we can't—"

Zamia heard a familiar voice scream from the next room. *The Doctor!*

With lion-speed she flew forward into a great columned chamber, Raseed moving beside her. She was still weak from her earlier injuries, and holding onto the shape took every bit of strength she could muster.

The room was a riotous mix of scents and sights. The Falcon Prince and a boy sitting on a throne, shouting. Men's corpses. A wall of light. More of those gibbering monsters. A gaunt, black-bearded man who smelled of unnatural filth.

Zamia shut it all out and focused on what had brought her here—Mouw Awa the manjackal, hunched over the body of the Doctor. She pictured her band's bodies, and drew new strength from her rage.

She shot past Raseed, never taking her eyes off of Mouw Awa. "This one is mine!" she growled.

She slammed into the shadow-creature, raking out with her claws and knocking the thing yards away from the Doctor. Raseed turned to face some new threat and was lost to her sight.

The manjackal's eerie voice filled her head. *The*

*Kitten! No! She hath been slain by Mouw Awa! The savage little lion-child hath been slain!* Mouw Awa's shadowy shape backed away as Zamia approached.

Zamia snarled. "Not quite. You are afraid, creature? Good!" She felt bold, as a Badawi tribeswoman ought to. It felt as if her father were speaking through her. She tensed herself to strike.

She leapt, but Mouw Awa moved too quickly. It scrabbled back, and her claws cleaved only air. The monster snapped at her once, twice. But she was ready for its every desperate strike. Mouw Awa was fighting fearfully. The thing was truly part jackal—cruel to a helpless foe, but cowardly when facing one who could kill it.

She slashed out again with her claws and made deep gouges in the shadow-flesh. Mouw Awa howled in pain.

*No! She hath hurt Mouw Awa!*

The creature lunged and missed again. Her counter-strike only grazed it.

They circled each other, each searching for an opening. It tried to rattle her with that mad mouthless voice.

*Dost thou remember the pain? The sickness when Mouw Awa's fangs sank into thy soul? Yes! Thou dost recall it.*

She paid little attention to the words in her head. Her vengeance was at hand.

Mouw Awa feinted, then, more quickly than she'd thought possible, snapped at her again. Its jaws found only air but it grappled her to the ground. Corpse-stinking, shadowy claws dug into her flanks. The pain nearly made her black out.

She could feel more than see something that was once a man sneer somewhere within those shadows. *The kitten doth hope to baffle his blessed friend's plans! No! Mouw Awa's mangling maw doth—*

She saw her chance and struck. Swooning with pain and calling upon the Ministering Angels, Zamia twisted violently. Now her forepaws pinned the screaming monster to the ground.

*No! Cheated! Mouw Awa the manjackal hath been cheated!*

The rest of the room melted away. Zamia saw nothing, heard nothing, smelled nothing except the foe before her. Bracing herself, she plunged her maw to Mouw Awa's throat and tore, ripping away shadows as solid as flesh. The manjackal, howling without words now, punched and clawed at her sides.

But she sank her teeth deeper and deeper until she tore Mouw Awa's throat out. The manjackal's clawing briefly grew stronger, then stopped completely.

She choked, the foulest of foul tastes filling her mouth and nostrils. Without willing it, she shifted out of the lion-shape.

She rose shakily to her feet.

The shadows that Mouw Awa had seemed to be formed from swirled and rose like smoke. Some unseen, unfelt wind tattered the shadows until they were but dark wisps. Then the wisps themselves gusted into nothingness.

What was left on the palace floor was a man's skeleton. *Hadu Nawas. The Child-Scythe.* Instead of a man's skull, the corpse had the skull of a jackal. The sight brought to mind wind-stripped bones of the desert—and all she had lost among the sands.

She kicked the skeleton with a booted foot, and it instantly crumbled to dust. She closed her eyes against the agonizing pain of her wounds and sank back to the stone floor.

*My band is avenged. The Banu Laith Badawi are avenged.*

Zamia dared to tell herself that her father would be proud.

And then she was sick. Over and over again, until tears filled her eyes and her stomach ached, she was sick.

Raseed heard the Doctor scream and, heedless of whatever danger might lie ahead, shot forward as fast as his feet could carry him. He entered a vast columned room with a great dais at its center. He saw the corpses of the Khalif and a black-robed man—a court magus, he guessed—sprawled on the ground. A gaunt man in a filthy white kaftan stood above the corpses. Several skin ghuls were pounding on a wall of shimmering light.

Upon the dais was a high-backed throne of bright white stone. The Falcon Prince sat on the throne, hands clasped with a long-haired young boy by his side. Pharaad Az Hammaz was shouting. "It's not working. IT'S NOT WORKING!"

Raseed didn't know or care what the traitor was going on about. His attention was on the floor beside the dais, where Mouw Awa crouched over the Doctor, who screamed in pain.

He had to help his mentor. The manjackal was distracted and Raseed, moving faster than he'd ever moved in his life, flew at the thing.

But, fast as he was, Zamia Banu Laith Badawi was faster. A bolt of golden light, she shot past him, growling "This one is mine!" and barreled into Mouw Awa, knocking the manjackal from the Doctor.

Raseed spared a glance at the combatants, light and shadow battling in a tangle of claws and growls. Then he saw the man in the soiled kaftan—Orshado, it had to be—dash forward and calmly touch the wall-of-light. There was a flash of red, and the wall was gone. At a gesture from Orshado, the skin ghuls, no longer impeded, strode toward the throne.

Raseed reached the Doctor. Claw-marks had shredded the Doctor's kaftan, though Raseed could see no blood. Around the rims of the Doctor's eyes, Raseed could see a red that was brighter than bloodshot.

"Ministering Angels! Doctor, are you . . . What can I do?" he asked, ashamed to feel as frightened as he did.

"Raseed bas Raseed," the Doctor said, his voice hollow and vacant. "A good man . . . a good partner."

Raseed grabbed the ghul hunter by the shoulders. "Doctor, please! How can we kill these things?"

The Doctor's bright brown eyes seemed to struggle against the red light that rimmed them. "Hunh? Be . . . behead. Stop skin ghuls!"

"I *did* behead one, Doctor, it just—"

"O . . . Orshado." It was the last thing the Doctor said before he fell into some sort of sorcerous death-sleep.

*Orshado. Then the ghul of ghuls himself must be beheaded!*

Out of the corner of his eye, he saw gouts of magical flame—Litaz and Dawoud battling yet more skin ghuls. He didn't know what had become of Zamia.

Raseed laid his mentor's big limp body carefully upon the dais. He looked up and saw Orshado leap impossibly—magically—onto the throne itself. The ghul of ghuls backhanded Pharaad Az Hammaz with a, no doubt, sorcerous strength. The master thief dropped his sword and fell from the throne onto the dais. Then Orshado, one foot planted on the throne, grabbed the child—the Heir, Raseed realized—by his long, jet-black hair and drew a knife.

*He's going to drink the Heir's blood, just as that scroll said.*

Orshado's curved knife darted up and down, and the Heir screamed in pain. A red spray spattered Orshado's kaftan.

At the same time, the half-conscious Falcon Prince spoke a single word and made a strange gesture. Then he reached past the bleeding Heir and pressed something on one of the throne's armrests. Raseed heard a loud click and a groan of shifting stone.

*Another secret that the Khalifs never learned of?* It seemed so, for below him the floor swiftly receded as the throne and the entire dais it sat on—with Raseed, the Doctor, the Heir, Pharaad Az Hammaz, and Orshado all on it—rose on some sort of column.

Raseed gave the Doctor's limp form one last pained

glance, then looked back to Orshado. The ghul of ghuls plunged his knife into the Heir's chest a second time.

Raseed leapt toward the throne. *Almighty God, though I know I am unworthy, I beg You to grant Your servant strength!*

He flew at Orshado. But the ghul of ghuls waved his hand, and then something strange—something *impossible*—happened.

The throne room around them ceased to be. Where stone walls and ceiling had been there was only swirling red light. Raseed's companions were gone. Orshado and his monsters were gone. Raseed was alone.

*What foul magic is this?*

Raseed looked around frantically, trying to find a ceiling, a floor, or a door. But there was only the churning whorl of red light.

He went into his breathing exercises, and with them came a degree of calm. He recited scripture. "Though I walk a wilderness of ghuls and wicked djenn, no fear can cast its shadow upon me. I take shelter in His—"

The Heavenly Chapters died on Raseed's lips as a man appeared before him.

The man carried a spear. He was roughly dressed and had a gruesome sword wound through his middle. He should not have been able to stand. Something about his face was familiar to Raseed . . .

*One of the highwaymen!* When Raseed had first left the Lodge of God two years ago, he had been ambushed by three highwaymen on the long road to Dhamsawaat. He had slain them with ease.

This was the first man Raseed had ever killed.

The man looked at Raseed with empty eyes and spoke.

"'O BELIEVER! KNOW THAT TO MURDER ANOTHER MAN IS TO MAKE GOD WEEP!'"

At the sound of that voice quoting from the Heavenly Chapters, Raseed froze in fear. The man's mouth moved, but the voice that spoke the scripture was Raseed's own—the doubting internal voice he often heard in his head.

As the man spoke, the other two highwaymen whom Raseed had killed on that day appeared. One had half his head missing, the other bled from his chest. They joined in the chanting, each speaking in Raseed's own voice.

"'O BELIEVER! KNOW THAT TO MURDER ANOTHER MAN IS TO MAKE GOD WEEP!'"

Another mangled man blinked into existence beside Raseed. The magus Zoud, who had been kidnapping women, wedding them, then feeding them to his water ghuls. Raseed had killed the man on his first ghul hunt with the Doctor.

"'O BELIEVER! KNOW THAT TO MURDER ANOTHER MAN IS TO MAKE GOD WEEP.'"

Another wicked man whom Raseed had slain appeared. Then another. As one, the dead men stepped toward him. And at last Raseed felt movement return to his limbs.

He slashed out with his sword at the closest form, but the forked blade whistled through the highwayman as if through empty air. He feared the touch of those dead men's hands more than he had ever feared anything, though he could not say why. He backed away step by step, keeping his eyes on them.

Behind him he heard a great whoosh of fire. He felt his blue silks singeing. Prying his eyes from the dead men, he turned toward the horrible heat. He saw a vast chasm filled with water-that-was-fire.

*The Lake of Flame! I have been consigned by God to the Lake of Flame!*

The dead men advanced. Raseed backed away a few more steps and felt the heat at his back begin to scald his skin. From nowhere and everywhere he heard a soft weeping that sounded like the universe being torn in two.

But then, beneath that, he heard another voice. Dim and distant, he heard Doctor Adoulla Makhslood's words from moments ago.

"Raseed bas Raseed. A good man . . . a good partner . . ."

Raseed clung to the words as if they were the sheltering embrace of God Himself. He found power in them.

*No. This flame is not real. These men are dead. I have served Almighty God as best I can. I have failed at times, but "Perfection is the palace in which God alone lives."*

Around Raseed, the thick, roiling red glow wavered and seemed to thin. The dead men disappeared. For the briefest of moments, he saw a gaunt figure in a soiled kaftan before him.

*Orshado! This is his doing, not God's!*

It lasted only an instant, and then the dead men

were on him again, herding him toward the Lake of Flame. Raseed felt his flesh burn but he stifled his screams.

He forced focus upon his thoughts as he never had before. He pictured the Doctor, Litaz, and Dawoud. He pictured Zamia Banu Laith Badawi, who had dared to speak to him of marriage. He thought of the flaws they all had and the good they had done. And he heard himself chanting.

" 'Perfection is the palace in which God alone lives. Perfection is the palace in which God alone lives. Perfection is the palace in which God alone lives.' "

Again the churning red light wavered and thinned. Again he saw Orshado standing there.

Raseed flew forward, the chant on his lips, his head filled with thoughts of his friends. The red light dispersed. The dead men did not return. He slashed his sword at Orshado, and felt as if he were breaking through a brick wall.

He heard the gurgling scream of a man with no tongue. Then he was in the throne room again, on the rising dais. The Heir lay bleeding on the throne and Orshado stood before Raseed, clutching his temples in pain. It was as if time had stood still while he'd faced the death-specters.

The agony they'd caused was still with him. Pain blazed through Raseed's body, and his back burned. But he forced himself forward, slicing out again with his sword as he did so.

Manjackal, sand ghuls, skin ghuls. Again and again these past few days, Raseed's sword arm had proven too weak to vanquish the creatures of the Traitorous Angel. But now he felt filled with God's power. He was the Weapon of the Wisely Worshipped.

This was the moment that he had lived his whole life for.

The force of Raseed's blow carried him and Orshado both away from the throne and over the edge of the dais, which had now risen halfway to the ceiling. They plummeted to the floor as Raseed's sword sliced through the ghul-of-ghuls' neck.

The man in the soiled kaftan made no noise, even as he died.

Raseed felt his bones break as he hit the stone floor. He cried out in pain, but in his mind he heard only the Heavenly Chapters. *God is the Mercy that Kills Cruelty.*

Beside him he saw Orshado's headless corpse twitch once and fall still.

Raseed tried to stand but felt the pain pulling him down into darkness. He watched the dais—with the Doctor, the Heir and the Falcon Prince still on it—rise on a notched column of marble carved to look like the scaled length of a cobra. A stone block in the ceiling slid aside. The throne ascended through the resultant hole, the underside of the dais fitting perfectly into it. There was another loud sound of grinding stone and the contraption stopped moving.

For another astonished moment, Raseed just stared at the ceiling that had swallowed the Doctor. He noted with satisfaction that the skin ghuls were all falling to the ground.

Then the pain blazed again and darkness took him.

Adoulla Makhslood felt as if a great gray boulder were crushing down upon his soul, smashing to bits everything within him that had ever been happy. He half-sensed things happening around him—a lion running by, bursts of fire in the air, the soft footsteps of a man in a filthy kaftan, his own mouth mumbling words to a man in blue—but they meant nothing to him. He felt that he was dying and that he was being shoved from the sheltering embrace of God. In all his years on God's great earth, he had never felt such despair.

Then he heard the howl of a jackal that was somehow also the scream of a man. And the next moment he felt the merciful hand of Almighty God rolling the soul-crushing boulder away.

He blinked away tears of grateful joy. He heard a loud sound of grinding stone and a click like something sliding into place. He rubbed his eyes and sat up. His chest blazed with pain and his kaftan was shredded. But when his fingers felt for wounds they found none.

And then it all came back to him. The things his eyes had seen while his soul was behind a screen of shadow. Mouw Awa attacking him. Zamia attacking Mouw Awa. Orshado stabbing the heir. The throne climbing to the ceiling.

Adoulla struggled to his feet and tried to sort his thoughts. *I am alive. Which must mean that Mouw Awa has been destroyed. But what of its master?* He saw no sign of Orshado.

He was in a very small stone room without windows or doors. The throne-dais had somehow risen into this chamber, and it filled most of the room. The Heir's un-moving body was sprawled across the Throne of the Crescent Moon, which was spattered with the boy's blood. Pharaad Az Hammaz was hunched over the dead Heir.

And there was blood dripping from the man's lips.

Adoulla fell to his knees, and his joy at having dodged a dark death fled. He screamed wordlessly at the foul act he was witnessing.

The Prince looked at him, the guilt on his face as vis-ible as the blood was. "The boy *asked* me to do this, Uncle. He knew he was dying." His voice was a rasp, with none of its usual bravado. "The passing of the Co-bra Throne's powers through hand-clasping was a lie, it seems. Its feeding and healing magics were a myth. But the blood-drinking spell. The war powers. These are real. I can feel their realness coursing through me."

Adoulla wanted to vomit. He wanted to choke the Prince then and there. But it took all of Adoulla's strength just to rise to his feet. He bit off angry words as he did so. "He was a *boy*, you scheming son of a whore! A boy of not-yet-ten years!"

And, just like that, the madman's smug mask dropped. "Do you think I don't know that, Uncle? Do you really think my heart is not torn apart by this?"

"Better that your heart *were* torn apart by ghuls, than that this child should die. You are a foul man to do this, Pharaad Az Hammaz, and God will damn you for it."

The bandit wiped blood from his mouth onto his sleeve. "Perhaps. I did not kill the boy, Uncle. But he is dead now. His father is dead. There will be a struggle for this damned-by-God slab of marble, and I will need all of the power I can muster if I am going to keep it from falling back to some overstuffed murderer who lives by drinking the blood of our city. What was I to do?" The smug smirk returned.

The Prince's matter-of-fact manner made Adoulla furious. Without quite realizing what he was doing, Adoulla lunged at the bandit, throwing out the right hook that he'd mastered back when he was the brawniest boy on Dead Donkey Lane. The man was absorbed in his newfound power, or Adoulla would never have been able to lay a hand on him. But the punch connected with a crunch.

The master thief's eyes flashed with hatred and his hand went to his sword. Adoulla had doomed himself.

But then a slow, sad smile spread across the Prince's face. "I suppose I deserve that, Uncle. That and more." Pharaad Az Hammaz winced as he touched the corner of his mouth, which now dripped with his own blood. Adoulla looked at the floor, disgusted with the Falcon Prince, disgusted with himself—disgusted with everything on God's great earth.

"Look at me, Uncle, please," the Prince said. He sounded different, now—like a frightened child. Adoulla looked up and locked eyes with the man.

"Even . . . Even without the benevolent magics I'd hoped to hold," the thief continued, "there is a chance to begin something new here. This is why, before he died, the boy asked me to do this thing. The Khalif claimed that it was God who set his line on the throne. I now know that you spoke truly that this man Orshado was sent by the Traitorous Angel to seek the throne. But me? I am just a man, Uncle. Just a man trying to do what is right.

"When I saw Orshado stab the boy, I knew what I had to do. And thanks to a trick of the old stonework I was able to do what needed doing in private. Now the question is what will happen when I lower the throne back into place and try to wrest order from this chaos. There are still ministers who support me, and my diplomats and clerks-of-law will help me twist recognition from the other realms. There is still some small chance to avoid soaking the streets in blood. Given time, my scholars might even find ways to use the Cobra Throne's powers to help the people. But if word of this—" he gestured at the dead Heir and faltered.

The Prince swallowed and began again. "If word of this part of things gets out, even that small chance will fly out the window. It will mean another civil war, of that we can be certain. You and I are not here together through mere happenstance, Uncle. You would call it the will of God. I will simply say 'Great sailors sail the same seas.' But either way, I need your help. Your silence about what you have seen."

*Do you know what happens to whores in war?* Miri's question of two days ago echoed in Adoulla's ears. He looked at the limp form of the Heir sprawled on the Throne of the Crescent Moon. If he kept this vicious, villainous secret there was a chance—a chance only— that this could happen smoothly, without ten thousand corpses in the streets. Adoulla watched a small splotch of blood—whether the Prince's or the Heir's, he couldn't say—slide magically from his kaftan. Again he remembered his God-sent dream—a befouled kaftan and a river of blood. *Was* it Orshado that God had been warning him of? Or was it himself?

*What a damned-by-God mess.* He would keep the Prince's secret. It was wrong, and it was foul, and he didn't doubt he would answer for it when called to join God. But it was also the only way. And it might—right here and right now—save his city, his friends, and the woman he loved. He looked up toward Beneficent God, He From Whom All Fortunes Flow, and begged silently for forgiveness.

He looked at the Prince and made his voice as hard as he could. "If you turn out to be a liar, Pharaad Az Hammaz—if you don't do everything in your power to keep this city safe and to feed its people—there will be a price to pay. A very heavy price. Don't think that palaces and death-magics will protect you. If you betray this city, I swear in the name of Almighty God that *I* will drink *your* blood."

The Prince bowed solemnly to him and said nothing.

# Chapter 20

ZAMIA STOOD WITH HER COMPANIONS in the early morning sunlight, staring at the burned and broken wreck that had been the shop of Dawoud Son-of-Wajeed and Litaz Daughter-of-Likami. The stink of burnt wood and charred stone stung her sensitive nostrils, and she had to stand back farther than the others.

Litaz had finally stopped screaming. The anger in her voice now was cold but no less powerful. "The Humble Students. May God damn them all to the Lake of Flame. While we were saving this damned-by-God city from the Traitorous Angel, they were doing . . . they did *this*."

Raseed, his arm bandaged and his face bruised from the battle, frowned at the burned-out building. "This . . . this is not the work of God that they have done, Auntie. I am sorry."

"It is the work of wicked men," the Doctor said weakly, putting one arm around Litaz's shoulders and the other around the shoulders of her husband. Even before they had discovered this destruction, Zamia noted, the Doctor had seemed unusually subdued.

After the group's wounds had been treated by Pharaad Az Hammaz's healers, they had left the chaos of the Crescent Moon Palace stealthily and under escort, the quiet thanks and blessings of the Falcon Prince following them out the gates. Even Raseed had stayed silent as they left, though his eyes had been like swords leveled at the master thief.

And now there was this.

"All I can say," the Doctor half-whispered, "is what you said to me days ago: with weeks of work your home will be restored. You will—"

Dawoud held up a long-fingered hand and silenced the Doctor. For a long time they all just stood there staring.

Hours later the five of them sat in Mohsabi's teahouse, sipping nectar and cardamom tea, and nibbling unhappily at pastries. The teahouse owner, a well-groomed little man with a goatee, had, for a few extra coins, shooed away his other customers and left the companions alone to discuss in private the aftermath of their battle in the Palace.

"So is he still the Falcon Prince," Dawoud was saying, "or is he now 'The Defender of Virtue, Khalif Pharaad Az Hammaz?' Well, whatever he decides to call himself, the madman has his tasks cut out for him. I'd still bet a dinar to a dirham that there will be war in these streets before it's all over. And as great as Dhamsawaat is, it is only one city. The governors of Abassen's other cities, the Soo Tripasharate, the High Sultaan of Rughal-ba—how will these men respond? The Crescent Moon Kingdoms have always been stitched together with delicate threads. After last night . . ." the old magus shook his head, looking even older than he had before the battle. "What of the guardsmen, by the way? Orshado's spell must have seized the souls of a half-thousand men," Dawoud said to the Doctor. "Will the guardsmen survive now that this ghul of ghuls is dead?"

The Doctor shrugged. "According to the old books, it depends on the man. Some will die. Some will live but will not be what they once were—indeed, some will go mad. A few—the strongest, the closest to God, will survive whole, with only a few days' illness and a few hours' blank in their memories. But we have more important things to talk about. As we were walking over here, you and Litaz were whispering quite furiously about something. And twice now when I've brought up rebuilding your shop you've shut me up. Are you planning what I think you're planning?"

The magus stretched and looked at his wife, who smiled sadly, then nodded.

"You know us too well, brother-of-mine," Dawoud said at last. "It's time we left Dhamsawaat. Litaz has been saying for years that she'd like to see the Republic again, and now I feel much the same. We've always intended to make another visit. Other things just kept getting in the way. And . . . this last battle, Adoulla. It *cost* me. Weeks, months of life. Soon I'll be too old to make such a journey."

Litaz laid her small hand on her husband's shoulder. "This business with the Humble Students, the unrest in the city—maybe they are all signs from God. Perhaps it is time for us to return home."

"I . . . You . . . You'll be missed, my friends," the Doctor said, his eyes shining with unshed tears. "In the Name of God, you will truly be missed."

Litaz's own eyes were moist now. "You could come with us, of course, Adoulla. But I suspect you have business of your own to see to, now that our part in this foul madness is over. Perhaps you will soon announce a blessed event for us to attend before we leave?"

Zamia knew not what the alkhemist meant by this, but the Doctor looked suddenly embarrassed.

Litaz went on, looking less sad now. "In any case, on the walk over here, I must confess that we tried to steal away your assistant, asking if he'd like to join us. The young man needs to see more of the world," she said, smiling at Raseed, who lowered his eyes. "He politely declined, of course."

Litaz turned to Zamia. "What of you, Zamia Banu Laith Badawi? You could travel with us if you wished. The open road is not the desert, but you might find it less stifling than this city. Dawoud and I are a band of only two, but we would still be honored to have you as our Protector."

Zamia didn't know what to think, let alone what to say. Finding a new band to roam with—and roaming so far—was a strange notion, with nothing of the ways of the Badawi to it.

And then there was Raseed bas Raseed. She wished

that she and he could leave this frightening city together. With him, she thought, someday she might forget that she was Protector of the Band, might find a place where such things did not matter. A place where enemies never threatened. Surely there was such a place *somewhere* on God's great earth? She was ashamed that this sounded so appealing to her.

But she knew that these were only wishes. She could not allow herself to ever forget that she was Protector of the Band. Or that the world was full of the enemies of mankind. The Ministering Angels had not granted her the power of the lion so that she could shirk her duties. And she loved the dervish —*yes*, she told herself, *you* love *him!*—because of his own devotion to duty.

"I . . . I will have to think on this, Auntie," was all she could say.

She looked at Raseed. Despite his gruesome-looking injuries he sat crosslegged on the puzzlecloth-carpeted floor, his forked sword lying across his lean thighs. She nearly jumped when he stood with a pained wince and approached her.

"Zamia . . ." he said and trailed off, looking as if someone had stabbed him. She flattered herself that his expression was not merely due to his injuries. He continued. "I would . . . I would speak to you in private, if you do not mind." He gestured toward an unused side room away from the old people.

*Keep your mind on your duty*, she told herself. She gripped her left hand with her right, her fingernails digging into her flesh, and followed him.

Raseed bas Raseed struggled to keep his mind on his duty. He led Zamia into a private part of Mohsabi's teahouse, a small room out of earshot of the Doctor and his friends. The place was empty of other customers, due not only to the owner's facilitation but also to the fact that word of events in the palace—distorted, fanciful word—was already trickling onto the street. People were scurrying about, buying food and fighting-staves then locking themselves in their homes, making vague preparation for the unknown.

Raseed turned to Zamia. He looked at the tribes-woman for as long as he dared, then darted his eyes to the ground, only to bring them back up to meet Zamia's bright gaze again. His body ached, and his soul had never been more unfocused. Still, he had to speak.

"You fought fiercely yesterday, Zamia Banu Laith Badawi," he said, feeling foolish as the words flowed out.

"As did you, Raseed bas Raseed."

"Zamia . . . I . . . I wish you to know that, of all the women on God's great earth, you are the only one I would ever wish to wed." He felt his cheeks burn with shame, and he could not believe he had forced the words out.

Zamia's green eyes—the most beautiful eyes Raseed had ever seen—grew wide. But she said nothing.

"But . . ." he continued, wishing he were dead, "but the Order forbids Shaykhs to marry. If I asked for your hand I would be turning my back on any chance of advancement in God's eyes. I would forever remain a dervish in rank and would never be able to teach at the

Lodge of God. Until I met you, I was certain that to ascend from dervish to Shaykh—to become a fitter weapon of God—was the kindest fate I could possibly pray for."

Zamia's eyes were wet, but she shed no tears. She swallowed hard and it took every bit of training Raseed had to refrain from reaching out to her. "And now?" she asked at last.

"Now . . . now I do not know. Perhaps I will return to the Lodge of God. I plan to leave this wicked city. That much I do know. After that. . . ." He trailed off, not knowing what else to say.

"Raseed?"

"Yes?"

"What happened there? In the throne room?"

Raseed tried to speak, but the words would not come. For a moment, his weak body almost betrayed him by crying.

Finally he heard himself say, "A vision from a cruel man's magic. I will not speak of it, Zamia. But it . . . it has made me think about . . . about many things. Almighty God forgive me, but after these past few days I no longer know just what my place in His plan is. But I think that I must take some time to find out. Alone."

She ran a hand across her eyes and nodded once. "Then that is what you must do," she said. Then she smiled sadly at him, kissed him once on his cheek, and turned away.

His cheek burned like the Lake of Flame. If his Shaykhs had seen that kiss, they would have been scandalized. But Raseed could find no fault with Zamia

Banu Laith Badawi. All he could do was force back the tears he felt filling his own eyes, and follow her back to join the others.

Adoulla sipped his tea and looked at his oldest friends in the world. His heart nearly broke, looking at Dawoud. Adoulla was used to seeing his friend look bleary-eyed and haggard after a fight, but this was different. A day later and Dawoud's shoulders were still stooped. He had lines around his eyes and a hitch in his walk that hadn't been there yesterday morning.

*They're really leaving,* Adoulla thought, and he felt an almost physical ache. Everything had changed now, and not all of it for the better. He looked about Mohsabi's formally decorated teahouse. The place was fine enough—fancier than Yehyeh's had been, to be sure—and Mohsabi himself was a generous host, but the tea was a bit bland and . . .

*Oh, Yehyeh. My friend, you deserved a quieter end than what God granted you. But may your soul find shelter in His embrace.*

Adoulla silently mouthed lines from the last passage of Ismi Shihab's *Leaves of Palm:*

*So this is old age! I've seen half my friends die.*
*I say prayers at their passing, too tired to cry.*

Raseed and Zamia, both looking somewhat stricken, emerged from a side room and walked back toward the table, finished with whatever private talk they'd had. Adoulla looked at the two young warriors and sighed.

They frightened him and made him wonder about the future, these zealous children who longed to kill. Who considered killing a calling and a path to honor. *Would that we lived in a world that needed no swords or silver claws*, he thought. But that was *not* the world he lived in. Without meaning to, he moaned in pain, thinking of the world as it was.

He knew that Dawoud was right about the chaos that was likely to come. But regardless of what was coming, regardless of what building Adoulla lived in, or where he took his tea, Dhamsawaat was his home. At the end of the day, nothing could change that. And, for whatever it was worth, Adoulla did not think that Pharaad Az Hammaz could possibly make a worse Khalif than the last. He even dared to hope that the man—the blood-drinking usurper—might just make a better one.

As he moaned, his companions—not just his old friends, but the two youths as well—looked over at him. In each pair of eyes—tilted, bright green, rheumy, and reasonable—he saw concern for him. More—he saw love. It was disguised by degrees of gruffness and grim honor, but it was love nonetheless. Each met his gaze with a silent offer to lend him their strength. Four fine people who wished to save him pain.

*Perhaps this world is not in such bad hands, after all.*

He and his friends had faced their most powerful threat yet, and defeated it. And everything and nothing had changed. The sky had not split open to reveal the Ministering Angels singing that all ghul-makers were dead. There was no shower of flowers from a forever-safe populace. Tomorrow, or the next day, or a month from now, some fishmonger or housewife would come to Adoulla with more terrified tales. God had not rewarded Adoulla with retirement in a peaceful palace full of food and friends. The half-mad Falcon Prince, armed with the tainted powers of the Cobra Throne, ruled Dhamsawaat tenuously. And the people Adoulla cared about most were either leaving that city or dead.

But not Miri.

Not Miri, who mattered more than anything. He had made a sacred oath to her. More than once in his life Adoulla had found himself regretting a sworn oath, but he had never broken one.

His obligation to God had never felt so sweet.

And so, despite all of the horrors Adoulla had seen, despite all of the horrors that were yet to come, he felt a small smile steal across his lips. There were ways to help men other than ghul hunting, he told himself. Men had managed to survive without him once. They would do so again. He had paid his "fare for the festival of this world."

Now it was his turn to dance.

That evening, Adoulla again found himself standing on the doorstep of Miri Almoussa's tidy storefront. The brass-bound door was closed, a rare sight. No doubt some of her Hundred Ears had brought her tales of the battle in the Palace. If that was the case, pragmatic Miri was likely preparing herself as best she could for the chaos that was to come.

He pounded on the door, and when it opened it was not Axeface but Miri herself who stood there. Adoulla's breath caught in his throat, and he found he couldn't speak.

Miri said nothing, but she looked at him, her eyes bright with an unasked question.

Adoulla swallowed hard, clutched at his kaftan, and nodded once. As Miri took a step toward him, he allowed himself a small smile.

Then Doctor Adoulla Makhslood got down on his knees, touched his forehead to the ground, and wept before the woman he would wed.

# C.S. Friedman
## The *Magister* Trilogy

"Powerful, intricate plotting and gripping characters
distinguish a book in which ethical dilemmas
are essential and engrossing."
—*Booklist*

"Imaginative, deftly plotted fantasy...
Readers will eagerly await the next installment."
—*Publishers Weekly*

## FEAST OF SOULS
978-0-7564-0463-5

## WINGS OF WRATH
978-0-7564-0594-6

## LEGACY OF KINGS
978-0-7564-0748-3

To Order Call: 1-800-788-6262
www.dawbooks.com

# Sherwood Smith
## *Inda*

"A powerful beginning to a very promising series by a writer who is making her bid to be a major fantasist. By the time I finished, I was so captured by this book that it lingered for days afterward. I had lived inside these characters, inside this world, and I was unwilling to let go of it. That, I think, is the mark of a major work of fiction…you owe it to yourself to read *Inda*." —Orson Scott Card

## INDA
978-0-7564-0422-2

## THE FOX
978-0-7564-0483-3

## KING'S SHIELD
978-0-7564-0500-7

## TREASON'S SHORE
978-0-7564-0634-9

To Order Call: 1-800-788-6262
www.dawbooks.com

# Tad Williams
# The Dirty Streets of Heaven

"A dark and thrilling story.... Bad-ass smart-mouth Bobby Dollar, an Earth-bound angel advocate for newly departed souls caught between Heaven and Hell, is appalled when a soul goes missing on his watch. Bobby quickly realizes this is 'an actual, honest-to-front-office crisis,' and he sets out to fix it, sparking a chain of hellish events.... Exhilarating action, fascinating characters, and high stakes will leave the reader both satisfied and eager for the next installment." —*Publishers Weekly (starred review)*

"Williams does a brilliant job.... Made me laugh. Made me curious. Impressed me with its cleverness. Made me hungry for the next book. Kept me up late at night when I should have been sleeping."
—Patrick Rothfuss

*And watch for the sequel*, Happy Hour in Hell, *coming in September 2013!*

The Dirty Streets of Heaven: 978-0-7564-0768-1
Happy Hour in Hell: 978-0-7564-0815-2

To Order Call: 1-800-788-6262
www.dawbooks.com

DAW 207